ZODIAC RISING

VICKI PETTERSSON

www.vickipettersson.com

1

USE YOUR WORDS, MORON.

The perfect kiss forms the words 'I love you.' It is a kiss powered by epic intention, potentially life-changing, and never forgotten.

I read this once while sunbathing in the sand as I scrolled the 'gram between sets. Scoffing, I swiped away, thinking it sounded more like a kiss powered by wishful thinking and too many Disney movies.

I wish I'd paid a little more attention to that meme tonight, though. Because tonight I'm standing in the dim lamplight of a cliff-side gazebo, riding the tailwind of a summer that doesn't want to end, while surf god Beckett Lux—he of the strangest surname and the biggest biceps—is leaning over me.

The *intention* in his gaze is, indeed, totally epic as the waves crash like cymbals below us.

His palm is firm on my neck as the stars blaze like distant bonfires above.

His attention is totally on me ... which would be great were it not for the tight knot of men sneaking up on us behind his broad, muscled shoulder.

The man in the lead slips into the pooling lamplight, and Beck whirls at my gasp. The light reveals less than half of that hulking body, yet catches in the deep pits of his scarred skin as the stranger stares at us. His smile deepens, seeing he has our undivided attention. Without warning—without reason—he lets loose a roar so loud it blots out the crashing surf below.

No meme can describe *this* sound. It's a bellow made for comic book scrawls ... bold, red, and unconfined by a tiny dialogue bubble. It's a sound that demands blood, a war cry, and for some bizarre reason ... it's aimed directly at me.

It's also cut short by the tin can that comes out of nowhere to strike the screaming behemoth squarely between the eyes. Beckett and I both jump.

Furious, the man shakes his head, droplets of soda whipping from his beard. The four dudes behind him wheel toward the darkness. There, a slight figure materializes like mist.

"Two surfer kids against what looks like an entire biker gang?" The voice is silken, slivered, and unafraid. "That doesn't seem fair now, does it?"

The leader's muddy eyes fly wide beneath brows so bushy they loom like a hedge. Surprise and fury fight for dominance on his face as he steps forward and raises a gleaming machete. The men behind him square up, too, and I gasp again as the pavilion's lamplight finally draws them all into view.

"Hey, I know you guys," I say, pointing. I ran into them on the street earlier today. They'd been dressed as construction workers then, with hats and bandanas covering their entire faces, but they're bare-faced now, and even in the meager light, the sight is a full-on gnarly-fest. Bulbous black formations bubble from their cheeks and foreheads, and I take a step back when I realize, dude. That's their *flesh*.

"Nasty."

Beck's hand tightens on my arm, silencing me. Probably wise, I think, and allow him to ease in front of me while simultaneously pulling me back. Not that there's anywhere to go. Beckett tries to keep going, but the gazebo's edge cuts into my calves. Surf pounds the sand far below.

Yet the men ignore Beckett and me, their attention trained on the woman who's emerged along the cliff's edge. Though encased in shadows, the outline of her soft skirt and smooth shoulders and uplifted chin remain hard.

"Yes," she says finally, formally. "They are the nastiest."

Although she's standing across from five giant, armed, misshapen men, a smile edges that voice. The desire for hard and fast violence curls in her unseen grin like the foam in the surf pounding behind us. And Beckett Lux—i.e., Beck, the hottest guy in the world (or at least Laguna Beach), who is almost as good of a surfer as I am and who'd been about to deliver me that epic kiss —squints into the darkness. "Who's that?"

"That's my ... Zoe."

I never call her grandmother. For multiple reasons, the title doesn't fit her at all.

Hearing the name, the giant growls again.

"Don't," Zoe says, inching nearer the gazebo's railing. The light catches and sparks in the small gems of her chandelier earrings, and bounces off the bracelets that clank along her wrists. "By the stars, do not make that Mother-Loving sound again. I know you think it's tough, but you sound like a moron. Can you imagine if women went around forgetting how to use our words?"

She roars in example, flinty eyes flaring like blue stars, glossed mouth revealing rows of perfect, white teeth. I slump while she continues to howl like a banshee.

So embarrassing.

Still, it surprises the five men long enough for her to hop the gazebo's railing deftly and reach my side. Great. Now there are two surfer kids and a bipolar, neo-hippie surf shop owner against an entire biker gang.

"Zoe Archer," the leader finally says, proving Neanderthal is only his first language. "I knew we'd find you someday."

His voice isn't as deep as his roar, which is kinda disappointing, though the record player scratch sound in my mind overrides any real dismay.

"Whoa." My attention swivels between the two of them. "He knows you?"

Zoe ignores me, her upper lip curling with disdain. "Yeah, you're a real genius, Vasari. It only took you fifty moons."

"So, like, you know him?" I try again, but the giant named Vasari bares needle-sharp teeth as he takes a step forward, and his distorted flesh parts to reveal mucus beneath rotting skin.

Gnarly!

Zoe halts him by merely holding up one finger.

Maybe it's nerves at being held at knifepoint, or annoyance at being followed by my grandmother—or, most likely, distress at losing what I'm sure would've been a life-changing kiss—but I let out such an unladylike snort that it belongs on a farm. I try to cover with a cough, but it's too late. Vasari's lava-hot gaze shoots my way, and my mouth immediately dries to bone.

"Find me funny, daughter of Chaos?"

This time, his voice is markedly lower.

Yay?

"Daughter of—?" Never mind. Dude is obviously sketchballs, and besides—who the hell argues with the guy holding the knife? "Nope. Not funny at all."

This time, his whole body vibrates with his rumbling growl, and a scent hits me at once, warm and fetid, like he's boiling inside. I fight the urge to shield my nose as he shifts the blade to his other hand and pulls out a short, pronged spear. Awesome. Matching utensils.

"I am going to flay the skin from your bones with quick flicks of this blade. I will carve the chaotic nature from your body in strips, and your cries will ferry my greatness to the gods."

He runs his tongue across those barbed teeth and lowers his head to charge. I back up until the gazebo's railing smacks my thighs. Beck, who hasn't said a word throughout this entire exchange, is right there with me. I can feel him shaking with the need to turn and run, yet Zoe just reaches out, curls her fingers around my shoulders, and pulls a gun from the voluminous folds of her skirt.

I wish I could say I'm surprised, but she's been known to do this before.

Cocking the gun at her hip, she points the barrel into the vaulted night sky. She looks like the flower-child version of Annie Oakley, but at least the walking slab of meat across from us has halted in his tracks.

Zoe tilts her head, fiery curls swaying as she strains to make out a far-off sound. "Hear that?"

Vasari cocks his foul, rancid, rotting head. "What?"

I hear nothing but the resounding gong of the town hall clock. Its toll reverberates in the air before rippling out to be eaten by the sea.

"That's the sound of midnight, boys," Zoe says, and now she bares her own teeth. "It's the sound of planets moving into alignment and fates clicking into place. And it's one of the last sounds you'll ever hear."

The kiss she blows Vasari doesn't even come close to forming an 'I love you,' but there's no time for him to reciprocate anyway because that's the moment that Zoe pivots, levels her .22 my way, and surprises us all by shooting me right through the center of my silk-clad, heart-thudding, B-cup chest.

Not. Awesome.

2

BUT BEFORE ALL THAT.

Sixteen hours earlier, and I'm dozing on the beach when the shadow first passes over me.

I'm only feet away from Joe's lifeguard stand—a touchstone for us locals and one that means friends and security ... and sometimes free snacks.

It's too early in the day for that, though, so I'm chilling solo, my damp sweatshirt tucked beneath my head for support, and my right arm splayed atop the longboard still beaded with water from the ocean. My wetsuit is peeled down to my waist to reveal my bikini top, and I'm not wearing my shades. (Tan lines are way bogus, am I right?)

It's the combination of the Pacific's relentless heartbeat, the soft sand, and my loud thoughts that keep me from hearing the stranger's approach. I've been alternately brooding over having to man the counter at the board shop for an entire Saturday, and lazily chasing the idea of catching a few more waves before my shift begins when I finally realize someone's blocking my sunlight on purpose.

I know it's a man before I even open my eyes. Every girl over the age of twelve knows that weighted stare. It's like being studied as if you're some sort of exotic bird, and then being told it's your fault for being able to fly. It always makes me wish for a pair of claws to go with my invisible wings.

Yet, I'm rarely approached so directly. I have surf-chick swagger, I am clearly comfortable in my body—a totally effective defense mechanism, by the way—and besides, my grandmother drilled into me long ago that I am never, ever responsible for someone else's dark intent.

Those people who can't control themselves will always try to control you.

Know what she never told me, though?

Why *I'm* the one who has to learn a whole new way of moving through the world just because other people can't control themselves.

Like this guy.

Creepers usually stick to Main Beach, where they can watch the chicks who are watching the dudes playing volleyball. Yet Thalia Street is mid-town, almost exclusively local by summer's end, and reserved for surfers only. I've surfed and skimmed here almost every day for five years, which is why I'm more annoyed than afraid when I finally crack an eyelid at the ray-blocking kook still looming over me.

The sunlight's thrown his silhouette into relief, so I can't cop a good look at his face, yet his arrow-sharp outline surprises me. Not only is he big, he's wearing a full business suit, glossy and black, all the way down to his dress shoes, which are buffed and shine in the sun, and are probably pretty pricy. (I can tell you exactly how much a good pair of flip-flops costs, but Wall Street chic is totally beyond me.)

The creeper smells expensive, too. He reeks of some spicy cologne I'll never be able to name ... and something else, something almost sickly sweet. I don't like any of it. Patchouli, cocoa butter, and the salt-kissed sweat of the boys who run this strand are my jam.

Shielding my eyes from the sun does little to improve my view, but I can still tell the jerk's gaze is pinned to my chest.

I speak before I can stop myself. "Lose something there, goob?"

The chuckle billows from him like a cloud. "Or found it."

I shift, wishing for my sunnies. Or a friend. Or a towel the size of a state.

Creeper notes my discomfort, but instead of backing off, he takes one more step forward, spraying sand over my left ankle.

I flinch before my eyes narrow into slits. I should get up and leave. Run away exactly how society says a sixteen-year-old girl should when faced with a bigger, stronger threat. Yet I haven't been raised by society.

I've been raised by Zoe Archer.

So it's probably just as well that one of those salty-skinned strand boys comes along at exactly that moment and knocks my Peeping Tom right off his perch.

"Hey, Ash," the newcomer says to me. "S'up?"

I push to my palms and really wish for my sunnies now. Six feet of sun-kissed Beckett-freaking-Lux. Wave king. God-in-training. A mystery man who allows his surfing to talk for him and who's been making the girls at Laguna High swoon for the past year. I've shared a few sets with him, but he's never even deigned to look my way outside the ocean. I didn't even know he knew my name.

Yet here he is, hair damp and dark and threaded with sand, his own wet suit drawn tight over his shoulders, but unzipped to reveal a smooth, broad chest. His fine face is closed and serious, like he could go all Bruce Lee on this nugget, and I suddenly understand why every girl he's dated and discarded is said to spend weeks weeping in her bedroom.

"He is perfect-o!" my best friend, Julia, once said, hands fluttering, hair flipping as she threw herself atop my bed. "Beck's, like, the proverbial flame. I could totally see myself spreading my arms like wings, and letting him draw me in close, and poof!"

Moth. Flame. *Poof!*

It was the dumbest thing I'd ever heard.

Yet now that Beckett Lux is right here, shifting on tanned feet, forcing the creeper to dodge the wet surfboard swinging precariously close to that bazillion-dollar suit, I can't help but smile. A knight ... wearing a wetsuit as armor and riding a short board in lieu of his trusty stead—totally my kind of hero.

"S'up, man?" Beck says to the creeper this time. "You look lost."

I can't see the look Creeper shoots Beck, but my errant knight responds with his infamous grin—the one the teachers hate, the one all the flitting moths can't resist, and the one that has nerves now curling in my belly.

I smile more widely, too, because Beck's words are so close to my own. "Lamo thinks he's found something, actually."

"Oh, I sincerely doubt that." Beck sharpens the words into bite-sized pieces, and his body goes even more rigid, if possible. He fixes his gaze squarely on the older man.

Yup. Moth. Flame. *Poof!*

Creeper, though, seems immune to Beck's charms, as well as the threat in his voice. He turns back and gazes down at me for another too-long stretch.

"How amusing," he finally says, "that you don't see yourself as lost."

His voice is like flames over gravel, and the words trigger a memory that fades as fast as it comes. Before I can chase it down, he tucks his hands into his pockets and spins away. The sun sits full on me again, yet I can't help but shiver.

I never did see his face, but even with the ocean breeze, the overripe scent that clung to him still lingers behind like rot in his wake.

"How long's that guy been bothering you?"

The creeper is now just a black speck disappearing around the jutting bluff leading to the shoals, and I tear my gaze from him to find Beck watching me closely. Even though the stare rockets through me, even though he doesn't blink, his gaze doesn't bother me the way Creeper's did. This look is more considering, and Beck's brow is furrowed in concern, like he wants to say something but doesn't know what.

"He didn't bother me. Just stole my rays," I reply, hoping to erase the frown while still sounding cool. Yet I've never been cool; if Beck knows my name, he'll also know that. I'm too tomboyish in my tees and board shorts, and too laid back in school ... which is really just a way to hide my shyness over a learning disorder that no one can seem to name.

I also happen to be totally clumsy outside of surfing, which is why I pull my legs up and wrap my arms around my bruised shins. I heal pretty quickly, but it's rare that a day goes by where I don't wake with another rash of bruises.

"So you've never seen him before?"

"Nope." A suit on the strand. Get real. I hope the sand and salt destroy his expensive shoes. "I'd remember a nutter like that."

Beck drops his board and squats. His skin possesses the same burnished beauty of the sand, sun-kissed and smooth for miles. His eyes rival the blue waves cresting behind him, and are filled with the same restless intensity of the tide rolling into shore. If he were a movie star, this would be his close-up. I half-expect music to swell in the background along with the next crashing wave.

Tilting his head at my board, he says, "You're pretty good on that."

"I'm from Laguna," I retort, leaning back on my palms, which isn't what I want to say at all because I'm not just good, *I'm awesome*.

It's also not technically true. I've only been beachside since I was twelve, just five short years. Before that, I'd been raised in an ironically named desert city: Las Vegas.

But I don't remember any of that.

I've been here longer than Beck, though, and that's all that really matters. He was a late transfer from what had to be some sort of military school. He arrived with a farmer's tan and buzzed hair, though it wasn't long before he was on dawn patrol, shacking out of his mind with the rest of us. He's good. Almost as good as me.

He also graduated this past spring, but shows no signs of going anywhere. I'm only a year behind him in school, but the difference feels monumental right now. For some reason, this summer has stretched impossibly long, and not in a good way.

Leaning back on his palms, Beck stares out at the water as if we chill like this all the time. "You live above that surf shop that looks like a garden, right? Hummingbird House?"

I blink. "You know it?"

"Everyone does. It's, like, magical."

It's, like, fortified.

I don't say that.

"I've seen you ride," he says, making me glad I hadn't bragged. It's way cooler that he's brought it up himself. "You dig the single-fin lifestyle?"

He means longboard versus short, and I do. Searching out the fat swells calms my busy mind and lets me live in the moment. Surfing is the only time my mind isn't fighting itself. Outside the ocean, I feel like I'm fleeing a past I can't even remember.

I nod. "And you like the thrusters."

"Why hang ten when you can attack the nose?" Beck grins, worry gone. Now he just sounds like a surfer.

"You're all shoulder-hoppers," I scoff. Every surfer who ignores right-of-way and drops in on someone else's wave is always a short-boarder.

"You're all wave hogs," he shoots back.

"I'm surprised you've seen me at all. I don't usually skim Main Beach."

It's a dig at how he and his friends like to hotdog for the summer touries, and I grin when his eyes narrow at the edges. "Yeah, I don't usually ride Thalia. You kids hang out here under the guard stand, right?"

My smile fades. He says 'kids' like he's no longer one of us. Maybe that's how it is when you've graduated and are finally free to roam the world, but I don't see him going anywhere. He's still here, hunting the same crests as me. It makes me wonder what he's looking for out there, or if he's just biding his time like I am —waiting to catch a wave.

Waiting for life to really begin.

I don't realize I'm staring at him until he grins, which does totally amazing things to his face. "How old are you, anyway?"

"Almost seventeen," I say, even though it's August, and my birthday isn't until November. I'm closer to it than not.

"Young," he says, almost to himself.

"Older than I've ever been."

Chuckling, he nods to Joe, who's finally arrived for duty. "So you're an older-than-you've-ever-been wave-ripper who causes grown men to stop dead in their tracks."

"Hey, I didn't ask for that."

"No," he says quickly, and then more softly, "No, you wouldn't have to."

Heat floods my face so quickly, so unexpectedly, that I have to look away. I still feel Beck's gaze like a flame, but again, it's not the same burning touch as the creeper's. It doesn't feel like he's just looking.

It feels like he's seeing.

"So." He rises to his feet. "Think you can run with me?"

I cock my head like I'm giving it serious consideration, and I am. Surfing is pretty much the only thing I'm serious about, but pitting my skills against Beck's is dangerous. He's tall and strong and rides quad, which favors the fast and short waves. Yet riding long means I can paddle in and get the jump faster, and that's totally in my wheelhouse.

I stand and begin shimmying into my wetsuit. Beck chuckles in a way that has my heart kicking, and as I grin back, I think, maybe *this* is the way life actually begins: a chance meeting, a glimpse of something that may or may not be dangerous to you.

And a headlong rush in that direction anyway.

3

HE KNOWS MY NAME.

So I forget all about the creeper, about my shift at the board shop, and even about Beck's total radiant hotness as I zip up my wetsuit.

I'm already scoping the sea as I pick up my board, and sense Beck doing the same as he secures his leash. My longboard doesn't have one, not that it matters. Wipe out in front of Beckett Lux, and I'll pretty much have to drown myself, anyway.

The wind is swooping in from a perfect north/northeast direction. The swells are glossy and lay up like they're daring me to make a run. I make the mistake of glancing at Beck and momentarily lose my breath again. He looks as entranced by the ocean as I am, making me wonder if the water feels alive to him, too.

Does he sense it breathing along with him? Does it seem more like home than any place on land?

A smile tugs at one corner of his beautiful mouth, and without looking at me, he says, "If you're wondering whether I'll go easy on you, the answer is no."

Julia's voice—so frothy when she spoke of moths, flames, and fires—intrudes again, but this time it's honed. *Never be too opin-*

ionated, too loud, too aggressive. Her advice is never to be too *anything*, which sucks.

The things I'm "too much" of happen to be my favorite things.

"Just try not to cry when I catch the first roll," I say, breaking into a grin that's too-wide, too-me. "I hate it when the big boys get the sads."

"Pretty confident for a kid," he retorts, eyes still pinned to the roaring sea.

"That's right, old man," I reply, scouting my ride. "Besides, false modesty is the eighth deadly sin."

"That right?"

"That's fact." It's another thing Zoe's drilled into me. Never put yourself down. Never hold yourself back. False modesty is not a feminine virtue...it's just another form of playing dumb.

No, I'm not big on holding back ... although I might be slightly over my head here. I've seen Beck ride the rail. He's aggressive, which only causes his buddies to push him more.

Always with a different girl at his side, too. Sand bunnies, content to sit on a towel and cheer him on from just beyond the fingers of the surf. Long, bronzed limbs attached to long blonde hair. With my dark curls tangled up in a bun and my self-congratulatory cheers, I am most definitely not his kind of girl.

"When's the last time you bit it?" Beck asks, clearly trying to rattle me.

"I rarely bite it."

"I never do," he shoots back, and when I look over this time, he's staring directly at me.

I guess that's why I spot the fat roll first. It's been all mushballs for the last few minutes, and while this wave is soft and placid on top, it's bursting with energy underneath. I rock to the balls of my feet, but Beck's noted my attention and is already sprinting—no, not going easy on me at all—and I have to hurtle myself atop the ocean's back at full speed.

We duck dive the breaking wave simultaneously, boards and

bodies submerged, and come up gasping on the far side of the crashing wave, already heaving ourselves forward. Beck's breath comes hard as he paddles, and suddenly the idea of holding anything back—of listening to Julia's mild-mannered warnings, or sitting on the beach while the waves pass me by—seems insane.

Try not to be "too much" of anything, and you might end up being nothing at all.

Weighting the right rail of my board, I pivot with my left hand on the nose, then pin my gaze on the blue bulge bearing down on me like some giant, distended belly. It's a strong one, the kind surfers wax on about over late-night bonfires, and I rest my bent elbows along the outer edges of the board—waiting, waiting— until it's time to kick hard into the pocket.

I've just gotten ahead of the surge when a strange flutter tickles through the wave's belly. I've only felt something like it once before, when I ran up alongside a giant tuna two years ago in Punta Mita. Yet other than a careless nutter or two, I've never collided with anything out here.

I jerk my foot from the water, a distraction that costs me. Beck sails, prone, in front of me, and I have to fight to catch my rhythm again, paddling whip fast. I've just braced for launch when that fluttering thing in the ocean returns, this time climbing from the water to encircle my ankle.

Shark, I think, salty water rushing into my mouth as I yelp.

Instinct has me clinging to my board—it's all I have; without it, I'm lost—but it's like being jerked back on a fisherman's line. The more I flail, the harder I'm pulled.

Not a shark, I realize as I go under. There's no acute pain or thrashing to accompany the hold. That gives me enough nerve to kick hard, and I feel myself jar something loose beneath the waves. I float, momentarily free. Yet when I try to kick again, *both* ankles are wrapped up tight, pulled together, and dragged straight down.

I thrash in my watery jail, but it's like being placed in iron manacles. The surface recedes, and the ocean depths drown out the sun. I hold my breath, but my lungs are already screaming. I'm already so deep beneath the waves that the ocean has lost all choppiness.

One of the manacles moves to my waist, and the other climbs to my shoulder. In the dimming light, I realize that the figure materializing before me is not a giant fish but a man's face. More importantly, the limbs encircling me are covered in a billowing dark suit, and deeper below—I know without looking—are expensive, shiny shoes.

The creeper grins at me underwater, and I can see his features fully this time. His skin lies across his face in knotty ropes, and pockets of black bone are visible along his cheekbones and temples. His teeth are a slab of white beneath cracked lips, and his eyes are lidless, corneas gone entirely black. He lets me study him for one shocked moment before he chuckles.

Then, he speaks as clearly as he did on dry land. "The Zodiac world is set to rise again, Ashlyn Archer. Are you ready?"

It is not my name—at least, not the one I go by. Yet I recognize it all the same, and that—along with the way the man snarls each syllable—makes me scream.

NOT TO STATE THE OBVIOUS OR ANYTHING, BUT IT'S FREAKING HARD to scream underwater.

And with no air left in my body and my vision already gone spotty, I'm only half aware of the projectile that bullets into the creeper, knocking him backward and freeing me. Though hoping for a Russian missile, I don't wait around to see what's blasted him. Instead, I kick to the ocean's choppy surface, where sweet air floods my stinging lungs.

Luckily, my board bobs nearby, and I pull myself atop it, gasping as I begin whipping my arms along the waves. It's fast-going with the current at my back, and I've almost found my feet when I sense another object closing in on me from the shore.

"Ash!"

I'm pressing the rail of my board to angle away from it when I recognize Joe's voice. His rescue can is beneath his arm, and his whistle pierces the air in shrill beats. I blink stinging saltwater from my eyes as he stumbles into the surf, and Beck suddenly appears on my other side. Together, they help pull me to shore. Beck takes my board while Joe rambles on about an undercurrent.

Yeah, *that's* what you call a dude who laughs while dragging you to the ocean's bottom!

"Damn, Ash," Joe finally sighs. The early morning dog walkers are gawking, and I'm almost recovered enough to feel embarrassed. "You scared the snot out of me. I've never seen anyone get tubed like that."

"Did you see him?" I try to ask, but it comes out in a breathless sputter. I push strands of hair from my face. I must look like a waterlogged rat.

"Him?" Joe draws back, gaze drifting to Beck's. "No, dude. I meant the wave. You totally took it on the head."

"It was a beast," Beck agrees.

It was a *man*.

Finding my balance on the packed sand, I whirl back to the endless ocean ... and see nothing out of the ordinary. No rogue waves. No monstrous men beneath them whispering my name without breathing.

How'd he know my real name?

"But I..."

Joe cocks his head. I feel Beck's presence looming large and silent on the other side of me, and shame floods in to displace the fear.

"Nothing. I'm okay," I tell Joe.

He squints, but something in my face must tell him not to

press. He pats my shoulder instead. "Cool, but maybe lay off for the day, yeah? You're too pale beneath that tan."

"Sure."

With an uncertain backward glance and a nod to Beck, Joe heads back to his stand.

"Is that really all you saw?" I ask when Joe's gone. "A big wave?"

Beck squints. "What else was there?"

I shake my head, sending water flying. Now that I'm standing on terra firma, the whole episode seems totally loco.

A man in a full business suit pulling at my ankles? The ability to talk underwater? Some stranger uttering a name no one knows?

Yes, it all happened, but how to explain it? I take back my board. "Nada."

Trudging back up the strand, I pick up my sweatshirt and yank it over my wetsuit. My hands are still shaking, and while a part of me wants to turn back around and make another run at beating Beck, all I can think of is that man, that *thing*, and his strength as he dragged me away from air and light.

"Hey, Ash. Everyone gets dumped." Beck misunderstands my body language, my silence. "It's nothing to be ashamed of."

He reaches for my shoulder, but I shake off his touch. So much for cool.

That's all right...I'd rather be alive.

"Gotta go." I race up the stairwell leading from the beach to the streets above, moving as fast as I can—which, compared to that thing under that water, isn't fast at all. Even with my thighs pumping hard, I still expect powerful hands to come out of nowhere and drag me back down the stairs. I make it to the top of the landing, though, and only then do I dare glance back.

Beck is no longer where I left him, and why would he be? A guy like that probably has a million other places to be. I finally spot him striding away, black wetsuit down around his waist again, board tucked beneath his arm. With his sun-kissed back glistening with saltwater and muscle, he looks like every surf rat who's run this beach for the past fifty years. Dudes like that roll right over any problems that come their way. The stuff beneath the surface never seems to touch them.

For a moment, I'm envious.

A group of junior high girls appears below to take up residence around Joe's stand. He chats with them as they drop towels and lotion up, but his eyes stay fixed on the sea. I scan it, too, all the way to the southern point, where my gaze snags on the jutting bluff.

There, at the pointed tip, stands a man wearing a full business suit. He is dripping from head to toe, and though it's impossible from this distance, it's like he knows the instant my gaze lands on him. His chin lifts, he leans forward at the waist in an exaggerated bow, and then blows outward as if sending the wind my way.

A second later, I'm engulfed in the scent of rotted fish.

I've read about this, I remember, even as my mind rejects the thought. Even as I stagger and whirl and run. The part of me that's sane fights against the thought ... against the indoctrination that my grandmother preached for so long.

This is not happening, I think, even as I break into a sprint. It's not possible to scent the evil in another living being.

Yet I can't help but listen for the sound of pounding footsteps behind me. It's five entire blocks before I outstrip the stench of death and decay. It's another five before I stop hearing the accompanying laughter, as jagged as that rocky outcropping. They both cling to me, though, and in the late summer wind, I even think I hear the faintest whisper.

I will find you again, it says. And I will drag you under.

4

YOU TALKIN' TO ME?

I've been so preoccupied with my near-death encounter—and wondering what to tell Zoe, if anything—that I don't even hear the catcalls at first. Even if I had ... what sane girl acknowledges wolf whistles arrowing up the street?

"Hey, baby! I'm talking to *yoooou*!"

Annoyance finally flares. "Oh, come on."

I am breathless, sweating, and carting a surfboard on my head. My hair is plastered to my cheeks—at least the portion that isn't springy with wind or snarled from the sea—and my ratty sweatshirt is two sizes too large. Outside of my face—which I assume is a blank slate of stunned bewilderment from being tumbled in my beloved ocean and simultaneously attacked—the only bare part of my body are my calves, visible beneath the lines of my spring suit. My toenails are unpainted; my feet calloused from roaming the streets and sand barefoot all summer. There is literally nothing attractive about me in this given moment.

But that isn't the point, is it?

"Why you runnin' so fast, baby? I'm right here."

It's the construction crew that's been tearing up the south side of PCH for a month. They're listening to classic rock and having their own street party, complete with hardhats, jackhammers, and unwanted innuendo.

Get out of the situation. Flee if it makes sense ... fight only if it makes greater sense.

I grit my teeth as Zoe's advice flutters through me. Surfing the ocean. Walking down the street. Where the hell don't I have to worry about strange men coming after me?

Then I spot *her*.

She's strolling on the other side of the road, rocking pink and pigtails, and tiny in that way you forgot you once were. She's walking—get this—a kitten on a leash that glitters, which is strange but not unheard of, yet it's also somehow so innocent that it makes me stumble in my tracks.

Because she's also headed directly to the construction zone.

The biggest man, the one who yelled, either doesn't see her or doesn't care ... but he sure sees me. "Yeah, baby, come and get it!"

The little girl has paused and is now watching me, too. I pivot slowly, then lean at the waist, cocking my head just slightly. "What did you say?"

The man is bent over an open pit, his face covered with a red bandana and plastic sunglasses shading his eyes from debris. He also wears a hard hat, rendering him completely featureless, but I see him jolt in surprise. The other four men pause, too, and though their faces are similarly covered, I'm sure their mouths are agape.

Shocked that this object can form words, no doubt.

The big man glances back, sees the rest of his crew watching him, and snorts loudly. "I said come and get it, honey."

He doesn't even glance at the little girl in pink.

I take another step forward and cast my voice even higher. "What?"

The worker repeats himself, adding a lewd back-and-forth motion with his hands and hips, just in case his friends are too stupid to know what 'it' is.

"What?" I say again, drawing the word out, feigning confusion. Yeah, my chest burns like it's on fire, and the burnt rubber heat of my anger has me breathing hard, but I'm not moving until these Neanderthals *really* see me. Of course, I'm conscious of the kid, too. She's here, and there's nothing I can do about that, but I can show her ...

Just because other people toss crap your way doesn't mean you have to walk in it.

The dude is starting to feel stupid but can't back down without losing face. He insults me again—this time with a phrase he would never use on a friend, a sister ... his mother. That's okay because they all see me now. I know because I suddenly see all of them.

The shortest guy has red hair that sprouts beneath his helmet in tufts. The skin of the man next to him is coppery in the sunlight. The whack-job yelling at me even has a thin gold band on his ring finger and a cross around his reddened neck. They're all looking me over, maybe noting the freckles spattering my nose or wondering where I've gotten my dark hair and eyes. Who knows? Maybe they even see the obvious...

That I should be able to walk down the street in broad daylight without being accosted by strangers.

That I should be able to swim in the ocean without being attacked.

That I should be able to live my life without having to tame every extraordinary thing about me.

The construction workers have all fallen silent by now, shifting under my unblinking gaze. Then the little girl—one they'll think nothing of leering at in just a few short years—starts to laugh. Her giggle bubbles into the air, fizzy and loud, and after a moment, she doubles over, still going hard.

It deflates the ego that's replaced the big guy's heart because he finally drops his head. I shake mine as I turn to the girl, who's still laughing but turning back the way she came, hopefully headed home.

I do the same, and I do it in silence, broken only by the music from the radio. Somehow, the run-in has calmed me, and I don't look back, even when the jackhammer thunders down the street. I certainly don't flee like I did with the creeper. Instead, I head home as I'm meant to.

At my own chosen pace.

ARCHER'S BOARD SHOP IS TUCKED SHOULDER-TO-SHOULDER WITH A clothing boutique on one side and an indie coffee shop on the other, all facing the beautiful Pacific Coast Highway. I ignore the storefronts, though, and instead make my way into the easement tucked behind the block, entering our yard through the back gate.

I'm used to the sight, but my breath still stutters at the greenery exploding behind the white picket fence. My grandmother, a woman with little use or care for most people, adores plants of any kind. Verbena and impatiens waterfall out of giant terra cotta pots, while bougainvillea and honeysuckle attempt to leap the side fences. Lichen and moss sprout between the random brick walk, while kitchen herbs scent the air in orderly rows near the fence.

Zoe dedicates most of the space to the plants she uses in her homemade soaps and essential oils, but her heart secretly lies with the ornamentals, especially those that attract the hummingbirds. I duck and dodge fifteen feeders on the way to the house and slip my board behind another next to the door before stripping off my wetsuit. I yank my sweatshirt back over my bikini and grab a pair of board shorts I'd left outside to dry the day before.

There. I'm ready for work.

Thump-thump, thump-thump-thump.

The sound hits me as soon as I open the door. Muffled and

syncopated, the pounding is the exact antithesis of the ocean's waves, and I frown as I glance at the wall clock in the mudroom. A quarter to nine in the morning?

"She never trains this late," I mutter and detour up to the second floor.

Ignoring the beachy, slip-covered comfort of the living room, I keep close to the wall as I peer around the corner. Zoe expanded and encased the balcony in glass when we moved in five years ago, turning it into an enclosed second-story greenhouse.

"This flora is different," she replied, caressing the fragile pink petals of an oleander when I asked her why. Everything grows wild and raucous in the California soil. "These flowers are my sentinels. The vines are my thorned guards."

Companions in a fight against enemies only she could see.

"Besides, the vegetation obscures the view inside our house, releases new oxygen into the air, and sucks the carbon dioxide released from my breath."

Zoe is obsessed with concealing her breath.

"If you don't want anyone to see in," I asked. "Then why do you keep the windows so spotless?"

She'd narrowed her eyes at the mention of this obsession. "Because if someone *does* happen to be looking in? I damn well want to see them, too."

Cat's-claws climb to the rafters. The bitter orange plants—used for petitgrain—line the perimeter in stumpy pots. Herbs imported from the "old world" fill the spaces in between. The tinctures she makes would've gotten her burned at the stake in another age, but she also distills chamomile for teas, lavender for salves, and dried cloves for candles that burn woody and herbaceous. She's made a name for herself locally and sells her essential oils in the board shop, but that's all just a front.

What she's really into are the poisons.

Thump-thump-thump.

Oddly, the center of this green oasis is adorned with a large mat and a heavy bag. The vines block the direct view, but Zoe's shadow stretches tellingly as she dodges across the sun-streaked room, a lithe outline of sharp jabs and light feet. Even her silhouette is martial and focused.

I bite my lip, wondering if I should try to talk to her now. Zoe has the sleep habits of an octogenarian. Three a.m. isn't her witching hour; it's her *watching* hour. She's fully caffeinated by five every day and hits this mat, literally, a half-hour later without fail.

I'd heard her working out when I left for the beach this morning. That she's still at it four hours later can only mean one of two things: she's either worried—about money or bills or me—or she's entering one of her manic phases.

I decide to wait to talk to her until I can better gauge her mood. The muffled pounding follows me back down the stairs, shifting overhead as soon as I enter the shop where Kai, our only other employee, is manning the counter.

"Late, little mahina!" he accuses, but shoots me the shaka sign anyway.

Surfing tends to attract one of two types: first, those who pull out their longboards after a long week of being a responsible adult, and who use the weekends to chase waves and the feeling of being young and free again.

Then there are the Peter Pan types, the Lost Boys and their ilk, who think responsibility is some kind of disease. Kai Levine is one of these.

Over six feet of shaggy hair, calloused heels, and tan lines. He speaks mainly in monosyllables and is one of those rare people who isn't always looking down into their smartphone ... mostly because his vacant-eyed stare is perpetually trained on the horizon.

His real age is lost to history, but my guess is anywhere from his mid-twenties to mid-thirties. He's also kinda hot ... if you don't mind someone who lives paycheck-to-paycheck and always has sand in his shorts. I'm fine with all that, but I've known him for too long to consider him anything other than a goofy, and often smelly, older brother.

The best thing I can say about Kai is that I want to be just like him when I don't grow up.

"Sorry, dude," I tell him, "but it's so sick out there right now."

The shop smells like cocoa butter and is bright with a slivered ocean view. The place comforts me as no place outside the water can, and something inside me unclenches despite the morning I've had.

Kai's blue eyes flare. "Tell me."

Poor Kai. Forced to labor indoors in hopes of a walk-in surf lesson. It's torture this late in the season, so I blow out a hard you-wouldn't-believe-it whistle as I push past him to start the coffeemaker.

"Almost every single wave held its shape. I swear, you could hang forever. I rode one nose for, like, a year."

The coffee begins brewing as Kai groans and clutches his chest. Zoe drinks tea brewed from her herb garden, natch, but I set aside some of my board shop earnings to buy a machine that brews hot mugs of heaven by the cup. It's the most expensive thing I've ever bought for myself, but my mother—not my birth mother, but the one who raised me—once told me she started drinking coffee right before college.

Maybe that's why Zoe doesn't press. I only have a handful of memories of my parents, after all.

"What beach? Rock Pile?"

"Thalia."

"Swell?"

"South." Which means it sits straight up.

Kai ragdolls it to the other side of the counter, where he pretends to fall over in mortal pain. I sip my coffee and lean over the counter to watch him flop around the ground. He squirms for a while before peering up to make sure I'm watching. "What else?"

I could tell him a bulldog peed on that exact floor mat the day before but sip my coffee instead, grimacing both at its heat and the seriously pathetic display before me. "Why don't you go see for yourself?"

His head pops up like a seal's, and I spew laughter that chases away the last of my nerves.

"Seriously?"

I shrug. "Shop's gonna be dead today, anyway."

The construction work has driven the tourists away from south Laguna; only the locals catch us now ... mostly because they prefer construction over tourists.

Besides, I'm not worried about strange men here. I know all of Zoe's secret hiding places.

For example, the faux bamboo pole dividing the center of the room conceals a sword. Each of the shop's four corners also has stools parked beneath loose ceiling tiles that sag under the weight of serrated daggers. Each clothing carousel sports metal tops that extend into steel batons.

In short, there's an accessible weapon within five feet in any direction, a fact that usually embarrasses me. Yet an image of Creeper's disfigured face flashes in my mind, and today I am soothed.

Kai's hopeful expression falls. "Shaa-a ... Zoe practically had a conniption the last time I bogied out."

I nod. She reamed him out for over an hour and told him he could go work down at the Saddleback if he didn't want to follow her rules.

"You'll be in a uniform," she'd hissed cruelly. "You'll have to bathe regularly and cut the dreads from your hair."

He was a model employee for weeks after that.

I jerk my chin at the ceiling, where the thump of the heavy bag still rumbles on its chains. "She's still working out. She'll go up and take a shower after this. You don't tell her that I got here late, and I won't say you left early."

Kai's on his feet before I finish the sentence. He belly flops on the counter, plants one large hand on each side of my face, and yanks. It's like being slobbered on by a puppy. When he's finished attacking my face, he pulls back and studies me for a reaction. "Ever been kissed like that before?"

"No."

Misunderstanding me entirely, he beams.

As Kai snags his backpack from behind the counter, I search out the reading material I'd hidden there the day before. Panicking when I find the shelf empty, I'm bent over and scrambling with my fingertips when I hear the soft chuckle behind me.

"Looking for this?"

Kai's grin widens at the narrowing of my eyes. Payback sucks. "Give it to me."

He raises the comic too high for me to reach. "Say, 'My name is Ashlyn James, and I read comics, which makes me an uber-geek.'"

"Shut up. The Signs of the Zodiac series is a collectible now. I could get good money for that."

"Geek," he sings, his gravelly voice breaking on the single syllable. Early puberty. It's Kai's resting state.

I cock my head and look toward the ceiling. "Listen. She must be finishing up."

I barely save the comic from my coffee cup as Kai bolts back around the counter. He threatens to kiss me again, but I dodge. He shrugs off the dis by doing the wave instead and clears the front door just as the shower starts upstairs.

I wait until I'm sure he's gone, then push my coffee cup to the counter's edge. Slipping the comic from its protective sheath, I take a moment to study the man on the cover. "Stryker. Agent of Light."

Then I sigh, flip it open to the first panel, and begin reading.

Yeah, in case you're wondering, I'm totally searching for clues to what happened to me this morning in the pages of a comic book.

I'm also looking at what Zoe so adamantly, wildly, and consistently claims is my true and extraordinary and *super* ... family history.

5

OH, LOOK. IT'S A SIGN.

There are things that haunt Zoe Archer, things she refuses to talk about, including those hazy months after the car accident that claimed the lives of my adoptive parents. I know she's just trying to protect me. She's done this ever since I emerged from the numbness of a near-catatonic state to find her hovering over me.

Yet even after she took over as my guardian, she refused to tell me about my birth mother. It was like she wanted me to believe I had sprung up only in relation to her. The past was never to be referenced.

Not until I accidentally found the first manual.

"Why do you have comic books?" I asked her, holding up a stack from the box I'd just opened. We were moving into Hummingbird House, though it wasn't called that yet. There were no attractive plants or feeders. There was no second-floor green-house hiding fauna meant to kill.

"You weren't supposed to see those yet," she said, and though her expression was schooled and placid, her face had drained of color.

I glanced down at the cover, confused by her reaction. *Signs of the Zodiac.*

It meant nothing to me. "Why?"

"Because that," Zoe finally said, giving the world's weariest sigh, "is why your name is now Ashlyn James. It's why we moved to a beach town where the ocean breeze can ferry away your scent. It's why we have to hide. That is your history, Ashlyn. Your birthright ... and the reason your parents were killed."

My stomach churned as I waited for the sick punchline, but she didn't smile.

Over a comic book?

I shook my head. "That was an accident. The brakes failed. I was there. I—"

"Remember? Do you?"

I searched my mind for even a small detail, something to prove the story I'd been told after waking in the hospital was true, but I'd hit my head with such force that it took me months even to recall my favorite color. The neurologist said that there were likely ways in which I would never recover.

Zoe had a different explanation.

She sat me down with a warm cup of hot chocolate and proceeded to tell me that my birth mother's name was Joanna and that she'd given me up at birth for Andie and Dennis McCormick to raise me as their own. Yet Zoe had kept an eye on me all those years ... which was how she knew about the accident.

"You are special, Ashlyn," she said as the shadows grew long outside, turning the ocean into something heard but unseen. "You come from a long line of heroes. Not policemen or firemen or any real-life warrior, but superheroes who are impervious to mortal weapons, who can run faster, leap higher ... and who battle villains on behalf of all of humanity."

Go ahead. Roll your eyes. I did.

"I swear by the stars that it's true," she said, walking me through the pages of that first comic. "Have you ever caught a flicker of movement from the corner of your eye? Or have the feeling of being watched only to turn and find that no one's there?"

"Yes."

"That means an agent of Light or Shadow, a *Zodiac* agent, has been checking you out. Yet they move too quickly for mortal eyes to see."

Zoe went on to say that while there were great male super-heroes, it was the women who were the most powerful players in the Zodiac world.

"Our lineage is matriarchal, back to the First Mothers. Back to the times when Greeks still wrote about heroic things."

"Are you a...a superhero?" The word felt new and raw on my tongue. I felt silly saying it, but Zoe didn't laugh.

"Once." She nodded and produced a comic with a woman drawn in slashing strokes of black and white. "I was an agent of Light."

I read the issue title: *The Archer of Light.*

The woman depicted there was younger and dark-haired, while Zoe was red ... but even I had to admit the resemblance was uncanny. Her weapon was strange, a palm-sized crossbow, and the symbol on her chest—a glyph, Zoe called it—glowed with the distinct Sagittarian outline of an arrow. Her name was Zoe Archer.

At twelve years old, I didn't yet know a person could legally change their name to whatever they wished.

"What happened to you?" I asked, wide-eyed.

"I gave it all up. Relinquished all of my powers to save my daughter's life."

She had another comic—she called them manuals—depicting *that* story, and after locating it within the stacks of those dusty boxes, she flipped to the end where she was shown floating in a state resembling a black void, unable to move, react, or think.

Reborn as a mortal.

"I lost everything that made me super, but it was worth it. Joanna was special. She defeated the most powerful Shadow leader in the world and, in doing so, changed the Zodiac world forever. She is the greatest superhero who ever lived. And you are her daughter."

Of course, I believed her. What twelve-year-old wouldn't?

She gave me more manuals, all carefully curated and stored for years. I devoured every one, internalizing the heroic narrative that gave me a past beyond the tragic story of a girl who'd been orphaned twice. I did this the same way other girls studied the Bible, the Koran. Teen Vogue.

The comics backed up everything Zoe said in illustrated form: a heroine named Joanna Archer had a girl child when she was only a teen, and she named her Ashlyn. In an issue entitled *The Harvest*, Zoe orchestrated an adoption to keep the baby—me —safe.

Because despite my mother's superhero status, my birth father was nothing more than your garden variety mortal. Zoe was very clear on that.

"So I'm weak?" I asked, still eating up everything she dished out. I already knew I had no powers—no ability to fly or jump or fight—and maybe this was why.

"Oh, honey. Try not to think of it that way. I like to believe that we're super *because* of our humanity, not in spite of it. But..."

She trailed off, and an alarm bell went off inside my gut, the first of many.

"But?"

Her gaze darkened. "You are a target for those who would see you as a pawn in a paranormal war."

And to a girl who'd just lost her short-term memory—along with the only parents she'd ever known and loved—this was a way to make sense of senseless loss.

The only problem was that the manuals were no longer being

written. Zoe claimed it was because the Zodiac world was broken, that it was undergoing a re-ordering of the likes of which no previous generation had ever seen. Yet someday soon, the manuals would be written again, the heroic stories would be told to a new generation, and the Zodiac world would rise.

I believed this up until the summer before I turned fifteen. I was in the kitchen, watching Zoe grind down some herbs with her mortar and pestle, listening to her voice grow breathy as she ranted about our "enemies" and how desperate they were to scent us out. The tincture she was creating would shield our "signature scent," and the next one she made would delay my glyph from emerging until later.

Until, she said, I was powerful enough to fight them all.

I remember looking down at the smooth and unblemished skin on my chest, the blank space where she was so sure my glyph would soon be, and realizing ...

My grandmother was totally and certifiably insane.

So that's it. That's how my life shifted beneath my feet again, transferring me from the terrible story of an orphaned superhero to the terrible story of an orphan raised by a wacko. One day I believed Zoe, and the next day I didn't.

Our "hiding"—having no close friends or genuine relationships outside of one another—is how her paranoia manifests itself in the real world. Does she look like the woman depicted in those old, thumbed-through comic books? Yes ... because it's the world's most elaborate cosplay. There's no supernatural underworld based on the signs of the Western zodiac. My grandmother —who clearly suffered trauma as great as the car accident that forever rocked my world—retrofitted our names to match those in the old comics.

So why play along?

Simple. I need her. Zoe might be certifiable, but I have no one else. I love Laguna—my sea and my surf—and while I might be too tomboyish and strange to be popular, I'm dialed in at school. I can stick out one more year of teachers treating me like my scrambled brain is a character fault.

If there's one thing the ocean taught me, it's that there's a time to beat against the world and its forces ... and a time to ease back and ride the wave.

"You know, when a guy saves a girl's life, she usually doesn't run off without saying thank you."

The words jolt me from my trance, and I look up to find Beck silhouetted by the morning sun, body spanning the whole of the doorway. He's changed into a fitted tee shirt that looks soft to the touch and matches his blue eyes. His hair is wet, but from the shower, not the ocean. He looks buffed instead of burnished. He also seems a little more, I don't know, *real*. Solid in a way I hadn't allowed myself to think of him before.

"What are you doing here?" I blurt, suddenly self-conscious. My hair is still tangled and threaded with sand, and peeling my wetsuit from my body probably doesn't count as a real change of clothing. I wonder what the sand bunnies Beck dates usually wear. Then, I forbid myself to wonder anymore.

"Usually," he continues, advancing on me with that same unblinking intensity, "the girl is even grateful."

The Girl. As if we're interchangeable. Every one of us, moths to be burned by the flame in those blue eyes. I choke down an instinctive snarl.

"And let me guess," I say, and fold my arms over my chest. "You're fond of gratitude."

Touching a hand to his heart, he feigns affront. "You're tough."

I could be, thanks to Zoe, but Beck doesn't know that. Besides, he says it in a way that makes me think he might like tough. That alone softens me.

"Why'd you run off like that?" he asks, ambling forward. His gaze settles on the comic before I can hide it, and he snatches it before I realize what he's done. I wait for him to make fun of me, like Kai, but after studying the image of Stryker atop the cover, he only holds it up. "What, are you saving yourself for the next hero that comes along?"

"Actually, I'm a save-myself kind of girl," I retort, swiping at the comic. He dodges easily with the counter between us and takes a step away. I'll have to go after him if I really want it back. I glance down at my still-bare feet and sigh.

"'Cept when it comes to rogue waves," he corrects, slipping the comic into his back pocket with a lazy, sideways grin. I refold my arms over my chest. No way am I going to beg. "I can see I'm going to have to get your attention in a more conventional way. How 'bout letting me buy you a real cup of coffee?"

Moth. Flame.

Interchangeable girl, I remind myself.

"I gotta work."

"Dinner, then." His voice is deeper than it'd been in the open air, huskier. Lower, too.

My heart leaps, but I say nothing.

"C'mon, now." He inches forward again, a half-grin growing beneath those still-blazing eyes. I wonder what it's like to be so sure of yourself all the time. "Don't make a real-life hero beg."

The thought of him begging is laughable, but the scrape of sound behind me has me freezing instead. A prickle works along my neck, and I shift to keep my body between Beck and the hallway behind me.

"You haven't spoken to me once in the entire year you've been here." My voice is harder than before and more formal, too. If you'd just walked in on the conversation, you might even think we'd never met at all.

I hope.

For some reason, though, Beck smiles. "Yeah...but you know I've been here a whole year."

I ignore the way my cheeks burn. "So why now?"

"Maybe now it's time." His shrug is easy, but he keeps his gaze fastened on mine, like asking me out is something he's been waiting to do forever.

For a moment, I feel spotlit, like this is a part of my own epic story ... not a fantasy concocted by a damaged mind to make sense of the world, but something that makes sense all on its own. A reality that belongs only to me.

Then, the voice slaps at me from behind. "Time for what?"

Only Beck jolts in surprise. After all, I knew Zoe was there all along.

SHE ENTERS THE SHOP ON LIGHT, SLIPPERED FEET, HER HAIR cascading down her back in a damp red stream. A cashmere sweater is wrapped atop a fitted tank, and a flowing peasant skirt covers her legs to the ankle. Most people assume she's a hippie—crunchy and granola and green all the way through—some flower child nostalgic for an era past, but she wears these things to hide her bruises ... and her strength. If anyone saw the real Zoe Archer the way I get to see her?

They'd either run away screaming or stand up and salute.

"Zoe," I say warily, trying to feel her out. I move smoothly, keeping my voice even and light, as you would with a horse that easily spooks. Her eyes flick to me like she knows what I'm doing. I tilt my head behind me. "This is Beckett."

"My friends call me Beck." He shoots her a friendly smile, his first mistake ... but how can he know that Zoe doesn't trust men who grin? She considers it suspect. Then again, she considers everything suspect.

"Hello. Beckett."

He swallows hard and glances back at me. "So ... you call your grandmother by her given name?"

"How did you know I'm her grandmother?" Zoe asks, the

sides of her mouth lifting in a way that's too edgy and iced for a real smile.

"I made a point of learning all I could about Ashlyn James," Beck says, and I want to groan. Mistake number two.

"How rude," Zoe says, floating forward, "that we haven't done the same."

She extends her hand as if to introduce herself, but I know what she's really doing and hold my breath. Beck smiles the whole time she pumps his hand, not knowing that she's breaking his body into strike zones, looking for weaknesses and tells. Never suspecting that she's testing his grip or that she's come up with five different ways to kill him before he lets go.

I clear my throat in warning.

Zoe tightens her hold.

"Your granddaughter is the best surfer chick on the strand," Beck says when he finally gets his hand back. He frowns as he rubs it. "But I s'pose you know that."

"I do ... though I don't think her being a chick has anything to do with it," Zoe purrs and turns away. Slinking along the counter to join me, she squares up on Beck like a queen would a subject. Despite the time spent with her herbs and beakers, oils, and poisons, she only ever smells like one thing: burnt roses. Her unpainted fingers hover atop the counter. Right next to the dagger she's buried among a vase of daffodil stems.

Does Beck sense the danger lurking, loose and jittery, just begging for an excuse? Can he see her trying to chisel him with that prying look? Did he feel the way she used too-smooth fingertips, ones shaved of prints, to determine if he'd done the same? Does he know she's wondering if he's a part of *her* world?

"I didn't quite catch your surname, Beckett."

Names have power and meaning in Zoe's whack-job mind. Nothing can just be what it is. It takes all my self-control not to pinch her.

"It's Lux," he answers, a frown appearing between his eyes.

The light in them begins to dim. My heart grows heavy in my chest. It's one thing for me to turn Beck down. It's another for Zoe to decide for me.

"Lux." Zoe draws the sole syllable out, overly long. "That's Latin for light."

"Is it?" He tilts his head, no longer smiling.

I shoot her a warning glare. Knock it off.

Zoe ignores me completely. "What's your lineage?"

I groan. Now she's just trying to run him off.

"I'm a little of this," Beck answers gamely. "A little of that."

"So you're a mutt," Zoe says rudely, and I elbow her in her ribs. She doesn't even grunt.

"My mother says it means I got the best of everything."

"Funny." Zoe pushes from the counter and turns away. "Mine always told me they make the best pets."

I fight the urge to throw my coffee mug at the back of her head.

Instead, I turn back to Beck, hoping the apology is clear on my face. "I gotta get back to work."

"Right," Beck says, easing backward toward the exit. I'd like to think he just can't keep his eyes off me, but he probably doesn't want to turn his back on Zoe. Good call.

Watching him go, I'm sure I'll never see him up close again, but then he flashes the comic he'd stashed behind his back while Zoe's is still turned, along with that ill-advised grin. "Pick ya up at eight."

I grin back. Not the last time I'll see Beckett Lux, after all.

"Come around the back," I call, as Zoe's gaze burns between my shoulders. Beck gives a totally gratifying fist pump, then pushes out the door and disappears before Zoe can protest. It makes me want to pump my fists, too.

"Think it hurts to have that much testosterone tripping through your body?"

I place my hands on my hips and whirl. Zoe blinks rapidly.

She thinks this makes her look innocent, but it really makes her look like a caffeinated owl.

"Would it kill you to be normal?"

She moves to the front window to study the street. "Normal has never been one of my aspirations."

I'm about to comment on her rudeness when the light catches on the hollows beneath her eyes. Were those there yesterday? Her hands are fidgety too, her nails bit down to the quick. Worry is her eye shadow. Obsessive thoughts are her liner.

"You really going out with that surf rat?" she asks suddenly, trying to distract me. She sees me watching.

"He's nice," I say, and Zoe sneers. Nobody is "nice."

Yet maybe she feels bad for running Beck off, or maybe she's hoping I won't notice how her jaw keeps clenching, but she changes the subject herself. "You were late."

That's the thing about Zoe. She can be totally crazy and utterly lucid at the same time. "I lost track of time."

"You should never lose track of that which is finite."

I roll my eyes and busy myself with refolding a stack of tees. Any argument will invite a greater tirade, and I decide against telling her about the creeper until she's acting more stable. Feed into her violent fantasies, and there's no way she'll let me go out tonight.

And while Zoe might not want to be normal, I do. I want to go out with a hot guy and have it just be a date, a spot of luck before my senior year. I want to forget all about superheroes, villains, and a grandmother who hits things and fashions poisons and looks for the fist in every outstretched hand.

I want to have at least a chance to get over what happened to me five years ago.

"You should just stay home with me," Zoe says darkly, like I've spoken aloud, but we both know that being careful doesn't mean being safe.

After all, my parent's death is proof enough of that.

6

OF GOD AND (WO)MEN.

I'm in the mudroom at eight sharp, poised to lunge for the back door at the first sign of Beck's approach. I wear a jean jacket over my white tank and a black skater skirt. I feel slightly off-kilter outside my usual board shorts and tee, but I throw on my diver's watch and feel more like myself. I also like the way I look.

Like I'm going somewhere for once and not just treading water.

Of course, Zoe's also keeping a close eye on the time. She slips downstairs, takes one look at the length of my skirt, and immediately sends me back upstairs to change. Her voice chases me.

"Where in this Mother-Loving universe are you supposed to hide weapons in something that short?"

In revenge, I slip on her silk harem pants, which she's already forbidden me to wear. Though her eyes narrow when she sees me in them, she's also outfitted them with custom pockets, so instead of ordering them off, she fills each one with a different-sized blade. This is Zoe-approved date attire.

"What do you do when someone reaches to secure your hand?" she asks as she hands me a kubaton.

I interlace my fingers with his.

"Bend their pinky finger back until it breaks," I say as I tuck the steel baton into my ankle boot.

"Unless you have enough leverage to go for the wrist," she corrects, handing me a bobby pin with pointed tips. "And when you're grabbed around the middle?"

Let that special someone pull me close for the kiss of my dreams.

"Arch backward for a head-butt or tuck for a roll." I slip the weapon in my hair where it will do the most damage in either of those cases.

A noise sounds outside the alley, and Zoe whirls, fingers twitching as she peers out the curtained window. I frown. Maybe I shouldn't leave her alone tonight. It looks like she's headed for one of her manic phases. She turns back to me as if she's heard the thought.

Then she reaches into her pocket.

"Wait!" I say, too late.

She spritzes me dead center in my face with a perfume atomizer, and I flail, coughing out the scent of wood bark, lavender, and something spicy I can't name. The particles tickle my nose and cause my eyes to water at the corners, threatening to undo all my careful work with the mascara wand. "Geez! Zo!"

Despite my sniffles, she grabs my wrists and spritzes them as well. I yank them back. "Not so much!"

"Relax. The ocean breeze will lift it off. You'll smell like a rare orchid."

It's already dissipating into something petal-soft, but I still try to wipe it away. "I want to smell like me."

Wrong thing to say.

Zoe's head does this dangerous auto-tilt. I swear, it's like there are springs and hinges in her neck. "You must never smell like you, Ashlyn. You must smell like nothing, like wind. Like ocean and sand. Never attract attention, not in word or deed or—"

"Or body or breath." I keep my expression neutral and force my jaw not to clench.

Definitely a manic phase.

"Are you okay?" I ask, though I don't want to.

She gives me a hard once-over, pauses, then snaps her fingers. "You need a belt."

And she takes off hers. It's shiny and silver and would resemble a sword if its honed edges weren't covered in a thick plastic glaze. She loops it around my waist, and I fight off the feeling of being yoked to her forever.

Nine more months, and I'm out of high school. Six months after that? I'm eighteen and can finally start living my own life.

Right now, though? It feels like I'll never be allowed to leave.

"I found a dead hummingbird this morning," she says, fastening the belt.

My heart sinks.

Zoe's never allowed me to have a cat or dog—she sees pets as a weakness that can be used against you by your enemies—but at some point in the last few years, she's grown inexplicably fond of the tiny birds.

"Whatever murdered that bird had first to penetrate the eucalyptus and the protective nectar of the garden. It even invaded the spider's silk to slip into the tight webbing of her nest." Finished with me, she once again peers out into the dark garden. "I found her inside. She looked like a little mummy."

Horror and pity for Zoe war inside of me. I want to stay and hold her tight. I wanted to push her away from me and run and forget how fervently she believed.

"I knew her. I invited her into my garden with my feeders and flowers. I watched her build the nest, and when her babies were born, she left and returned over a hundred times a day to feed them. I sat one day and counted."

I don't doubt it.

"Always busy," Zoe said absently, her gaze far off now. "Always on guard. And now she's dead because of—"

Me. You. Unstoppable evil.

I don't know what she would have said because the door rattles with a knock, and Zoe jumps right out of her slippers. I go to put a steadying hand on her arm, but she's already reaching for the handle.

"Your patio's kinda crowded," Beck says when the door opens. "And kinda dark."

I push past Zoe to flip on the porch light. Changing from skirt to silk has been a good choice. Beck's dressed in a sports coat, jeans, and boots. I have to blink a few times to make sure I'm not dreaming. If I recall correctly, Beckett Lux wore board shorts to his graduation.

He gives me an appreciative once-over. "Hello, Ashlyn James."

I grin. His insistence on saying my full name is becoming a habit I'm starting to like.

Zoe isn't quite as charmed. "Do you make it a practice to pick up your dates late, Beckett Lux?"

Tellingly, she says his full name, too.

He glances at his diver's watch. "It's just five minutes."

"A lot can happen in five minutes," she says. "A girl could even change her mind."

"I haven't changed my mind," I say, pushing forward. I note Beck straining to see inside, but I motion for him to follow me back through the garden maze while yelling over my shoulder. "We'll be back before midnight."

The 'twelves' on the clock are one of Zoe's greatest obsessions. They are a time of great magic in her imaginary world.

"Don't make me come after you," she calls back. "And remember. Listen to the wind."

Sure. If I don't die of embarrassment right here on the spot.

"Day-um," Beck says when she finally closes the door and flips off the light.

"She's usually more chill," I lie as we thread our way past a pot that's tilted on its side. Zoe's rigged it to make a nasty boom if anyone tries to set it upright. "I mean, she makes essential oils, for God's sake."

Beck shrugs as we hit the main street and surprises me by immediately taking my hand. Call me crazy, but I do not bend his pinky finger until it breaks. "I guess there are other things that are simply more essential."

And even though I know we're being watched through the shining glass of our greenhouse, at that moment, I'm not only stoked ... I even feel a little bit normal.

WE DINE AL FRESCO AT THIS HIPSTER ITALIAN PLACE OVER ON Forest Street. I recognize the hostess as a newly graduated senior who takes one look at Beck, spares a second for me, and rushes back to her stand. Her thumbs are flying over her phone's touchscreen in seconds. I don't know who she's texting, and by the time we're done with our bruschetta appetizer, I don't care.

This date rocks.

"So this isn't so bad, right?" Beck grins, echoing my thoughts. "Aren't you sad you ran away earlier today? Aren't you just mortified that you kept turning me down?"

I refuse to laugh, even if the smile hits my eyes. "Speaking of...don't you owe me a little something?"

"Owe you...oh, yeah." He reaches into his sports coat and pulls out my stolen comic. "I went ahead and read it—"

"Of course you did," I murmur, tucking it into my bag atop my secondary kubaton and pepper spray.

"Just to see what you were more interested in than me." The candlelight shifts over his jawline and catches on his cheekbones as he leans forward. I literally can't think of anything more interesting than him right now. "So why do you like it?"

"What? Comic books are below you?" I try to change the subject. "Too busy oiling your pecs?"

"No, I'm serious—though gratified that you noticed my oiled pecs." He props his chin on his hands. "What do you like about those things?"

I push the pasta around on my plate. I should let it go. We're having such a great night, and if he laughs, I'll have to hate him a little. Zoe's stories of a superhero lineage have messed me up that much. "Are you familiar with the Zodiac series at all?"

"Have they made a movie out of it?" he asks, and I roll my eyes so hard he laughs. "Then no. But I got the general idea from this one. Superheroes, right?"

"There's more to it than that. It's been written for—" Centuries. "A long time. I can give you the entire history lesson some other time, but the gist is this: Once upon a time, in ancient Greece, there were two sisters who were very close until..."

"Along came a man," he guesses.

"That's right, Lux," I feign shock. "But not just any man."

"Course not." It's Beck's turn to roll his eyes. "How else would he spawn a whole series?"

"This was a God. Ophiuchus. There's a constellation named after him—"

"Why?" Beck interrupts while chewing. "I mean, two sisters? Really?"

My laughter catches the hostess's eye. She begins texting furiously again.

"Anyway, one of the sisters tattled to Zeus about the other's relationship with Ophiuchus. Gods disapproved of co-mingling with mortals, you know."

"Gotta keep that bloodline pure."

"It tends to be a reoccurring theme," I say wryly. "But Zeus, while impulsive, wasn't stupid. He sensed the betraying sister's real motives and realized Ophiuchus had been courting both mortal women. So he cursed each one with a fatal illness."

"'Cause it's always the chick's fault, right?"

"Also a reoccurring theme," I concede. "Yet that's when our hot, if noncommittal, hero finally stepped up. Still wishy-washy on the commitment front, he gave both sisters an elixir that restored their health and made them superhuman, thus protecting them from the gods."

"So they all lived happily—if illegally—ever after."

"Wrong. He was punished instead."

Beck's eyebrows arch up. "Oh, a progressive fairy tale."

"Myth," I correct, taking a sip of my water. "Anyway, the women went on to beget two lines of descendants, Light deriving from the good sister—"

"Duh."

I smile. "And Shadow from the betraying sister. Since then, every generation has seen twelve men and women born in every major city, raised and trained to battle their opposites on the zodiac wheel. But just like those First Mothers, we follow the stars, and they tell us how to live."

Question marks bloom in Beck's blue eyes. "We?"

"They," I say quickly, heat spreading through my cheeks. Zoe and her stupid neuroses.

Beck doesn't say anything for a long moment. "Well, that's ..."

I wait and finally sigh when he remains tongue-tied. "Go ahead. Say it."

"Okay, totally geeky." He blows out an intentionally hard breath but holds up a hand as he laughs. "But I like it on you, Ashlyn James. It balances out all that hot action on the waves. Brains and brawn, as they say."

"I don't know anyone who says that," I retort, but I'm secretly relieved.

"Wanna hit Main Beach?" Beck asks afterward as he drapes his coat over my shoulders. I hesitate only because Zoe forbids me to go near the water at night, and not because she's crazy.

Some dangers have nothing to do with the supernatural.

"Sure." And, smiling, I let him steer me north. I know where we're going. The hilltop gazebo atop Heisler Park has the best view of the entire strand, and even if we can't see the surf at night, we'll hear it crashing directly below the pavilion's rocky perch.

"So, one more year at Laguna High," Beck says as we head up. "And then, what? Maui? Bora Bora?"

"Yes! I mean, I wish." It's every surfer's dream. "I'm not sure where I'll start."

"Not here, though?" He says it softly like he's testing.

Zoe's here, I think, shaking my head. I love Laguna, but I can't stay here and be free. Like a rip current, her psychosis would pull me under. "Just someplace with a beach. I can't be without my waves."

"You love it."

"The ocean healed me." I glance up because I want to read his expression. Julia is the only person I've told about the accident, and though she tries to understand when I explain how the waves taught me to live and trust and hope again, she doesn't share my love for surfing. "I was in a car accident when I was twelve. I lost my parents. They were my adoptive parents, but the only ones I'd ever known."

He stops on the incline, his face half-eaten by shadows. It makes him look older and graver ... and somehow sad. "You mean you didn't even know Zoe before, what? Twelve?"

I shake my head. "I don't remember the accident. The doctors say it's my mind's way of protecting itself. Everything right before it is a blank spot. The week that followed was completely gone. It's like my family was there, and then..."

And then nothing. And then I am alone.

"Were you injured?" Beck asks as we begin walking again. "You don't have any scars."

"My mind works ... differently. My teachers dismiss it as dyslexia or ADHD."

His voice softens. "Most of the best surfers are."

I smile at the compliment. "Concentrating is hard, school's a nightmare, but I don't know...maybe it would be harder if I remembered."

I wrap my arms around my middle, pulling his jacket tight. It smells of his cologne, the ocean ... and something else I'm beginning to recognize as Beckett Lux.

"All I know is that there's a blank spot whenever I try to access that time. None of it matters when I'm surfing, though."

We've reached the gazebo. Lamplight casts shadows into the initials other late-night strollers have carved into its supporting beams. The city regularly whitewashes the sentiments into nonexistence, but like the waves, the marks keep coming back.

Beck slips his hands beneath the jacket and slides them along my arms until goosebumps rise atop my skin. His coat slips from my shoulders to pool at my feet, but his body heat chases away the cool bite in the air, and neither of us moves.

"Don't worry about those blank places, Ashlyn."

"No?" I feel him lean closer, and his scent—that thing that is him—causes me to go dizzy.

"Nah. I mean, look up. The stars shine more brightly because of the darkness, not despite it."

I look up, but it's into his face, stars forgotten. He moves closer, and I think of the perfect kiss, how amped I am, and what Julia would say if she could see me right now.

And that's when Vasari and his misshapen henchmen appear.

That's when this fragile freedom blows up in my face.

Because that's when my psycho grandmother shows up and shoots me dead right before midnight.

7

RISE AND SHINE.

I don't know what it feels like when other people get shot, but the bullet from Zoe's gun gut-punches me like the world's tiniest, sharpest fist. The dense iron rips through my soft flesh, burning as it tunnels through shocked organs. I'm so focused on that searing heat that I fall in slow motion, jerking mid-air as the bullet lodges next to my spine.

"Open to it."

It takes me a moment to recognize Zoe's voice, but as soon as I do, I know ...

That psycho's been planning to shoot me for years.

I'm too busy dying to care. I'm also kinda distracted. It feels like legs are sprouting from the bullet, tiny prongs snapping out and locking onto my vertebrae. I'd scream, but my breath is long gone, and lightheadedness roars through my skull in bright, carbonated bubbles before flipping to pool in my toes.

Suddenly, I'm upright again, momentarily weighted to the ground. Then the base of my skull explodes, my head snaps back ... and I float.

I open my eyes to find the night sky blazing down upon me. The sea is there, too, but compared to the Universe, it's surprisingly inconsequential. So am I ... or I would be if every constellation hadn't turned its shining gaze upon me as I began drifting into the sky. My body is stitched to space, limbs dissolving in the blackness. All that makes me *me* melts away except for one thing.

That bullet. Whatever's inside of it tugs me directly into the heart of the blinding cosmos.

The stars roar in recognition. They blink, bending light, bowing as if they recognize me. Gazing back, it's like I'm seeing my soul. I gasp, inhaling stardust, particles, and atoms as old as the Universe's birth.

Then my vision snaps to black and white, my limbs jerk back to life, and—with starlight humming in my skin—two words flash with the speed of light: *Feet. Earth.*

I somersault, spot the ground with the ease of a lioness, and land back on my feet just as lightning splits the earth. Right between the five attacking men and me. Their bodies momentarily burn in a one-dimensional sketch, outlines penciled in red. Two other shapes—Zoe and Beck—are drawn white against the stark night, but I keep my attention trained on the five beings staring at me through a blood-red hue.

A second clear thought whips through my mind.

Kick. Ass.

Vasari is closest, a bright cherry silhouette of fetid muscle and brawn.

"Don't worry, boys," he calls out. "She's been flooded. It's just temporary."

"But it's enough," Zoe says, and it is.

I lunge without thinking because I already know what to do. Stardust explodes as my fist connects with Vasari's mangled jaw, and he rockets backward. The other four men sprawl like bowling pins, but he doesn't move, and the whites of his eyes stay fixed on the night sky. His scarlet outline fades.

Zoe screams something I can't quite hear, and Beck shoots back a frantic reply, but the sound is just energy, zinging between my teeth like fillings. I taste the residue of centuries on the tip of my tongue. I am still connected to the stars.

I also suddenly have a weapon in my hand. Zoe's belt is in my right palm, yet I have a new name for it as the other men scramble.

"Urumi," I say in Zoe's voice as I drop the thick protective shell around it to the ground. I crack the flexible metal against the cement; it's both whip and sword, and the pavement ruptures beneath my practiced hand.

"Shit! She's got a conduit!" The four men draw close, snapping tight like a chain.

"That's right, Mother-Lovers." The smile bleeds through Zoe's voice. "Time to Rise and shine."

I don't know what that means, but the redhead on the end mutters to the others, his breath like brimstone, all charred gristle and heat. I can't hear him clearly—my ears are still filled with the language of the stars—but years of surfing have made me an expert lip-reader.

On three, boys.

They fan out to cage me in, their red outlines slowly replaced by smoke. Beck and Zoe back away, one protecting the other, though I can't tell which. Thunder rumbles overhead, and heat lightning lashes out to reveal four charred skeletons, eye sockets black and empty. They are all looking at me, and they are grinning madly.

I give them my best pageant-girl smile and begin whipping the urumi around my body in arching figure eights.

Back to the sky, back to the stars, I leap. My newly strengthened thighs are fueled with astounding power, and—suspended just for one extra second—I can't help but laugh as all four men's heads turn up to me. I aim for the brightest danger, a man with spiked hair and the scent of a faulty exhaust pipe, and fall.

Gravity bends for me, and I drop faster than he expects. The urumi whips out, extending my reach, and the blow sings up my arm as it sinks into his charred skull. The explosion of scorched funk is so satisfying that I totally miss the fist rocketing my way from the other side.

I thud full-force into the gazebo's support beam, shaking the small pavilion on its pilings while the urumi bends around it, jerking from my grasp. The blow should knock me out cold. The pain should steal my breath.

Instead, I jerk my head, lick the blood from my mouth, and rear back up.

We fight in the center of the shaded building, where darkness devours the redhead's features. Without the stench, I wouldn't know where to strike.

"Hurry, Ash!" Zoe calls from somewhere. Everywhere. "Your power's abating!"

It is. We trade blows, and while I block most, the ones that land burn like flame. It's also becoming harder to catch my breath in the increasingly dense smoke. I finally drop to one knee beneath a wild left hook and lunge to wrap my arms around both of his legs. He topples, head striking the ground with a fatal crack.

Just to be sure, I catapult him the other way, releasing him so that he flies over the rocky hillside and onto the beach below.

I sense rather than see the next man rushing me, but as I cringe to take the blow, a whistling shot rings out from my right. Turning, I find Zoe standing wide-legged and holding an object that's a cross between a pipe and a flute. The man falls without ever finding another breath. Poison.

The last man takes one look at her, spares me a second, and whirls to run. I yank at the leather strap above my boot, take aim with the throwing star nestled there, and whip it tail-over-end through the air so it sinks into his spine.

Or would have ... if Creeper didn't catch it in his fist.

He looks the same as he did this morning ... yet different, too. The skin wrapped over his skull is even ropier, and the black bone beneath has gone marbled with decay. His teeth have also turned ebony, which I only note because he smiles as he whips the star back at me lightning-fast. I barely have time to dodge.

"We meet again, daughter of Chaos." This time, the man's breath overwhelms the oxygen in the air. I feel the plants wilt and brown around me. I also begin to choke. His every word is singed.

He looks at the man I would have killed and jerks his head at Zoe. "Get her."

I take a step toward her, but the creeper intercepts, whip-fast. "Don't even think about it."

I don't have to. Just as the other man reaches for Zoe—which she, in her humanity, never even sees—Beck darts to intercept. The two tumble down the hillside while Zoe whirls back to fire another poisoned dart. Yet the creeper's feet are hydraulic springs. By the time she's lifted the blowgun to her lips, he's already leaped the gazebo's ledge with me tight in his grip.

I reach for Zoe, scream for Beck, and scramble for the power that was so strong just moments before. Yet I'm a rag doll in this guy's grip, body slamming against the cliffside as he bounds to the beach. We fall the last fifty feet into the dark voice of the surf, Zoe's scream chopped short as water closes over my head.

So much for my short stint as a twenty-first-century superhero.

8

FREEZING, FRIGHTENED, FREAKED ... AND A FEW OTHER F-WORDS.

I cy, moon-drenched water attacks my limbs and floods my throat. I manage to suck in one greedy gulp of air before Creeper alters his grip and rockets directly into the face of a cresting wave.

I've duck-dived thousands of times but never bulleted into the ocean like this. The pure force of it creates drag, and saltwater stings my eyes as I struggle against the ocean's weight.

Creeper pinches me more tightly around my neck until black dots appear behind my cold eyelids.

I shouldn't even be conscious ... which gives me hope. I shouldn't be *alive*, not with the force of the giant hand palming my neck. So maybe if I can survive long enough, there'll be another miracle in my immediate future.

If only I could see the stars.

Creeper halts suddenly, and I slam against his chest harder than should be possible when fully submerged. Wrapping one strong arm around my core, he drags me back to the surface, and I scent the bile staining his breath when I gasp.

The dude is no prettier up close. His lidless eyes remain

unblinking, and his petrified skin stretches like dried jerky atop the blackened bone.

"Now," he says, his rot billowing hotly over me. "Where were we before we were so rudely interrupted this morning?"

We are miles from the shoreline. The lights of Laguna have been reduced to flickers, mere fireflies on the distant shore. Yet the stars above are raw and sharp.

"Don't you remember me, daughter of Chaos?"

"I remember the funk," I reply without thinking, and the next thing I know, I'm beneath the waves, his immobile hand palming my skull as I flail.

I wish for my belt, my urumi, because that would make this a more even match. Yet it's lost on the hillside, and the stardust that so ably powered my limbs has dissipated in the saltwater. My ears are buzzing by the time Creeper finally drags me back to the surface.

"Yes!" I gasp as he looks at me expectantly. "You were there today."

"Stupid, freakish spawn! I mean, five years ago."

Memory flashes, white-hot. My father and mother cuffed at the neck like I am now, one lifted high on each side of this man's leering face.

I clear my head of it. That's not right. My parents died in a car accident ... and I was unconscious through it all.

The creeper chuckles. "And you say I stink? Your confusion smells like soured milk, bad enough ... though it's absolutely rancid when melded with your humanity. Even if your mother hadn't upended our world's natural order, you would never take her place in the Zodiac. Not in that befouled mortal skin. That's why Zoe has kept you hidden."

"Zoe's kept me safe," I sputter. He's teasing me with air, letting the waves lap at my mouth.

"Zoe's ashamed of you. A quarter Shadow, a quarter Light...

but the other half of you? Human." He spits the word like it tastes terrible. "Your weakness requires hiding ... even from yourself."

Play along, I think, the knowledge from all the comics Zoe has fed me filtering through my mind. Play along, and stay alive long enough to think of something.

Fortunately, Creeper isn't even close to being finished. "Where did you get your conduit?"

I shake my head. "It's just a belt—"

Stupid answer. We both know that's not true. He dunks me so that I struggle ... so that I almost stop struggling.

"Zoe," I rasp when he lifts me again.

"Zoe Archer." If he had a proper upper lip, it'd curl. "That woman just doesn't know when to die. Can you touch any others?"

"What?"

"Conduits!" He shakes me so hard my teeth rattle. "Can you touch any more of our world's magical weapons?"

"I don't know."

"By the stars, Archer," He leans close, spitting his maggot breath into my face. "You're a failure in every Mother-Loving world."

I fall dead still. There are many things about this situation that I'm having trouble wrapping my brain around, but my being a failure ain't one of them. "Screw you, rat vomit. I'm half-super."

And as soon as I say it, I know it's true. Perhaps I've always known. Maybe my need to pretend I'm normal is *because* I know it.

The creeper's blackened skull pulses like a heartbeat, pressing against his skin until one foul cheekbone actually pops. "What you *are*, Ashlyn Archer ... is half-dead."

He pushes me deep underwater this time, first with his arms and then by wrapping his legs around my neck, thrusting me lower. Eyes squeezed shut, I kick harder as the cold depths of the ocean reach up to thread between my legs. I try to wedge my palms between my neck and those strong, unyielding legs.

"Hold still."

Get tubed, I think, struggling harder. No way am I going down without a fight.

Yet the hands around my wrists are too strong ... and somehow out of place. I fall still and crack open one eyelid to find another face before me. It's also misshapen, but only due to the water pulsing in the inches between us. I open my mouth to scream anyway.

Beck moves one hand atop my lips. "Shh. His hearing is honed. He'll hear you and love it. Also, do me a favor. Stop running away from me, all right? I'm trying to help. Oh, yeah ... another thing. Breathe."

I shake my head, panicking all over again at the reminder that I can't breathe, and Creeper's legs tighten around my neck, fingers tensing atop my skull. He thinks I'm still struggling.

"Ashlyn, trust yourself. You can see me. You can hear me. Trust that you're super." Beck raises his brows like I'm being unreasonable, then points to himself. "Now, trust that you can breathe."

This time, when I try to shake my head, the creeper holds it tightly in place.

"Breathe," Beck coaxes again, and I'm so busy watching him do it—even while it hits me that he knows about all of this—that I don't even register how he eases forward and firmly places his lips atop mine.

It's the kiss I was hoping for on dry land.

It blooms in light of my newly enhanced senses, and color explodes behind my eyes. The scent that only teased at my brain before is now rich and dizzying as it swirls inside my mouth. I breathe in ripe, sun-warmed grapes, followed by a sorbet's bright, lemony coolness, and then something loamy and rich, like dark, churned earth.

I inhale deeply, wanting more, chasing that taste, and that's when it hits me.

I *can* breathe.

Beck pulls back as I open my eyes, awed. I can still taste him on my lips.

"Okay?" he asks.

"Okay," I reply, as if it's natural. I don't remember reading about this ability in any comic book, but I'm not about to—

The creeper yanks me back to the surface.

Cold air attacks my skin, and my shudder convinces Creeper that he's just pulled me from the precipice of death. Leering close, he studies my face, and I realize that if I live through this, I'm gonna owe Zoe a big apology. Forget that she was telling the truth the whole time ... *this* is what crazy looks like.

"Titan should have killed you five years ago," Creeper snarls, spittle hitting my face.

"I don't know who that is," I choke. Play along, stay alive.

And where is friggin' Beckett?

"His failure has cost us much in the reordering of our world." Apparently, Creeper is gonna give me a history lesson while I catch my breath. Awesome. "We would have ascended to the god state, but instead, we languish among the mortals we were meant to rule. And now, a new generation is supposed to rise up and take our place?"

His voice plunges to a serrated whisper.

"Do the Mothers really believe I'm going to relinquish my position and power and birthright to some snot-faced neo-agent who doesn't even know she's a child of the stars?" He turns his mangled face directly to the sky and screams. "Do you hear me? I am not going anywhere!"

A shadow shifts over his left shoulder.

Creeper lowers his burning gaze down to mine. "It's too bad you lost your conduit on that hillside. I'd like to erase you from existence the way you once tried to doom me."

That has a shudder ratcheting down my spine. Turning a conduit on its owner—if that's what I was—turned their personal power against them. In evil supervillain shorthand? It'd blot out my life like I'd never existed.

"That's okay." His gaze turns almost fatherly as he reaches into the front of his leather vest. "Mine is sharp enough to kill everything you think is super in you."

His is a one-inch thick stake, and as long as his forearm. I get the feeling he's spent a lot of time honing it to that wicked point. "What? You didn't think you were the only person able to touch the conduits, did you?"

I didn't think there were such things as magical weapons, but there's no time to say that. The thin stake winks brightly in the hovering moon, and only two things keep me from fighting as Creeper lifts it overhead. One, he expects it and has already adjusted his grip. Two, that familiar figure is closing in over his shoulder.

Instead, I pull myself close. I cut off his angle, erase the space between us, and wrap my legs around his. Then I hold him in place. Beck's arm, appearing from nowhere, steals around Creeper's throat and squeezes.

I struggled in his arms, but Creeper thrashes in mine. Beck arcs back to cut off his air supply—and to keep clear of that deadly stake—but there's, like, an endless supply. Twice, I'm hit by an errant fist and have to readjust my grip. Two against one proves totally helpful, though, and the onslaught slows as Creeper finally, slowly, passes out.

"Watch out!" Beck suddenly cries.

Too late. I glimpse the stake flashing in the moonlight and can only brace against it. I struggle to wedge that arm high, but the dude is right. I'm half-mortal, he's not, and even with Beck at his back, the stake closes in on my face.

"Enough." Beck rears back and head-butts the man right in

the nose. Blood and soot pour from it before his eyes roll into the
blackened skull. His whole body falls slack.

I stare at Beck. "Now what?"

I hope he doesn't expect me to help him hold this guy under.
Fighting off a murderous super-villain is one thing, but killing
someone outright is not my jam.

Beck shakes his head. "All I have is a blade, and that won't kill
someone from our world."

The Zodiac world. Right.

"Then what do we do?"

"Same thing we've been doing since the Reordering." His look
cuts through the darkness. "We run."

WE RUN.

Or, in this case, swim. I focus only on that, trying not to think
too hard, even with this newfound ability to breathe underwater,
and as I reach the beach faster than ever before. What the hell
happened to me on that hillside?

You know what happened.

But even now, the idea of Zoe unlocking latent powers inside
of me—and doing it with a key that looked and felt a lot like a
bullet—is too much to take in as we stumble onto the down-
turned mouth of the empty beach.

I place my hands on my knees and glance back at the dark
ocean as I catch my breath. Water undulates beneath my strong,
new eyes as far as I can see while the ancient sky pulses above
like an expansive heart.

I turn back to the beach just in time to spot something
streaking along the sand ... and headed right for us.

"Um?"

"Oh, sh—"

Beck can't even finish his curse. The thing plows into him like
a smoking tire, catapulting his body into mine and blasting the

breath from my chest. The accompanying war cry cracks open the ocean air. Even the waves stutter-step on their way to shore.

Vasari. I recognize the stench and the sound.

Palming Beck's face, Vasari slams it against my chest and holds it there as he edges around to pin me with a gaze that's too bright for the evil lurking beneath that ruptured skin. When Beck attempts to rise, Vasari double-taps the sand with his skull. I grunt beneath all that weight.

"We have unfinished business, daughter of Chaos. I was about to flay the skin from your body, was I not?"

Yeah, and carve the chaos from my bones, I think to myself, but I'm kinda hoping he'll forget about that part.

I try to struggle since Beck seems to have given up, but the starlight in my blood has dimmed. The power that seared my every nerve has been doused by the ocean and exhaustion and fear and the creeper. Beck begins gurgling atop me as Vasari shifts, straddling us both as he rears back.

His teeth gleam against the soot of his charred face, sharp stars filed into mean chips. It's a neat party trick, but my attention is on the blade arching high over his head, and then down as he screams again and keeps on screaming...

Until his head topples from his erect body.

"Ugh." Beck cringes, getting the worst of it.

Nasty.

"Get off me," I gag and turn my face to the sand, using it to wipe away the hot, wet streak I feel burning my forehead and cheek.

I'd crawl to the water's edge to let the waves lap away the blood and heat, but I don't trust that the creeper won't appear there, so I finish wiping my hand over my face and turn back to find someone else looming.

She's clad in skintight black leather, with moonlight that blazes through her tight onyx curls, and a sword steaming at her side. She wears a hard expression as she takes in my wet, ripped silk and shocked face. Then she extends her free hand to me, and in it—carefully held in its protective sheath—is my urumi.

"You have to finish him off."

"He's not a plate of peas!" I back away, but Beck is behind me, and for some reason, he's pushing me forward.

The girl forces my urumi into my hand. "We can't kill a full-fledged agent with my sword. It's mortal-made."

"Then I guess Vasari will live to roar another day."

I dig in my heels, literally. They sink into the wet sand as the girl pulls me toward the prone man.

"Do you really want Vasari to live to roar another day?" Beck's voice, warm in my ear, sends chills down my spine for entirely different reasons than I ever imagined. I glance back at him, and our eyes connect in the moonlight for just one moment.

I see nothing of the boy I went on a date with earlier this evening. Gone is the guy who shredded summer waves like he was born to it. Instead, there's this severe dude with a sharp gaze dusted with dark matter. A flash of revulsion hits me because it looks more like the creeper's than any I've ever seen.

So does the girl's ... who is suddenly forcing my palms around my urumi. In a single move, she removes its sheath. "The Mother-Lover is mending. End it already."

I look at Vasari convulsing, *mending*, on the ground and shake my head. "I don't th—"

Wrapping her hands tight around mine, the chick uses her strength to power through my weakened limbs, rocketing the urumi overhead. It lands right where she wants, finishing the job her sword started in one thunderous crack.

The accompanying scent is like the plague took a bath in gangrene and then dried off in a towel of butt funk. We all choke until the ocean breeze finally drives it away.

"That," the girl finally says, a crisp bite to her voice, "is how you take down a Mother-Loving Elder."

Beck high-fives her, then holds a hand out to me as she uses the sand to wipe off her sword. Her *sword*, I think, wobbling on my feet.

Beck moves to steady me, but I jerk away. "What the hell was that?"

I mean all of it. The hillside ambush, the second near-drowning of the day. Oh yeah ... forced murder! Beck knows about it all. Suddenly, I want my friggin' kiss back!

But I'll settle for an answer.

"You okay?" he asks instead.

"See this?" I gesture up and down my body that was, only moments ago, pinned beneath a headless man. "This is totally the opposite of what okay looks like!"

"You're breathing," he points out, unhelpfully.

I give him a wry double-thumbs up. "Awesome."

Beck sighs. "Please calm down. Your panic smells like rotten eggs. And if I can scent that, so can they."

"Ditto." The girl hands me my urumi's protective sheath. "So whatever you're thinking, stop."

"Leave her be, War."

Eyes widening, I hold up my hands. "Her freaking name is *War*?"

"Your freaking name is *Archer*?" she retorts, crossing her arms. The moon is shining brighter now, so I can make out her features: dusky skin, wide eyes, and a full mouth pursed in disapproval. I'd call her hair windswept, but I bet it always springs from her head in untamed coils. In fact, I bet *untamed* is one of her greatest personal traits.

"No," I mutter, sheathing and belting my urumi. "It's not."

But it is in the Zodiac world. *Her* world.

Screw that. I give the Black Joan-of-Arc and her bloody sword a one-finger salute and stalk off in the opposite direction.

Beck jogs to catch up. "You gotta come with us, Ashlyn."

I dodge away from his blood-soaked chest. "Wrong-O, freaky Zodiac-liar-bastard-jerk."

Don't judge me. I'm totally mad.

"I'm going to find Zoe and get myself out of here." The last I'd seen, she'd been hurtling off the cliff, too. There'd been a flash of movement, then nothing. "And by the way? That was the most bogus date ever!"

"Your matriarch is safe," War says, flanking my other side. I eye her sword warily. "Which is more than I can say for us if we don't find a secure location."

"Please. Trust us, Ash," Beck tries.

"Yeah," War adds. "We're not the ones trying to flay the skin from your bones."

But she's not exactly friendly, and it also occurs to me that Beck could've saved me the hassle of being attacked—*twice!*—if he weren't such a two-faced liar.

Crossing my arms, I stop dead. "You already knew Zoe when you came into the shop today, didn't you? Have you been watching us? Do you even really like to surf?"

"I knew *of* her," he corrects with a sigh, and how would he not? The Zoe Archer of comic book lore was one of the most famous heroines ever. But that's not the point. The point is that Beck hadn't been interested in me at all. Not for his own personal reasons. Certainly not for mine.

Determined not to let him know how much that stings, I finally turn away. "Screw this. I'm outta—"

My heart gives a meaty double-tap and flips. The surf rears up to make a roaring home inside my head as I hit the sand. Heat flashes through me, and someone lets out a blood-curdling scream. I whip my head side-to-side, but all I see are the stars squinting back at me. "Who was that?"

"It's the blowback," Beck says, and even though he looms above me, his fake surfer voice is far, far away.

"That was fast," War adds, but she sounds tinny, too, even as she leans close.

Beck's eyes lay worried on mine. "Just breathe, Ashlyn."

God, he's so pretty for a total liar.

"What's happening?" I croak.

Beck's pretty eyebrows draw low. "You didn't just regain your hereditary powers when Zoe shot you. It's all returning ... including your memories."

I shake my head because now I know where the screaming is coming from. It only increases the spinning. "No, I don't want —"

"I'm sorry, Ash. I'm so sorry..."

And as the scream—my mother's scream—fills my mind again, I am totally sorry, too.

9

WHAT YOU DON'T KNOW CAN KILL YOU.

"See how they interlock? Purl one, knit two."

I am dreaming. I know that much because, in the dream, I am almost twelve years old and sitting next to my mother, who is teaching me how to knit. I do not yet surf. I have never been to Laguna.

All I know is this.

"Where's Dad?" I ask, but the sound goes scratchy in this, my memory. I have gone off script because almost twelve-year-old me knows exactly where Dad is. The same place he always is on this day of the month. His Friday night poker game—which mom doesn't understand but supports—leaves us curled together beneath a task lamp on the slip-covered sofa. Across from us, the curtains lay open to the unblinking eye of a full summer moon.

Spotlit for those who move in shadows. For those who *are* Shadows.

"Purl one, knit two. That's it." The enormous needles obey her hands, and the yarn bends and takes shape beneath her dancing fingers.

It's like magic to me, how she can will something with no form at all into something beautiful. I felt like she does this with me sometimes—because I am still forming, too, my potential being constructed with her careful guidance.

I frown at the beautiful yarn in my hands. I picked it out. Under her watchful eye, I've already learned how to sew by hand and machine, but this is my first go at knitting. It's just a simple scarf, but we keep backing up and unwinding the work we've already done. I try to imitate her deft touch, but I can't keep the rows straight. I keep lifting my elbows to jam the hook through the yarn, a habit she gently corrected by stroking my shoulders and arms.

I finally drop the entire heap onto my lap. "It's the yarn. It's too scratchy and stiff."

I loved the color at first sight, a salmon pink sparking with threads of silver—but now it seems babyish. After all, in less than twenty-four hours, I'll be twelve. "I don't even know why I chose it."

"There's nothing wrong with the yarn." My mother caresses the few finished rows like they're the finest she'd ever seen. "Sometimes it's hard to envision a finished piece, especially if you've never done it. The trick is to imagine it as tangible before it even exists. It takes a while, but trust yourself, keep going, and I promise it'll come."

A totally unsatisfying answer.

I wrinkle my nose but settle back in close to her side. Truth is, I love this. She's always flitting around, mopping or spraying or cooking something on the stove. Usually all at the same time. Having her to myself, sitting still and soft and warm at my side, feels just as good now as when I was small.

Especially now that my sense of smell has begun to bloom.

Purl one, knit two.

Inhaling deeply, I catch a whiff of the spearmint gum she's no longer chewing. That'd been a startling revelation. That I could smell things that were already gone. I still smell the rose scent of her soap from her morning shower, now gone soft and powdery, while the bitter chamomile from the tea cooling beside her is a soft cloud around my head. My mother is a garden of soft scents.

The woman at the library, Zoe, was right.

I've seen you here before. I have some comic books I think you'd like...

Purl one, knit two.

Fast forward two months, and I practically live amongst the stacks. By now, I know the entire history of the Zodiac series, I've read every manual. And I want more.

Someday, you'll run as fast as a cheetah, Ashlyn. Jump from rooftops without injury. Scent your enemies with a bloodhound's nose. You're not just special...you are super.

Purl one, knit two.

By now, Zoe is more than just the librarian. We meet secretly after school because she says I also need martial training. She shows me the dojo she built in the library's basement. She goes easy on me, working more on speed and flexibility than outright combat, but she's still purposeful. Tai chi and drills for my body, mediation for my mind.

The Zodiac world is one of good and evil. Your friends can only access it through their imaginations, through comic books. Yet mark my word ... you will have a place of glory within it.

My mother makes an approving noise, and I know without looking up that she's smiling. "That's great, sweetie. See? You can do it. You just need to trust yourself more."

And an explosion rocks the street outside.

"What on earth?" Mom rises to cross to the front window, where she is silhouetted between our thin curtains.

I lower the yarn to my lap. "What is it?"

"I don't know," she murmurs, pushing the curtains open more. "I can't see anything. The moon has disappeared."

Watch the planets. Watch the stars. They will warn you that change is coming.

My knitting needles clatter to the floor as I stand. "Mom?"

And Ashlyn? You are a child of the stars. You will feel the change inside of you.

Mom presses her cheek against the window, angling her head to get a look at the sky.

"Mom, I don't think you sh—"

The back door crashes open, and Mom yelps and whirls, but it's only my dad entering from the attached garage. He slams and locks the door behind him, breathing hard. He smells like burning fuel.

Fear.

"Andie! Away from the window!"

Her hand flutters to her chest. "Denny? What's—?"

"There's a man." Dad rushes forward, reaching for her and the curtains at the same time. Outside, the gloom thickens. It clouds the glass like pressing fingers and seeps through cracks in the door. I sniff and scent something burning ... something already dead. "He's watching through the window. He ran when I pulled up and opened the garage, but now—"

The windowpane explodes, and a large, bare arm shoots out to seize my mother around the face. She squeaks in the din of falling glass.

Dad screams. "Andie!"

The arm jerks back, and my mother disappears with it. The rest of the glass shatters around her body, and a scream finally fractures in my mind. Dad lunges for me while the front door rockets from its hinges, thwacking against the floor like a mallet and clipping him on the way down.

A man appears on the other side. He spans the width of the doorway. Striding evenly, barely breathing, he takes three steps into the room, bends, and throws the door aside so that it cracks the dining room table in two. Then he lifts my unconscious father from the floor by his neck.

No more! I don't want to see any more!

I don't want to see the expression on the man's face as he comes after me.

I don't want to watch my parents die again.

THE KNOT OF PAIN INSIDE OF ME IS BOTH OLD AND NEW ... A RAW, sorrowful thing that once caused me to cry until I vomited, and scream until my vocal chords went ragged.

How could I ever have forgotten?

"Because I erased your memory."

The answer is zipping through me before I even realize I asked the question aloud, and though I keep my eyes shut, I can suddenly smell Zoe everywhere. She's here in the room, but she's also in the past ... Zoe coming to me after my parents died, holding and rocking and calming me until I could finally hear the words through the animal noises in my throat.

I can take the memories from your mind, Ashlyn. You can deal with them later when you're older and more able. But you'll have to forget the rest of it, too. The Zodiac world. Your powers. It'll all be taken from you.

I agreed. Of course I did ... I was a kid.

And everything I'd loved had already been taken from me.

I don't know how she found me now. Maybe Beck and the murderous girl on the beach called her, but the familiar Zoe-scent of burnt roses is amplified in my nose ... although the sour milk smell is new. Panic, Beck had named it.

And tacos, I think, cracking open one lid. I smell tacos.

I open my eyes and find I'm lying in the corner of a small settee in what appears to be a giant tin can. Beyond a wide, frosted glass window, I can make out two figures moving about the perimeter outside. One has a sword.

I blink. "Are we at The Taco Tavern?"

"It's your favorite snack shack, right?" Zoe is hunched over a steel prep counter, loading up a backpack. Not with tacos, but things.

My things.

"Yeah, but I come here for the carne asada." I sit up. "Not superhero cosplay."

Zoe's wearing the same clothing as earlier tonight, her hair glowing flame red in the security lights, but it's still a very different Zoe Archer than the one I left at Hummingbird House.

This one has bare arms tight with muscle, and wears her weapons outside her boho skirts, at the ready. Her hair has also been knotted into a tight, low bun, and I've only ever seen her wear it flowing and free.

But that isn't the real Zoe, is it?

I swallow hard against my bitterness and stand. "You knew me before my parents died. You were training me to join a troop, even back then."

"Of course." She stops moving and stares at me. "After all, you are Ashlyn Archer, daughter of Joanna Archer, the Kairos, whom our enemies have named Chaos. You'd be the new Archer of Light in Troop 175 if troops still existed. Yet you're still a daughter of the Zodiac ... and that makes you dangerous."

I don't feel dangerous. "And you never thought to tell me?"

A laugh bursts from her, and I can sense her reply in the burnt-rose smell. It's all she thought about. "Did you really want to know?"

That the Zodiac world was real? That evil beings were after me? That I was being trained to kill?

"That's what I thought," she mutters when I don't answer, and turns away.

I rub my chest as I step forward. "You freaking shot me."

"Sorry." Zoe peers into the backpack, mumbling as she studies its contents. Given the subject, she's kinda more distracted than I'd like.

"You shot me point blank." I enunciate each word as I move across from her.

Zoe shoots me a quizzical squint. "I didn't want to miss."

I stare at her. This boho vigilante who tricked me into thinking she needed me even while she crafted potions and fashioned weapons and played with my life.

"All this time," I say, shaking my head. "You let me think there was something wrong with me."

Zoe's gaze zips from my hands to my face and back down my body. Maybe I appear unfamiliar to her, too, because she blinks before releasing a hard sigh. "You're angry."

"I'm. Furious."

"I know." Her gentleness is a slap in contrast to my heated growl. "You look just like your mother."

The flashback slaps at me again: my poor, mortal mother being dragged through a glass window. By her *face*.

"No." The syllable wavers, and that's what breaks me. "No, my mother died in the crossfire of a war that should have never touched her!"

"And that is why we're here!" Zoe slams her hand down onto the metal table, sending it ringing. "We were born to keep this war from touching the innocents, the mortals, and it's time you took up that fight!"

"I don't want a fight! I want a life!"

"Oh, stop pouting." Zoe turns away with a scoff. "You're like a toddler who sticks her fingers in her ears and screams so she doesn't have to hear the truth. All that does is make you powerless."

And Zoe loathes anything that's powerless. I know this better than anyone.

"Beckett says you two met only yesterday."

"Yes." She hesitates for the first time. "But I suspected who he was as soon as he used your love of surfing to get to you."

Which confirms that Beck has been watching me ... though not for any reason I've ever dreamed.

I think for a moment, then squint up at her. "Kai?"

"A gray." A rogue agent. An independent. A superhero. I shake my head.

"I expect you knew it, too," she says, watching me closely. "You knew what he was. You sensed our world in him."

"*Your* world," I correct, and then just because I'm still angry, "and I don't even know who you are."

Her stance widens, her eyes narrow, and she lowers her chin. "I am Zoe Archer, the former Archer of Troop 175, Las Vegas division. I am Light and always will be. I am also your grandmother. Any other stupid questions?"

Yeah. Did you ever love me?

I don't ask her that. The question would sound childish—powerless—to her.

Besides, I'm not sure I want to hear the answer.

"Let me ask you something," Zoe says after a minute.

I don't yet trust myself to speak, so I just blink.

"How does it feel knowing you can jump ten, twenty feet off the ground in a single bound? Or leap a cliff and survive?"

I felt my biceps bunch and forcibly relax them. I should be covered in bruises after doing just that, but I feel fine.

"How does it feel knowing you can lift a grown man right off his feet?" She jerks her head. "That you could toss me across the room right now, one-handed?"

"I would never move another human being around like they're a pawn in some supernatural game."

Like you, is what goes unspoken between us.

"But you can." She angles her head, searching my face through narrowed eyes. "And the knowledge feels good, doesn't it?"

I don't answer.

"I know it does," she finally whispers. "I remember."

I remember. The power that flooded me tonight had been a part of me once before. I flex my fist, tensile with all this new strength, and admit she's right. It feels normal.

Zoe turns away. "These are your things. I packed them as soon as you left for your date tonight. Beckett will take you someplace safe."

"You're just going to leave me with strangers?"

"You need allies. You won't be safe alone or with me. Not until the Zodiac rises again." She looks at me from the corner of her eye. "Besides, weren't you leaving soon, anyway?"

Zoe, never one for sentiment, still stuns me with her coldness. I jerk my head before it can freeze me in place. "So what am I supposed to do? Learn to fight?"

"You know how to fight." And she points to my belt—the urumi—that managed to kill a man from another world. I look at it, and suddenly, I can remember every minute of every hour of every year I've spent mastering it.

It's the blowback, Beck said.

I can suddenly remember it all.

Now I know why I wake with bruises every morning and why I'm so tired that I fall asleep in class. Zoe had ways to make me remember ... and she also had ways to make me forget.

Her herbs ...

I have so many questions ... yet Zoe is suddenly lifting a second backpack from the floor, and she's turning to the door and away from me. All at the same time.

"Wait." It's all too fast. I rush to keep up with her. It isn't hard; I'm fast, she's mortal. "So I'm just supposed to move away from Laguna? Change my identity? My life?"

"Yes."

"Just be someone else?"

God knows she's an expert on that.

"No, Ashlyn." She finally looks at me. "It's time to be yourself."

"Wait!" Despite my anger and confusion, I panic. *"Wait!"*

She pauses, and I scramble for something else to say.

"What about you? Do you have a plan?"

Zoe gives a small smile. She knows I'm stalling—she knows why—yet her amusement shifts almost immediately, turning her expression predatory, foxlike. Oddly, I've never seen her look more sane. "Kid, I've got backup plans to my backup plans."

And then she leaves because, apparently, none of them include me.

10

NAME IT TO CLAIM IT.

Comic books.

Villains with ancestral connections to the gods and stars.

Superheroes.

I wrap my arms around my body and bend over myself in Zoe's wake, as if my stomach has cramped up and I'm in pain.

I am in pain.

A knock comes at the door a few seconds later, and I know it's Beck because the girl named War doesn't seem the type to knock, and Zoe is gone.

Zoe is gone.

"Hold on," I call because I don't know what else to do. I do know that once that door opens, my life will change forever.

Which is when my eye catches on the trailer's secondary exit. I fall still.

Weren't you planning on leaving soon, anyway?

Yeah, I think, gaze shifting between the opposing doors. I was. And since all the bad, smelly supervillains have decided to converge upon Laguna, now seems as good a time as any.

The knock comes again, more insistent.

"Please." I force a warble in my voice as I secure the backpack over my shoulders and glance at my watch to mark the time. "Just five minutes."

There's an audible sigh from the other side of the door, but it remains shut, and I almost manage a smile. Zoe expects me to do what she says, as always, probably because she's the one who cast me in the role of ignorant, young girl.

But I'm no longer ignorant or that young, and now I know ... the Zodiac world is real.

"Get a grip, Ash," I whisper as I cross to the back of the trailer.

Because that's what I do in the real world when facing the impossible. Like the first time I ran over-the-head waves. I stayed focused, targeted the barrel, and clawed my way inside. Then I rode that gnarly slide all the way home.

But how do I get in the barrel on something like superheroes?

I giggle at the thought and have to cover my mouth, my giddy hysteria, with my hand.

Focus.

And attack it head-on.

Because I'm going to get older and stronger. I know that much, and I also know how to hide. Nighttime combat sessions under hypnotic suggestion, or whatever Zoe used, isn't the only skill she imparted. Paranoia is totally part of my DNA.

Besides, I don't give up on my dreams that quickly.

"I'm not missing out on Kauai." I'm reaching for the back door handle when my gaze snags in the mirror above a small wall sink. It's funny, but I look just like me. No more or less. I'm kinda surprised at that.

"What are you going to do now, Ash?" I ask the girl in the mirror before immediately amending the question. "What are you going to do now, Ashlyn Archer?"

A tingling races along my skin, and suddenly, my reflection is smiling back at me. I know exactly what I'm going to do.

"I'm going to chase down ... the gnarliest waves ever."

. . .

I HAVE TO BE QUICK. OH...AND, LIKE, *SUPER* QUIET.

Piece of cake. I move with such stealth it's almost a dream, and when I open the back door and the cold air of what is now a very early morning hits me, I smile and rocket away from the building. I don't bother shutting the door behind me. My new speed gives me a fantastic head start.

There's only one place outside of the ocean that has always represented safety to me, and I use the winding, hillside backstreets to return to it under the cover of darkness. I leap as high as the rooftops a couple of times just because I can't help myself—it feels so sick!—but chill out in case the neighbors are looking.

The plan is to lay low at Hummingbird House until dawn, knowing I can count on Zoe's multiple booby traps to stop anyone from entering. I'll shower in the morning and repack my belongings, along with the surf shop earnings I've hidden for this sort of getaway. I'll snag a ride to LAX from there.

Except there is no "there."

My home—and the surf shop—have been yanked at the root like a pulled tooth. The entire structure has been cut away with such precision that the buildings flanking it are cardboard cutouts in the night. Only stars and sky loom where Zoe's greenhouse once was. Not one ropy vine remains.

It's burned to the ground, I think, whirling around and searching for someone to yell to for help. Yet there are no firemen on the street or neighbors peering from the hillside deck homes. In fact, I think, sniffing, there's no smoke. So where the hell is my home?

Stepping onto the sidewalk, I inch my way onto the property.

"I wouldn't do that if I were you."

Tidy pools of lamplight mark every property but ours—even that is gone—yet nothing moves in the blank spaces in between. Then, a bit of shadow detaches itself from the darkness closest to me. I react without thinking, kicking out with more instinct than finesse. The arm stretching my way immediately withdraws.

"Jeez! You wanna kill me or something?"

"I don't ..." I don't kill people, is what I want to say. Instead, I squint at the shadowy figure. "I don't know."

"Here's a little hint," says the voice, calmer now, but tight and clearly male, "You're supposed to protect the humans. Unless you've decided to cave to your Shadow side?"

"No. What? Wait." It's too much to take in all at once. I shake my head. "You're mortal?"

"Head to toe, which is more than I can say for you."

This time, the guy sidesteps into the nearest square of light, motioning down his body like that's supposed to comfort me.

He's dressed entirely in black, biceps bulging beneath his fitted sweater, turning the skin above his neck and below his wrists almost translucent in contrast. Not one freckle mars his face, ethereally pale and framed in jet-black hair. He is more like Count Dracula than any actor to play Dracula since the beginning of time.

I wondered if he plans on biting me.

I wonder if I'd mind.

I banish the thought with a shake of my head. "Sorry. I've been attacked more times tonight than in my entire life."

"I know." His smile completely transforms his face. Out goes Dracula, in comes every leading man who was ever filmed in black-and-white. "Let's try a handshake. I'm Carl Kenyon."

"Ashlyn James," I reply, shaking.

"Archer," he corrects. Oh yeah. "If you're going to claim your place in the Zodiac world, you must also claim your name."

"I wasn't planning on claiming anything."

He huffs lightly. "Then I guess you weren't planning on staying alive, either."

I scowl as I take a step closer to what used to be my home.

Carl makes a sound that's both a warning and a taunt. "Seriously, honey. Don't touch the supernatural funk."

"Don't call me honey, mortal spawn."

"My, we learn quickly," he shoots back, joining my side. We both stare at the thick gloom.

"What is it?"

"A black hole." His voice is all nonchalance, like it's a natural occurrence. Like a rainbow or dust devil. Something incredible that makes sense. "Don't you remember?"

"Should I?"

"You've seen it once before." I feel him studying me as I squint into the gloom. "Think."

There's a freeze frame, quick as a blink—a room encased in steel, a deep, black well carved in its middle—but it's gone before I can truly grasp it.

"See how dense it is?" Carl's saying, with a jerk of his head. "Even a fingertip on the surface will pull you in like quicksand. It'll hold you there like flypaper."

That seems right ... which unsettles me. How do I know this? What else am I supposed to remember?

"For how long?"

"Until your enemies find you." Carl shrugs, then lightly adds, "Or until its centrifugal force tears apart your limbs."

I grimace. Neither one of those things sounds awesome.

"Anyway," Carl continues. "None of the bad guys are here now because they figure you'll either get stuck in the black hole or you're too smart to come back here at all."

He gives me a pointed look.

I return the stare and cross my arms. "So where is my freaking house?"

"They took it."

"You can't take a whole house."

"You can't breathe underwater or survive a bullet to the chest or commune with the stars, either."

All good points.

I give Carl another careful once over. He's still Goth-boy good-looking, and his scent tells me he's not lying about being completely human ... so how does he know all this?

Carl turns back to the void. "They're going to search every inch of that place. Every closet and drawer, even the air ducts and wall planks. Bet they even sift through your fireplace ash."

"Good. Then they'll stumble upon every booby trap Zoe ever laid." Hopefully, the hard way.

"They're looking for clues. Where are you now? Where will you go next?"

Alarm sizzles in my veins. Posters of Kauai's north shore blanket my bedroom walls. Longboards in the mudroom, board wax and shorts and suits ... everywhere. Oh, God. They'll know how much I love to surf.

"So," Carl says slowly, still watching, "where will you go next?"

Where do you go when your home's been sucked up into a black hole?

When part of your mind has as well?

What's the next step when you find out your whole life is a lie ... or worse, a comic book?

Everything that made me *me* is in that black hole, I think, gaze flicking to its edges, and that's when I spot it.

I watched her build the nest. She reinforced it with silk, tight enough to keep the elements out, elastic enough to allow room for her growing family. She incubated them. She did it all alone.

"Oh, Zoe," I whisper, leaning down to scoop the empty nest into my hand.

Carl's voice blooms beside me, and I startle. "We should go."

I don't look at him until I've made room for the nest in my backpack, which is as much of an admission that he's right—and that I need him—as he's going to get. "Fine, but just so we're clear, I'm not gonna be some *lamo* superhero."

I'm just going with the flow until I can get my life back on track. I still don't want any part of the Zodiac world.

"Of course not." Carl agrees, then shoots me a grin. "You're a chick. The proper term is heroine."

CARL LEADS ME SOUTH ON PCH, PAST THE CONSTRUCTION SITE where I ran into Vasari and his crew that morning. It seems like years ago instead of hours. We're facing the backside of a free-standing liquor store, empty but for a Dumpster and a motorcycle that appears to have been built using wishful thinking and old twine.

"The hell is that?" I ask, tilting my head.

"Our getaway vehicle," Carl replies, pulling a buttery black leather jacket from the handlebars.

"Really?" I wrinkle my nose as he slips it on. "Got something a little more flash? Maybe a Schwinn?"

Carl tosses me a second helmet. "Just get on."

"I don't know, dude," I say, remaining where I am, "You're ruining that whole neo-Goth vibe you've got going there."

Of course, I'm really stalling because of where this bike leads. I don't need details; whatever it is, it's a future I never wanted. So I turn one last time to stare into the darkness where the ocean's voice beckons ... and spot a squat shadow dart behind the Dumpster.

I leap to the padded seat just as Carl fires up the engine.

"They're here," I hiss into his ear.

"What?" he yells, unable to hear me through the padding of his helmet and the chugging of the bike.

But other things can hear me, and the street behind me suddenly swarms. I punch his padded shoulder. "Go, go, go!"

To Carl's credit, he goes.

I've barely caught his waist before the little crotch rocket shoots off into the night. He pushes a button as we jet around a corner, and I catch a second of static before his voice appears in my ear.

"They still there?" he asks through the wireless speaker.

A lumpy figure careens off the nearest building. "Yes!"

And, God, whatever they are, they're fast. It's like watching popcorn kernels explode into view.

"Hold on!" Carl swerves, narrowly avoiding a gnarled knot of muscle that swipes at me as we rocket past. We're headed west, everything but the nearest homes and buildings blurring into darkness, and I can feel my beloved beach disappear behind me like it's been swallowed by a black hole, too.

There's no time to mourn the loss. Glancing behind me, I see half a dozen creatures pinballing across the road. They're on foot, but they're catching up fast.

I scream this to Carl, who places my hand atop his chest.

"Take it," he yells, and I'm somewhat gratified to hear that his deep voice had gone panicked and tinny in my ear.

Gratified and *freaked* because 'it' is hard, gun-shaped, and probably loaded.

"No!" I push the weapon away, recalling Creeper's rant about conduits ... and how War forced me to use my urumi. If I take this, my life will definitely change ... and I might not be able to get it back on track. "I've never shot a gun before."

"Yes, you have! You just don't remember!" He shoves the gun my way again. "Now take it, or we both die!"

Gee, since he put it that way. I take the gun, feel my trigger finger itch, and know immediately that he's right. Even with the wind battering my face at fifty miles an hour and no conscious memory of firing a gun, I know how to do this.

"I don't kill people!"

"They're not people!"

It's the way his voice shoots up a notch that causes me to aim. Hooking one hand beneath Carl's arm, I steady my sights on the closest attacker. Wait, says something inside of me, something with Zoe's voice.

Wa-a-ait...

I ground myself with a deep breath and let it out on a slow three-count. Only my arm moves, tracking the beast that now dodges across the empty lanes. Only one car length back, its burning red eyes are fixed on me. *Wait...*

I sight down the barrel and exhale... just as it jumps. The shot flashes bright blue and flips my attacker head-over-tail, where he ricochets into two buddies in mid-air.

Carl lets out a whoop. I have to fight not to do the same. That felt good. "What kind of bullet was that?"

"An effective one," Carl yells.

A magical one, I think, sighting another lumpy figure. I can't help how my heart kicks as I repeat my feat—sighting, exhaling, shooting blue fire—so that another attacker drops, and another. I'm on a roll...

Until Carl suddenly yanks the moped, and I nearly topple off.

The weapon flips from my hand and clatters somewhere behind me while the back wheel skitters dangerously below me. As we wheel toward the pavement, I catch sight of another half-dozen creatures barreling down on us, a snapshot that momentarily etches their mangled face in the air.

Carl rights the bike just as I realize what's happening. "They're pushing us toward the canyon pass!"

Laguna Canyon is the most direct route into California's heartland, but the narrow pass is also the perfect spot for an ambush.

"Then we let them," Carl says, and I decide I prefer him panicked.

"Are you crazy?"

"They'll never expect it!" He howls with laughter in front of me.

Holy crapcakes, I'm piggybacking on an adrenaline junkie's sled!

"That's not funny!"

"Nope," Carl says, still laughing. "But this is."

He flicks a switch on the handlebars, and the moped's single headlight vanishes. For a moment, we have to trust that the road is still beneath us, but then a strange glow flickers through the windshield. It's infrared... or is it ultraviolet?

Whatever, it's just like the movies, and it illuminates falling rocks and leaping creatures. They rain down on us from every side.

Carl zigzags, cutting one corner so close that I feel the mountainside on one shoulder and the hot breath of an attacker at my leg. Then something explodes beneath us. A scream replaces the breath, and I cringe as not one, but two skeletons fry in the air in front of us, mid-leap, mutilated faces frozen in pain.

The bike levels off while everything is arrested around us, and we just glide for a few moments before jolting back to earth, leaving the debris and smoking body parts far behind. The motor has shifted to near-silence, but glancing at the speedometer shows the red needle sitting just past the triple-digit mark.

"I knew it would work if you were on it!" Carl laughs, and I slump as we glide past the dusky hillside. Another conduit.

It's another ten minutes before I realize we're not stopping. Yet I'm so tired by then that I can barely keep upright, much less question where we're going. Instead, I tuck my head low and let Carl's body take the full force of the wind's breath.

Sensing my fatigue, he mutes the speaker in my helmet and replaces it with a song. The girl's voice alternates between melodic and rasping as she sings of parting and sorrow and goodbyes.

I didn't even get a chance to say goodbye to my beloved ocean, yet all I can do by then is close my eyes and let the bike and the song ferry me away.

11

I WILL SURVIVE (SING IT WITH ME...)

Vast stretches of highway have disappeared behind us before the bike begins to slow. I've actually fallen asleep behind Carl, which scares me enough to have me jolting upright as we bypass a green sign showing we're not far from Los Angeles. Carl gives my hand a reassuring pat and turns away from that known destination in favor of a winding mountain road.

We climb into the altitude along with the nascent morning sun.

Dawn arrives as we emerge in a clearing flanked by dogwoods. Soon, we're overlooking a storybook village, complete with brown wooden gables and carved posts. Beyond that is a vast lake that glistens with steely blue strength. The signage pointing to the village reads *Lake Arrowhead*.

Carl rolls to a stop and removes his helmet, which I take as a sign that we're finally safe. He shakes out his hair, which, if anything, grows even inkier in the sun's rays. "Pretty, huh?"

Yawning loudly, I lift my arms high and stretch. "Sure. Which one is Hansel and Gretel's house?"

"Oh, we kicked those cottage-eating jerks out years ago."

"And why are *we* here?"

"It's secluded but still only forty-five minutes away from Los Angeles, if you know how to drive."

And, as I'd already seen, he did.

"This place used to be teeming with Hollywood royalty. All the silent movie stars came here to escape city life. It's not exactly hopping with nightlife, but the pine and cedar pump continuous fresh oxygen into the air. The animal musk doesn't hurt, either. The altitude, seclusion, and even the icy winters make tracking and locating you harder. You'll like it."

As if I'm going to stay long enough to endure an icy winter.

"Don't bet on it," I mutter. "Glamping isn't really my thing."

"Is breathing your thing?"

"Lead the way."

Pushing off again, he motors down a winding hillside, quiet and cool in the morning air, and into the village. It's little more than an outdoor mall with cafes and cutesy boutiques all hunched beneath a long wooden awning. Carl points the puttering moped past the empty shops to the far corner of the long gallery, which also sports the brightest signage in the village: The Lion's Den.

"Crap." I let my head fall, helmet banging Carl's shoulder blade. "You're going to make me go in there, aren't you?"

"Welcome to my humble abode."

I jerk back up. "Wait, you live in a *comic book shop*?"

Carl silences the motor and turns to me with a sigh. "You still haven't figured it out, have you?"

"What?"

He stands and crosses his arms, looking at me like I'm sketch-balls. "What human is entrusted with the secrets and stories of the Zodiac world?"

"Don't know." I remove my helmet.

"What mortal is bound to tell the truth and resist favoring either side of the Zodiac?"

"How about you just tell me?" I snap because I'm tired and hungry and don't even really want to know.

"Who can color your stories, choose the words to describe your reality, and without whom you wouldn't truly exist?"

I jolt and involuntarily rise from the bike. His left eye twitches under my close stare, and suddenly, his pale coloring, his strange and somewhat formal demeanor, and his casual acceptance of this weird world make sense. "Oh my God!"

"Goddess," he corrects.

I point at him. "You're a geeky, weirdo, all-knowing record keeper!"

The record keeper is a human who creates the comic books—the manuals—that detail the actions of the warring sides of Light and Shadow. At least, back when there were still sides, and they were still written. I'd always wondered how the record keeper knew about every major event, but Zoe always made it sound like some strange mix of telepathy and voodoo.

Carl clenches his jaw and lifts his chin. "I penciled Zodiac activity for the west coast troops *before* the Reordering. I have more knowledge of this world's ethos than any other human. I know things practically before they happen ... which is how I knew you would be attacked at your beloved Hummingbird House. Lucky for you."

"Goddess," I exclaim, to which he gives an approving nod. "Four hours."

A frown appears between his brows. "What?"

"That's how long I've been clinging to the leather-clad back of a total freaking geek!"

His all-seeing gaze narrows. "We'll go in the back way."

Leaving the moped out front, we slip into a hallway so well placed it's almost indistinguishable from the front. Seconds later, we exit at the back of the property. The walkway back here is still shaded, dark, and narrow, and the wooden planks creak under our feet. Given what we went through to escape Laguna, each sound is like a saw down my spine.

I wince and decide to leap to the grass.

"Don't!" Carl's hand is rough on my shoulder as he jerks me back. "Don't ever touch the grass."

"Why?" The back of the village opens up to a wide rolling field, making it markedly cooler than in the building's front concrete lot. The green grass swaying high in the morning air is also beautiful.

"Because your footsteps will vibrate through the earth, calling to those who live in the fields, and you're not ready to meet them."

I shudder and open my mouth to tell him I won't ever be ready to meet *things that live in a field* or respond to vibrations, but he's already keying open a rickety wooden door. Before entering, he reaches for my hand.

"I got it, dude." I shake him off...right before I'm catapulted backward onto my butt. It takes me a moment to uncross my eyes from whatever power was just shot through my every nerve.

"It's shielded. *Dude.*"

Carl extends his hand again. I give him the evil eye but take his hand.

Touché, geeky-but-sorta-hot record keeper. Touché.

CROSSING THE THRESHOLD IS LIKE STANDING ON A LISTING SHIP. The dizziness rocks through me like a wave but vanishes when I'm safely on the other side. Carl points out the button that lifts and lowers the shield of butt pain. Then he flips its sister switch and strides into the room, leaving me gaping in his wake.

I'd expected to enter a storage room at best, something

crammed with racks and boxes of unsorted comics. Maybe some tilting cartons of Superman figures. Instead, I've been plunged into a cosmos fired by candles and recessed light. The pattern is easily recognized as constellations of the western sky, the false brilliance of the stars augmented by walls that've been painted and curtained black.

"Someone's been taking design tips from the Addams family," I mutter, venturing further inside. The only furniture adorning the room is a giant mahogany desk so shiny it appears oil-slicked in the candlelight. It's parked below the Milky Way and flanked by a black-tufted velvet chair that reminds me of a throne.

I complete a full circle turn, taking in the whole room again, and stop in front of Carl, who has been watching. "You're not going to suck my blood, are you?"

His left eye takes on a weird, slight twitch. "You sure you're the Archer's daughter?"

"You sure you're the record keeper?"

"Got her attitude at least," he mutters, pulling out a phone.

"What are you doing?"

"This is called texting. Humans do it instead of reading the stars."

He rolls his eyes when I tell him what he can do with his phone. Probably because it's not *human*ly possible.

"I'm letting Beckett the Great know you're okay."

"Wait. You know..." Of course, he knows Beck. I slump and fight the urge to slug him. "Traitor!"

Carl points to himself without looking up. "Savior."

Oh yeah.

Sighing, I return to my inspection. Now that my eyes have adjusted to the room's dimness, I realize that what looked like an enormous black box theater—save for the 3-D constellations studding the room—is a room with regular entrances and exits. The back wall behind the desk is curtained entirely, but the one opposite the entrance has a black velvet panel the same size as a door.

Carl stops me before I can peer inside. "That's my bedroom. Nobody enters but me."

"Love them boxers, huh?" But I don't push. I remember one thing about record keepers now: aside from being total geeks, they hold a lot of power in the Zodiac world.

Carl smirks, but holds out his hand again. I smirk back before taking it. His touch is already familiar due to our time on the bike, yet places inside me begin to ache as soon as he pulls me forward and through the threshold leading into his room. I'd pull away, but his grip has tightened, and it's not until I'm on the other side of the door that I realize those aching places are my organs.

I brace myself against the wall. "I feel weird."

"Try that solo, and you'd feel weird and dead. You can only enter if you're touching me," Carl says, flipping on the lights.

I immediately realize there's more worth guarding here than his boxer shorts. A back curtain covers most of one wall, like in the larger room outside, but otherwise, comic book drawings cover every surface. Panels, splash pages, and two-page spreads... sheets and sheets depicting a world my birth mother was supposed to have destroyed.

Only Carl's hand at my back keeps me from accidentally stepping back across the dangerous threshold.

"I thought the manuals weren't being written." My voice is suddenly so small. I barely get it out.

"They're not being published," he murmurs, eyes not meeting mine. He knows he's freaking me out. Why not? He knows everything. "These are all unrecorded."

The girl named War is posted on the wall in front of me. She is training in a forest with her sword, sweat on her brow above sharp, purposeful eyes.

Beck is learning to surf on another. Taking it on the head,

trying again ... and watching a girl with dark curls catching slides in the distance. I shoot her, *me*, the shaka sign before moving on.

In the far corner, I discover a drawing of Zoe muttering under her breath, brewing poison ... and a shadow—mine—observing all of it from a darkened hallway. Swallowing hard, I glance back at Carl, and he doesn't just look tall, dark, and dorky anymore.

He looks dangerous.

I trace my fingers along the walls until I reach the corner, where I hover over a second plain, cluttered desk. There's a drawing of a boy I don't recognize, cowboy hat tipped low as he lassos one of the creatures that chased us last night. I also see Vasari filing his teeth into points. Pages upon pages depict strange weaponry, zodiac glyphs, and bright eyes peering out from dark places ... all ominous and all drawn by the same unwavering hand.

Carl slips up beside me slowly, as if afraid I'll startle. "When your birth mother destroyed the Zodiac world, she toppled a system that'd been in place for centuries. It wasn't Shadow versus Light for a time, but everyone for themselves. Back then, I couldn't write a haiku, much less a manual."

That certainly wasn't the case anymore. "So what happened?"

"I gradually started seeing fragments."

"Like visions?"

"More like I'm right there..." He trails off but shakes himself of his thoughts when he feels me watching. "There's no clear storyline yet, no narrative to link any pages together, but the fevers are stronger lately. A story is rising. I feel it."

I gaze at the drawings splayed over his desk. It's a black-and-white sea of carnage. Of troops and weapons and war. There is nothing lovely in sight.

"I just draw what I see," he says when I swallow hard.

"You see a lot."

"It's how I knew you'd be at Hummingbird House tonight. Alone."

So he saw what would happen, or guessed at it, and made the trip to Laguna on his magic motorbike to save my argumentative, ungrateful butt. I survey the walls, gaze flitting over the hundreds of drawings until it snags on one. I move to it, stare hard, and shudder. A man's face takes up the entire page. It displays black bone beneath every tendon. Beef jerky skin cross-hatches his skull. Hate practically bleeds through the page.

Same as last night.

"Hey," Carl says softly. "You look dead on your feet." His voice gently pulls me back into the room.

I don't know if he's reading my thoughts—I don't know how his gifts work—or if he's trying to change the subject, but he's right. When have I last slept? I can barely remember, but my eyelids feel lead-lined. My arms hang slack at my side.

"The bathroom is through there." Carl points, but I only have eyes for that clean, large bed. "It has a full shower and a fresh toiletry kit beneath the bathroom sink."

"So you regularly rescue damsels-in-distress?"

Carl looks at me, and I slump where I stand.

"I'm sorry." I'm tired, scared, and alone with a strange dude in a world I don't know—yet one who saved my life. "I meant ... thanks."

"I'll leave something for you to sleep in on the bed," he says, turning away.

"What about you?"

"I'll keep watch. The shop is armed, but I want to be sure we weren't followed."

Meaning, he's not sure. "So I guess you don't know everything, huh?"

He almost smiles. "I know that after keeping you safe for five years, Zoe Archer will kill me if I lose you in one night."

"She might just kill you anyway," I mutter, rubbing my chest where she shot me.

"Oh, that?" Carl smiles as he turns to leave. "She was just making a point."

"What?" I snort. "That I can survive a bullet through the chest?"

Carl pauses in the doorway, his dark gaze flicking from panel to drawing to page, then back to me like it's all the same.

"That you, Ashlyn Archer, have absolutely no idea what you can survive."

12

I KNOW YOU ARE BUT WHAT AM I?

I dream I'm back in my childhood home, right at the edge of the memory that ambushed me on the beach in Laguna. My poor, unarmed father is jerked from our home, his body following my mother's screams in the night.

I run after them. Of course, I do.

My parents are my safety net when I fall and scrape my knee, have a run-in with the mean girl at school, or need reassurance that the monsters in my dreams—ones that've been chasing me for as long as I can remember—can't reach me upon waking. I run to them for solace, comfort, and love ... yet it's not until I bolt onto the porch, searching for the man who'd lifted my father like a rag doll, that I realize this time is different.

This time, to be safe, I need to run *away*.

It's too late. My gaze is fastened on a trail of acrid smoke hanging in the air, thickening as it hooks around the corner. It smells like things dying underground. Like the man who crashed into my home moments before. I take two wobbly steps forward and am snatched into the air so fast there's no time to draw breath.

This is how violence feels. Like even the air in the sky doesn't belong to you.

Only the even, syncopated beat of pounding feet tells me I'm not flying. The wind whips at my hair, and my hair lashes my face, and my face slams against something hard. You are not just special ... you are *super*.

Like this man, I think, mind immediately winging to what else Zoe told me. It isn't hard, even while being kidnapped from my own life. She'd drilled the response into me.

Do this if you're ever caught in a dangerous situation, she said. If you're ever within reach of a Shadow.

I pull into a tight ball, hugging my limbs and forcing the Shadow to adjust his grip around me. Blindly, my fingers scramble for the ring Zoe gave me. I press the pink tourmaline protruding from its top, and a latch springs open.

"It's like a key," Zoe smiled while showing it to me. "Activate this button—and, of course, say the keyword—and I'll come running."

I press it and yelled the word Zoe told me never to say unless I'm in trouble.

The man carrying me thinks I'm screaming, and he laughs, the sound booming from him like a cannon. I curl further into myself and wait for Zoe to save me.

I don't have to wait long.

I remember that now. I remember what happened next, too ... and I wake screaming.

I SIT UP STRAIGHT, PANTING HARD. THE PILLOW IS SWEAT-DRENCHED beneath me, and the covers tangle about my legs. It takes a minute to clear my mind of the dream, and the raw, violent images bursting from every wall don't help. How can Carl sleep like this? With this violence in his head?

In his *life*?

Plus, I've always been a deep sleeper. Once under, I'm as good as dead to the world, dreamless in a total abyss of consciousness. Sometimes, I wake with a start, sweating and chasing the tail end of a dream that feels real, but the details are always fuzzy at best. No matter how hard I try, I can never recall them, and they sink back into the murky waters of my mind within minutes.

"Guess all that's changed," I mutter and throw my legs over the side of the bed. I pad across the room barefoot, wearing nothing but Carl's oversized tee shirt.

"You're not supposed to use your knowledge to choose sides, Keeper."

"The name's Carl, and someone had to keep her alive."

I yank back the curtain over the bedroom door to find a storeroom brightened by an open door and the amber rays of the late summer day. Carl's behind the enormous desk, back facing me, but he somehow senses me and raises his head.

Or maybe it's because Beckett Lux falls eerily still across from him. I both recognize him and don't, and have to blink to align the streaks in his sun-kissed hair with the de facto uniform of head-to-toe black that everyone in the Zodiac world seems to favor.

The surfer persona, I know now, was all a lie.

"Nice leather," I tell Beck, so he knows I mean the opposite.

He's kooked out if he thinks I'm gonna apologize for ditching him at the Taco Tavern. He must've considered the possibility that I'd do so again because he's brought backup—not just the girl named War, but two other likely wanna-be superheroes-in-training—a boy and a girl. They're all seated in a cluster of club chairs in front of Carl's desk.

"Just getting comfortable," Beck replies, giving my cotton-clad body a once-over so tight it hurts. "Like you."

I glance down at Carl's tee-shirt. I've worn oversized tees atop my swimsuits on the beach for years, yet I tug at the hem now. Context is everything, I guess.

"How do I get out of here?" I ask Carl as he turns. His expression, at least, is as blank as one of his unwritten pages. *Try it solo, and you'll feel weird and dead.*

"While entry must be granted," he says, with a mock bow, "exiting is always voluntary."

"Generous," Beck mutters, but Carl says nothing as he turns back to his desk.

I inch through the doorway, prepared to jerk back at the first sign of imminent death, yet there's only the faintest tug at my skin ... as if I've separated myself from my shadow. Then I'm free.

"That's yours." Carl jerks his chin at the corner of the desk as I approach, and I can't help but smile.

"My favorite." Coffee with a bagel is my Sunday morning ritual...though I usually enjoy it oceanside with gulls peppering the sky.

"I know."

I glance at him sharply, but my stomach is running the show now, and I reach for the food without comment.

And may the First Mothers bless the hot, weird, Goth boy ... the coffee is fresh and hot, and the bagel is so thick with cream cheese that it seals itself to the roof of my mouth with the first bite.

Eyes fluttering shut, I groan.

"Better?" Beck asks as I thumb cream cheese from the corner of my mouth. He's been watching/not watching me this whole time with a downward turn of his too-pretty mouth.

"*Super*," I say, giving him a thumbs-down, which makes him scowl even more.

He starts to gesture to the newcomers, but the lone new boy beats him to it, jumping to his feet. His skin is dusky, and his eyes are shaped like almonds, and when he stands, he keeps on going. He's big underneath his tee-shirt, too—less martial arts expert than football player. There's also a pretty dusting of freckles on his nose, which means the whole package is distracting enough to get me daydreaming.

I wonder how the surfing is in Asia?

"Thayer Storge," he says to me. "I'm a Libra. Nice to meet you."

I ignore his outstretched hand and, still chewing, say, "You're wearing a cape."

All the pretty distracted me. The dude is actually wearing a cape.

"Right?" Thayer says, as if I said *beautiful* cape.

Then, inexplicably, he takes off to circle the room.

"Is that normal?" I ask, keeping an eye on him, leaping, momentarily taking flight.

War snorts as she throws a leather-clad leg over one arm of her club chair. "Thayer's never been accused of that."

Thayer completes his second lap and lands back in front of me with a flourish. "I'm wearing it all the time now. Just in case the record keeper starts drawing again."

"I never stopped," Carl mutters without looking up.

"See?" Thayer says like he already knew that. "So what do you think? I look dapper, right?"

I shrug one shoulder. "In a Jack-the-Ripper sort of way."

Thayer glances down, shocked. "You don't know what you're talking about. Batman wears a cape. Superman, too. It's standard superhero fare."

"The Elders will never fear you in a cape," the girl calls out.

Thayer turns to me for validation. I wince.

His hopeful expression falls. "You'll see. I'm going to rock this look so much that once it shows up in all the manuals, even the mortals will start wearing capes. The cape is the new duster coat."

Actually, I think it's the precursor to the duster, but before I can say so, he's off on a new tangent. "So. Beckett says you're going to help us save the world."

I shake my head. "I'm not really the 'save the world' type."

"Yeah." Thayer is careful not to look at me as he adds, "That's what War said."

I glance over at War. She shrugs. "Your mother destroyed a centuries-old system that obliterated the troop system, fractured our matriarchal lineage, and upended the entire paranormal underworld."

She has a point.

The other girl rises, but not far. She's what Zoe would call pocket-sized, though she's also dressed entirely in leather. "I'm Afthonia Koine," she says, offering me her hand. "Nia for short. I'm a Virgo."

Specific.

I look her over. Despite her attire, she doesn't appear remotely martial. Her build is slight, and her hair is so dark and shiny that the light practically bounces off it. I note with some jealousy that she has also perfected the effective, yet elusive, skill of applying cat-eye liner, the ebony slant accenting nut-brown eyes beneath ruler-straight fringe. Basically, she's a kick-ass mini Snow White.

"So is that how you guys introduce yourselves? By your zodiac signs?"

"Historically," Beck allows. "It was a shorthand way of letting another agent know where you were from, if you were Shadow or Light, and other identifying attributes."

"Funny," I say, glancing at him. "I don't remember you doing that."

Beck opens his mouth to answer—to defend himself, no doubt—so I turn back to Carl. "Have you slept?"

Carl shrugs, but the answer is clearly no. "Beast needs to be fed."

"You have a dog?"

Thayer laughs, though it doesn't sound like he's laughing at me. I just get the feeling he laughs a lot.

Carl's giant black chair creaks as he leans back and offers me a wan smile. "I mean, I have to draw."

"Wait, you drew all of this..." I motion over the sketches covering the desk, half a dozen thick in some places. "in a few hours?"

"You slept longer than you think," Beck interrupts, and another glance at the open door proves he's right. Dusk isn't far off.

"I can't sleep until every last image is out of my head," Carl says, bending back to his work. "Occupational hazard."

My gaze catches on one drawing, and I stop chewing. The coffee sours in my throat. The bagel turns over in my belly. It's the face of the man who attacked me in the ocean. The same man whose scent was in my dream ... my recovered memories. "So who's the creeper?"

Carl tilts his head, amused. "That's what you call the guy who took you for a midnight swim?"

I just sip at my coffee and wait while Carl looks at Beck. Beck looks at War. Nia and Thayer look at each other. What's really telling, though, is that no one looks at me.

"His name is Cassius," Beck says after a long pause, "and he's been searching for you for a long time."

I wrack my fractured mind, but the name means nothing to me.

Nia steps in to help. "He leads a group who belonged to the generation of star signs your mother displaced when she destroyed our world. We call them Elders."

"The Reordering," I murmur, and drop the page back onto the desk with shaking fingers.

"Right, " Beck says. "Except these guys refuse to let go of their powers or their lineage or any of the old ways. They feel they've missed their turn, and they're trying to get it back."

Do you really believe I'm going to simply relinquish my position and power and birthright to some snot-faced neo-agent who doesn't even know she's a child of the stars?

I shake off Cassius's ocean-logged voice. "Is that possible?"

"It's the Zodiac world," Beck replies tersely.

Right. Anything's possible.

"But it's a broken world," Nia adds, and there's a warning in her voice. "Those who were full-fledged agents at the time of the Reordering, meaning all the Elders, still have an immunity to manmade weaponry. Initiates, and that's all of us, don't."

"Which is why you shouldn't have run from us."

Beck stares at me stonily. Gone is the guy who called me a geek and nearly kissed me under the hot, starry sky. There is nothing in him that speaks to the boy who took me to dinner— no romantic look, flirtation, or smile.

There's only this severe, serious boy I've never before seen dressed in black.

My thoughts must be splayed openly on my face because at least he has the decency to blush. "Listen, I know you're angry. I know you're scared. You probably have a million questions, but that's why you must come with us."

"Okay," I tell him.

"Really?" He looks surprised, which warms me so much that I decide to do it again.

"Sure. Lead the way, dude. Now or never."

He must think I mean it because, after only a glance at Carl, he turns toward the door. I put down my bagel on top of the drawing and follow as Carl curses, lunging to save his artwork. Beck remembers I'm barefoot just a second too late.

"Hold on—" He turns just outside the threshold, but I've already pushed the button, and he face-plants into a shield that has his eyes flipping like slot reels beneath his eyelids.

"That's for not telling me about Cassius," I say while he's still uncrossing his eyes.

And as I turn away, I silently add, *And for making me want to kiss you while all you did was lie.*

W<small>AR LETS</small> B<small>ECK BACK INTO THE SHOP.</small>

"Real mature," she mutters as she passes me.

"I know you are, but what am I?"

Thayer laughs again, the sound so infectious that even Carl cracks half a smile, but War halts short of her goal, and when she spins on me, she's definitely not laughing.

"Okay, Archer, listen up. I know you've been all hang ten or loose or whatever you say while working on your tan every day—"

"My kick-ass tan," I amend.

"But *we've* all been busy trying to stay alive in the world your birth mother destroyed. So here's what's going to happen next. You're going to get on board and help us force the Zodiac system to rise again. Got it?"

The others hold their breaths to see if I've got it.

I nod my head. "No."

War's eyes slit. "I said--"

"Noooooooo..." I sing it. I sing it with my arms outstretched and coffee on my breath. I sing it loud, and I sing it proud.

"Wow," Nia says when I'm done. "You have a *terrible* singing voice."

Thayer grimaces. "Yeah, that is totally not your superpower."

War just curses under her breath—the way they do in her world; *Mother-Loving this* and *Mother-Loving that*—and slams the button beside the exit to let Beck back in. I wait until they've both returned to make my own awesome, Mother-Loving speech.

"Now *you* listen up, you super-duper teens." I clap my hands like I'd actually ever want their attention. "I get that you've all been raised to protect humanity from the influence of those who'd like to see the globe burn, and after what I saw on the strand last night with Vasari and his gnarly henchmen, I'm totally on board with that. But here's the deal. I am almost seventeen years old, and do you Mother-Lovers know what *that* means?"

The dumbfounded superheroes-in-training—and the self-proclaimed record keeper—just stare.

"It means that I've been saving surf shop paychecks for two freaking years, minus taco and strawberry shake money, in order to spec out some seriously macking sets half a world away after high school, and there's no way I'm giving all that up for the zombie apocalypse!"

Beck, recovered, squints at me. "There is no such thing as zombies."

"Vampire war, then."

War rolls her eyes. "No vampires."

"Kid armies forced to fight to a death in an arena by adults too chickenshit to do it themselves!"

Thayer and Nia look at each other again, and even Carl shakes his head. "I don't even know what she's talking about now."

"You guys have never read The Hunger Games?" I ask them.

"We only read manuals," Thayer says formally.

"Geeks." I grab my coffee.

"You read them, too," Beck points out.

"Because I'm dyslexic, and I like pretty pictures." I look at Carl and point at the bedroom door that holds my belongings, but that I can't access without his assistance.

Carl rises, but Beck moves with us, still trying. "You're not dyslexic, Ashlyn. Removing your powers and memory messed with your learning abilities, but it'll be much easier to comprehend and retain information now."

"Not if I'm dead." Then I brighten. "Oh, look. I totally comprehend that!"

"Cassius has your scent now," he calls from behind us. "He'll track you again and won't be alone."

I juggle my coffee so I can stick my fingers in my ears until Carl assists me over the threshold to his bedroom—buzz, buzz, buzz. Then I yank the black curtain closed behind us. Then I slam the interior door just because I want to slam something.

Carl sighs and leans against the back of it, the only spot in the room that isn't covered by drawings of heroes and villains. "You know they're not leaving here without you, right?"

"Yeah, I know." I sigh, then brighten. "Hey! Let me stay here with you."

After all, Carl is the only person here who really knows what it's like to be human.

"No."

"You're like my touchstone, dude. My one link to the real world. The only one who truly understands me."

Carl rolls his eyes. "That wasn't even remotely convincing."

"Come on! We'll eat bagels and watch people face plant into your security shield when they try to come and kill me." I give him my best pouty-lip. "It'll be fun."

"You don't understand." He pushes off from the door. "What I did last night was technically against the rules. Record keepers aren't allowed to interfere with events in the Zodiac world, but I figured since there really isn't a fully functioning world right now..."

"You would save my life," I guess.

"Yeah."

"But you can't keep doing so," I guess again.

"Yeah."

"Because you're human?" I know this one.

"Because the Zodiac world *is* rising again, Ashlyn." He crosses the room to sit next to me. "And soon, we'll all have to play by the rules."

I fall into a slump on the bed. "Bummer."

"Hey." He pats my knee. "Zoe has prepared you for this. You're ready."

"I know." The confirmation thrums like a gong in my chest. It's why I wake with bruises but heal fast. It's why I know hand combat, how to use the urumi, and how to shoot. And ...

"It's why they hate you, Ashlyn."

Truth smells the same way the sun feels when it's scorching your skin, and Carl's words are scalding enough to take away my breath. *Hate?*

"But I'm just a surfer chick. I'm cute. And I'm a good per—"

"You exist."

All the humor drains from me, and I swallow hard. "That's it?"

"It's enough."

And I don't need a comic book, a crystal ball, or even a fortune cookie to tell me that I'm not enough—not alone.

Everything that happened yesterday is a part of something bigger, and I need help from people who know what that is—people who are strong and who can teach me how to defend myself against the Elders.

"Fine." Sighing, I stand. "But can I at least come visit?"

"Bagels and face-planting." He nods, and seeing the smile that grows over his pale, strong face almost makes me feel better. "Anytime you want."

13

UP, UP AND AWRY.

Evening has woken up by the time I exit Carl's bedroom, changed, and with backpack in hand.

"Oh, that's not fair," Nia says when I finally reappear, her eyes wide and fixed on my gray sweatshirt. "That actually looks comfortable."

I make no apologies. "Yeah, I'm not wearing one of those sausage suits you're all so fond of."

"These are vintage troop uniforms from before the Reordering," Beck informs me sharply.

"You look like a GI Joe figurine," I say and watch his face fall as Carl snorts.

"But taller." Thayer pats his shoulder consolingly.

Nia gazes down at her body, encased in leather from neck to boot. "It's supposed to make us look tough, dark, and mysterious."

"Does it make you *feel* tough, dark, and mysterious?" I ask.

"Actually, it kinda makes me feel like a boiled sausage in the winter." She tugs at the pants. "And I always get swamp-butt in the summer."

"Can we go now?" War snaps, exchanging exasperated looks with Beck.

"At least I have this cool cape to differentiate me," Thayer fake-whispers to me as we follow.

"It is rad," I fake-whisper back.

"Yes," War calls stiffly from in front of us, without turning. "I'm surprised you didn't bedazzle it."

We exit Carl's shop under shadows that lengthen like fingertips over the sky, keeping to the porch, footsteps thudding until a pebbled path comes into view. It's flanked by the long grasses and weeds that Carl warned me not to touch. Meanwhile, birds chirp from every direction, pine and dogwoods sway in the breeze, and the air sits thick with the scent of sap and green things.

Other than all the nature crap, there's nothing around for miles.

Oddly, a wheat stalk bows before us, dipping low like the savannah in some far-off country. The only thing marring the pastoral view are giant, black boulders that randomly pop up throughout the field, and the sole path cutting through it like an elongated scar.

I shudder and wish again for my ocean waves.

"Our cottage lies on the other side of the blood wheat," Beck says, pointing across the field.

Blood *what*?

"And you call it that because ...?"

"That's what it is. Any blood spilled on this land infuses the wheat with color. It's kinda pale now, but you should've seen it when we first claimed the territory."

He gives me a sidelong smile that's almost wistful, then plunges headlong down the path.

"Psychopath," I mutter, too low for human ears ... though Beck stutter steps and half turns. I point at the ground. "I mean, it's totally a psycho *path*."

"Don't worry," Nia says, motioning me forward. "It's perfectly safe if you know what you're doing. The wheat is meant to fortify the cottage against the Elders. It's one of our more creative defenses."

"And I assume 'creative' means 'deadly?'" I glance from her to the path as we catch up to the others, who've stopped at the wheat's entrance.

"Creative *and* deadly." Beck motions to a cairn of stones that've been stacked waist height at the side of the path. "Nia."

Nia reaches over and, very carefully, twists the top rock clockwise. Everyone else is gazing expectantly at the field, and I turn back in time to see a pearlescent fog rising to twinkle atop the wheat heads, where it lingers and burns.

"That's ... normal," I deadpan, as the scent of lavender and anise and something duskier drifts over to tickle and blunt my sense of smell.

"There are underground ducts spread throughout the field," Beck explains.

I nod. I stop nodding. "Why?"

"Because the incense calms the homicidal creatures who dwell within." War flares her eyes at me and then plunges into the wheat.

"That was kinda mean," I mutter as she disappears.

Nia laughs, following. "Don't worry. You can't be touched or harmed as long as you stick to the path."

Thayer pats my shoulder before trudging off after Nia. "Just don't touch even one stalk of wheat. And if the incense ever fails while you're in the field? Run."

I look at Beck, the only person who isn't yet headed into a wheat field that thrives on blood and holds beings ready to murder me if I touch their gluten.

"Hey," I say to him, "remember when the gnarliest thing I had to worry about was stepping on a jellyfish?"

"This is kinda the same thing ... except that you die if you're stung." He jerks his head for me to follow him into the wheat.

"Totally not the same thing," I mutter, watching him walk away.

Yet I have to marvel. This is the same guy who slayed hearts and ripped waves for the last year in Laguna. It's as if his body has been snatched by an alien who's severe and stoic and doesn't smile or laugh or flirt with me. Or kiss.

"Oh well," I mutter, finally following. "At least his walk is still good."

THE WHEAT IS SHOULDER HEIGHT AT ITS DEEPEST, AND I AM BURIED within feet of entering it.

The stalks are still and calm, trapped between the sinewy fingers of the iridescent mist, and with darkness falling, I have only the dual ends of the path to anchor me in place. My hearing grows muted as if I'm wearing headphones, and I can't shake the feeling of being watched.

I fight off my rising claustrophobia by keeping my head down and concentrating on moving forward on the slim path.

Fortunately, the others are moving quickly as well, and I see the outline of the cairn marking the far end of the blood wheat, and whatever creatures it holds, right as a scream tries to bubble up in my chest. I turn as Nia twists the top stone and watch with the others as the mist of incense drops away.

As soon as the shimmering veil settles to the ground, an agonized howl rips the night.

"Oopfh." War stumbles as I careen into her.

"Sorry," I say, as we both straighten. "I was fleeing the murderous sound behind me."

"By the stars, just look up," she mutters.

"I was trying to keep to the path," I complain.

"I mean now. Look up."

I do ... and the breath I've just barely caught leaves me on a ragged whoosh.

It's not particularly impressive for a cottage. Simple wood slats rise skyward in the same nut-brown color as the trees, and moss drapes the roofline like it's been growing there, darkly, for centuries. I can't see the building's depth, but it's as wide as my former home in Laguna, and light glows from one curtained window like a fixed star.

Again, not spectacular, and somewhat homey ... if the whole thing weren't also floating forty feet off the ground.

"Whoa!" I breathe, neck craned to the sky. "Best. Treehouse. Ever!"

War groans next to me. "Don't call it that."

"But--" I wave to the house held up high in the arms of the trees.

"We call it the cottage," she informs me coolly.

"You can call it a lollypop if you want, Black She-Ra ... but that's totally a treehouse."

There's a scuffle as Beck rushes to intervene. I back away, hands up. "Half-mortal over here! The kind you're supposed to protect."

Thayer does exactly that, tipping his hand to my back to keep me from accidentally stepping back into the wheat.

He waits until Beck has led War away to the treehouse before shaking his head. "Black She-Ra? Are you nuts?"

"You live in a treehouse on the far side of a field of mist and blood, and you're asking if *I'm* nuts?"

Thayer tilts his head. "Fair point."

"She's just so ... intense."

He resettles his cape over his shoulders. "You know the drill. Lineage used to mean everything in the Zodiac world, and War's a second-born daughter."

My eyes bug out. "You mean there's another one of her?"

"Yeah, and if you think War's intense, wait until you meet Rometra." He shudders.

"Not warm and fuzzy?"

"Let's just say she's not a hugger," Thayer jokes, but there's a telling pinch at the corners of his eyes, some memory that bothers him.

I'd ask what, but Beck is back by then—sans the girl named after violence and bloodshed—and for some reason, he's spewing his exasperation all over my personal space. It smells like soured peppermint.

"Can you at least *try* to get along? I mean, since you're here and all?"

"No." I cross my arms and give him my best resting bitch-face. "I hate it here. It's ugly."

Only his eyes move as they tighten at the corners. He takes in the verdant beauty of the natural forest and looks back at me.

"Fine," I relent and cup my hands around my mouth to shout. "Sorry I called you Black She-Ra!"

"By the *stars*," he mutters, rolling his eyes and reaching into his back pocket. To my sadness, he does not pull out a chocolate bar. "Put this on."

Before I can say no, laugh in his face, or throw the friggin superhero mask into the expanse of blood wheat behind us, he adds, "It's for your protection. Ever hear what happened to your birth mother when she tried to enter her troop's sanctuary without her mask?"

Oh yeah. It was described in a manual of Light. '*The Boneyard Surprise*' or '*Light is Might*' or something like that. Basically, the sanctuary's security system detected the Shadow side in her and attacked. The drawings were pretty gnarly.

"You think that'll happen to me?"

"You want to risk it?" He quirks one eyebrow. On someone else, it would come off as owlish. On him, it's just owlishly hot. Overcome by all that hotness, I nod and put on the mask.

Plus, I really don't want to get microwaved from the inside out. It's already been a long day.

· · ·

BACK IN THE OLDEN DAYS, SUPERHERO HIDEOUTS WERE ALWAYS underground. Yet, as we near the dense copse of trees to slip beneath the gloomy underbelly of the cottage, Beck and the others explain that they've decided a new world order requires a new way of living and thinking.

"Why should those born to save the world hide underground like moles?" War says as my heightened eyesight adjusts to reveal an enormous rounded grove.

Swiftly, I count the supporting trees. Sure enough—the same number as the star signs on the western zodiac—twelve, all evenly spaced, with trunks tarred black and enough foliage to obliterate even a hint of the sky above.

I'm about to ask where the elevators are when Thayer gestures me around the thick bole of the closest tree, where he disappears much faster than he should. Nia and War follow, never appearing on the trunk's far side, and I'm rushing to keep up when the ground gives out beneath me, and I fall directly into the hollowed-out shell of the elm.

"Come on, Ashlyn!" Nia's voice sounds from above me, and I squint up and into the darkness.

"I've got her," Beck calls back, coming up behind me.

It's the first time we've been alone since ... well, the last time we were alone. The closeness, coolness, and darkness remind me of that seaside cliff. I'd be more weirded out about it if I weren't so weirded out about this.

"You gotta jump. See?" He's close enough that his body heat warms me in contrast to the cool night air, and the smell of him washes over me, a scent I've only been unconsciously aware of until now. It's that kickass, loamy, earthy smell, the one that's both bright and rich at the same time.

Resisting the urge to sniff at him like a bomb dog, I jerk my chin up. "Is that a ladder?"

He nods. "You just capture the bottom rung and start to climb. When you want to exit, you drop to the ground."

"But that's at least thirty feet straight up!"

"So?"

Point taken.

I still miss the rung on the first try and end up pinballing across the hollowed-out trunk and back to the forest floor. I make sure to catch the rung on my second attempt, fighting for pride's sake to whip my legs up and over the bar as my backpack works to strangle me from behind. The rungs are coated in black, forcing me to use nothing more than blind trust to keep moving forward.

"Same as surfing," I mutter, placing one hand over another.

Same as *living*.

Finally, an opening. Not exactly a light, but the whisper of one where a giant circular door has been carved into the cottage wall like in an old cartoon.

Beck calls out from below. "Mind the—"

I stumble as I step inside, catch myself, and trip again to land on my butt with a grunt.

"Limbs."

Beck's there a second later to give me a hand up. I take it, careful not to meet his eyes.

"Sorry. I should've warned you," he says. "The cottage was built within the crowns of the trees, but with the supporting branches incorporated into the design."

Which is why everything blooms inside as well: greenery climbing the walls, flaring buds that blossom with abandon, while the branches act as a root system that curls untamed along the floor. I'm getting used to my amplified senses, but the riot of scents in my nose is dizzying.

I have fallen into Alice's rabbit hole ... but in totally the opposite direction.

I gaze up at a ceiling littered with bright yellow blooms while Beck plays tour guide. There's a cantina where we take meals together, weapons and training facilities, and a whole wing of rooms that far outnumber the four superheroes-in-training I've already met.

Beck motions me around an ivy-strewn corner, where another circular door appears, this one slightly ajar. "This is yours."

I duck past a splash of honeysuckle blooms to push the door wide. The supporting branches line only two of the triangular walls, massive boughs that cup the room in between to keep the floor clear. A good choice, considering how groggy I am before my morning coffee. Also held within: a bed with a simple but full duvet, a side table, and a small writing desk—all carved of wood.

Probably by elves, I think wryly. Using the sharpened horns of unicorns and pixie teeth.

An enormous Persian rug covers most of the floor, but the long, sole window takes up the exposed third wall. The forest outside is absolute in its darkness, making the late hour known. The one piece of furniture not made of wood is a giant locker like one might find in a gym, although this one has a symbol—the glyph for the Sagittarian star sign—my sign—punched into the steel top.

Dark and blank, the symbol reminds me of a closed eye.

"What do you think?" Beck asks from the doorway.

"Fragrant." Because the greenery still dips from the ceiling, trailing palm-sized leaves above like a living chandelier.

"It's another defensive layer. It keeps the Elders from--"

"Scenting us out so they can murder us in our sleep. I know."

It's the same reason Zoe hid me in a greenhouse located in a beach town where the ocean breeze could ferry away my signature scent. It's why she sprayed me with fragrance every time I walked out the door ... and probably at night while I was sleeping.

Beck clears his throat in the elongated silence. Every part of me tenses up. I realize we're about to have The Talk. Address the ol' elephant in the room: We-Almost-Kissed-But-Didn't-And-Now-It's-Awkward.

My nerves spike, so I busy myself with my hands, which I realize still hold the mask. I try to hand it back.

Beck waves it away. "You'll need it to enter and exit the cottage, and you should probably wear it anytime you're outside since Carl clearly intends to draw you."

"Is that what you guys were arguing about in the shop?"

Beck's eyes go flat. "Among other things."

"Carl's cool," I goad, trying to get him to say more.

"He's not exactly who he seems."

"Neither were you," I say sharply, then clear my throat. "Besides, he saved my life."

"I saved it first."

I huff, and even though I can't scent my own emotions, I know my laugh must smell bitter. "Maybe if you'd told me about Cassius earlier ... approached me on the sand at any point in, say, oh, the previous year, I wouldn't have had to fight him off at the bottom of the ocean."

Twice.

"There wasn't really a chance," he mutters, not looking at me.

I fist my hands on my hips. "You let me explain the basics of the Zodiac world to you over a plate of carbonara." I shake my head. "God. I bet you were laughing so hard at that."

"Never." He steps closer, his voice still low but tight. "But I couldn't make a move until Zoe decided to--"

"Shoot me in the chest?"

"Return your powers to you," he corrects, then sighs. "Return you to our world. Ashlyn, you have no idea how hard it was to watch you on the waves, completely unaware of what you can do. What you *will* do."

"Look, I haven't said I'm going to be the next caped crusader. I'm happy to hang out here and learn some magic tricks that will help me stay alive as long as Cassius is out there, but after that? I'm totally outta here."

"No," he says softly, like he's afraid to hurt my feelings. "You don't have a choice in this, Ash."

"Yes. I do." I say, equally soft, and put a hand on his arm. "And I choose to eat fish tacos. On the beach. In Kauai."

Beck closes his eyes. At first, I think he's trying to keep from smacking my hand away. Then he opens them again, and I realize he's almost too calm. Whatever he's about to say? He's been about to say it for a long time.

"What if I told you that I believe you were born for this? Cassius and the other Elders? They hate even the possibility that you might be great. Your humanity is repulsive to them. The human race is an affront. They consider themselves lords who rule over you with—"

I hold up a hand. "Got it, dude."

But Beck doesn't stop. He steps so close that his breath rustles my hair.

"But I believe the very thing they hate in you, the humanity they mistake for weakness? That will eventually become the source of your greatest strength."

I shake my head. "How can you know that?"

Something moves in the shallows of his gaze. "Because I've watched you for a year."

We lock eyes and hold them through a moment that feels like the one on the cliff. For the first time since we were both bowled over by Vasari and splattered in his blood, I see the guy I thought I knew. Or, at least, the one I thought I wanted to know.

Then he points at himself and gives a lopsided smile. "Plus, I'm your friend. Potential superhero, remember?"

It's his attempt to keep things light, but it reminds me who he really is, so I don't smile back.

"That doesn't make you my friend. That just makes you a potential superhero."

His face falls. I'm being hard on him. Deliberately difficult.

But there's still the issue of that unmentioned kiss and all the lies that came before that.

Beck knows it. "I promise things will be different now that I don't have to keep secrets from you. And I really am sorry about ... before."

Sorry he lied? Sorry I almost died, twice, on his watch? Sorry he pretended to like me and made me want to kiss him?

I'm supposed to fill the silence with a smile, tell him it's okay, don't worry about it, or do something else that will loosen the tension between us, but honestly, I'm not feeling it.

I'm not comfortable with any of this ... so why should I try to make him comfortable at all?

"I think I'll rest for a bit," I say instead of offering up the forgiveness Beck so clearly wants.

Disappointment flashes across his brow, but he only nods. "Dinner's in an hour."

I don't watch him walk away this time. Yet even amidst all the lush greenery of the treehouse, I make out the scent of damp ash mingling with citrus gone sour.

Yet Beck's right. I'm still new to this world. I have a ton to learn. So I shut the door firmly behind him ... with absolutely no idea what those mingling scents might mean.

14

YO, MIRROR. WHO'S THE DEADLIEST OF THEM ALL?

I 'm glad Beck's gone. I'm happy to finally be alone.

A part of me wishes I'd been more chill, easily blowing off his claims that I'm supposed to be part of this world forevermore. I'm usually less reactive, but then again, I'm usually totally sure of my place in the world.

I just need to get my bearings, I think as I drop my backpack down atop the duvet. I've gone from Hummingbird House to a treehouse in one day, and I literally recognize nothing around me.

Including myself, I think, catching sight of my reflection in the mirror of the small adjacent bath. The girl reflected there has circles beneath her eyes from the weight of real-world problems. She looks like a girl who remembers things best forgotten. She also really needs to brush her hair.

Turning away, I unhook the urumi from around my waist and test the latch on the locker. It opens easily to reveal two jumpsuits, four tops of varying sleeve lengths, and three pairs of pants. All black, and—you guessed it—all made from a cow.

"You people really need to get over this leather fixation," I say to no one.

I shut my urumi inside the locker but save the rest of the backpack for later. Right now, I just need to keep moving.

I don't want to be that girl in the mirror.

Beck is right about the flowering blooms and vines. They do a rock solid job of masking all other scents, and even though I think I'm headed toward the dining room I saw upon our arrival, I end up having to backtrack from three separate dead ends.

Finally, a room reveals itself, its doorway encircled by the limbs of a vine with palm-sized leaves so thick and large it's like they're giving it a giant hug. I'm about to peer inside when a voice surprises me into stillness.

"Oh, baby. That's what I'm talking about."

"You're in the wrong spot."

"I'm not. This is great."

I recognize that bouncy cadence immediately and feel myself flush. It's Thayer, and he's clearly busy.

"No, it's not, and if you keep jerking around like that, you're going to injure someone. Probably yourself."

And that, I realize with a start, is War. More relaxed than I've ever heard, her voice lacks the harsh rasp she affects when addressing me. She even sounds playful.

A mood that seeing me is sure to ruin, I think, backing away. I have no desire to interrupt whatever's going on in that room. The mental flash alone is enough to give me new nightmares.

So, of course, I trip right over the tubers threading the floor, land on my butt with a grunt, and curse in a sudden, all-encompassing silence.

War's head appears around the door a moment later. I let out a relieved sigh when I see that she's fully clothed, but freeze again because she's also fully armed. Luckily, and a little reluctantly, she sheaths her sword when she sees only me. "Figures."

I sigh as she disappears back inside.

Rising, I dust myself and poke my head inside the doorway. It's colder in the room than in the hallway, more sterile. A faint humming sits in the air, like the sensation that goes through your jaw when biting on tinfoil. Yet, instead of being repelled, I'm drawn forward.

The space is nothing like the rest of the cottage. The floor is concrete and bare, and the ceiling and walls lack the natural greenery that lingers just outside the door. It's like the boughs are just as repelled by the buzzing as I am ... or as I'm supposed to be.

It's not natural, I think, advancing farther within. Nothing inside is natural. The walls are steel-encased, ditto the ceiling and floor, and even though I've never been here before, I know exactly where I am.

"The weapons room."

"Did all the weaponry happen to give it away?" War asks, but her sarcasm is muted, and she's watching me from the corner of her eye. I don't care. She could be watching me from halfway across the planet ... I only have eyes for the arsenal.

It's like a supernatural museum in here. Knives and batons and guns and arrows and swords—all piled atop steel tables and lined along the metal shelves. Most are rusted over with disuse, but all once only existed in the pages of comics.

My fingertips itch with the need to touch them, but no one has been able to touch supernatural weaponry since the Reordering. An agent is more likely to blow off their own hand than hurt anyone else by attempting to use supernatural weapons. Still, something inside of me feels like it's urging me forward, pressuring me to touch even just one, to see how it works, what it does.

What I might be able to do with it.

Like Thayer. Cape and all, he squats in the room's center, gloved hands prying back a lever on something that looks like a cross between a bazooka and a bayonet. Careful not to let the weapon touch any of his bare skin, he props it between padded knees and gives it a hard yank. War's right. He does look in danger of losing a limb.

"I didn't mean to interrupt," I say, wrapping my arms around myself to hold back the desire to inspect everything.

I've only ever felt like this while scoping massive waves—greedy, gluttonous, ready to start. I edge to a table with strange bullets shaped like acorns or needles or filed screws, along with other projectiles. Some are as long as my forearm. Others span the length of my body, times two.

"You're not interrupting. We're just trying to tear this thing apart to see how it's made."

"You," War corrects coolly. "Not we."

"Why?" I ask.

Thayer shrugs, tugs. "So we can learn to make new ones."

New conduits for a new generation. My fingers twitch involuntarily at my side.

"It's better and safer to stick with mortal weapons and fists," Zoe said when she first told me about conduits.

Yeah ... but then she gave me a urumi made of a strange flexible steel.

One I used yesterday to kill an Elder.

I swallow hard, also remembering the way the Elders who attacked Beck and me on that clifftop totally freaked at the sight of that urumi. In a flash, I recall how War wrapped her hands around mine to dispatch Vasari. She hadn't wanted to, or couldn't, touch the urumi. But I can, I realize, and as if reading my mind, the humming grows in strength.

Slowly, I begin backing from the room.

"But can you do it without blowing yourself up?" War is asking Thayer. He's too preoccupied with wrenching the rusted knife from its socket to answer.

Yet he does look up when I reach the threshold. "Where you going?"

"To find cover," I say, but the joke falls flat. Probably because of the way my voice wavers.

Or maybe, like me, they can hear the buzzing of the weapons, too, because it intensifies even as I exit. It follows me down the hall as I search, ever more frantically, for my room. It chases me when I begin to run.

When I finally find my room again, I lock myself inside it, and when the questioning knocks sound at the door—first Beck, then Nia—I pretend I don't hear them. They eventually stop.

I skip dinner.

I shower for the first time in two days and don't leave until the water runs cold. When I finally finish, I rub the steam away from the mirror and catch my own eye.

"The Zodiac world is real," I tell the girl in the mirror. "And you're a part of it whether you want to be or not."

Beck is right. I need to know how to defend myself. I need to learn what I can and can't do as a half-mortal. It doesn't mean I have to stay here forever, but right now, I need these people more than they need me.

"I know," the girl that I both do and don't recognize replies ... and damn the twisted childhood that Zoe Archer somehow made me love because a little thrill rises up to drown out the fear in my chest.

In the morning, I close my bedroom door behind me and take my time winding through the verdant hallways, using my honed sense of smell to ferret out the dining room. The scent of waffles lures me up a flight of stairs, while bacon strings me forward and French Toast ferries me home. A sharp left turn brings an open door with an ivy welcome mat into view.

When I step inside, the room falls still.

The cantina is made of smooth, hewn planks, as plain as a country church, but made beautiful by an explosion of rainbows that spark atop the equally rustic tables and chairs. The skylights are cut from crystal and sharply angled to represent every constellation in the zodiac and their location in the sky.

The night sky, and our mythos, loom over us this way, even in the day.

War blinks in surprise, giving me a good up-and-down. I've thrown on a clean tee-shirt because it smells like home, and some cargoes Zoe packed me in deference to the chill in the mountain air. "You look ... good."

"Thanks," I say, and hesitate a moment before adding truthfully, "You still look scary."

I'm tired of trading barbs with this chick. Yeah, she is hard and cold and biting, but I lived with Zoe Archer for five years. I know more than anyone that people with solid defenses usually have a good reason for them.

She considers my words for a moment. "You think I'm scary?"

"Totally. You have muscles and a really big sword. Even your hair is strong."

She nods after a moment, and I feel some of the tension that's been building between us loosen like slack in a line. "Cool."

Her reaction, this small acceptance, calms me enough for what I need to say. To get them to understand that my needs are as valid as theirs. Even, or especially, when they don't intertwine.

"So I need to tell you all something, and when I'm done, I'll go back to being chill and awesome, but for now? Just let me talk."

Thayer nods, but the rest of them only wait. I think I see Beck swallow hard, but it might just be a rainbow shifting in the light.

"I was thirteen years old the first time I was attacked," I say, in a rush of words that don't even sound like me. "Zoe sent me to the corner store for milk, and this guy jumped out at me from the bushes. I got away, and not long after that, she told me to go outside and play. Another guy charged my bike from around the corner. Even so, Zoe kept sending me out."

"She paid them." Beck's voice is different, too. Deep with disgust and something else. Something that seeps into his gaze as he watches me. I think about asking him if he ever witnessed this, but I nod instead. It doesn't matter.

"I was "trained" to consider the world a very dangerous place."

This is how we live. Knowing something hunts us, but never when it's going to strike.

"I don't know if you guys can imagine what it's like to walk down a warm strand on a perfect summer day, barefoot, with ice cream in one hand and a skimboard in the other, then suddenly be flipped to your back atop sand that's no longer soft, and forced to fight your way free, but ..."

"It sounds awful," Nia says softly when I don't finish.

It was like being abandoned by God.

"Fortunately, another feeling kicked in right after the initial fear," I take a deep breath to stay on top of the memory. "My knee and my head came up at the same time. My fists came up after that."

"You were good at fighting back." It's War's way of consoling me. Like me, she's saying. Like us.

"No. That's the problem. " I stop shaking my head and frown. "I wasn't good. I was awesome. And the only reason the dude got away was because I eventually got sick of the sound my knuckles made while meeting bone through flesh."

I don't tell them I spent the next half-hour puking into the surf, and not because I'd been scared. Because I wasn't. The only thing worse than living in a violent world was getting used to living in a violent world.

"After that, I went home and confronted Zoe."

A girl shouldn't have to walk through the world afraid she will be attacked!

But that's the world we live in, isn't it?

"I don't like violence," I tell these future superheroes now, just as I told Zoe then. "Hurting another living being might kill their desire ever to touch you again, but a little piece of you has to die in the process. Yet, I also know I can't block out this world anymore. My senses are stronger. My reflexes are faster. Even my memories ... the blowback?" I ask, and Beck nods. "It's all brighter in my mind, like it happened only yesterday. I also know you're right. That dude, Cassius? He's not done with me."

It's the conclusion I came to at some point in the hours-long shower, or in the night, or in my not-dreams. And ...

"Last night. In the weapons room. I felt this strange buzzing. Like the conduits were alive somehow. Like they were—"

"Calling to you." A burning scent accompanied Thayer's words. Jealousy?

"Yeah."

It'd taken me the whole night to work it out, but it's so clear now that even with a Swiss cheese memory, I can't believe I didn't see it before. "Not just one conduit, either. All of them."

"It's very exciting, Ashlyn," Nia says with near reverence. "So far, the Elders can't be killed while we can, but this could change everything. Plus, no one has been able to touch the conduits since the Reordering. Five long years..."

"But someone else can, can't they?" Or, I should say, he. I look at Beck. "When Cassius had me trapped underwater, he was holding that big-ass stake of death. He said he was going to kill me with it."

This time, Beck does not lie. "We don't know where he found it or why he can use it when no one else can, but he's been carrying it since he began assembling the Elders."

"They say he's killed dozens of initiates with it," Thayer adds. "And mortals."

And the only thing that can stop him is if the Zodiac world rises again.

So I tell them the second realization I came around to after a good night's rest. "I need to learn what I can do. I need to train with real weapons. Zodiac weapons. I might not like violence, but I know what kind of world we live in."

Zoe taught me that much.

"We'll help you," Thayer offers immediately.

"We'll train you," Beck says, eyes shining.

"Train with you," Nia corrects.

We all look at War.

Squinting, she considers me. "Are you going to take it seriously?"

I have to smile ... mostly because she's taking it seriously enough for both of us.

"C'mon, Black She-Ra," I say, shooting her a conspiratorial wink. "Where would be the fun in that?"

15

MY WORST IS THE BEST I CAN DO.

The fun in that—or at least my training—will be in the forest. My gut clenches upon hearing this because even though we're going outside, there's something about the dense layers of greenery that I find totally suffocating.

I'm a surf rat. I thrive in the sand, beneath the sound of gulls, and with the world's heartbeat thrumming in my ears. I have no sense of direction amidst the moss and grasses, the shrubs and thickets, the trees ... and even bigger trees.

We hit the ground, and my breathing immediately becomes shallow because, unlike in Laguna, I can barely see the sky. Oh—and being surrounded by three people wearing head-to-toe leather instead of flip-flops and board shorts totally doesn't help. They stride around the forest floor, looking like they're being strangled by their own clothing.

I try to slow my breathing to keep them from sensing my panic. I tell myself the forest is just the upside-down version of the beach. That we're at the bottom of the ocean floor, and the plant life is really algae and grasses and seaweed. As for the leather-clad beings, they're just strange ocean creatures with smooth hides instead of scales.

"Here. Put this on." Beck tries to hand me a cropped jacket with padding and long sleeves, clearly meant to protect the arms.

"But I'm already wearing this super cool mask," I say dryly.

We all are. Beck has figured Carl will want to draw the story of my training, so our appearances must be kept hidden in case he includes this day in the manuals that are finally published and recorded. That's what we're trying to do, after all.

Bring about a new Rising.

War steps up, arms crossed, and I can tell she will side with Beck even before she speaks. "Do you know how hard it is to acquire an authentic zodiac-era troop uniform? Every single one of these is made of—"

"Suck. They're made of suck," I interrupt, gesturing to her get-up. "What you're wearing right now doesn't even make sense."

"What in Mother-Loving hell are you talking about?" she snaps back.

"It's kinda true," Nia speaks before I can. "You have side-boob. It's ten o'clock in the morning."

"Yeah," I say, shaking my head. "Why do you have side boob at ten o'clock in the morning?"

War looks like she's going to punch me in the face ... at least until her own expression falls. It looks like a sandcastle being kicked in.

"I don't know," she wails. "But I hate it no matter what time of day it is!"

Nia and I exchange glances. See?

Beck growls under his breath and turns away, pulling at his hair. This amuses me enough that I calm down ... at least until Thayer drops from the cottage and into the grove. He's holding a bag that bulges and looks as old as the uniforms of suck, and my heart rate picks up again. I already know I'm going to hate what-ever's inside of it.

Yet the buzzing that comes from whatever's in the mysterious bag also makes me want to hold it.

"Some of the things we can all do," Beck begins, ticking them off on his fingers, "Breathe underwater, super speed, extra strength, enhanced senses—"

"You do know all of this already, right?" War asks, and I give her a look like, *shut up*.

"Trust me, if Zoe Archer could've pulled me from school and educated me solely using comic books, she would have. We had every issue in the 'Signs of the Zodiac' series from *The Scent of Shadows* to *The Reordering*."

I don't say that the final manual was the only one I wasn't allowed to read. Zoe kept it tucked away in one of her endless hidey-holes and told me only that I wasn't ready to see it. That's how I know there's something important inside of it.

Something about me.

"We have the Reordering issue," Nia says as if reading my mind. "That's how Beckett figured out you could touch the conduits."

Because my birth mother could touch the conduits, too.

"So, do you think it's hereditary?" I ask Beck.

He shrugs. "You're the only one of us who can do it, and Cassius believes you must die."

"No." I shake my head back and forth, hard. "I must not die. I must eat poki, wear too many puka shells, and surf the North Shore. But not die."

Beck jerks his head at the bag. "Thayer."

Thayer steps forward, reaching into the bag to pull out a silver orb a little smaller than the palm of his hand. My hands immediately begin to tingle. I have to lace my fingers together to keep from grabbing it, but he holds it out, and, noting that he's not wearing gloves this time, I take it. Something inside of me gives a quiet, inward sigh, and the itching in my palms immediately ceases.

"Ever seen a demi-cannonball before?" he asks, pulling out another.

"Sure. My local gym offers an early morning superhero boot camp. It's right after Mommy and Mini-Me and before cardio yoga."

"Really?" Thayer, handing the second ball to War, looks up.

I roll my eyes. "As if I go to the gym."

War, standing across from me, just squints. "Do you ever. Take anything. Seriously?"

I nod my head. "No."

"You might want to start," she advises. "Because drop that, and you'll never joke again."

I freeze.

"Just kidding." She even almost smiles. "Go ahead. Drop it."

I look at her like she just stepped on my cat. "No. You drop it."

She does, causing my stomach to leap to my throat, but the ball just tumbles across a patch of gravel, gets caught in a bank of pine needles and dead leaves, and stops.

So I drop mine. And then the forest really does flip upside-down. I'm blown into the air like I've sprung from a trampoline, which would be kinda fun if I'd had some sort of warning. And if I didn't bean my head on the arm of a low-hanging elm.

Hoots of laughter ring out around me, and I briefly see the others, also air-bound, before I'm bracing for a faceplant that never comes. A thin, sooty mist has bubbled up below me, and it shifts with my involuntary movements to cushion my impact, catapulting me into the air again.

At least this time I don't hit my head. I find my bearings on the third bounce, and I'm in control by the fourth. I land on the fifth, mist dissipating around my toes. Everyone else lands in a pile of giggles, fighting to catch their breaths for an entirely different reason.

Thayer's fist rockets into the air. "That was awesome!"

"I don't think you know how that word's used!" I bend over and put my hands on my knees, still breathless. "That was not awesome! That was ..."

Everyone waits.

I pinch my mouth shut. "Okay. That was totally awesome."

"Yeah!" Nia and I high-five.

Beck is beaming, which is a totally new look on him. It has my heart racing with more than adrenalin. Even War smiles, which turns her pretty in a way that shouldn't be possible for someone still sporting a sword.

I do it again. And again. It doesn't take long for me to learn how to control the balls, the angle and speed at which to throw them to achieve my desired result.

"They go where I want them to. Like they can read my mind!" I don't know how the demi-cannonballs respond to my will, but they do.

Which makes me, I think with an inward laugh, a badass cannon.

"Of course. That's what conduits are," Beck says, grinning so widely it looks painful. "They're an extension of your body, like a surfboard on the waves. Learn how to use them--"

"If you can touch them," Nia interjects.

"And they'll do your will in any situation."

Awesome. I hold out my hand, bat my eyes at Thayer, and say in my best Oliver Twist accent, "Please, sir. I want some more."

USING THE DEMI-CANNONBALLS TO BOUNCE HIGH INTO THE AIR IS the closest I can come to surfing big waves all the way out here in the wilds of the mountains. Beck must sense that I need it because he indulges my hoots and hollers for another half hour, allowing me to flip in circles, twists, and other tricky maneuvers I'd only ever tried on the ocean's wet back. This is even better, though, because while the ocean eats up my painful belly-flops, the mist moves to support my limbs, augmenting my balance no matter what I do.

It's magic, I think, grinning ear-to-ear, and it's mine. I bounce higher and higher, stoked on the power, my first in this new world—or, at least, my first that doesn't involve beheading a murderous Elder.

I'm slowing down, wondering how many balls are left, when Beck suddenly claps his hands to gather us into a circle. Thayer's face is so flushed that his cheeks burn red. Nia's eyes sparkle even in the dim light of the forest. War's hair springs from her head in buoyant coils. My ability is theirs, and we are all amped with our success.

"Okay, Ash. You ready to train?"

It's not like I didn't know this was coming, but I still grimace and feign a slump. "I guess. And I do feel stronger than ever."

"Of course." War waves this away like it's natural, which, of course, it is in this world. "And your hearing? What about the birdsong in your ear?"

"Sharp," I answer immediately. "Shrill, even."

"And colors?" asks Thayer.

"Even sharper."

Nia grins. "And the bagel you had yesterday in Carl's shop? I bet it was the best you'd ever tasted."

My mouth starts watering at the mere memory. "Yeah, but then again, I hadn't eaten since..."

I falter and am very careful not to look at Beck. He knows I was about to mention the date that wasn't really a date, a reminder of his deception, which I'm not quite over yet. You don't need supernatural abilities to know that.

"Your heightened senses are your new baseline," Beck says, smoothly transitioning to a new subject. "You'll be able to build on and strengthen them, just like the rest of us."

Nia puts her hand on my arm. "You'll never feel weak again. I promise."

She's sweet, and obviously remembering what I told them about being attacked as a kid. Her concern causes tears to flood my eyes unexpectedly.

"Nia, you have your plastic throwing stars on you?" Beck asks, and she pats the pockets of her leather pants.

"Don't worry," she tells me. "They're mortal made."

She suddenly looks a lot less sweet.

My tears disappear as a gnarly little alarm goes off in my head.

"War, use the flat of your sword, okay? Thayer, you and I will rush her head-on."

"Hand-to-hand." Thayer nods approvingly before his eyes narrow on me.

A record player scratch arcs across my mind. "Wait. You're *all* targeting me?"

Nia nods. "We just need to get a baseline reading of your speed, strength, and instincts."

Call me crazy, but this reassurance isn't very reassuring.

"Don't worry," War says, noting my frown. "You get to use the cannonballs."

"Yeah, hold that thought." I grab Beck's arm, yanking him into the underbrush. "Is this necessary?"

"It's just training."

"But you saw me on the cliff in Laguna. You know what I can do."

"I saw you react with the power of the stars in your blood," he reminds me.

"It's more than you did that night," I mutter, crossing my arms. I'm stalling, obviously bringing up the past so I don't have to face Nia's throwing stars, the flat edge of War's sword, and Thayer's fists.

Beck's fists, I think, with some shock.

"I was biding my time," he replies softly.

He was waiting for Cassius to appear, which left me vulnerable. However, it also kept Vasari and the others from attacking him, freeing him to save me beneath the ocean's waves.

Sighing, I frown up into his face. "Is Cassius really that strong?"

"Yes and no," Beck says. "He was born a Shadow at a time when that actually meant something. They were formidable back then, and the Shadows had the advantage before your mother came along. So he has experience on his side, a chip on his shoulder, and his sights set on you."

"You know a lot about him," I comment lightly.

"You could say I've made a study of him." He gives me a wry smile that I can't read. It belongs to this new Beckett—whom nobody but me calls Beck—in this new world ... and there's so much still that I don't know about both. "But I've also studied you, and you have a gift Cassius lacks."

"Because I can fold my tongue into a three-leafed clover?"

"Because you know how to live in the moment better than anyone I know."

I snort, suddenly finding the seriousness War thinks I lack. "Never much choice in that."

I can't exactly trust the future will come when I don't even remember the past.

"You take each wave as it comes. You rely more on instinct than those of us who've always possessed extraordinary senses."

"That's why you think I was born for this?" I ask, observing him carefully.

"Evolution has turned your humanity into a weapon," he shrugs. "Or it will, once you learn how to use it."

Use what Zoe honed in the midnight hours using deceit, drugs, and potions. I have to admit, it'd be nice to move and train in the open. I already know my slow-twitch muscles are well-developed because of surfing. I can endure a long wave and a lengthy foot race.

Yet I can feel that my fast-twitch fibers have also gotten a boost. I look down at the tendons in my right hand as I make a fist. I am stronger than any boy or man in Laguna. I am stronger than any man who isn't, well, super.

It feels good, doesn't it?

I remember ...

"Come on, Ashlyn," Nia calls out, overriding the memory of Zoe's voice. "Just do your best."

I scrunch up my face. "I might only have a worst."

Beck just holds out the bag of demi-cannonballs. I look from face to expectant face, then back at the spheres that only I can use. Finally, I roll my eyes and take the bag.

The others shout so loudly that their cries lift and tangle in the branches overhead. I can't help but picture Carl bent over the shiny black desk in the middle of his shop, readying himself to sketch the story of my first training session. It makes me grin even while my new friends draw their weapons and scatter in the wild forest.

The looming trees in this upside-down world settle into their roots to watch the show.

THE BAG HOLDING THE DEMI CANNONBALLS IS CUMBERSOME— something Santa might carry, whereas I'm going for more of a Navy S.E.A.L. Vibe. So I load my cargoes with as many demi-cannonballs as possible and drop the bag at the base of some tree I can't name. I have nine spheres in all, the first already palmed. Instinct has me wishing for my urumi, but of course, I didn't bring it ... we're not really fighting.

Which, apparently, no one told Nia.

The first throwing star impales the oak to my left, so close that I'm cross-eyed as I look at it. Sure, it's plastic, but it's also hard enough to puncture bark and have me jumping a whole foot off the ground.

"That's your warning," she calls out right before I whirl, my first cannonball already in hand.

"And that's yours," I say as she flips into the air on a percussive blast that shakes leaves from the trees above her.

Mean plastic stars tumble from her pockets, and for a moment, I worry that she'll impale herself in the fall. Yet the gray mist from the sphere eats them whole while forcing her to spot the unforgiving ground for a hard landing.

Cool trick shot, I think, even though she still manages a three-pronged crouch.

"You throw like a girl!" Thayer calls, voice admiring.

I ignore the compliment since he happens to be rushing me at the same time. He'll plow me down if I try to shift the ball into my dominant hand, so I fast-pitch it directly into his body. It blows him backward with the strength of a really tiny cannon.

War's voice keeps my laughter at bay ... and registers too late. "You'll have to learn to watch your blind spots, though."

Her sword whistles behind me, and I barely have time to duck. If she were trying to kill me, the blade would sink deep into the same tree as Nia's star. Fortunately for the tree, she follows Beck's instructions and uses the flat of her blade. Unfortunately for me, this leaves her able to pull back quickly for a second strike.

Without looking, I toss a sphere through my legs, a move that blows us in opposite directions on a percussive thrust. I already know I'll land near Beck because my heightened sight has caught movement from the corner of my eye.

Maybe he's right, I think, scrambling for a low-hanging branch to stay my fall. I swing only once—Nia and her throwing stars have to be near—and drop a ball atop a briar thicket that would otherwise score and scratch my entire non-leather-clad body.

The mist is as much an extension of my body as the racket in a tennis player's hand. It goes where I want, does what I want, just because I will it. I bounce softly atop the resulting gray mist, keeping low, and then disappear behind the tumbling thicket.

And land directly in front of Beck.

My head whips back and forth from where I just saw him on the other side of the rough hedge. Damn, he's fast!

"War's right," he says as we start to circle one another. He's watching my hands, clearly intent on rushing me as soon as I reach for another ball. "Not paying attention to your blind spots is dangerous."

"Yeah? Well, up until recently, dangerous meant forgetting to wear sunscreen."

I edge left, where a small clearing will afford me space to retreat. Space means time, and that's all I need.

"Wearing sunscreen *is* important." Thayer's voice is on the thicket's far side, but not for long. No escape that way. I alter direction again.

War and Nia's locations are unknown to me, but they're out there, recovering, and they know exactly where I am. I only have seconds before they converge, and the instinct they're so intent on testing has me darting behind the nearest elm.

I shove my hands into my pockets and yank out the remaining demi-cannonballs. Five.

"Here goes nothing," I mutter and, taking a hint from the heavens we so greatly revere, I begin hurling them all around the elm in the pattern of a five-point star while using the tree's base to brace against the explosions.

Four distinct cries of varying insult rise through the air, along with bodies I can't see through the tangling mist. I want it to obscure me, and it does my bidding, rising high as I crouch low, both hidden and blinded by the soot that has leveled into a gray veil. It's only after half a minute, when there's no other sound, that I know: I have won.

I'm just about to stand and suggest we all go watch reruns of The Bachelor on Netflix when a figure materializes before me. The mist is still a translucent shroud, and my allies have been blasted too far back to reappear this soon, so I alone see this new person emerge like a specter from the blanketing fog.

"Just for the record, blind spots are generally more important than sunscreen."

The figure grows taller, elongating like a shadow, still obscure, though that doesn't hide the voiced smile.

"Because they can be everywhere."

16

PARTY TIME … OR NOT.

The mist is still thick enough to mask the sound of each encroaching footstep, but *this* is the figure I saw on the other side of the hedge. This is the person I mistook for Beck, although the knowledge does me no good. I have no idea who it is.

I'm just happy she doesn't seem interested in partaking in today's fun and games because I don't have any cannonballs or, apparently, allies left.

And it is a *she*. Her shoulders are wide set, but taper into a core that flares at the hips, strong thighs flicking down into the earth like twin black flames with each stride. None of that is reassuring. This is the Zodiac world, after all—a matriarchal world.

And this chick is clearly a part of it.

The girl saunters right up to me so that I have to crane my neck to look up at her. It's either the way she parks her fists on her hips or her smile—amused but also patronizing—but I get the feeling she likes the view. The mist is finally clearing, but that does nothing to lighten her skin, and I feel like I'm still looking at her outline—opaque, super femme, and totally unyielding.

"Ever hear that staring is rude?" Her voice is as dusky as her skin.

"I'm trying to figure out if you're photoshopped," I mutter truthfully before a branch cracks underfoot behind her.

"By the stars," comes Thayer's voice as the girl turns. He stutter-steps at the sight of her, causing Nia to crash into him with a muffled curse.

"Watch it, Th--" She falls as still as Thayer. The only way they could look more thunderstruck, I think, is if they'd been struck by thunder. "Oh."

"Not exactly the welcome I was expecting," the girl says dryly, "but how can I be anything but pleased when my presence inspires such awe?"

Before Nia or Thayer can answer, a curse bounds across the thicket, and everyone turns to the far edge of the copse, which Beck has slipped around unnoticed. "What the hell are you doing here?"

The mist has cleared by now, giving me my first good look at the girl's face. It's still as smooth and polished as ebony, but with a genuine smile pulling it wide. Not like when she'd been gazing down at me. "Long time, Lux."

I roll my eyes. Of course, Beck knows her.

At least the uptick of his mouth doesn't reach his gaze. "Doesn't seem you missed me, though."

"Oh, honey." She swivels completely his way, and I know I'm forgotten. "Take a deeper breath."

Beck does not, but I'm wondering what a long-limbed, dusky goddess smells like, and am about to venture a whiff when War steps into the clearing across from us.

"Rometra."

If anything, the girl's stature grows even more rigid. "Little sister."

My mouth falls open, and I look to Thayer.

If you think War's intense, wait until you meet Rometra.

He hadn't been lying that first day, then. There really were two of them! I gesture back and forth between them but stop when Thayer gives a slight, almost pained shake of his head. Apparently, this family reunion is taking place in a No-Humor Zone.

As for War, her shoulders straighten as she squares her chin and strides directly toward the other girl, though she doesn't return the smile. Despite the obvious tension in the clearing, I feel better as I reach Thayer's side, and we all wait for the two girls to embrace, or at least shake hands.

Instead—without smiling, speaking, or warning—Rometra reels back and slaps her younger sister across the face. The sound pinballs between the tree trunks, and War's knees nearly buckle.

"That's ..." I search for words.

"Abusive and disturbing?" Nia mutters as War recovers and slaps Rometra across the cheek in return. Rometra takes the blow without blinking, and her smile never leaves her face.

"And how is my ambitious little sister?" Rometra asks like she's asking a disinterested third party, not the person in question —certainly not her sibling. "Still working hard not to be seen as second best?"

To War's credit, she doesn't even blink. "Can't fight my destiny, Rometra."

"Not once it gets you killed," Rometra agrees.

When she breaks their shared stare, it's like she's dismissing War entirely. She proceeds to spare Nia only a short, considering glance and passes right over Thayer as if he's a ghost. Then her gaze is back on me, kinda making me wish I were see-through, too.

"This is your Archer?"

That rubs.

"I'm *an* Archer," I say, and a buzz lights up within my skin like a landing strip. My vision pulses, everything brightens, and I'm forced to gasp so that the particles in the air sting the insides of my mouth.

Worried, I look at Beck, only to find him smiling. For some reason, so are Thayer and Nia.

"So. You've claimed your birthright." For the first time, Rometra stops grinning and takes a step forward. "Anxious, then, to take up the mantle of the woman who left our world defenseless?"

"Joanna Archer is a legend--" Nia tries.

"Joanna Archer is a ghost," Rometra shoots back, not even glancing at her.

I remember what Thayer said about Rometra being trained to lead since birth, and realize my birth mother's erasure of the matriarchal dominance—and lineage—probably put a big asterisk's mark next to that inevitability. *Whoops.*

"My grandmother says otherwise," I say, because if anyone knows about this world, not to mention the woman who dismantled it, it's Zoe.

"Zoe Archer." Rometra scoffs, confirming she already knows exactly who I am. "Another mortal."

Something dormant, something I usually know how to keep dampened and dark, sparks inside me, and I fall too-still. It's one thing for me to insult Zoe. I have a right to my anger. Yet Rometra's disdain doesn't just rub me wrong. It's like she just slapped Zoe in the same way she had War ... and nobody touches Zoe.

"You say that like it's a bad thing." My voice has gone flat, as leveled out as my emotions.

Beck steps between us, and I lean to one side to fuse my gaze back on Rometra's. Yet she feigns a yawn as she studies her fingernails and doesn't even look up.

"It's not anything."

"It's what we're fighting for," Nia points out, edging near me. Rometra looks at her now, and Nia swallows hard.

"We're not *It*." I bite off every word and step back to square on them all. I'm surprised to find I'm shaking, and the feeling inside of me is hot and raw, like skin rubbed too long. The only thing I know how to do with this feeling is run or surf until my limbs give out ...

Or kick Rometra's ass, some foreign part of me says.

I ignore it and point at my own non-leather-wearing chest. "We're not things. We're people."

"So." Rometra sneers openly this time. "*It* has a backbone."

"And what the hell would you know about mortals?" I jerk my head at her, but suddenly, I'm angry at them all. I've been pulled from my world and life without my permission, and everyone in this clearing is acting like that's normal.

Like *this* is.

"Let me guess, you studied us in a book? You Googled our mating habits online?"

"Ash—" Thayer tries.

"Outside of Beck, I bet none of you has even had a token mortal friend before," I snap.

"Our job is not to befriend you," Rometra's mouth has thinned out like she's going to hiss. "Our job is to save you."

"People don't want to be saved," I say before I know I'm thinking it. "They want to learn how to save themselves."

For some reason, Rometra's intense face blooms at that, and she tilts her head like she's glad to hear it. "Then you're in luck, Archer. Because I've got a lesson just for you."

ROMETRA INSISTS ON PRIVACY BEFORE SAYING ANYTHING MORE, SO we're back in the cottage before she reveals why she's here. This time, we're in a den with ample buttery brown leather seating bunched under a jumble of climbing vines. Tiny, white flowers bloom along walls that slant sharply to culminate in a sheer apex, like a pyramid, and the sun slants in from the crystal peak, causing the fragile petals of the blooms to glow in the resultant beams. The entire room is infused with a blanket-warm honey-suckle scent.

It may be pretty, but it's still not calming. Rometra's presence has cast a heaviness over our mood, and as I watch her pace before us, I wonder: are the blooms here to keep our enemies from scenting us out ... or to keep us from ferreting out each others' strongest emotions and secrets?

Nia and Thayer have taken up club chairs, which leaves me with a sofa too big for my body alone. At first, I'm fearful that Rometra will plop down next to me, but she and Beck seem to be having an unspoken stand-off of sorts, pacing and circling each other in the room's center. All that's missing, I think, watching them, is the actual OK Corral.

War stands by the only door leading out of this inverted pyra-mid, but I can't tell if she's guarding it or readying to bolt.

"I'm going to hold a festival," Rometra finally says, arms crossed. "And I want you all to be a part of it."

Thayer tilts his head as he leans back into the chair. ""Festival like a party? Or festival like a party with medieval jousts?"

"How do you even know about medieval festivals?" War calls across the room.

"He wears a friggin' cape," Rometra says flatly, staring straight ahead. Only the mention of the cape proves she's seen him at all.

Sadly, she has a point ... which sucks because even though I just met her, I am totally Team Thayer. There's something about Rometra that I instinctively dislike, the same as those girls in high school who look like spun sugar but whose actions fall on the heavy side of cloying. It's repellent in a homecoming queen, but chilling in someone who can toss an automobile over her shoulder with one hand.

Thayer pulls the loose ends of his cape more tightly around him as he shrinks back into his seat. This bugs me enough that I happily move to take a little of the heat off of him. "What's a festival?"

"A gathering of all the available agents in a given region." Beck's voice is quiet, and he's frowning, almost like he's explaining it to himself. "It's one of the ways the earliest troops would fill their ranks when lacking certain star signs."

"Or form a new troop," Rometra puts in, "like they did in emerging cities."

Only in this case, it isn't the mortal world that's new, but ours.

Seeing she has our attention, Rometra continues. "Most festivals would last about a week. Long enough for all the free agents in the region to gather for a series of trials. It was zodiac sign against zodiac sign. Aries against Aries, Taurus against Taurus, and so on. The twelve victors formed that city's first troop."

So what? None of us need this history lesson. The old ways were dead. "But the troop system has been—"

"Destroyed in the Reordering." She waves impatiently. "I know. And the Elders have repeatedly tried to replicate it in several ways. Twelve men or twelve women or even thirteen, in accordance with the sidereal zodiac system."

Because that had been a "thing" for a time—thirteen star signs instead of twelve. But even that failed after the Reordering, and since the Western world followed the tropical zodiac, which was fixed on seasons and not constellations, the thirteen star sign system had since been debunked.

In other words, that old dude, Ptolemy, was still right.

"Anyway," Rometra continues, "Every time I heard they were trying something new and failing, it made me think: what if the only way to form a new troop is with initiates and star signs from *this* generation?"

I wait for someone to protest or argue. Or even make a weird face. Yet all I see is shock and consideration instead. That kinda shocks me, too.

Is that even possible?

"You mean ... a neo-Zodiac?" Beck asks, still working it out like it's a puzzle.

"I think it could work," Rometra says, crossing her arms. "In fact, I think it's the only thing that can work, and the Elders know it. Why else would they be so adamant about hunting us down?"

It makes sense. Hunting down initiates and killing them is a lot of trouble if there's no obvious reward. And the Elders can't merely be trying to hang onto power ... because there is none.

But if we were all dead? If no new generation of star signs existed to replace the troops that my birth mother destroyed?

"Of course, if you'd rather hide out in a glorified tree house and wait for the Elders to find and slaughter you en masse, be my guest." Rometra smirks. "But I think it would make for an outstanding manual if we're shown forcing the Zodiac to rise again. Together."

"Why now?" Beck says suddenly, blue eyes flickering, searching. "We've offered to join forces with you against the Elders a dozen times. You always said no."

"Yeah, what happened?" War barely holds back a sneer. "Have you lost a few potential star signs to the Elders?"

The muscles in Rometra's jaw flex as she clenches her teeth. "Actually, we only have one zodiac sign left to fill."

"And let me guess?" War gives him her bitterest smile. "Beckett's destined to stand at your right-hand side?"

"Stand there again, you mean?" Rometra snaps, and I feel a twinge in my gut that has nothing to do with nerves. "No. The only star sign we're missing is the Virgo."

"Me?" Surprise has Nia springing up straight. She almost looks dazed. "But I always have to fight for everything."

"The festival gives the rest of you a shot as well, and isn't that what you want?" She looks at her sister here, and her smile is sickly—cloying, just as I thought. "An opportunity to be seen? To be counted even though you are second-born? To be great?"

It is. It's what they've been raised to do since birth and what they've dreamed of since my mother's actions destroyed that.

"Of course," Rometra says, "you won't be the only five initiates gunning for immortality."

I raise my hand and correct her math. "Four."

"Rometra could be right," Beck says, ignoring me. Rude. "If we can form a troop, we can usurp the Elders here and now. We can stop hiding. Not in ten years, but now."

Nia is warming to it, too. They all are. I can see it. "Then other initiates would rise up across the country and do the same," she says.

"And," Thayer adds, "we could once again make the world a better, safer place for the mortal race."

For my friends back in Laguna.

For Zoe, who can no longer do it for herself.

And for myself, when I finally get loose of this forest and this world.

War narrows her eyes from the spot next to the door, and I don't need super-scent to smell her ambition. The hope of becoming part of a troop is palpable in all of them. And don't they deserve the chance? I might not want to be a superhero, but these people know nothing else.

"What about you?" Rometra points at me. "You in?"

"Don't see how I could help," I say honestly.

"Can you run as fast as a train? Leap as high as a building?" She names things that everyone can do until ... "Can you kill?"

There it is. That's the difference between her and War. War would never say that with a hopeful smile.

"I can pat my belly and rub my head at the same time." I demonstrate.

She stares at me, unblinking, for so long that it's uncomfortable. She is clearly amazed.

Finally, her upper lip curls. "Not even going to try to be a hero, then?"

"I'm not even going to try to be a grown-up."

Disgust rolls off her in noxious waves. "Zoe Archer did you no favors by coddling you."

I snort as a succession of Zoe's "coddling" methods—the surprise attacks, the drugged and hypnotized training sessions, the weapons training—roll through my mind.

Yet maybe this *is* my place in the Zodiac world, I think. Maybe half-mortality means that I'm just a bridge between the past and the future—a way to mend the rift that my mother broke between the supernatural world and the mortal one. I have to admit, the thought is poetic.

"Ash," Beck finally says, jerking me back to the present.

They're all still waiting for my answer.

"Sure," I shrug and plaster on a smile. "I'll try to help in any way I can."

Because if I'm merely fated to help in the rebirth of the Zodiac world, maybe I can get to the java-stained hills of Kauai faster than I think.

"Man," Thayer says, rubbing his hands together as he grins. "I sure hope Carl's writing all this down somewhere."

I'm sure he is, I think, as everyone stands to shake on it.

Because I just agreed to help the Zodiac world rise again.

17

THE GOLDEN RULE.

Beck and Rometra remain in the den to hash out the festival's details while the rest of us wander back into the hallway, silent and stunned.

Every so often, the branches twining along the walls break off long enough for me to glimpse the outside forest. The floor is stacked with oak and elm, emblazoned with ferns and grasses, while a blue, cloud-dotted sky hovers above it all. The grove of evergreen that lifts our cottage high conceals everything else within its big, broad-leaved arms.

This treehouse totally takes its job seriously.

"Your sister sucks," I finally tell War ... though I make sure Thayer and Nia are between us when I say it.

But War doesn't look happy either. "At least she's not complicated."

"Neither is bacteria."

But it's still freakin' deadly.

"A new troop system, though," Nia points out, "You have to admit, it's exciting. And it's fair of her to give us all a chance when she only has one zodiac sign to fill."

"Rometra doesn't care about being fair," War mutters.

"What does she care about?" I ask.

"Power and control."

"Plus, Los Angeles is lousy with mortals," Thayer adds. "If the Zodiac world does rise again, it will be one of the premier territories in the country. She's smart to claim it."

Nia looks at him hard. "Which means we're lucky for the opportunity to be a part of it."

"Easy for you to say. You're the shoo-in star sign."

"It's not Nia's fault," War says quietly before Nia can retort. "Conflict is all my sister knows, and if she can't yet have a real war, she's happy to manufacture one."

"You don't trust her."

The statement could get me body-slammed if I'm wrong ... but I'm not wrong.

War huffs. "Rometra never means what she says."

"Sure she does," says Thayer, looking at War. "When she's being mean, nasty, vindictive, and horrible, she means exactly what she says."

So why would Beck even consider joining forces with her?

Before I can ask, Thayer sighs and rustles the honeysuckle dipping from the walls. "I'm going to the weapons room to play with something sharp. War?"

"Sure." She pauses to shoot me a knowing look, one eyebrow raised. "Anyone else?"

I shake my head. "I'm going to visit Carl."

I haven't seen him since that first day in the shop, and besides, I want to hear his take on this festival.

Yet War thinks it's for another reason. "Thinking about running away?"

"Should I be?"

"After meeting Rometra?" She shakes her head as she turns away. "You wouldn't be the first."

Nia and I watch them pick their way through a hall choked

with bulging fauna. It tickles their shoulders as they disappear around a final soft, green corner.

Nia turns to me. "Want me to walk you to the cairn?"

"Sure."

We don our masks just in case the forest holds any other surprises and emerge from the cottage into a forest gone quiet with the sleepy sounds of late afternoon. There's the rustling of scurrying things in the brush, and the wind makes a whistle of the reeds trying to remain dignified and upright, but for the most part, the forest naps.

Something inside of me unclenches.

It's not the ocean, I think, slipping through the dappled shade, but I guess it doesn't totally suck.

"Does War ever talk about Rometra?"

Nia shakes her head.

"Strange."

She knows I'm waiting for more but stares straight ahead. Then, finally, "My mother used to say that there are two reasons why people don't talk about something. Either it means nothing to them at all, or it means absolutely everything."

I can't help but think of Zoe immediately. How she shot me dead center in my chest without blinking. How she left me in the taco shop without turning back.

Do I mean anything to her at all?

"What if we all lose to the LA initiates?" I say so suddenly that I have to correct myself. "I mean, to you. Them."

"That's probably what Rom hopes," Nia admits, frowning. "The initiates who follow her are all first-borns. That's why she and Beckett parted ways. She still believes we'll rise again through the lineage of first-borns."

I cock one eyebrow. "And what's Beck's grand master plan?"

What I'm really asking is, why did he spend a whole year watching me?

"Ever hear the saying 'what doesn't kill you makes you

stronger'?" She waits for my nod as we clear the last of the forest's canopy. The blood wheat appears around the next bend. "Beckett only musters teens who've survived an attack by an Elder. He thinks it turns on some power inside of us."

"Like flipping a paranormal switch?" I joke.

"Like evolution," she returns, all seriousness.

"But there are so few of us."

"Exactly."

I frown. Could that be true? I thought it was my natural power returning to me in Laguna, but maybe Beck's right. Maybe my powers appeared because Cassius triggered a supernatural fight-or-flight response in me. I'd ask Nia how she was attacked and got away, but I'm distracted by our arrival at the wheat field.

"It's so quiet," I say, scanning the tall stalks. The wheat barely moves, and the stillness weighs heavy on my eardrums.

"Don't mistake that for peace. They're not the same thing at all."

Nia's expression has soured. Her lip curls as she stares out over the motionless stalks, and something I can't understand is going on behind her eyes. A scent rises, too—it's warming wood, minus the crackle. I don't know what it signifies, but I'm pretty sure I don't want to be near her when it ignites.

She pauses, hand hovering atop the stacked stones that will cause the mist to rise. "Want to see them? The creatures, I mean?"

My eyebrows shoot up. "Is it safe?"

She turns to me, unblinking. "It's inadvisable, incredibly dangerous, and possibly stupid."

"Like everything else in this world, then," I mutter and make sure my mask is tightly secured.

Nia's grin is tinged with bitterness. "Now you're getting the hang of it."

. . .

THE WHEAT IS SHOULDER HEIGHT AT ITS DEEPEST, AND THICK, AND it's not long before I feel buried inside the field. The afternoon takes a hard dip toward twilight in the depths of the looming stalks, and with only the dual ends of the path to anchor us in place, claustrophobia threatens to shorten my breaths.

I also can't shake that feeling of being watched again, yet there's no one around but Nia. I'm about to ask her if the field's somehow monitored when the stalks suddenly rustle to our left.

"Here we go," she mutters as the long wheat parts directly ahead of us. A short, stout creature lumbers into view. The thing is at least twenty yards away, yet in a blink, it's at the path's edge.

I wish I could say that dim light obscures its features, but that's not what's happening. Everything is situated correctly on its face—eyes, nose, and mouth right where they're supposed to be —but its features are scrambled, like they've been softened and quick-whipped before hardening that way. It wears no clothing, and its soft belly is bowed with the weight of whatever's on its back.

It carries a red high-top Converse shoe in one hand.

It's the shoe, its normalcy, that brings me back around. This is one of the creatures that chased Carl and me into Laguna's canyon pass, and as the realization takes hold, the path before us suddenly looks as wide as a tightrope. "What the hell is that?"

"We call them hermits because they have to live alone, but they're really law-breakers."

My body chills over at the word.

There is one law that no one in the Zodiac world can break, meaning if the Zodiac world has a Golden Rule, this is it: Light or Shadow, good or evil, no agent is allowed to take a mortal's life.

The creature is still ahead of us, watching with shining eyes. "That thing used to be an agent?"

"There were a lot of law-breakers just after the Reordering," Nia says, motioning me forward.

I take a step. The hermit doesn't move. I can't tell if it was once Shadow or Light because it doesn't even look human.

"Agents were testing every boundary back then," she continues, "searching for more power, but it quickly became clear that one rule still stood. Killing a mortal doesn't just weaken you ... it turns your own power against you."

I'd read accounts of Shadows tricking humans, influencing them, indirectly affecting the actions of someone already inclined toward evil ... but none had ever dared kill a mortal outright.

Now I knew why.

"So did this one's power turn against it, or did it pistol-whip him first and shove him in a footlocker?"

Because its skinny, flaccid arms hang to the ground, and its wide, hunched back appears to be mounded, all the muscle in its body rearranged on top. Its legs, too, are thin with tendons.

In the single record I'd seen depicting such a crime, the agent had been kicked from the troop, stripped of his name and star sign, and then of his human nature. Zoe once tried to explain to me what happened when someone's power attacked from within.

"Think of the Big Bang happening again, except inside your body. Every molecule inside of you heats up, expands, then explodes. When it cools again, nothing's where it's supposed to be."

In other words, the agent was no longer a he or she, but an *it*.

"Just don't look it in the eye," Nia says. "They're sane enough to know that they're hideous, and it enrages them."

Maybe the hermit can't touch us on the path, but it keeps pace with us on its bowed, stumpy legs, darting forward every few feet to bend low and try to catch the eye I'm not supposed to be turning its way. I train my gaze on the muddy path, but it sticks close, leering and breathing its sewer rat breath directly up at me.

Then, suddenly, it's gone.

"That's the end of its land," Nia explains, and even she sounds relieved. "Hermits are very territorial."

A rustle sounds up ahead, and another hermit darts to the path's edge. The little light seeping through the wheat is both a blessing and a curse because I can easily see the creature even though I don't want to. Nia, however, is suddenly transfixed. She halts in her tracks and does exactly what she warned me not to.

She narrows her eyes and stares directly into its melted face.

"This is the one."

The hermit hisses. It's as ugly as the other one, made more hideous by crossed eyes and the spittle oozing down its chin. "What one?"

"The former Shadow agent that killed my whole family."

I gasp, but the hermit doesn't even blink. I'm not sure it feels anything. I can't even tell which direction it's looking in, but I feel like there's an extra attentiveness between them now. It tilts its head at Nia as her hand lifts and floats in the air ... and she very softly, gently caresses the head of one thick stalk of wheat.

The reverberation thrums through the earth.

The beast with the red shoe howls somewhere behind us. A handful of answering cries pop up throughout the field, yet the creature before Nia doesn't move an inch.

They are locked in a memory that only they share.

"It was before the Reordering," Nia murmurs without breaking eye contact. "Before it murdered a mortal and became ... this. But when I first saw it out here, I knew. After all, I witnessed the whole thing. Didn't I, you wretched, wicked, law-breaking beast?"

She reaches out and plucks the head of wheat again. Furied howls rebound through the field, but this hermit only narrows its eyes.

"Careful," I warn her. "It has a weapon."

And I curse myself suddenly because I don't. I've left my urumi back in my room, and the only thing protecting me now is my mask.

"It's not a weapon. It's a fork."

I tilt my head and see she's right. One deformed hand holds tarnished silver, with one tine missing. "Odd choice for a weapon."

"It's a talisman. It belonged to his human victim."

I think back to the red shoe the first hermit was carrying and can't help but shudder. "Why would it want to hang onto that?"

"No choice. Talismans are physical reminders of a hermit's sins. They can't let the item out of sight lest they forget what they've done. Lose it, and he'll begin to weaken and die. Isn't that right, you rancid ass?"

Again, the hermit takes her abuse in stony silence.

"And you guys are fine with them just hanging out near your cottage?"

"Beckett invited them."

She begins to walk forward slowly, daring the creature to grab her. It doesn't, but its breath rattles in its twisted lungs as it tracks us, and spittle lands on my arm as it jogs to keep up.

"The agreement is that they guard against the Elders or anyone else getting through to the cottage, and we allow them to dwell within the wheat. Don't mistake their agreement for goodness, though," Nia warns. "Their only real joy is trying to lure us into the blood wheat to kill us."

"The one back there just looked at you," I point out.

"It's just biding its time." She smiles suddenly, and the warming wood scent begins to burn. "But don't worry. So am I."

She turns away, leaving me gaping as I trail behind her. Forget the hermits ... and forget Rometra.

The look in Nia's eyes as she talks of revenge is the scariest thing I've seen all day.

18

FOR HUMAN EYES ONLY.

I arrive at the shop to find the back door flung wide, a broken tooth in the building's long, wooden smile. Lamplight puddles on the wide porch, and Carl sits on the worn steps, a sketchpad on his lap and pencil box at his side.

It would appear picture-perfect, Rockwellian even, if I didn't suspect him of drawing bloodshed and conflict and, possibly, my own death.

"Did you see that crap?" I call out, pointing to the field behind me as I trudge up to him.

With a sigh, Carl sets aside his pad and tucks his pencil behind his ear. It disappears into the length of his jet-black hair, which is more mussed than usual. I envision him running his fingers through it as he works, which has me relaxing with a smile.

Leave it to the lone human to make me feel at home.

"Is that the only shirt you have?"

All my good feelings for him are flushed away as I glance quizzically at my totally awesome sweatshirt. "I haven't unpacked yet," I reply defensively.

"Why? Planning on going somewhere?"

"You mean you don't already *know*?"

I flare my eyes at him dramatically but drop down beside him with a pained groan. Training with the others isn't like training with Zoe or being suddenly attacked from behind by a mortal, both of which I'd long ago mastered. I've forgotten what it's like to get that pump of adrenaline when the outcome is uncertain, how it makes me tighten up, turning my limbs stiff and slowing my reactions instead of the opposite.

And that's while training with my *allies*. No one has to tell me I'll feel much worse while helping the Los Angeles initiates.

Sighing, I lean over to see what Carl's drawing. He makes a feeble attempt to shield his sketchpad, but I knock his hand away.

It's Rometra, emerging from the wheat on the cottage side, a skein of mist rising in the treetops before her on what had to be just this morning. Her face is tilted up in the morning light as if she's just caught scent of something, and she wears a smile as if she likes it.

My gut tells me it's me.

"She doesn't like me," I tell Carl, handing the sketchpad back.

"Nope."

"That's it?" That's all he has to say?

"No." He resumes drawing. "She dislikes you so much she's likely to use training to kick your ass."

Groaning, I lean back on my hands and dangle my foot above the grasses he warned me not to touch that first day. I think about tapping the ground, just to hear the rumbling screeches of someone—something—more annoyed than me.

More scared than me.

"Don't expect much better from the other firstborns," he tells me, tilting his head as he feathers a skein of trailing smoke into the drawing. "I mean, you're the daughter of—"

"Chaos?" I provide the first name that Cassius called me.

Instead of providing the sympathy I'm so clearly angling for, Carl shrugs. "Hey. If the name fits..."

"Dude, it's not my fault that Joanna Archer blew up--"

"Yadda, yadda," Carl interrupts, already bored by the rant I've barely begun. "Cassius wasn't referring to her when he said that. He was referring to *your* actions. Want to see?"

He meant five years ago.

"No. Just tell me."

"No. Hearing isn't remembering. It isn't knowing."

"Exactly." And I don't want to remember jack.

I expect Carl to argue. Zoe would have. She'd have told me that knowledge must be earned, yet he just shrugs.

"Fine," he says. "Once upon a time, like five years ago, you tossed Cassius into the endless depths of a black hole that he created ... then left him there to rot."

"I WHAT?!" I rocket to my feet so fast my head spins.

Then I feel my sore muscles and sit back down.

Carl watches it all with a flat, bland expression. It must be nice to know everything. "Why do you think they tried to lure you into a black hole back at Hummingbird House? Cassius would love to finish you off himself, but trapping you in the same way you once trapped him? Totally satisfying as well."

I'd have liked to erase you from existence the way you once tried to doom me.

I shake off Cassius's words. "But that's not me. I mean, I'm not, like, evil and pushy."

I'm laid back and 'live and let live' and other totally chill mottos.

"You were grief-stricken." He clears his throat and looks out across the wheat, his gaze another shadow stretching there, like he's seeing the past even now. "Out of your mind with it, actually. You wouldn't have dared to touch him except--"

"He killed my parents." I might not remember the event, but I lived with the grief.

"I know what you're thinking," Carl says after a long moment.

"Great." Still kinda stunned, and drawing a total blank, I flare my eyes. "Tell me."

"You're wondering why Cassius didn't turn into a hermit?"

"Oh yeah!" I give myself a mental head slap. I mean, I just saw what happens to those who dared to murder the humans whose energy fuels the entirety of the Zodiac world.

"It's because everything is suspended in the heart of a black hole," he goes on without prompting. "You're alive, at least for a while, but can't breathe. You just spin, frozen, until you reach the hole's center. You're also usually stretched like spaghetti before your body is ripped apart, yet if you can somehow escape like Cassius did? You do so unchanged."

"So by pushing him into the black hole that *he* somehow created, which," I clarify for the record, "I totally don't remember —I didn't kill him, but saved him?"

"You trapped him," Carl corrects, propping his chin in his palm as he looks at me. "For four years. And guess what was the first thing he set out to do once he was free?"

I don't have to guess. I remember.

"That's why Beck came to Laguna?" To protect me. He knew Cassius had gotten loose and would be looking to exact revenge.

Carl nods. "And that's why Cassius hates you so much. Not because you can touch the conduits, but because you once dared to touch him."

"I don't remember." I frown because it's probably the kind of thing a person shouldn't forget.

"But he does," Carl says, flipping the pages on his sketchpad closed. He stands noisily, dusts himself off, and stares down at me. "So."

I gaze up at him. "So what?"

"Wanna go do something boring?"

I squint up at him. "I don't follow."

"I mean, no fighting. No conduits or treehouses. Something normal. Human. Mundane."

"No reading the stars to foretell my impending doom?" I say in a dramatic voice.

One side of his wide mouth quirks up. "You don't even have to read your horoscope."

"Seriously?" I hold out my hand for a lift up. "Best offer I've had all day."

CARL GUIDES ME TO THE BACK OF THE ROOM, WHICH IS TO SAY HE leads me nowhere ... or so it seems until he yanks back the floor-to-ceiling curtain to reveal a whole other room. I gasp when I see the enormous leather sectional, the black velvet walls, and the shelves brimming with actual, physical copies of movies.

"Whoa! Does this generation of superheroes and villains know about this?" It's a full-sized theater, complete with a big screen and popcorn machine.

"Hell, no. This is for human eyes only." He points to a sign that says exactly that. "Besides, *they* only care about duty or jockeying for power or training to fight epic battles. They're so busy trying to gain immortality that they don't have time to go to the movies or do anything cool."

"Exactly what I've been trying to say!" I prop myself on the sofa's edge and start going through the videos stacked atop the coffee table. *Breakfast Club. Pretty in Pink. Weird Science.* "Man, these are ancient."

"I think the adjective you're looking for is classic." Carl corrects and glares when I make a gagging sound. "Have you ever even seen a John Hughes movie?"

I stare at him blankly.

"Molly Ringwald? The Brat Pack?"

"Nope." I shrug one shoulder as I cross to the professional-grade popcorn machine. "This is incredible, though."

Red-and-white striped bags, along with a metal scoop, are stacked next to it, and flavored salts. Below is a glass case that

Carl has repurposed with movie theater candy. Milk duds, Junior Mints, Hershey's bars, and Mike and Ikes.

"My mom used to take me to the movies on Saturdays." His voice blooms over my right shoulder, soft, almost wistful. "She'd pop the corn at home and hide it in her purse because it was cheaper than buying. Then we'd put our heads together and scour the Internet to figure out how to see three, sometimes four, movies in one day. We'd buy one giant soda when we arrived and then sneak from one theater to the next."

This is one of his fondest memories? "That's dishonest."

"Very." He flares his eyes, then shoots me that crooked grin. "But it was our escape. Just hers and mine. I'd look up at her as the light from the screen moved across her face, and I could see the stress melting off her with each passing hour. By the end of the day, she looked like one of the heroines on the screen, scrubbed free of worry. I remember wishing I could capture that."

I scent something then, not heated or threatening, but a whispered smell—an old sorrow. I tilt my head up at him. "That's when you began to draw?"

He nods, then sighs the memory away. The smell washes over me. It's musty, an old room rarely opened. I shiver in its wake. "Then she remarried and ... that was that."

"Your stepdad didn't like movies?"

"My stepdad didn't like me."

Carl chooses the movie, *Pretty in Pink*, and we pop corn, pick out one of each type of candy, and plop down on the giant sofa, where I'm immediately swallowed by the soft pillows and the leather cushions and the story of a girl from the wrong side of the tracks who just doesn't fit in.

Gee, doesn't *that* sound familiar?

For the next ninety-six minutes, I am mesmerized by the horrors of what was high school in the Dark Ages. Or, the eighties. Same diff. By the time the movie's over, my fingertips smell of butter, salt, and chocolate, and I've completely forgotten a world where heroes and villains battle for dominance at the behest of the stars.

"So weird," I say, as Carl brings up the lights. "They didn't even have cell phones."

"That's your takeaway from one of the most iconic teenage films of all time?"

He's teasing, but his voice lacks its usual edge. I look at his silhouette, glowing in the light of the big screen. It's then that I realize he's done it again. Just as in my first night here, when he gave over his bedroom to me so that I could sleep safely and in peace, he's taken me into his space, sharing the familiar world of mortal worries and cares with me, a touchstone and respite in a world where everything else is unfamiliar.

Despite his faked indifference, it's way kind. And much needed. Maybe that's why I suddenly blurt, "I'm not sure I can do this."

I don't explain what I mean. I get the feeling he knows about all these new powers welling inside me ... and that I have no idea how to use them.

Or maybe it's the opposite, I think, swallowing hard. Maybe I'm afraid I can. "I'm afraid—"

"Of everything," Carl says softly, and of course he knows. He's the freaking record keeper.

"What you said earlier? About my parents and me pushing Cassius and the black hole?" I pull my knees tight to my chest as I turn to him on the wide sofa. "I don't want to remember any of that."

"So don't."

I pull back to study his face. "Really?"

"Or do." He shrugs one wide shoulder.

I slump, which is hard because I'm already slumped. "Nice wise-man act."

"Nobody can tell you what to do, Ash."

My nickname rolls off his tongue like we've known each other much longer than a week. Maybe it's because we're the only two people in this world who understand what it is to be human. Or perhaps because he's drawn me, which I guess I don't mind so much anymore.

It's nice to be known. Even in a small way.

"Does ignoring the past make me weak?" I finally ask.

"The real question is, will remembering it make you strong?"

Okay, so I guess that is a little wise.

"Want my opinion?" he asks, and I nod, trusting him. I don't think you should let one moment in time forever define you."

"Even a terrible one?"

"Especially a terrible one." He reaches out and touches a hand to my cheek. "Your past is something that happened to you, Ash, and it's awful. But it's not who you are."

Chills whip down my arms, and even though I'm sitting, I go a little lightheaded with relief. As tough as Zoe was on me, she always treated me like I was injured. Like I couldn't trust myself because I couldn't remember my past. Often, when friends or teachers would learn that I was orphaned, they'd do the same.

Only now do I realize how those feelings held me down, tethering me to my past. Nobody'd ever given me permission just to let it all go.

I lean back, sinking into the sofa so that our arms touch. He's warm, smells like popcorn, and looks at me not like I'm injured, but like I'm strong—just as I am.

I smile up at him and ask, "Can we watch another?"

"Duh."

So, while the rest of the Zodiac world prepares for festivals and battles, we binge-watch eighties movies the same way he and his mother used to, both of us facing forward and—at least for now—letting go of our pasts.

19

DREAM ON.

The Pacific Ocean has a singular scent, and every wave that touches the shore wafts like the effervescent top note of a classic perfume. Yet it's the base note, and the heart, knitting those waves together, that speaks to me.

It smells like home, even in my dreams.

Yet, in *this* dream, there's also a bright red longboard. I've never owned this board, but I reach for it, knowing it's meant for me.

Who else? It's my dream, right?

I hop onto the back of the ocean as I have a thousand times before, and its roar immediately turns seismic in my ears. It's different this time because I know I have powers that half-mortality can't shake.

I hear the anemone sway in its depths.

I smell seaweed on the ocean's breath.

And as I flip my board around, I feel the swell of a big wave burrowing up behind me long before it thrusts me forward. I know I'll catch it even before I start paddling.

I've just gained my balance when the sun's rays suddenly intensify, attacking the ocean's surface in thick, golden slashes.

They momentarily blind me as they bounce off waves that've gone still and extra silky beneath my weight. Then the water turns icy, and a gust of rotted fish replaces the clean ocean wind.

Cassius, I think, and still blind, I topple.

Then I'm underwater, fighting to hold my breath and figure out which way is up, all while looking for the Elder who smells like graveyard funk.

Relax, I tell myself. I can now breathe underwater, and I take my first breath of the icy depths while staring down into the darkest, blackest hole I've ever seen. As soon as it hits my lungs, I'm whipped back as if on a bungee cord. I get a momentary bird's-eye view of the hole ... and then plummet directly into it.

I try to wheel away, succeeding only at the last moment. It's not a hole at all. Instead, it's a deep well placed in a cold, steel-lined room. As I drop down next to it, everything flashes silver.

Except for that circular void.

It roils thickly with a fog that laps over the well's sides, the edges waving like tattered black flags.

I realize that's the stuff that ate up Hummingbird House. Carl called it a black hole, and instead of being surprised, I think, *of course.*

Where else would Cassius—an Elder, a Shadow—be?

Yet it's not Cassius who appears at the well's side. This man is tall and kind of sad-looking, and he looks right through me as if I'm unimportant.

No. I amend the thought, shivering. He's looking at me like I don't exist.

"Titan."

I jolt, but a hand of steel clamps onto my shoulder from behind before I can run. The smell and sound and touch of the ocean are suddenly far away. We're in some sort of steel silo, and my dream has shifted into a nightmare.

"Well done, Cassius," Titan says, and as his gaze finally finds me, as if Cassius's touch has made me real. His expression is no longer sad. It's no longer anything because nothing lives in that gaze.

Nothing lives in him at all.

"Give her to me." Titan holds out his hand.

Cassius's grip tightens. "You said we'd trade."

The silence between them grows taut enough to pluck.

Titan lowers his hand and grins. "Careful, Cassius. Your weakness is showing."

Cassius growls. "You promised I could have them once I found the girl."

"Fine." Rolling his eyes, Titan reaches down to two mounds on the floor. The strange black substance has previously obscured them, and that's what really sends my heart racing.

What is so strong that it could reduce the two people I love more than anything in the world into mere shadows?

Titan drags my half-conscious parents to their feet. "I'm just teasing. What would I need with these mortals now?"

I sway, threatening to topple. It's my fear, yes, but it's also because Cassius has stepped forward so quickly, leaving a fetid gust in his wake. I'm not even sure he realizes he's moved, and that's when I begin to shake.

"No." My voice is so small. So small.

Cassius hesitates in reaching for my dad ... but it's not because of me. "Do you think it'll be safe?"

"You mean, will you be marked as a law-breaker?" Titan shrugs, causing my parents to jerk like puppets in his hands. "Our world has been completely Reordered. As far as I can tell, none of the old rules apply."

And as he holds my parents out to Cassius, a pounding rockets through my skull.

I jerk upright on Carl's sofa so fast that I dizzy and topple to the floor. I grunt as my shoulder torques painfully beneath me. The giant movie screen has gone black. The pounding continues.

"Kenyon!" Beck's cry ripples through the curtained room

before being eaten by the velvet walls. I bolt upright again like I've been caught doing something wrong.

"It's for you," Carl mutters, wiping sleep from his eyes as he pushes into a sitting position on the sofa. Yet the first person to round the curtain isn't Beck. It's Nia, her outline rigid in black leather.

"What time is it?" I ask groggily, pushing up from the floor.

"Attack," she answers instead and throws a knife at me. She expects me to catch it, but I dodge it instead, and it impales the sofa where my legs rested only seconds before.

Sighing, Carl swings his legs to the floor. "And *this* is why we can't have nice things."

He reaches for his sketchpad. That can't be good.

"It's almost ten o'cl—" Beck steps around the corner then, blinking as he takes in the aftermath of our movie marathon. The sight stuns whatever he'd been about to say from his throat. "I didn't know you had a theater in here."

"Because I didn't want you to know."

Even I'm taken aback by Carl's sharp tone. Gone is the dude who distracted me from my worries. In his place is the more familiar brooding, mysterious, and kind of creepy record keeper.

"You forgot to seal the door." Beck seems to be having a hard time tearing his eyes from me. Maybe because I'm sleepy-eyed with mussed hair and buttered fingertips. Maybe because I'm so close to Carl.

"I wasn't worried," Carl mutters, but he frowns, and I get the sense that he did forget.

"No, just distracted." Beck's chest rises and falls unevenly, likely because he's run the entire way from the cottage.

Right?

Shaking his head, clearing it, he holds out my sheathed urumi. "The hermits have gotten loose from the blood wheat."

"What?" I look at Nia, wide awake now. "How?"

"I don't know," she answers, but won't meet my eye. "They

were secured when I left you, but now they're in the village. Looking for humans."

I am not a superhero. I know that much in my gut, and if I'm honest, I don't want to be. Yet the scent of Shadows—of Elders, of Cassius—is still thick in my nose. All I have to hear are the words "human" and "attack," and I'm slipping on my boat shoes and heading to the door.

WE CATCH UP WITH THE OTHERS AT THE MAIN EXIT. DESPITE THE late hour, they're armed and dressed. War even wears headgear. Maybe she sleeps in it.

Beck tightens the laces on his leather forearm guards. "The horde likes to congregate in wide open spaces, so they'll most likely be in the village square, but you have to be extra vigilant when the blood lust is up."

Thayer whoops and transfers his weapons, all regular knives, to one hand before throwing back his cape with the other. "Let's roll!"

"Why are you so stoked?" I shake my head.

I mean, the blood lust is *up*.

"We're just going to drive the hermits back into their designated territories," Beck says matter-of-factly, but I can tell that even he's on a high and itching to move. His fingers tap at his sides, and he stares into the night, bouncing on his toes.

I startle when Nia comes up behind me and secures a utility belt studded with locked pockets around my waist.

"That doesn't really match the rest of my outfit." I motion to my slip-on shoes, cutoffs, and trusty sweatshirt, which I'm admittedly going to have to wash soon. Still, I know those belt pockets contain demi-cannonballs, so I let her fasten it around me since my urumi is back at the cottage. "And why would the hermits listen to us? I thought they wanted to kill us."

Beck grins. I think it's supposed to be reassuring, but his teeth are clenched tight, and he's practically vibrating with the need to throw himself into the night. "They follow the orders of those who've either bested them in battle or given them refuge. We've done both."

"The problem is," War says, pounding her open palm with an arm-length club, "They're so brain-addled that they occasionally forget that."

"We're going to remind them," Thayer says, shooting me a grin that perfectly matches Beck's.

For a moment, I have to remind myself that these are the good guys. I do that by remembering the way the hermits—murderers of humans like me, law-breakers—tracked me like prey through the blood wheat on their bowed, stumpy legs.

I do it by remembering that my dream wasn't a dream at all.

"It'll be good practice for battle against the Elders," Beck assures me, which is totally not reassuring.

"Just try, Ash. It's fun, I promise." Then Thayer gives a loud whoop as he rushes the exit. The last thing I see is the hem of his cape trailing behind him. War rolls her eyes but follows, quick on his heels.

"You coming?" Beck waits for me to decide, though he's clearly anxious to follow.

"Promise you got my back?"

Beck's expression melts into pure relief. "I won't let you out of my sight."

And then he promptly disappears.

Nia clears her throat. "That was unfortunate timing."

But then she disappears, too.

"Better hurry," Carl says, holding out the knife that Nia embedded in the sofa. "Or you'll miss all the fun."

"Wouldn't want that," I mutter, tucking it into a waiting sheath. Taking a deep breath, I turn to go.

"Ash." Carl remains unblinking when I look back. His pencil

is nowhere in sight, but I know ... he still sees everything. "You know how to do this."

I nod. "I know."

That's probably what scares me most.

VIOLENCE HAS A TANG TO IT, LIKE LEMON GONE TO ROT. I'M NOT sure what hits me first, that too-citrus taste or the cries coming from the village square, but by the time I get there, the others have scattered.

Nia's closest, having just surprised a hermit into crushing the hood of a car as he stumbles away from her throwing star. "How'd they get out of the wheat?"

"My guess? Someone swiped their talismans." Eyes narrowed, she aims at another silhouette lumbering across the lot, bulging in all the wrong places. "Told them to attack the mortals if they wanted them back."

I want to ask how the hermits are supposed to protect us from the Elders if it's so easy to swipe their talismans, but an unholy screech rises behind us, and we duck and turn toward it simultaneously.

Of course, Rometra is already there. Three living mutations surround her... yet they appear to be the ones under attack. Nia rushes to help, but Beck yells my name from my left and points to two creatures lumbering toward the cute, indie coffee shop that is the cornerstone of the sleepy little square.

"Got the cannonballs?" he calls, and I'm already on it. I vault one overhead, and it sends the hermits wheedling overhead like Ferris wheels ripped loose from their hinges. Pulling out another sphere as I run, I follow the rank scent of a hermit in a full-on flight.

Like the one about to mount War's back. I pivot and launch the little ball forward just as Thayer encourages, "Do it, Ash!"

The hermit is still leaping as the ball explodes beneath its feet. It's catapulted directly into the air while War only wobbles, looks up, and readies herself to club the beast as soon as it hits the ground. I still don't understand how the balls respond to my will, but the cheers of my allies rise with every measured throw while the remaining hermits screech and scatter.

Together, these sounds mark the first time I hear the true war cries of battle.

A knot of dust rises from the lot as the skirmishes shift. I loosen up with each successful blow but remain careful to watch my blind spots, just as Beck and War warned in training.

That's how I catch sight of the hunched figure slipping around the corner of the village market. It's the opposite direction of the wheat, and I do a quick calculation, remembering the layout Carl gave me that first day. I realize the lake's premier hotel lies that way, and if the creatures are under orders to attack humans, then that's the honeypot.

I give chase.

The mealy odor of unwashed fur, soured skin, and fresh blood tells me exactly which way the hermit has run. It also grunts as it flees, a sound that makes it hard to believe it was ever human, let alone super. It's as if someone sliced its vocal cords lengthwise, turning them into a string instrument that trembles and bleeds in its throat. Pushing against my instincts, I dive into the forest flanking the hotel.

You know how to do this.

Branches and thorns tear at my arms as I push through the underbrush. In Laguna, the sky sweeps overhead, ever-arching, but there are just green smells piled atop deep shadows, and I fight my way through both as panic wells up inside me. I try to outrun that, too, but I am lost in a strange forest that, for all its expansiveness, seems intent on closing in around me.

Finally, the wall of trees relents, and I skid to a halt in a dell that has been scooped out and cradled beneath an onyx cliff. The rock face rises above me like a raw black gem in the starlight, and the full moon and reflective rock work in tandem, causing the tiny grove to glow. The stars above are equally bright chips, and my heart flutters as the Universe wheels above me.

I remember how the stars roared in recognition as my power reentered my body ... and I know I am made of stardust at my core.

You know how to do this.

Then, the enormous black rock next to me moves.

Yelping, I back up and knock into a tree with a thick covering of moss and leaves that mute the impact and my step. I realize that no one knows where I am as the rock grows eyes and teeth and is not a rock at all. It turns to me, panting with the breath of the unwashed dead, and all I can think is, I *don't* know how to do this.

But I'd better figure it out fast because the advancing hermit has saliva dripping from its teeth ... and a hatred in its eye that sparks like heat lightning.

20

NOW YOU SEE ME, NOW YOU SEE ME.

Even if I could will myself to reach for another ball, the hermit is already too close. Its eyes track me like prey. It'll be on me before I move.

As it is, the gnarled being shifts to block my way out of the grove. In the wash of moonlight, I can see it's a man—or used to be—though it looks and smells like it has been Dumpster-diving for the last decade. I can't see what's in its hand—that's lost to the shadows—but I'm pretty sure whatever it is can easily kill me.

"Stay away, law-breaker!" I yell, hoping someone will hear me.

I let my hand fall behind my thigh. Maybe I can reach Nia's knife at my back. The hermit doesn't growl, but its throat rattles as it breathes, and that's close enough. Ignoring my command, it wobbles closer, and the slashing moonlight reveals his weapon of choice.

A grimy teddy bear with matted fur and a single button eye.

The hermit widens its stance in the monochrome light, then tilts its head with a resounding crack. "That's it?"

I blink.

"You." It bares teeth so stained they don't even reflect in the moonlight. "I thought a firstborn girl-child descended from each

of the First Mothers and cross-bred with the mortal race from which this world derives its true purpose and power would be ... I dunno. More."

Is this gnarly creature judging me?

Annoyance wars with my mortal fear. "Hey, I'm not the one drooling on my bare feet, which you might notice if you could uncross those eyes."

The hermit's sneer has the effect of almost rearranging his features back into place before they bungee-jump back into their twisted form.

"A smart mouth. Typical Archer. Does your mother's capacity for violence live in you as well?"

"I'm not like you, law-breaker." I shoot back. "I don't kill."

"You don't kill *yet*." The hermit's eyebrows wing halfway up its forehead and threaten to stick there. Its voice goes sly. "I wonder what your Beck would do if he knew how powerful you could become? If he knew, as I do, who you're destined to destroy?"

"You must have snakes for brains," I snap, sounding nothing like myself. Instead, I sound like Zoe. Yet Zoe is exactly what's required in this situation, and I point at him with my weapon. "I'd keep the hissing to yourself."

It lifts its chin. "I'll have you know I was a Seer before the Reordering."

I swallow hard because I know exactly what a Seer is. They could read the fates of others being played out across the skies ... and not like Carl, who merely records our deeds for an audience of greedy little mortal minds.

Seers blend science and superstition much like Zoe blends her potions. Mathematics, natal charts, astronomy, astrology, casting lots, and reading cards. A good one is worth their weight in gold.

This one was probably worth its weight in excrement.

It wobbles forward on its bowed legs, and I think of the demi-cannonball tucked into the pocket of my cutoffs. I might be able to reach it ... if I can keep the thing talking.

"Are you saying you knew I'd be the one to follow you from the village?"

"I wanted to warn you," it says, jerking its head in a nod. The time for hiding is almost over. Elder Cassius recognized your unused power, and he will try to seize it. I can't See if he will be successful; that is not yet written, but I know this: the Elders will draw first blood."

I shake my head. "No—"

"Your failure is fated." The hermit intones. "It's written in the stars, yet none of you know how to look."

"NO!" I forget my fear and point at him with my empty hand. "I am fated to wear puka shells and learn how to play the ukulele!"

A branch snaps in the brush behind me, saving me from having to answer. The hermit startles. Guess it didn't see that coming. I reach for my cannonball just as something rockets through the bright dell, and then the hermit's black-bottomed feet whip through the air with a bloodcurdling shriek.

"Rometra!"

Rometra ignores me completely. She's latched onto the hermit's arm and is shaking the creature so hard that its spittle flings side to side. Still, the hermit refuses to relinquish its talisman, and a crack echoes through the copse. The hermit's scream turns almost human. I cringe at the new looseness in its shoulder.

"Stop!"

Rometra doesn't stop. Without thinking, with a mind only to end the violence, I throw my last demi-cannonball their way.

Up until the moment it hits, I would swear I was aiming for the hermit. Yet it's Rometra who goes rocketing through the air and out of sight, her cry just as alarmed as the hermit's, who's dropped its talisman in the blast. I'm totally alarmed, too.

That was my will?

Breathing hard, I stumble toward the prone creature. I half-expect it to launch itself at me, but the run-in with Rometra has sucked the fight right out of it. It's bleeding and cradling its dislocated shoulder, and only looks resigned when I reach for the teddy bear at its feet.

It also looks completely dumbstruck when I give it back. "Get out. Go back to the blood wheat and stay there."

It doesn't have to be told twice. It snags the bear and stumbles from the bright dell without another word, disappearing into the black tangle of forest just as Rometra reappears. Beck must have seen her aerial act because he's right on her heels … and thank the Mothers because she instantly pins me to the onyx cliff.

"Stop!" Beck has to push her away from me. Twice.

"She gave it back its talisman!" Rometra yells, coming at me a third time.

I hold up my hands. "What should I do with a flea-infested stuffed bear, anyway?"

"That's how you enslave the hermits, you idiot!" Rometra informs me. "The Elders make a habit of hoarding every talisman they can."

"We don't enslave anyone, Rometra," Beck quietly says.

"And I'm not an Elder, am I?" I say, not quietly at all.

She bites back her retort but is still vibrating with anger. "Then why was I the one who was blown away by your Mother-Loving blast?"

"The real question," Beck interrupts again, "is why didn't the hermit kill Ashlyn when it had the chance?"

I'm not ready to tell them that the hermit attacked me with words instead of weapons. After rocking Rometra with a weapon that only I can touch, how am I supposed to casually mention, "Oh, the thing used to be a Seer before it was befouled by sin said that Cassius is going to use the power in me against all of you?"

I throw up my hands and turn to leave. "I'm not doing this anymore."

"Why not?" Rometra snaps.

"Because I'm not like you!" I whirl back around. "I'm not some supernatural vigilante out for vengeance!"

"We know." Rometra's eyes go slit-thin as she appraises me, up and down. "You're just out for the next wave."

Then she pushes between Beck and me, bumping us both. The only comeback I can think of as I watch her go is, *I wish.*

"She does *not* like me."

It's the same thing I said to Carl, but Beck responds with a laugh so bitter I scent lemon.

Wincing, I cross my arms. "She seems pretty chill with you, though."

Beck rubs a hand over his face and sighs. "We have a history, Ashlyn."

I can tell, I want to say, but now isn't the time to push. Although the sounds of battle in the village have ceased, and insects chirrup around us once again, I'm still shaken by my run-in with the hermit. I need Beck to understand and tell the others why I can't do this anymore.

I *don't* know how to do this.

"I didn't want to say it in front of Rometra, but that thing said it used to be a Seer."

Everything about Beck sharpens. For a moment, he even projects fear, a mirrored spark, and I can tell he has to force lightness into his voice. "Did it prophesy?"

I groan because that means it can. "Yes! And it said I am totally not helping you by being here!"

What it said was, You don't kill *yet.*

Beck's gaze darts around the little dell. He's thinking fast. Either that or planning escape. "That's not true. You can become someone else with one action. In a mere thought."

"Then here's a thought for you. I think I'm going back to being a kick-ass surfer!"

Not a superhero-in-training. Not a killer.

"Fates aren't always preordained," he tries, and I shake my head. "They can twist in an instant."

"Like when Cassius killed my parents in front of me?" I blurt. "That instant? Or like when I responded by pushing him into a black hole?"

"Carl told you." Beck's expression grows hard.

"*You* should've told me!" It's out before I even know I'm thinking it.

It's useless to rail about things that've already happened, and if I were feeling more chill, I'd remember that, but I'm not. I'm scared. I'm pissed.

And it's Beck's fault.

He changed my fate.

I wonder what your Beck would do if he knew ... who you're destined to destroy?

I give in to that, the grief of all I've lost flashing inside of me for just a moment. Pulling at my hair, I whirl. "God, Beckett! I was doing so well before you came along!"

"I know." He says it like he didn't have a choice.

Like he'd do it again if he had to.

"I was working on my longboard reverse walk," I tell him, hands falling to my side. "I was so close!"

He steps close then, and I feel the warmth in his breath and touch as he grasps my arms and forces me to look into his face. "And I bet you would have perfected it."

The apology is there, unspoken but plain. Yet I can see, still, he'd do it all over again.

I clench my teeth. "Look, I've been trying to fit in," I tell him. "And to learn to use these powers to help you guys, but honestly? The lesson that Zoe really drilled into me was how to run."

All I really want to do is run.

Beck knows it. I might as well have a neon sign over my head flashing, "Gone Surfing!" He gives me one of the saddest looks I've ever seen, causing tears to pinprick my own eyes. I've been playing along like this has been one big joke, but Beck's obvious pity—coupled with the hermit's totally jacked prophecy—comes crashing down on me like the ocean's biggest, gnarliest wave.

This can't be my fate!

Images wash over me in quick succession.

My parents screaming, my parents slumped.

Zoe creating poisons with wild zeal, Zoe turning her back on me with utter calm.

Beck kissing, Beck lying.

Rometra yelling ... the hermit screaming ... my waves.

Missing.

I feel like I'm in the tube, taking a donut, losing my rail, cartwheeling to the bottom of the ocean. My legs give out right then and there, and for the first time since being attacked on that clifftop, I break.

But I don't just cry ... I dissolve like foam on the beach. There's snot. There are tears. Puffy eyes.

I am pretty much disgusting by the time I'm wrung out.

But Beck is still there. Waiting in the middle of a dark wood gone silent with my grief.

I pull in a deep, full breath and sigh it out. A person can't smell their own emotions, so all I smell is the green scent of the falsely reassuring forest, and that thing that is Beckett, too.

The one I used to like.

In that dense, green expanse of silence, Beck finally speaks. "Can I show you something?"

I sniffle. "Will anyone want to kill me for seeing it, knowing it, or being with you while viewing it?"

Beck refuses to meet my gaze. I take that as a big yes.

"If you still want to leave after seeing it, I'll take you to LAX myself."

Hope leaps in my chest, and yet ... his confidence is telling. It means he thinks whatever I see will change my mind. And yet...

I could be in Hawaii by tomorrow.

I'm not sure what to think of that. Will leaving make the hermit's prophesy come true? Or will staying?

Beck holds out his hand.

I gaze up into his face from the sad little nest of tears I've made on the ground. He's still beautiful. Still intense in that warm, watchful way, and still totally hot ... even if his tan has begun to fade.

So I make a small, resigned sound, wipe my face with the hem of my sweatshirt and, pulling in a deep breath of the crisp night air, finally take his hand.

21

A NEW STORY.

W e borrow Carl's motorcycle. He's not thrilled about handing over his keys to Beck, but he either knows or guesses where we're going because he doesn't ask. His fingers also twitch at his side, clearly itching for a pencil.

I don't bother telling Beck how the bike can glow and glide when I'm on it—that it's actually a conduit. I'm sure he already knows.

So instead, I hold tight to him for the body heat as we move from mountain air to the smog of exhaust fumes, street lights gradually replacing the night stars and sky. The fast food signs, the billboards ... all of it is jarring after the treehouse hidden across an expanse of blood wheat.

We finally roll into a brightly graffiti-ed lot next to a trendy West Hollywood brunch spot. No, it's not the beach, but it's near enough that my amplified senses perk up.

The ocean is near.

I'm also pumped by the sights and sounds of the vibrant urban sprawl. Beck leads in silence, watching me take it all in. He's already assured me we'll be back at the cottage by morning, and he must know I want to enjoy this hermit-free time while I can.

We wind our way into the interiors of a neighborhood spattered with LA's iconic bungalows, tucked beneath the shadows of the more modern and imposing high-rise apartments. Our silence evens out as we slip along the side streets, the hum of the freeway traffic disappearing, and for the first time, Beck's presence is ... unloaded. Easy. Like a fierce rain, my tears have washed everything clean between us.

Until Beck ruins it by bringing up the past.

"How do you feel now that you know Cassius killed your parents?"

I blink at the suddenness, the bluntness, of the question. I don't look at him as I answer. "You know I can't remember that."

"I'm not talking about remembering," he says, pausing before a dark wall cascading with bright purple bougainvillea. "I'm talking about feelings. How do you feel now that you know your mortal parents lived in a world with people like Cassius?"

The question sits on the air like a stain, and yes, it hurts, but he's not trying to be cruel. I can tell he's getting at something, and it's only by answering honestly that I'll know what.

"Helpless. I know I was only twelve, but I had powers. Zoe was teaching me. Yet I still couldn't do anything to save them."

"That's right," he says, shocking me. "You didn't have a shot. You were a child, and powers or not, you didn't have a chance of saving them after a Shadow like Cassius targeted them for death."

I go light-headed. My breath comes easier, and something I didn't even know I'd been carrying falls away. "Thanks."

Beck inclines his head and raises his hand to the wall covered in flowers. "Of course, that was then. This is now."

And he pulls back the great swaths of flowering vines to reveal a small hidden doorway. It's round and wooden and clearly original to this neighborhood. I'm already getting Secret

Garden vibes when he twists the stubborn handle. Laughter immediately overwhelms the fractured squeak of the door, and I'm greeted by the sight of warm lamplight pooling amidst clumps of greenery.

"It's ... a playground?" I say, spotting teeter-totters, seesaws, and swings that would've been new circa 1950. Then I squint into the layered gloom, even more surprised to find children bounding across the lawn, jumping rope, and forming teams to play hopscotch. "What the hell? None of these kids can be older than eleven."

"Ten," Beck corrects, watching me carefully. "Ready to walk?"

I nod, and we skirt the wooden edge of the hidden park. "But it's so late."

"Right before midnight, actually," he says, and I look at him sharply. Midnight. One of the twelves. It reminds me of Zoe. "They're always out here at this time. And they disappear within minutes of the new day."

"Are they mortal?" I ask because I sense nothing otherworldly about them. Beck nods as I spot a little girl with a leash. She looks vaguely familiar. She's also walking a cat. "They should be in bed. They should be dreaming."

"They *are* dreaming. Listen."

I pick out one voice and focus on it until the others fade. It's a boy with a bowl cut, barely into double digits, if that, playing in a sandbox with a friend.

"Everyone thinks the Shadows were evil, but they were simply willing to do what others couldn't. I mean, sometimes when you want something, you just have to take it!"

"Or smash it!" agrees his friend, then demonstrates on his buddy's sand castle.

Unmoving, the boy stares down at his destroyed work. Slowly, his gaze works its way up to the other child's face. "But if you do that, you have to face the consequences. Just like Zoe Archer."

He tackles his friend, and both kids go flying to the ground, but I jolt at the sound of my grandmother's name coming from some strange kid's mouth.

"Forget the Archers," growls the second child, grinding his friend's face into the sand. "Those Mother-Lovers just don't know when to die."

Without willing it, I'm suddenly there, pulling the kids apart. I hold each one up by the back of the neck. "Where did you hear that?"

Instead of struggling, the boys surprise me by falling still. Everyone else in the yard—around a dozen kids in all—quickly gathers around. Each child's face is like a lotus flower in bloom, turned up to me and wide with hope.

"Do you have more?" the first kid asks. The left side of his face is covered in dirt, so he has to squint at me with one eye. "He said if I was good, if I thought about him and cheered him on, that he'd tell me what happens next."

"Who? What?"

But before he can answer, the girl with the cat tugs at my shirt. "He told *me* that if I was *really* good, I'd get to see."

"Shut up, Tavi!" One of the little boys kicks out at her. "You're just a girl! He won't want you--"

I drop the little brat on his butt before he can finish. Tavi bursts out laughing.

"Please." A fourth kid with a pronounced lisp tugs at my sweatshirt. "You have to talk to him for me. I can't sleep. I can't think. I need more!"

"Please, please, please --"

They gather around, their cries earnest. I drop the second boy back into the sandbox and quickly back away. I'm being mobbed by short people.

"It's the Elders, isn't it?" I ask Beck over their dulcet cries. "They're trying to harness these kids' imagination."

"They're powering up," he corrects, with a certainty that

sends a ratchet of dread down my spine. "They can't physically touch the children because, hi, mortals ... "

"But they can use them."

Touching these mortal children would turn the Elders into hermits, cutting rather than doubling the power they so desperately seek. But catching them alone, whispering the secrets of the Zodiac world in their little ears, *that* would give imaginative, impressionable little minds something to gnaw on.

Beck lifts his palms, one on each side, holding off two yammering kids at once. "I guess they finally decided that if the manuals weren't going to be written, they could just cut out the middleman."

Because young minds are the most impressionable and flexible. That's why the mythos and lore of the Zodiac world are passed down in comic book form, after all. Children believe with a fierceness that is lost in adulthood ... and belief is fuel.

"There were only five kids when I was here last month, but there's gotta be triple that now." Beck turns to face me in the dark, and I get a flashback of Carl looking haunted in the comic book shop as he claimed he could feel a story rising.

Because of these powerful little minds. Because of their energy.

Horrified, I look back over the playground and at all the kids waiting for the Elders to show up and whisper terrible secrets in their ears. "You've known about this for a month, and you haven't tried to stop them?"

He holds up his palms. "There are a lot of Elders, Ash."

"How many?"

"Eleven. We think."

We, meaning him and Rometra.

"Cassius?" I ask, piecing it together fast.

"Yes," he says quietly. "Listen, about him--"

I hold up a hand, cutting off whatever he wants to say.

Cassius, solo, is an old problem—or, given my dreams, maybe one for later. *Eleven* displaced Elders, all once full-fledged agents, all hanging out with mortal kids—there's only one reason for that.

"They're trying to form a troop."

It's not a question.

"Which is why we need to form one first."

Thus, Rometra and her group of carefully culled first-borns. "You think we could take them on with the Los Angeles initiates?"

"No, Ash." Beck doesn't even blink. "I think we could *rise.*"

But all I want to do is run...

"We could be the first group in our generation to form an actual troop," Beck is saying, even as I shake my head. "The record keeper would *have* to write about that. Then we'd own the narrative. *We'd* shape the story. *We'd* be the heroes that kids like these mentally feast upon."

I look around at the children still eyeing us, circling, waiting for that story.

But what would beating Cassius entail? Killing him? Could I —a cute, kinda sloppy, but totally chill surfer chick—do that? Kill a man?

Not a month ago, I was more like one of these kids then. Zoe'd fed me the stories of the Zodiac world, too. I'd think about the agents, dream about them, and continue giving them energy even through the passions of a truly devoted mind.

But I had a choice. I knew what Zoe was doing and why. It makes me sick of these kids wandering a playground at midnight, being fed bits of stories like poisonous crumbs, always left hungry for more.

I glance back at the private playground. The smallest girl was picking weeds that masqueraded as flowers. She was muttering to herself, and I could almost feel the words twisting her mind. I knew what it was like to have my mind and life hijacked.

But this time, you can do something about it.

How can I just go surfing now that I know what—who—was at risk?

I finally sigh and give Beck the same answer that Zoe would—paraphrased, of course, and accompanied by a reluctant sigh. "So much for puka necklaces."

And we leave the children in the midnight playground and head back home.

Rometra takes off the following day to gather all the Los Angeles initiates together, promising to return to the cottage before the full moon wanes.

"The symbolism is heavy with that one, folks," I say, but nobody laughs. The moon and its many moods are no laughing joke to any of them.

Meanwhile, we train. While the others prepare to face off against their opposing star signs in Rometra's gang, Nia takes it upon herself to single-handedly fill in the holes Zoe left in my martial education. In short, this tiny half-pint of a chica becomes the sole reason I bleed at least once a day. By the end of the week, I'll never look at petite chicks the same again.

I do my best. I leap, I fall, I cut myself, I heal—over and over again. Every night I go to bed with severe injuries, and every day I get back up, good as new, and head back to the dojo, telling myself I don't have a choice.

What I don't admit is that I like it.

Ever since the encounter with the hermit in the forest, something has come to attention inside me, and it has been standing at alert ever since. It's the same feeling I'd get when I was stuck in the surf shop all day, dry and still, muscles twitching while the waves peaked on the Pacific outside.

There's a longing inside me, and while I can't name exactly what it is, I do know one thing: I want more.

Enter Zoe's still unpacked backpack. She knew I was entering a world of superheroes and villains. She's probably had this thing prepped from the day she took me in, and I've been too angry with her to open it before now. Yet I know there's something inside of it she thinks will prepare me for battle.

After all, she'd been doing that my whole life.

So I excuse myself one night after dinner, lock my door, and pull the pack in front of me on the bed. Since Zoe Archer's idea of "practical necessities" can mean anything from a toothbrush to a sword, I proceed carefully.

The first thing I pull out is the hummingbird nest I found next to the black hole that ate Hummingbird House. I place that on my bedside table and reach into the zipped side pocket. What I pull out is both alarming and familiar: a thick roll of bills, mostly twenties, wrapped within a pink hair band.

My get-away-from-Zoe stash.

"Ah, irony," I mutter because, in the end, she was the one who left me.

I tuck the bills back in the pocket where I discover my favorite lip balm and one of Zoe's favorite weapons, a short blunt kubaton. It's the one she used to thread through her ponytail when running on the beach.

How sweet.

I also pull out a tube of lipstick that, while not my best shade, snaps out into an edged blade when twisted the opposite way. For the classy assassin, I think, and set both weapons aside for *never*.

Underwear, tee shirts, feminine products, and another pair of board shorts come next...I toss it all in the locker before lifting out one final item, an ornate wooden box that I definitely don't recognize. Nerves run through my belly at its unfamiliar heft, though when I finally work up the nerve to unlatch the clasp and lift the lid, I just stare.

Inside is a petal pink crystal bottle cradled in satin padding. The cuts along the glass front and the stopper are shaped to resemble an ornate star. I unfold the tiny card tied to the stopper by hemp string, and Zoe's large, looping script leaps up at me: *To Remember.*

"Alice in Wonderland crap," I say aloud, but my breath is suddenly shallow, and my hands are shaking.

I'd pour the contents into the bathroom sink, but it'd be just like Zoe to concoct something that works upon inhalation. Then I'd have to remember the whole of my parents' deaths, and I will never, ever do that.

Because that's what lies in the bottle. *That* memory.

I know it like I know my true name. Just as Zoe had ways to make me forget, she had ways to make me remember, too. My re-entry into the Zodiac world has been steady and immersive. I'm remembering more with every day that passes, every new skill and power acquired. It's like building a web. It grows and strengthens with each additional strand.

But not that day. I'd rather it be sucked into the same black hole as the one that swallowed my home in Laguna than remember another instant of my parent's death.

I cup the crystal carefully in both hands and look around for a safe place to store it. The nightstand is too close to the bed. I'd be worried about knocking it over in the middle of the night and getting hit with a face full of violent forget-me-nots. Ditto the bathroom with its hard basin and floor.

My gaze finally lands on the windowsill, beyond which lie black trees, a pitch forest floor that unfurls in the darkness, and midnight mountains. The only light is a pale glow from a half-empty moon.

I place the bottle in one dim, slivered ray, and pink spills weakly to the sill from the glass's sharp etchings. It reminds me of a pastel sunrise, Laguna at Christmastime, and I'm both wondering if I'll ever see one of those again—and getting a little teary at the thought—when a sudden movement catches my eye. As I scan the tree line, an entire section of still-shadowed under-brush shifts into view.

Not undergrowth, I think, as a figure emerges in the gloom. I jerk back from the window when it grows gnarled and hunched —a hermit.

Inching forward, heart pounding, I peer out the window again. The hermit sits below my window, the ugliest Romeo to my relatively fine Juliet. Its chin is turned up to my window, revealing beady, hateful, unblinking eyes ... and a really disturbing mole protruding from its neck. It makes a motion like it wants me to come outside.

I shake my head. "Get bent, dude."

It makes a lewd motion like it heard me, then points at me and back to the ground outside my window.

I look at the creature, now tapping its calloused foot.

I look at the stunning array of trees and ferns and green crap piled atop the verdant mountainside.

Then I look at the gorgeously dangerous perfume bottle next to me, in a room so poorly decorated it's part army barracks, part dorm room.

"I hate this place," I mutter aloud.

But I still leave the room. I don't tell anyone where I'm going, but take my urumi. I'm stronger than I was even a week ago, and if this walking, talking ball of phlegm lifts a finger to even scratch his nose, he's gonna know it, too.

22

MY TOTALLY GNARLY IOU.

The night is glorious, the air so fresh it's almost an assault, and the silver moon blasts the landscape wide while leeching it of color. I've always loved the moon, but I've never seen it this giant and glowing, looming over the Earth like it owns it.

My heart doubles in size at the sight of it.

Yet it seems to shrink again as the scrub brush rustles behind me, and a scent like black rot assaults my pores. Whirling, I unbelt my urumi.

"Don't hurt me!" The hermit cringes and throws its one good arm across its face.

"Stop sneaking up on me!" I tell it, but lower my urumi a degree. "Jeez, I'm going to have to stick a cowbell on you."

"That is a cruel punishment," it snaps, misunderstanding me, "even for one who is already cursed."

Its talisman teddy bear is tucked beneath the armpit of the shoulder Rometra dislocated, which has yet to heal. Maybe that's part of the deal when you're a law-breaker. Maybe you never get better, only worse.

"Besides," it adds, unfurling to full gnarliness, "touching your skin would be like bathing in razors. Every strand of your hair puts me in mind of a viper. Even enduring your gaze is worse than being stripped of my title and my name and my home."

"Oka-a-a-ay."

"Your breath is worse than hellfire—"

"Got it."

"And your humanity is so repulsive it makes me puke in my mouth. It reeks of the sewers that stretch beneath graves and—"

"Seriously, dude! Shut up!"

It shuts up.

I wait. I wait some more in the lengthening silence and serious funk. Finally, I roll my eyes. "Fine. Speak again. But stop being such a loser."

"I'm just saying that you're half-human, and after what I've done, what I've become, it would physically hurt me to touch you." It eyes my urumi warily. "So can you please put that away?"

"Promise you won't hurt me?"

It nods.

"Shake on it?"

It looks at me like I've lost my mind.

"Just kidding." I sheath my weapon and tie it back around my waist. "So what do you want?"

"You saved me from the spawn of Shadows."

Rometra would hate being called that, I think ... so I don't correct it. "So?"

It lifts its chin. "So I do not wish to still owe the debt before your gruesome death at the hands of Elder Cassius."

"That's totally not fated," I tell it, remembering Beck's words. His conviction.

"It totally is."

"Fates can change."

It sneers. "So you're a Seer now?"

"Are *you* a Seer now?" I point out, and it scowls.

"I have known many Shadow agents in my long life. I know every tactic when dealing with the Light. I know offense. I know defense. I might be sidelined in this generation's war, but I See it all."

I snort. "Sounds more like a referee."

"Except this isn't a game." It screws up its face, eyes skyward, and I realize it's thinking. That Rorschach test of a face is it thinking. "I was more like a bishop entrusted with governing his flock."

"I don't care," I tell it. I don't. I just want to go inside and take a really hot, cleansing shower.

"Do you care that the Elders are still after you?"

"The Elders will fail," I say, even though nerves jump in my belly. "We're going to fill the zodiac star signs with twelve initiates."

The hermit huffs out a rancid laugh. "Then you will have twelve dead initiates."

"You're crazy." I turn to walk away.

It jumps in front of me, its bare, blackened foot almost touching mine. "No, crazy is trying to forge a new world with the failing ethos of an old one!"

"Well, what would you suggest, bishop?"

"I don't care about you and your lost cause enough to suggest anything!" It crosses its arms. Arm. "All I want is for you to tell me how to repay you for saving my life and returning my talisman so that I may be free of my debt and your miserable company!"

"Yeah, 'cause I'm totally the problem here!"

"Just do it!" it screeches, veins popping at its temples.

"Fine!" I yell back, breathing hard, trying to think of something. "So what's the deal? You have to do whatever I say?"

It raises its chin. Chins. "Anything that absolves me of this distressing moral obligation."

"Okay." I nod. "But I warn you, law-breaker. I won't go easy on you."

It squares on me like a soldier awaiting command. "I am prepared."

"Are you sure?" I ask it. "Because I can tell you right now that even in your time as a bishop or Seer or whatever .... you've never, ever done anything quite like this before."

The hermit swallows hard. "You can do nothing worse to me than I have already done to myself."

"Fine. There lies your future, and there lies your fate!" I send my voice booming into the dark forest as I point somewhere off into the distance. "Go throw yourself into the lake, and don't come out again until you've washed behind your ears!"

It gives me an almost-human squint. "Huh?"

I drop my arm. "You can wait until daytime if you want. The water will be warmer, which I totally get. I'm no sadist."

It doesn't even crack a smile. "That is your stipulation?"

"Yeah, dude." I nod solemnly. "You stink."

The hermit looks from me to the direction I've pointed and then back again. It is speechless with total gratitude. Then its already jacked-up visage skews further, and it begins throwing—I kid you not—the mother of all temper tantrums.

Its screams are a dozen nails on a chalkboard. Its spittle is acid rain as it shakes its head from side to side. It rages and curses and roars and finally bites its good arm with what's left of its teeth.

Like that's not crazy.

"That is not penance! That is not honorable restitution! It's not even a proper task!"

"You swore," I remind it.

It howls again, causing wolves to answer in the distance, and stomps its clubbed feet until its broken arm makes another raw popping sound.

"Nasty, dude."

"Stop calling me that!" It looks around for something to toss at me, stopping short of throwing its talisman on the ground. "I hate you!"

"Well, I don't know what to call you because I don't know your stupid name, and I hate you, too!"

"I am not allowed to utter my given name again," it snarls, bulbous chest heaving. "If I do, my tongue will burn and turn to ash in my mouth."

It falls eerily still, watching for my reaction and judgment.

I am careful only to blink. "Ouch."

One corner of its mouth twitches. It's probably involuntary.

"Okay, then I'll call you Bishop since I get to be the boss here." I grin as it startles. "Now. Go oversee the cleansing of thy flesh, Bishop, and don't forget to wash under your pits."

It looks stunned by my generosity. It's probably wondering how I can be so cool after it was such a spaz.

"What did you say?" it finally manages.

I hold my wrist up and make a show of tapping the watch I'm not wearing. "Really? All of it?"

It waves its good hand in the air impatiently. "What did you call me, daughter of Chaos?"

"Hey, Bishop is a lot cooler than law-breaker or cursed-beast-that-smells-like-fish guts-in-an-open-sewer. So deal with it!"

Bishop slumps before me, uglier than ever, mouth agape. I see things rotting in that unhinged maw that I can never unsee. When it becomes clear that it's just going to stand there, I shrug and turn back to the cottage.

"Should have named it Fungus," I mutter and leave the way I came.

IN PREPARATION FOR THE FESTIVAL-THAT-IS-TOTALLY-NOT-THE-SAME-THING-AS-A-PARTY, Beck gives the hermits scythes and orders them to cut a giant circle into the middle of the blood wheat. This will be our battleground.

Of course, the hermits protest the need to give over their land to us with howls and screeches that rebound through the night, but they ultimately do what he says. After all, he's the only reason they have a home in this world at all.

So the blood wheat is given a buzz cut, and the afternoon we're to meet the Los Angeles initiates finally arrives. The wheat rises on each side of a newly rent path leading directly into the center of the wheat field, blinding us to everything but the mountaintops, their browns and greens competing to smother each other in varying textures and shades.

Everything is soft, swaying, and densely layered. I guess I'm getting used to the place because, I have to admit, it's pretty in its own way.

"But not remotely beach-like," I remind myself as if atoning for the thought.

We finally spill out into a circle that is supposed to be an earthly echo of the sun and, eventually, the moon above. There's a secondary ring surrounding the battlefield where Nia and the other shoo-ins for superhero-dom get to watch the non-festivities.

The participants will stand opposite them in the same ring, waiting for their turn in the circle-o'-death. After the festival, a midnight claiming ceremony will bind everyone together in one troop, and that's that. The Zodiac world will rise again.

Or so we hope.

"So, who gets to choose the trial?" Nia asks, rubbing her arms as she looks left and right.

She's been on alert since entering the wheat, and War and Thayer have flanked her the whole way. Her hatred of the hermits is well known, yet there are no signs of them as we take to the circle.

"We'll pull from a hat," Beck replies, turning about himself, nervous.

I snort.

War hits me with a look that's as cool as it is steady. "Serendipitous restrictions are a centuries-old tradition for those who believe even simple things can herald great destiny."

Blah, blah.

"Yeah, grade schoolers and magicians with bunnies think so, too."

"You have a better idea?" Thayer asks. His dark hair is slicked back, shining. His freckles stand out, tiny constellations against his skin. He has ironed his cape.

"Draw straws. Pick a number between one and ten. Or," I hold up a finger here. "You could have, like, an actual game plan."

I'm pretty sure Rometra had one of those.

"Everyone has a plan until you punch them in the mouth," War mutters.

"Then fists up, Mother-Lovers." Thayer suddenly points off in the distance. "Because here comes the cavalry."

Although there're only eleven of them, the Los Angeles initiates appear to be legion. I shield my eyes against the midday sun as they approach, wondering why they look like they're walking above rather than in the wheat. They're also striding directly through it toward the battlefield, ignoring both the old and new paths altogether.

"I don't remember your sister being that tall," Thayer tells War just as Rometra breaks into full view, trampling the wheat surrounding the perfectly short battlefield.

Or as the hermit she's straddling does so.

Nia takes a giant step back, and Thayer puts a steadying hand on her shoulder.

"Guess we know where the hermits are," he says as the rest of the Los Angeles initiates appear, each one straddling the bulbous, deformed backs of the hunched creatures. They are haloed in sunlight and look so young and strong that the hermits beneath them are even uglier in contrast.

"That's inhumane," I say as I search for the hermit with the teddy bear.

"They're not human," Nia reminds me, and her voice is iron. Thayer squeezes her shoulder again.

I don't care. I feel like I'm looking at some kind of messed-up rodeo, where the bulls and the clowns have been mashed into one being, and the cowboys are leather-wearing bullies jacked up on their own superiority.

"Well, there's something not right about it."

The wheat parts one last time to reveal Rometra, rising high and as still as possible. She orders her hermit to a halt with a sharp kick to its ribs. I look around and am gratified to see the same feeling of disgust echoed on Beck's face, yet all he does is suck in a giant, fortifying breath.

"Come on, Nia. Time to meet your future troop mates."

"I SUPPOSE INTRODUCTIONS ARE IN ORDER," ROMETRA SAYS BY WAY of greeting. She's in her favored head-to-toe leather and masked, as are the three initiates who will also be competing.

Outside of Rometra, the most obvious shoo-in for future superhero is a beefy blond boy with round features and a menacing scowl. He stares at Beck with such intensity that I wait for a blood vessel to burst.

Clearly, they're dance partners.

The boy next to him, angular and dark-haired, has a gaze so flat that his eyes look like stones. The lone girl is bright-eyed and has hair as bright and red as Zoe. Each would look great drawn in a comic book penciler's black-and-white.

The field falls silent. I'm waiting for something to happen when I realize everyone's looking at me.

Of course, I think, startled into stepping forward. The Los Angeles initiates are probably more than a little curious about what a 'daughter of Chaos' looks like.

"Hey." I give a feeble wave and then point to myself. "I'm Ashlyn. Archer. So, yeah. Cool."

It is the lamest introduction in the history of introductions.

Especially once Rometra widens her stance, pushes her messenger bag to her back, and props her hands on her hips. She looks like an Amazon; her hair knotted down the center of her head in thick bands and leather clinging to muscles and curves. I realize I'd totally love to see her kicking butt and saving mortals and defeating Elders in the pages of a manual.

"I am Rometra, originally of Troop 888, Los Angeles division, which I renounced at the time of the great Reordering. I am first-born, female, and ready to use every power I have to assist in the rise of the neo-Zodiac. Mortals will dream of me, and future generations will speak my name with reverence and awe."

My shoulders slump. I wonder if I can get a do-over. That was a way better introduction than mine.

The large blond kid steps forward. "I am the firstborn of Malcolm Zobel, who died in the chaos of the Great Reordering. I will avenge his death and honor my matriarch's lineage as a direct descendant of the First Mother. My name is Talus."

The First Mothers. First-born. Nia was right about Rometra's agenda. There's a theme here.

Shaking his head, clearly thinking the same thing, Beck steps forward so that he's opposite Talus. "I am Beckett Lux, formerly of Troop 400, which I fled five years ago of my free will. I don't care who leads the neo-Light, as long as we all work together to defeat the Elders who would lay fire to the mortal world in their quest to see us all dead."

Cheery.

Beck and Talus exchange nods before the red-haired girl pushes forward. Outside of the flaming hair, she's fairly nondescript. If I saw her on the street, I'd mark her as nothing more than human.

"I'm Emerson Reyes. My lineage is that of the Libran." She

thrusts her hand Thayer's way. He takes it, eyes bulging when she tightens her grip. "And I swear to the First Mothers that I will never be drawn in relation to someone else's narrative!" Emerson lifts her chin, calling into the sky. "Hear that Record Keeper?"

"The Mother herself likely heard that," Thayer mutters before collecting himself. Clearing his throat, he throws back his cape. "I am Thayer Storge. I am also a Libra, obviously, and though first-born, I was raised on the fringes of Zodiac society as a gray. I have never known a real troop before, but I swear I will now."

Emerson and Thayer nod at each other respectfully, then step away without turning their backs.

Finally, War faces off against a boy who is dark-haired and golden-eyed. He has sable lashes any girl would kill for ... though I doubt that'll be War's primary motivation.

"My name is Cruz," he says, "and I am descended from—"

"Hold up." Rometra leans around the others to address him. "That's not your name."

"It is," the boy argues. "I'm dropping my first name and will only go by my surname now. I figure we all get a new start when the manuals are finally written again, and Chris is not a sexy name."

"I'll bet you a thousand Hemsworths you're wrong," Nia mutters, and she and Emerson give each other a knowing high-five.

Thayer gives Nia a disbelieving look.

"What?" Nia says but looks away, blushing.

"I was born and raised in a cosmic collective," Cruz continues, "and have never considered lineage, birth order, or gender as a means to greatness—only deeds."

Thayer catches my furrowed brow, and leans over. "A collective is a commune for agents and their offspring. They live off the grid, both mortal and supernatural."

"We had our own Seers and interpretations of the star signs,"

Cruz admits before giving a stiff shrug. "What we didn't have was frozen yogurt or WiFi. I had to get out."

War's introduction is similar to Rometra's but without all the first-born stuff. I note they don't look at each other as she speaks, a tension that breaks only once War and Cruz step back.

The tension picks back up again when Rometra holds out what is obviously a very old stack of cards.

"Want to go through them?" she asks Beckett. "Make sure all the trials are there?"

Beck already explained that there are dozens of possible tasks that we might be called upon to perform in the festival, including simple things that everyone can do, like running cheetah-fast and jumping in a way that defies gravity ... we just have to do it while holding sharp weapons in each hand, natch.

There are also trials like spike dancing, firing star muskets, or dodging lasers that represent supernatural bullets, which—I can now tell you from firsthand experience—really, really hurt.

"I trust you," Beck replies, pocketing the cards. "Would you like to measure the field dimensions?"

"I trust you," she replies as well. It's so obvious they're both lying that the ensuing silence is uncomfortable.

"This way," Beck finally says to the seven Los Angeles initiates who will merely witness the festival, motioning them toward the newly rent path. He and Rometra have agreed that all will dine, sleep, and prepare for tomorrow's battles at the cottage.

"Hold up," Rometra says, just as we've all turned away. "Don't dismiss the hermits just yet."

Beck's shoulders stiffen, not in a sudden jolt, but a slow hardening that reminds me of lava turning to rock. Thayer and Nia exchange a look behind his back. There's only one reason to hold back the others and hold onto the hermits.

Rometra's changing the rules on us, and she doesn't want to call for an Uber back to LA if we happen to disagree.

War, dead-eyed, appears unsurprised as we turn back. "What do you want, Rom?"

Rometra never means what she says.

Sure she does ... when she's being mean, nasty, vindictive, and horrible, she means exactly what she says.

"My allies and I were discussing the terms on the way up from LA."

Beck shakes his head. "We already settled on terms."

"It's just a small tweak." Her voice goes cloying, sap atop sugar atop honey. I look at War to make sure I'm not the only one who wants to gag.

"Here we go," War mutters.

Rometra ignores her. "Outside of Nia, who's guaranteed a spot since there are no other Virgos in the region, every single one of you must participate, and by everyone ... I mean *you*."

I must not have had enough coffee this morning because it takes me another moment to realize she's talking to me.

I snort. "Sure. If participate means wave pom-poms from the sidelines."

"You fight," she says slowly. "Or we roll."

Annoyed that I have to spell this out for a whole new group of initiates, I give an epic eye roll. "I don't wanna. Plus, you guys don't even need me if there's another Sagittarian initiate gunning for the spot."

Duh.

War gives a short, strangled laugh—one I'm not even sure she can control. "You don't get it, do you?"

Thayer puts his hand on my back like he's reassuring me. Or steadying me. "Rometra *is* the Archer of that troop."

I do get it then, and my mouth goes dry.

Of course, Rometra wants to fight me. Besting the daughter of the greatest heroine the Zodiac world has ever seen would satisfy her almost as much as beating Joanna Archer herself.

"Dude, you can just have the spot," I tell her, and she's in front of me so fast, chin thrust so far forward, it's like she's just begging me to tag it.

I won't lie. I'm tempted.

But I'm not stupid.

I step back instead.

"I don't want to *have* anything!" She snarls, pushing forward again. "I'm a warrior! I will earn my place in the annals of greatness!"

I snort again before I can stop it.

"What?" I say when Thayer clears his throat in warning. "She said annals."

No one laughs. I throw my hands into the air. "But that's not fair!"

"No," Rometra shoots back. "What's unfair is if you wimp out and none of your friends get a shot at greatness because you won't fight."

I want to remind them that I'm just a guest in this glorified treehouse, passing through on my way to the safety of Kauai's sun-kissed shores and all-you-can-eat sushi buffets. But then I remember Nia has never wanted anything more than this. Thayer, too, has already told me how much he's looking forward to finally belonging somewhere, no longer gray in a world of Shadow and Light. Beck hasn't told me much, but I know he has something to prove. Even War, who's as tough as anyone I've ever met, faces a lifetime of insignificance if I don't meet this condition.

This sucky, inconvenient—and probably excruciating —condition.

So, without overthinking it, I point before I can change my mind. "Well, I'm not wearing that!"

Rometra glances down at her leather halter top before squinting back up at me. "Your objection to participating in the festival isn't fighting me ... but the clothing while you do it?"

"Oh, I totally object to fighting you, too." I let the scent of my long, reluctant sigh reveal how true that is, then pluck at my sweatshirt. "But at least this way, I won't die of embarrassment."

And maybe it's for the best. By agreeing to fight Rometra, I will give Nia and the others their chance to build the first tribe of initiates in Zodiac history. I will help in the rebirth of this world the best way I can but after that? And I mean *directly* after that?

The java-stained hills and sky-blue waters of Kauai await.

23

THE HEIR AND THE SPARE.

The LA initiates disappear into the hollowed-out tree trunk of the cottage as soon as we enter the enclosed grove.

Of course, they're naturals at leaping up and away into the abyss. I hear murmured shouts to meet in the cantina, but I'm so preoccupied with what I've just agreed to that I miss the bottom rung—twice. Slumping, I lean against the hollowed-out trunk and cover my eyes.

There's no way I can beat Rometra.

I'd typically just grab my longboard and head to the ocean to ease my worry, but the sea is as far away as the moon right now, and the power that lit up inside me atop that cliff in Laguna might as well have been a dream.

"You're thinking of the ocean."

Beck's voice startles me back into the present. The grove looms around me, green and intimidating and quiet. I look around, quickly realizing we're the only two left in the pressing stillness.

"How'd you know?"

"I've seen that look before." His smile is thin in the dim light. "Is it torture?"

I shrug. "Only a lot."

His expression breaks, and he swallows hard. "I'm sorry."

"I know." Pushing from the trunk, I shove my hands into my pockets. "I'm going to get my star sign kicked to the moon and back, aren't I?"

He cringes. "Depends on which trial you're dealt. Maybe you'll draw the serrated cables. You're getting great with those."

"Yeah?" I offer up a wan smile because it's actually true. I've found my rhythm with the giant, razored ropes. Probably because their movement is so similar to my urumi. Too bad I can't use that. Unfortunately, since I'm the only one who can touch the conduits, using any of them is considered cheating.

"Yup. You were whipping them overhead like a supernatural cowgirl."

I give him a tilt of my imaginary cowboy hat. "Maybe someday I'll lasso myself an Elder and give that son-of-a-gun a piece of my mind."

"You have a terrible southern accent." He jerks his head back to the forest. "Come on. There's no ocean here, but I know a place that's almost as pretty."

"Impossible," I say, but follow him anyway.

It's not impossible.

We crest a hillock with a giant hole so well hidden by grasses that I nearly fall inside. Beck surprises me by leaping into that darkness, and when no sounds of agony rise, I follow.

It's only ten feet, yet instead of pine needles to soften my landing, the floor has been cleared, swept, and covered in over-dyed rugs, lavender hues piled one atop the other. Plump, jewel-toned pillows skirt the edges, and sheepskin throws and blankets sit in a pile to ward against the underground chill.

"We call it the grotto," Beck says as the underground cave's silence presses against me like cabin pressure in an ascending airplane. While the light is weak, that doesn't stop the mineral walls from sparking in white and silver speckles.

"Stalactites," I say, surprised. They hang from the ceiling at varying heights and angled points, while stalagmites rise from the floor in equally sharp tines. It gives the appearance that we're inside an enormous jaw. I run my hands along one shining wall. The sharp rock is icy under my palm.

"My sister used to cave dive. She'd find places like this, but underwater, and search out pockets where air might live ..." He touches the rock face, too. "She'd stay down there for hours. She wasn't afraid of anything."

I peer up at him closely. "I didn't know you had a sister."

"I'm a second-born son."

In a world that valued first-born daughters.

I freeze. "You weren't supposed to be an agent?"

"Ash," he finally sighs, "I wasn't supposed to be anything."

I just stare, and he gives a grim laugh before an old memory tightens the corner of his eyes. "But Juno ... she would have been a great and terrible Shadow."

I'm not just surprised this time. I literally lose my breath. I suck it back in on an indecipherable stutter. Beck, silent, only watches.

"Oh my God," I finally manage.

"Goddess," he softly reminds me, but I wave him off, putting it together, mental puzzle pieces clicking to form a complete picture finally.

It all makes sense now. "You were raised to be a Shadow?"

And if my calculation is correct, he was fourteen at the time of the Reordering. Fourteen years of learning to negatively influence the human race while hunting the Light.

I wasn't supposed to be anything.

Beck crosses the small clearing and drops to the floor next to the blankets. I follow, waiting for him to speak. He must know that Zoe taught me that Shadows were pure, enduring evil.

"People blame mortal vice whenever a major city falls to riot or ruin," she told me, "but when a city or world leader goes down a dark path, you can bet there are Shadow agents there to give it all a good, hard push."

Still, my birth mother was half-Shadow and half-Light, meaning I have a quarter of Shadow blood running through my veins. If I discriminated based on that, wouldn't I be eternally at war with myself?

"Who else?" I ask. "Rometra?"

He nods. "And obviously War."

"Okay, so what about you and Juno? Classic case of the heir and the spare?"

He inclines his head. "It's why she was named after a goddess, and they named me after my uncle."

I snort. At least he can joke about it. "Did she at least live up to the distinction?"

"And then some. She was to take up my mother's sign, the Shadow Libra. My mother," he hesitates to add, "who was killed while answering the call from a neighboring Shadow troop to defend against an Archer of Light, someone first known as the Kairos, and later known as—"

"Chaos." I sigh.

Oh, boy. My birth mother. Again.

"Awesome."

"My mother was," he says, deliberately misunderstanding me. "And I mean that in the original sense of the word. She was daunting, fearsome, dreaded. Every second she wasn't working to sway mortals to their darker inclinations, she was training Juno to follow in her stead." He pauses, frowning. "So you can imagine how excited Juno was to be the first in our troop to come of age after the Reordering."

It was called Metamorphosis. Midnight, age twenty-five. When a child of the Zodiac goes from initiate to full-fledged superhero.

Or villain.

I shiver in the cave's chill and shake my head. "But there were no more new agents after the Reordering."

"We didn't know that then," Beck says, pulling a blanket from the stack. The pile shifts as he pulls it around my shoulders. I lean back, immediately warmed. "It was before our weapons stopped working. We still thought the Reordering was temporary. Juno was so excited."

Excited to be an agent of evil sworn to kill superheroes and wreak havoc among the mortal populace. *Yippee.*

"The return of your supernatural abilities in Laguna was a powerful display, but nothing compared to true metamorphosis." He shakes his head. "It's incredible to see in person. The skies give over to storm clouds the color of new cement. The wind roars and thunder rumbles, and all that power is directed into you. Into her."

"I know." Zoe'd shown me such a manual, too.

Beck looks up through the hole that acts as the cave's natural skylight. "So at midnight on Juno's twenty-fifth birthday, my troop gathered on a small island in the middle of a manmade lake where the skies went gray, thunder rumbled, and lightning gathered overhead. I wasn't supposed to be there. I was only thirteen, but it was Juno. My sister."

Your evil sister, I think, but don't say.

"I reached the isle by rowboat to find our Shadow agents encircling her. I almost didn't make it, so they didn't see me at first. Their heads were turned to the sky, and when the Universe just changed its mind, backing away from the moment like it meant nothing, all eleven of them cursed the cleared skies."

I don't say a word. I barely breathe. I can see in my mind's eye the confusion on those demonic brows.

"The Zodiac world was an upturned snow globe," Beck whispers now, the impact of the memory thinning out his voice. "The lines between good and evil blurred like oils turned to watercolor.

Every agent could choose who and what they wanted to be, and their greatness was suddenly based on deed, not lineage. Even first-born daughters like my sister."

I shake my head when he falls silent. "So what happened?"

He blinks and refocuses on me. "They killed her."

Blood drains from my body so quickly that I shudder. "Your father didn't try to stop them?"

"Ash, my father led the charge."

Beck manages to hold my gaze, but his eyes are haunted. "She was a first-born daughter, yet she was powerless. But in death—"

"She'd be useful."

His words stir a memory. Zoe, again, schooling me in evil. "When a child of the Zodiac dies their personal power, everything that makes them great returns to their most powerful living relative."

"I tried to save her." He tried to save evil ... from evil. Just because she was his sister. "I leaped from the bushes and tried to block her, but they turned on me."

Horror pools in my gut. I put a hand to my stomach. "Why?"

"Why not?" That humorless laugh again. "If the greatest of the Shadow initiates were powerless, then the least of us were just fuel. So I ran, and I've been running ever since."

That's what we're up against. That's what Zoe had been trying to train me for all these years. A group of Elders so determined to hold on to whatever power remained to them they would kill their own children to do it.

"I'm so sorry. If my father tried to kill me—"

"That's just it." He cuts me off with a shake of his head. "My father was the fastest, the strongest. The meanest. He never *tried* to do anything. And there was a moment when I was fleeing that I felt him—his breath hot on my neck. His fingertips skimming my arm. But nothing happened."

"You think he spared you?"

"I think," he begins tentatively, "that if I can throw off my lineage and choose to be good, others can as well."

"Him?" I ask, the doubt coloring my voice.

He looks away. "Maybe not. But me. War. Rometra."

Because they'd all chosen what was good—they were choosing Light. I look at the black rock face, one sparking pure light. I blow out a hard breath and close my eyes.

I still wasn't looking forward to fighting Rometra, but what choice did I have after this story? The Elders, people who kill off their own children just because they're not useful—or because they are—cannot be allowed domination over the mortal realm.

Finally, I nod. "Maybe."

Relief floods Beck. I see it, blasting his face wide. "You'll see. We all have more in common than you think." Then he tilts his head. "Especially you and me."

I lift one eyebrow, questioning.

Beck lifts my chin with one fingertip, its softness matching the blue pools of his eyes, which've gone dark and liquid despite the light refracting all around us. It doesn't scare me. Maybe I'm crazy, but it doesn't make me think of Shadows.

Instead, it reminds me of my beloved ocean. It, too, is filled with things I don't understand.

"We both have childhoods," he finally says, "that should've been better than they were."

I momentarily soften against his palm. Then I snort and shake my head. "We're not the same at all, Beckett."

His hand drops. The light in his soft gaze dims. "No?"

"No." I lift my chin and lay the truth on him. "Because I am a much better surfer than you."

24

THE TEN SECOND RULE.

A month ago, I was content with fish tacos on the beach, wrapping my longboard around a super sick set, and a straight C-average in all my classes. None of that spoke of a girl hungry to change the world.

Yet a month ago, I didn't know Nia, who has a temper for reasons she won't talk about.

Or Thayer, who wants to be greater than the fate that he was born to.

I couldn't even guess at the real Beckett back then ... forget about his ability to "see" things he couldn't control.

Even the thought of War, fighting for her family's approval, would haunt me if I ran now.

No, the only chance I'd have at ever enjoying a real life again would be knowing that these *real* heroes were out there fighting for humanity. Becoming a neo-troop of the Zodiac.

Which meant that instead of a pleasant afternoon spent underachieving, I had to have my ass handed to me by Rometra.

Despite my total, understandable, and natural objection to this, I wake early the next morning, shower quickly, and shrug into one of the outfits in my wardrobe. It feels like being squeezed into a sausage casing, but I'm not stupid. Loose clothing would only provide Rometra with easy handholds.

Besides, I really don't want her ripping my favorite sweatshirt.

After that, I brush my teeth and tame my wild curls into a tight, low bun as I—get this—ready myself for freaking combat.

Staring in the mirror, I barely recognize myself. An idea flashes as I catch the unmistakable fear in the reflected gaze: I should escape from the cottage through the wheat and run away from my not-home. Yet the thought is like a match flaring before being blown out.

I won't run. Not because I'm a hero or think I have the slightest chance against Rometra. It's all the things that kept me up half the night.

I simply know too much.

Plus, I don't want Bishop's craptastic prophesy about the Elders drawing first blood to come true. I don't want mortal children treated like pawns in someone else's supernatural chess game. I certainly don't want the Elders to rise to power and lay waste to people like my parents just because they can.

It's only as I'm leaving my room that I even think to wonder...

Shouldn't I be more motivated by what I do want than what I don't?

Too late now. A dozen people wait, gathered in the main foyer, but I keep my gaze averted and head directly to Beck, who's pacing before the exit. Unsurprisingly, the leather fits him more naturally, reminding me of his winter wetsuit, zipped tight against the Pacific's froth.

My heart tightens in my chest. I miss the ocean more than ever today.

"You skipped breakfast," he says as soon as I join him. Nia slides up, flanking his other side. She is holding, but not drinking from, a coffee mug. She's not dressed for combat, but looks nervous all the same.

"You mean the Last Supper?" I mutter, just as Rometra spots

me. She gives me a little finger wave that has nerves flip-flopping in my belly.

"It won't be that bad," he says, though his gaze skitters away.

"I'm about to get pounded by a future superhero while wearing half a cow. It's already that bad."

"Here." Thayer arrives suddenly. His red cape punctuates his leather, and his shock of blond hair has been slicked into a peak atop his head. "I saved you a bagel."

"No, thanks," I say, pushing it away. Nia shakes her head as he offers it to her, and moves to stand shoulder-to-shoulder with me, which is somewhat comforting.

At least until the boy named Talus makes himself at home on her other side.

"You're not fighting today," Talus says, noting her nervousness. "Why aren't you eating?"

"This is eating," Nia muttered, sipping from her coffee cup.

"You should eat. I don't want someone scrawny and weak in my troop."

"Sorry," Nia says, not-sorry, "but all I consume in the morning is coffee and patronizing comments about my size."

"You should eat as well, Archer." The voice rises behind me and I turn to find Rometra so close she towers over me. Her boots are thick-heeled, but most of it is just natural height. Crap. "You missed dinner last night and now breakfast. You must be starved."

"Careful, Rom," War joins us then, her hair plaited like her sister's. They are so slick, dressed in all-black, that they look impenetrable. "Someone might think you care about someone other than yourself."

The room goes dead silent as Rometra turns to stare at War like she's never seen her before. I swallow hard and do the same. Is she ... standing up for me? Against her sister? In public?

"We'll be on the battlefield," Rometra snaps. "When you're ready."

I sigh as she walks away. Yes, she dresses like a female Terminator, but she has the muscle to balance out the curves and no doubt an earned confidence. She is the perfect heroine in every respect.

"Ten seconds."

The voice interrupts a disturbingly clear vision of me, the anvil to Rometra's hammer.

I frown, turning to War. "What?"

"Ten seconds of steady bravery." She crosses her arms and pierces me with an unblinking gaze. "That's all you need to beat her."

"She's right," Beck says as I begin shaking my head. "Being a superhero doesn't mean you have to be heroic all the time. Just when it counts."

"Plus, ten seconds is usually enough time to get you out of trouble," War says.

"Or at least into the next moment," adds Nia with an encouraging smile.

I frown at War. "I have to fight your sister."

She huffs. "I know how you feel."

"Come on." Beck drapes his arm over my shoulder and guides me to the exit. "Just remember that we're all going to be on the same side by the end of the day."

I hope *Rometra* remembers that, I think as we descend to the forest floor. I don't say it, though. I'm too busy counting to ten.

And, just like that, the next moment has arrived.

25

THE ANDEANS, THE SPARTANS, AND ME.

We enter the blood wheat single-file.

To my surprise, Carl is there, awaiting us all in the circle of shorn wheat. I blink twice when I see him, first because I didn't know he was allowed to enter the field, and second because he's positioned atop a wooden platform constructed sometime during the night.

Someone—most likely the hermits—has managed to drag his enormous black desk and red velvet chair atop the makeshift dais like he's some sort of literary king—which, now that I think about it, isn't too far off.

Yet more than all that is Carl himself. Gone is his disaffected indifference. His gaze is quick and darting, his back rod-straight, reminding me of a judge on a bench. Even his black leather jacket and jeans look stiff and formal now. Looking at him, I realize he's no outsider, not just a mere mortal among people who are stronger and faster than he is.

Suddenly, he fits in with these people in a way I never can.

Suddenly, I don't recognize him at all.

"Creepy," I mutter, causing his gaze to rocket my way beneath the brim of his black cap.

Oops. Outside voice.

He sets his jaw and waits until everyone has entered the circle. Then, he speaks in an equally unfamiliar tone that perfectly fits the new, creepy Carl.

"Welcome to the first festival of the neo-Zodiac. Thousands will see the outcome of these trials if and when the Zodiac rises again, and those in other cities may well use it as a blueprint to form their own troops. Thus, the record of this day will be shared for generations to come."

Yay.

"Competitors, please pair up and step forward for the drawing."

Eight of us move to the edge of the circle as Carl hops down to take the cards depicting the trials from Beck. Each is marked with a different glyph from the Western zodiac, and there's a set for both Shadow and Light. The remaining seven are stamped with planetary signs.

Carl gives the cards a perfunctory shuffle before slipping the hat from his head and dropping them inside. "There are thirty-one trials depicted in the ancient manuals, each written on one of these cards."

"That's a lot of ways to pick a fight," I mutter.

"Because there are so many fantastic ways to die," Talus growls, staring a hole through the back of Beck's head.

Carl goes on like none of us has spoken. "Just in case you weren't paying attention in supernatural Sunday school, here's a recap of the ground rules. Only the two battling initiates may step foot inside the circle at a time. If anyone attempts to assist a combatant, the hermits are under orders to cut you down."

On cue, the hermits shuffle from the wheat, breaking stalk to stand guard around the perimeter.

"Cut us down?" My gaze cut from them to Carl and back again.

"Don't worry, Archer. Mortal weapons aren't fatal to warriors of the Zodiac, though I can see where *you* might be worried." Talus sneers, encouraged by the laughter of the nearest Los Angeles initiates. "Which half of you is mortal, anyway? Top or bottom? Or are you split right down the middle?"

"Talus," War growls.

I snap my fingers like I'm trying to remember something. "Hold up. Zoe told me this once, and I wrote it down so I wouldn't forget."

"Ashlyn," Carl warns.

I search my pants pockets, growing almost frantic before I find what I'm looking for. Victorious, I sigh in relief, smile at Talus, and come back out with my middle finger held high.

"You—" He flounders, flushing red. "I hope Rometra stomps your ass."

"I hope Beckett stomps yours."

And I really do. I hate this guy. If he were a breakfast cereal, he'd be frosted dog shit.

Jiggling the hat to regain the spotlight, Carl raises his voice. "Additionally, combatants must not step foot outside of the main circle. Do so, and you're also fair game for the hermits."

In other words, don't slip and fall on all the bloodshed.

"You may fight as fair or dirty as you like as long as you adhere to the stipulation of the trial card. Which is ..."

There is no sound in the field except for the wind in the wheat and the laboring breath of the hermits. Carl chooses a card and lifts it high. "The Condor and the Bull."

A murmur snakes around the battlefield.

"Of course," I hear Beck say above the hissing sound. "A perfect marriage between the heavens and the earth."

I don't know what that means, so I look around, waiting for the wheat to part again and reveal a big, ugly bird or a red-eyed bull. Instead, all I see are drooling hermits and Talus's grin as he crosses his arms and glares at me.

"What the hell are the Condor and the Bull?" I ask as Carl returns to his dais.

Nia frowns. "A trial passed down from the Andeans."

"Nope. Don't know them."

"A pre-Columbian troop." Thayer clarifies, not looking at me. The smell of slightly rotting fruit tickles my nose, and I realize it's him. He's discouraged. "Back then, a powerful bull would be lashed to a sharp-taloned condor, and they'd fight to the death."

I grimace. "Why exactly?"

"The condor represents the celestial realm, and the bull represents the earthly one." War supplies. I don't scent worry on her, but her eyes have gone tight. "The duality of binding opposing forces symbolizes the wholeness of the Universe."

"Awesome for the Andeans," I say, "but what does that mean for us?"

"Well, seeing as how we're fresh out of condors and bulls…"

It takes me a few seconds, but I jolt when the realization finally dawns. "No way!"

Everyone's staring at me now, but I don't care. Whirling, I grab Beck by the arm and hiss, "You guys are going to tie me to that psycho?"

"It's the card that was drawn," Beck replies lowly. "We're just lucky we didn't get one drawn from the traditions of the ancient Greeks. Those Spartans were crazy."

Sadly, this is the sanest thing anyone has said all day … and it makes me want to cry. I glance over, following Rometra's imposing form as she turns her back. "So what happens after we're leashed together? A fight to the death?"

It's a joke, but Thayer looks at me like I'm a crazy Spartan. "No. Just until one of you is incapacitated."

Groaning, I rub a hand over my face. That sounds a lot like dead to me.

Carl locates the ropes and calls Thayer and Emerson forward.

"Ten seconds, remember?" Nia tries as I watch them each offer up an arm for binding.

I know this isn't her fault, but I'm not in the mood for platitudes. "Yeah, well, that's about five seconds longer than Rometra needs to crush me!"

Soon, we're all leashed together, forming four united pairs of combatants instead of eight initiates.

Carl returns to the safety of his dais, where he picks up his pen and sits. The hermits intersperse themselves equidistant along the battlefield's perimeter. Incidentally, they look happier than I've ever seen them. I wonder what's going to happen next.

"First combatants," Carl calls, without preamble. "Emerson and Thayer!"

Oh.

That's what.

26

SOMETIMES YOU'RE THE CONDOR, SOMETIMES YOU'RE THE BULL.

Thayer and Emerson face off across the battlefield.

The rope linking them hangs slack, cutting the circle directly in half. Thayer warms up by doing jumping jacks that have his cape jerking back from his shoulders, pushups that cause his grunts to be eaten up by the stubby earth, and a couple of sit-ups that may or may not have been cut short by the jarring sound of his ripping pants.

Emerson remains still, stoic, and unblinking, and the other Los Angeles initiates follow her lead. They don't breathe, they don't blink, and neither do I. Until...

"Let's do this thing!" Thayer yells, leaping to his feet.

Edging away from Rometra, I lean over to War. "Did his voice just crack?"

"Yes." War shoots a worried look over at Carl, who is drawing so fast that he can't be doing more than a rough sketch before turning each page. "The forces of evil will never take us seriously now."

Emerson is, though.

I can see her breaking Thayer's body into strike zones, just like Zoe taught me. She's already figured out that his dominant hand is tied to hers and makes up for it by looping their tethered rope around her fist. Still jumping in place, Thayer copies the move, but neither moves to begin the fight.

So how does it start? I wonder. A gunshot in the air? A ring-side bell? A war cry from the combatants?

No one seems to know. They've never been in this situation before either, and even reading about previous trials wouldn't reveal something so mundane. Manuals skipped the boring parts.

We all look at Carl, but his dark head is bent, his shoulders hunched around his ears as he works. Rometra clears her throat just as Carl's pencil falls still.

He blinks when he finds us all looking at him, almost like he'd forgotten we were there. "Go."

Emerson snaps her end of the rope like a whip.

Thayer jerks forward like a fish on the end of a line, and the crowd erupts. He rights himself immediately, digging in his heels, but Emerson anticipates this and allows the rope to grow slack so that he stumbles backward. The hermits nearest him howl and raise their scythes, hoping he steps from the circle. War tenses next to me, ready to run if Thayer needs her, but he wins his balance again.

When Emerson snaps the rope this time, she doesn't stop.

Hand over hand, she reels him forward, cutting the length between them by half in a blink. When Thayer finds his footing, she rewards him with a boot to the chest.

Rometra laughs, full-throated and loudly, next to me, and the rest of the Los Angeles initiates join in.

These are *allies*?

I glance at War, but she doesn't even know I'm there. She's too busy biting her bottom lip, staring at Thayer as if willing her strength into him.

It's not working.

With a yell, Emerson launches forward to take Thayer's back. Something inside of him—some instinct—kicks in just then, though, because, without looking, he kicks *out*. Emerson's breath blasts from her chest, but she arrests her tumble by wrenching the rope and pulling Thayer along with her. He wheels forward and trips on top of her.

I can't hear their labored breaths now—the crowd is too loud —but I scent the sour fear and whipped tang of adrenaline as Emerson jerks her bound hand overhead, lassoing Thayer's neck.

War's whimper is the girliest sound I've ever heard her make, and one that catches in my own throat as Emerson finds her knees, her feet, and then drags Thayer back to the arena's center by his cape. Holding the rope tight with the other hand, she lets the cape fall over his head and then proceeded to pummel his body and face with whipping kicks.

Fight as fair or as dirty as you like, Carl said, and Emerson has chosen the latter.

I can't watch. This world, this violence, is not for me. These people act like it's so normal to battle and fight and hurt one another.

But it shouldn't be normal, should it?

Yet I can't look away, either.

Instead, I look to Carl to stop it, but he's safe on his dais, like an untouchable king, and his head's back down as he does his job, scribbling fast. Everyone else just stands there like the beat-down has nothing to do with them, but it does.

It has everything to do with all of us. We're supposed to be on the same team.

"Stop."

It's not my voice. The only reason I hear it over Emerson's growls, or the dull thud of her body striking Thayer's, is because I've unconsciously inched closer to War so that our shoulders are touching. Though only a whisper, the word drops into my gut, wheels back up, and slaps me so that I stagger into the ring.

I push Emerson away before she can deliver one more steel-booted kick. "Stop!"

I catch her unaware and half-tipped, her right foot raised, and she backpedals wildly. She falls to her back with an alarmed cry.

Outside of the circle.

Surprised wails spring into the air as the hermits rush in. Emerson rolls just as a scythe embeds itself in the ground where her head rested. She reaches the arena in a crab crawl, and the two hermits nearest her rage with such blood lust that they turn on each other.

Oops.

"No interfering, Archer." These words hit me right before I'm yanked backward by my wrist. I hear the wheat rustling as the hermits anticipate my fall, but Beck's hand is suddenly at my back, steadying me before I can topple out of the circle. A hermit with a bright pink bow nailed to its mangled earlobe screeches behind me.

"She wasn't interfering," War snaps, pointing at the battlefield. "He's done."

Emerson looks dazed as she stands over Thayer's unmoving body. She blinks, head slowly swinging from the wailing hermits at the arena's edge, then back down to the boy she just kicked into unconsciousness. Putting two and two together, her hand floats up to cover her mouth.

I guess my mind isn't the only one that protects itself with big blank spots in the place of painful memories.

This is how good people can do bad things, comes the thought, unbidden.

Carl, one of those good people, calls up the next contestants.

THE NEXT FIGHT HAS NONE OF THE THEATRICS OF THE FIRST, AND once Thayer's immobile body is moved to the sidelines, even the spectators seem to remember themselves. Or at least that they're all supposed to be on the same team. Beck and Talus take to the field in an unnatural silence ... then Beck removes his shirt.

"Yeah," Rometra breathes from my other side. "I'd eat that up with a spoon."

I grit my teeth, and not just because her words mirror my thoughts. Of course, he just doesn't want Talus to be able to control him via his clothing. Thayer's cape was a good example. Yet the sun almost slams off his abs, and it curls atop the roll of his shoulders like it wishes to linger there.

I know how the sun feels.

Talus isn't quite as charmed. He snarls as he removes his shirt, too, though he chooses to rip it from his bulky frame and drop it to the shorn wheat with a menacing growl. The hermits beat the ground with their scythes in approval. Beck glances down at his black tee-shirt, which dangles from the tied rope at his wrist.

So maybe he hadn't given himself every advantage.

He shrugs and holds a hand out to Talus as if to say, hold on, but Talus isn't one to pause for breath, much less thought. He yanks Beck forward, giving another mighty roar, which he no doubt hopes will be splayed across the pages of a manual. I can almost see it arching in a perfect dialogue bubble above his head. I'm wondering if Carl is drawing it that way as Beck stumbles forward ... directly into the path of Talus's already-cocked fist.

It's not until later, replaying the incident in my mind, that I realize the dangling shirt is the perfect camouflage atop Beck's rock-hard fist. It's only in retrospect that I can see, as Beck already has, that while Talus is brutally strong, his knowledge of body mechanics sucks.

Or maybe Beck is just that good at disguising his intentions. He stumbles one-two-three—perfectly balanced steps—then plows his fist into Talus's jaw before the budding giant even knows it's raised.

All that bombastic bulk goes down like a plank of wood ... but dumber.

Beck pounds him once more for insurance, then straightens, turns, and climbs back into his shirt as he walks away.

Rometra gives him a slow, punctuated clap that brings the rest of the field—except for Talus—back to life. Even Thayer is recovered enough to sit up and give a weak fist pump. Fast healers, I think, and because I know my words won't be welcome once the noise dies down, I turn to War quickly.

"Good luck."

Either she doesn't hear me, or she's gone back to ignoring me. Either way, she stares unblinkingly at the empty arena. She's already fighting in her mind, imagining herself winning. Zoe used to look like that all the time.

"Next up," Carl calls after Talus has been moved, "Chris and—"

"It's Cruz!" Chris complains from War's other side.

"Cruz and War!"

"Wait!"

Thayer staggers to his feet. At this point, he's probably the only person War would wait for, though she does it with gritted teeth.

"What?" Her eyes dart between him and Cruz, who's crossing to the field's far side, where the Los Angeles initiates are already cheering him on.

"So I just..." Thayer, not great with words even when he hasn't been kicked in the head, trails off. "Well, I've been meaning to tell you—"

"Spit it out, Storge! I'm going into battle!"

"Okay!" He winces with the yell and grabs his head like it might roll off. "Just ... even though you have rancid Shadow blood coursing in your veins, and even though you're a second-born misfit in a world that honors only first—"

"By the stars, man, do you have a point?" War snaps.

"Even though you're all those things," Thayer continues, still holding his head. "You're also powerful and stoic and amazing. And no matter what, I'm glad that your powerful, stoic, amazing ass is on my side."

War stares at him, eyes wide and unblinking, and then shakes her head slightly.

"Unbelievable," she mutters as she takes the field.

Thayer looks at me.

I sigh and roll my eyes.

If we were in the real world—the mortal one—I'd feel bad for War, being matched against a boy already grown into most of his male strength, but this is not the real world. It almost makes me jealous of War's matchup, but to be jealous of anyone or anything in this unwanted realm is so messed up that I push the thought away.

They spring forward at the same time, rope forgotten.

War dodges low, attempting to trap Cruz's legs and climb to his back, but he widens his stance at the last minute and fumbles for the rope at her wrist. She circles back quickly, and he can't pull up the slack and block her fists simultaneously. He misses her straight punch but manages to stop what would have been a far more damaging hook and squares up on her immediately.

She's like a viper, I think, watching her fists whip out and back, her gaze steady between blows. Cruz is no Beckett, yet he's disciplined, and his strikes are equally practiced. They seem content to trade blows, mere pugilists, for a bit, an exchange that will show well in the series of panels that Carl is surely drawing now. I'm trying so hard to catch every movement with my half-mortal sight that I almost forget to breathe.

War double-pumps a straight jab, catching Cruz on the chin long enough to crowd in, but stumbles over the rope, and her cross lands short. She catches herself, but one boot heel edges from the circle. The hermit closest to her lunges, sickle high.

She doesn't flinch like Emerson had. Instead, she back-kicks the creature like a pissed-off mule, and the hermit flips head over tail with an exhalation that stinks up the whole field. War's pivoting back just as Cruz's uppercut catches her square on the jaw. Her head rocks sideways in a motion not meant for a neck.

It's like watching a god fall to earth.

Even Cruz has to blink away a moment of disbelief. Then he raises his arms high and turns his back on his vanquished opponent. The encircling initiates erupt in applause.

It's an outcome I never even considered. Open-mouthed, I stare at War's unmoving form. If *she* can't win, what chance do I have to survive?

I swallow past my suddenly dry mouth as Beck and Thayer retrieve War's body. The other initiates stop applauding. Cruz lowers his arms. And Rometra moves into the ring. Her sure-footed glide takes her right past her sister's prone body, but she doesn't look down. Instead, she crosses to the far side of the field, draws our rope taut, and turns.

And just like that, I'm up.

27

AN ARCHER IS BORN.

Once, when I was fourteen and feeling stronger and knowing more about the wind and the waves than ever before, I lost my rail in the tube of an epic wave.

It took me for a few cartwheels before it was done with me, and the feeling was like being whipped around the inside of a washing machine. For a terrifying few seconds, I had no idea which way was up or down, or even how I would catch my next breath.

It's how I feel now.

There's yelling on all sides of me, but I can't make out any discernible words. My eyes dart left and right, trying to make sense of the fists pumping in the air, but it's like the shutter-stop action on a camera. All I catch are the sharp teeth of the hermits as they leer, and the even sharper edges of their scythes winking in the sun.

"Hey, Archer!" A voice cuts through the sound of my heartbeat in my ears. "Aim straight and true!"

Thayer, who has just lost his place in the troop, is cheering me on.

Yet anyone can see it's hopeless. Rometra stands directly

across from me, our rope dividing the circle precisely in half. Viewed from above, it would look like a clock face projecting precisely six o'clock.

Too bad I'm not wearing my diver's watch because I wonder, in that detached way that you do when you know something bad is about to happen, what time it really is. What time will it be when she hits me?

What time when I fall?

The front of my mind is so occupied with this question that I don't even realize my breathing has sped up, and I can't seem to calm it. My feet are nailed in place—I'm not yet in the circle—and it looks like I'll probably pass out before Rometra even throws a punch.

Suddenly, something blocks out the images of blood splatter floating before my eyes. It is Beckett-shaped, and it seems to be trying to teach me how to breathe again. I take a few more shallow breaths, and Beck snaps into focus. The sounds he's making coalesce into words.

"You need to calm down," he's telling me. "Think of the ocean. Know that it's still out there, exists outside of this place, and is still a part of you."

The breeze that skims its surface. The waves that roll until they reach shore with a deafening crash.

My body being slammed against the unyielding earth until it's smashed to bits.

I whimper.

"Remember," he whispers, "Just twenty seconds of insane courage. That's all you need."

That penetrates my stupor. I tilt my head. "You guys said ten."

"What?"

"In the cottage." I panic at Beck's answering frown. "You said all I needed was ten seconds of insane courage and...and... embarrassing bravery... and you promised something great would come of it."

He glances Rometra's way. "Twenty is better."

"What about me, Beckett?" Rometra calls from across the arena. "Got any sweet words of encouragement for an old friend?"

"Yes." Beck steps back and turns. "Remember that you're one of the good guys now."

Rometra smiles.

I don't think she remembers.

"Shadow or Light, good or evil, you still need a killer instinct to survive this world." And she blows Beck a kiss that sits like oil on the air.

"Just go," I tell him.

"But—"

"Seriously, Beck." I shake my head as I look right past him. "You've done enough."

I only shift my gaze once he's moved from my periphery, and when I do, I see Carl finally looking at me. Unlike Rometra, he's not smiling, which makes me wonder what he knows.

My heart slams against my ribs as I step into the ring, and I instinctively begin moving counter-clockwise to Rometra's slow, steady stalk. The stubby wheat cracks under my feet. When Rometra switches directions, I do, too.

She switches again, taking her time. "I can smell you from here, Archer."

"Weird," I said, voice shaking. "I showered just this morning."

"Your nerves give you away." She jerks her chin. "You fear me."

"No, duh."

Rometra's gaze narrows as tittering pops up along the perimeter. Even if I could remember something from Zoe's midnight training sessions, what could prepare me for this? I try to think, what would Zoe do? But my heart is beating too loudly, and so are the cries of the other initiates as they urge Rometra on to violence.

I have no idea what Zoe would do. I *do* know what to do when someone tries to yank me forward and into their strike zone, though.

I run.

Momentum—and keeping as close to the edge of the arena as I dare—pulls the rope taut between us so that we swing around like weights on each end. I can hear the hermits grunt as I circle the perimeter, panting hard with breath that stains the air in fetid gasps. Some even tear at their own flesh because they want so badly to reach for me and can't.

But nobody wants it more than Rometra.

She finally stops rotating and takes two giant steps forward. I lose my balance with the unexpected slack, and the hermit nearest me shuffles into place, roaring with bloodlust. Two hands unexpectedly land square on my back, and suddenly I'm stumbling forward, thrown back into the arena before my foot touches one stalk of wheat.

"Initiates!" I hear as I pull upright. "No interfering."

"I just saved her life," comes Talus's lazy reply, and he may be right. The hermit he's foiled snarls its displeasure. I won't thank him, though, because he's also thrown me back into Rometra's path.

She doesn't dodge me—she's too pleased for that—but she is forced to adjust, which is how I see. Left ankle.

It's the smallest of movements—remember, we heal fast—but the weight shifting is there, along with the wince. She's hurt.

I lean right, put out my arm, and flip my weight atop it to kick out with my leg. It catches Rometra on her injured ankle, and I immediately kick my heel back, thwacking her Achilles tendon.

Someone calls my name. It's too faint to tell if it's male or female, but it's a bell clear, two-syllable beat. Suddenly, I am someone to root for.

I shift back to my feet, and as my name takes flight in the air, I imagine for a moment that out of the two combatants—the bull and the condor—I am the condor.

Rometra staggers to her feet, and as she balances, she pulls something long, black, and gleaming from her pocket. The condor in my mind hits the ground as Rometra yanks on the rope. I try to resist, but there's extra energy to the jolt, and though it's undoubtedly my imagination, I think something sparks around Rometra's frame. Either my hearing shorts out then, or the rest of the crowd has seen it, too, because an electric hush rolls over the circle, and it falls unnaturally silent.

She yanks again. I stumble toward whatever she's hiding behind her back, whatever's black and in her hand, and I plant my foot in the middle of the rope to stop the action. Rometra takes one impossibly long stride forward and punches me so hard that her laughter is still ringing in my ears as I fall.

That was a sprint, I realize, too late. Not a stride. I was just too mortal-blind to see it.

She also didn't hit me with her fist, though I only realize that once the metal baton falls to the ground in front of my nose.

A voice hisses hotly in my ear. "You are not an Archer, do you hear me? Not like me!"

Not like Joanna. Not like Zoe.

"You are a copy of a copy of a forgery."

I am. I know it.

I always have, I think … right before she pummels me into unconsciousness.

28

T.T.E.

There are places on the body that you only realize exist once someone hurts you. They are unmined depths that can be accessed only by those who want to cause you pain. I wonder if there are areas that respond to kindness in the same way, ones I don't know about ... but then I start puking and stop thinking altogether.

I've never wanted to escape my own body so badly. The throbbing drops along the inside of my skull in viscous drops, enveloping me in a tight cocoon of pain. I give in and drift away on the red tide.

The ocean awaits. Its waves rumble in my mind, unsteady at first but gaining rhythm with each ensuing ripple. I only know I'm dreaming when it dissolves and goes silent.

I shift to look for it and find my mother instead.

"Finally." Smiling up at me, she drops the sewing she'd been working on and pats the spot next to her on the sofa. It's the same one from my childhood; its cheery yellow and white stripes are untouched by age. Even my mother is as I remember, dark hair touching just below her shoulders in soft waves. I like this dream.

Curling up next to her, I tuck my feet beneath me and lean against her side as I've wanted to for so many years. Breathing deeply, I inhale the scents of roses, spearmint, and chamomile. The scents of home.

"I'm sorry," I say when I am so full of her that I feel like I will burst. "I didn't know you were waiting."

"Of course, I waited. I'm your mother."

Exactly what I've been trying to tell everyone. This is my mother. The mortal one. The one who sews. The one who waits.

"But why are you here?" I ask as her fingertips smooth back the hair at my temples.

"This is where I live now." Those light fingertips pause. "Didn't you know?"

"No." I shift into a sitting position but keep close enough that her body still warms mine. "I've never been here before."

"Oh." She returns her attention to the sewing in her lap. "That's sad."

I don't want her to be sad, so I search for a change in subject. "What are you working on?"

She smiles widely and holds up an intricate series of loops and knots that whirl around each other to create a useless but decorative pattern. "I'm tatting lace. Isn't it beautiful?"

It is, but it makes me frown. "It looks fragile."

She laughs like I'm joking, fingers moving like moths over her creation. "People always mistake what's beautiful, what's feminine, for weakness, don't they? But don't let that fool you. Look closer."

I see then that the rings are shaped like teardrops, and their points of connection are more intricate than a spider's web.

"It's as elaborate as a woman's worries," she sighs. "It's as complex as the way we love."

I reach out and test the stitches between my thumb and forefinger. They are silky, but they hold. "I thought it was just pretty."

"Sometimes. After all, there's nothing wrong with being 'just pretty.' You can never go wrong with being your prettiest self." She pauses, and the sides of her sweet mouth fall. But you must be yourself, Ashlyn."

Be myself.

"Here." She holds out the lace. "You try."

"Oh, no." I push it away. "I'll mess it up."

She laughs and places it back firmly in my hands. "It's impossible to mess up when you create from the center of your being."

That's where we are? That's where she lives?

Our fingertips touch as the thread passes from her hands to mine, and it's like being kissed by butterflies—gentle and light and too brief. I hold the lace like it's breakable, and hold my breath, too, at least until three new loops and whorls appear in the expanding pattern.

"See? The act of creation is your mind moving through your hands. It's like magic," she winks at me. Or power."

You're a copy of a copy of a forgery.

"I don't have any power."

"Oh, pish!" It's as close to cursing as my mother ever got, and I giggle, hearing it again. "Just because someone doesn't acknowledge your power doesn't mean it's not there. As long as *you* know who you are."

Who am I?

I'm a surfer chick who is now free to leave the cottage and go anywhere I want. I'm a friend who has fulfilled her duty here and can now say 'Aloha' to Hawaii or take that dream trip to Fiji or the Gold Coast.

As the next generation of superheroes and villains battle it out for supremacy over the world's population, I'll have my feet in the sand and my head in the clouds because I'm also the girl who did her job—who got her butt kicked—so that the neo-Zodiac could rise.

"Oh, look what you just did," my mother says in wonder.

My mind drifted away, but my hands did their work. "Did I screw it up?"

"On the contrary. You made good use of all that worry. You turned those feelings into something good." She beams with pride. "Clever girl."

Three distinct letters now thread the breezy pattern. TTE.

They don't fit at all with the rest of the design, but they look perfect there, as if they were meant to be. "I don't know how I did that."

"You don't need to know how. Just know that it's natural for you to create. Get it?"

I don't think so, but my mother suddenly stretches, threading her fingers behind her head with a yawn. "I like it here. I think I'm going to stay."

The whole room gives a white-hot pulse as my heart jumps. "I'd love that."

"Really?" She looks pleased, and I wonder how she could not know that. I've only wanted to be back here, with her, for five long years.

"Yes. I swear."

"Wonderful!" She claps her hands, leans forward, and then grasps me hard by the shoulders. Her smile drops, and her gaze barrels into mine. "Then, by the stars, Ashlyn ... wake up!"

It's the deep of night. That's the first thing I register. The moon slips into the room on bright, silent paws, slinking across the foot of my bed in its draping brilliance.

The second thing? I am not alone.

"Does it hurt?"

The voice brings me back to reality, concretely placing Rometra back in my consciousness, my life, and my bedroom.

She is silhouetted at my window, and the sight of her tight, coiled body drives away all of my mother's dreamy assurances. I glance around the room, but there's no one else in sight.

"Yes." My voice is still in dreamland, wispy and cracked, like wind over the desert floor.

She shrugs. "But you got what you wanted."

What, my ass handed to me by a future agent of Light? I wonder, watching her shift to face me. She is grace personified. She is bonded in steel.

I keep my gaze fastened on her as I shift in bed. A bolt of pain shoots across my temple, and I wince.

"You now have complete freedom from responsibility in this world." She tilts her head as she watches me struggle. "Nobody's going to want you now."

An unexpected pang hurtles through my heart at that. I ignore it and force my voice to be louder, stronger. "How did you get in here, Rometra?"

"I followed the scent." She jerks her head. "Eau de mortal."

That's not what I meant, and she knows it. Smirking, she picks up the pink bottle from the windowsill. I want to scream at her not to touch it, but I don't dare.

"They say your heart stopped for a moment out there."

I try to push myself into a sitting position, but even that tiny effort makes me dizzy. I fall back to the pillow and say, "I don't remember anything."

"Guess some things never change, huh?" She's looking directly at me, but with the light of the moon directly behind her, her features are wiped away like chalk from a board. There and then gone. "You know what I think happened? I think your human side died. In fact, I saw the light leave your eyes. It was like watching your soul escape on that final sigh."

She shifts to gaze at the fragile bottle in her hand, and I hold my breath, not daring to move. No matter what, I know I mustn't show Rometra how important that bottle is. Or how much it scares me.

After considering it for another moment, one in which I don't even blink, she sets it back down. "Pretty."

People always mistake what's beautiful, what's feminine, for weakness, don't they?

"You should leave, Rometra," I say lowly, my chest burning, my head pounding.

"Or what? You'll tell your mommy?"

She takes a step toward me, and I inch back against my pillow without willing it. The pain in my temple resumes a low throb.

"You know, I did you a favor by beating your ass," she says, now bedside. "Nobody should walk around thinking they have inherent greatness blossoming inside them."

"I was only fighting for my—"

"Troop?" She sneers the word.

"My friends," I say. "They're the heroes, not me."

She gives a sharp, little laugh as she turns to leave. "Then I guess no one told you."

I can't help it. I feed her the line even though I know whatever she says will hurt. "What?"

She regards me one more time over her shoulder, and I can't help but think that in the dark, in the night, she looks like a perfect example of what she was born to be.

A Shadow.

"There's no such thing as heroes anymore. Only survivors."

And then she lets herself out.

WHEN I WAKE AGAIN, BECK IS IN THE DARK, SEATED IN A CHAIR across the room. He rises when he sees me shift and tries on a smile. It's too stiff. That's how I know I look terrible.

"You're healing well," he lies, reaching my side.

I touch my head gingerly, pushing at my temple where Rometra struck. Nothing severe happens, so I throw my legs over the side of the bed, pausing to make sure they'll hold weight before I rise and limp to the window. Outside, the full moon bulges like it's about to burst at the seams, and the forest floor glows, though this time, nothing moves.

"Still think I was born for this?" I mutter, pushing into a sitting position.

"I still think you have your weapons."

Evolution has turned your humanity into a weapon.

I snort but don't answer. My near-death experience has robbed me of my excellent humor.

"I was worried," he says, making that two of us.

Rometra's taunt ricochets through my mind. "Because I'm human?"

"Because you're Ashlyn."

I don't know what to say to that. It's not just his words but the weight behind them... guilt, regret, and something else that feels like confession.

Still, the strange dream about my mother sits acutely in my mind. I don't know what TTE means or why I had the dream now and never before. All I know is I've done my duty. I'm now free to do and go where I want.

My silence tells Beck all he needs to know. "So what will you do now?"

I look at him sharply. He returns the look. Of course, he does. It's dark, I'm injured, but even so, the hunger for the ocean probably lives in my gaze. Rometra will fill the Sagittarian sign on the zodiac wheel. The neo-troop will rise. The human children will be safe. I'll be safe.

"The Zodiac world is in order," I point out.

"Yes."

His short answer causes an unexpected wash of loneliness to swim through me.

Weird.

Depression isn't my vibe, and being bummed over something I never even wanted makes no sense at all. I should be happy. I *am* happy. My life can now resume its regularly scheduled programming. Not like the other losers ... War or Thayer, or even that big kid, Talus. I can envision a life outside of a troop system and this world.

They're stuck in this one.

"I guess I'll just go back to being normal," I say slowly. "Just regular ol' Ashlyn."

"You think?"

Beck's doubt catches me off-guard. "What do you mean?"

"I mean, I was there. I watched you for a year. Sure, I thought I had the wrong girl the first time I saw you. Actually, I thought my enhanced senses had totally shorted out."

"Why? What'd I look like?"

"A waterlogged surf rat who subsided on sunscreen, board wax, and fish tacos."

I'd love to be offended by that, but I'm suddenly distracted. "Mmm...tacos."

"Then I saw you surf, and there it was—that drive, determination, and aggression that the Archer women are famous for—a stubbornness bordering on recklessness. That's when I knew. There was more to you than coconut oil and cheap flip-flops."

I narrow my eyes at his smile. "You've had a whole year to tell me this. Why now?"

"You might want to stay," he tries.

Ah, now I see where this is headed. "I might wanna do a header into shark-infested waters, too, but I doubt it."

"You might want to stop being such a smartass all the time."

"I doubt that, too."

He leans closer. "You might want to let me kiss you like I've wanted to since the first time I saw you racing down a mountain of water, dreaming with your eyes wide open."

All my expectations—what he will say, how I will answer— flips on me like I've been tubed. My breath catches short, like in the sea, even as my heart revs. Suddenly, it's like we're back

beneath that gazebo, and that's when I realize that a kiss interrupted doesn't mean a kiss *forgotten.*

Sometimes, it just makes it more desired than ever.

"Let me kiss you," he continues, his voice honey-thick, "while
we're alone and we have the chance, and I can show you exactly
how you made me feel for over a year."

I don't know if I let him, but we suddenly go from being
alone, together, to simply together. His lips are as firm as his
fingertips and as warm and soft as the feeling that blooms inside
me whenever I catch a smooth pocket ride on a roaring sea. The
ocean brought out my passion, but I am bringing this out in him,
which is a power all on its own.

Yet he possesses the same power.

My ears buzz, and my vision blurs. My skin tingles as his
palms slip to my shoulders and mine cup his elbows. His fingers
climb into my hair, and there goes the thought, whipping away
from me on a dizzying whorl of warmth as he pulls me closer. His
mouth fits and molds to mine like it was made to go there. He is
gentle but not cautious, steady but unrelenting.

"Wow." I'm breathing hard when we finally pull back, and I
have to wait until everything inside of me stops spinning before I
open my eyes. "You even kiss like a superhero."

"Have you kissed many superheroes?" His mouth looks even
more gorgeous after kissing me. How is that even possible?

"Only you. But a lot," I admit. "In my mind."

"Then kiss me some more."

I do as he says.

Hey, what do you expect? I am but a mere mortal.

"I'm glad you're okay," he whispers sometime later, and that's
when I know for sure that Rometra was right. I'm not supposed to
be okay. I'm not supposed to be alive. But I am. For some reason,
I've been given a second chance.

And I'm glad, too.

29

THE FALL-OUT.

Between getting beat up, knocked out, then kissed ... and then kissed some more, I'm pretty wiped out and end up sleeping for the rest of the next day.

When I wake, it's to a setting sun and a plate full of breakfast foods—eggs, bacon, toast, my beloved coffee left hot in a covered mug. Whatever's left of my sense of smell tells me it's Beck who's brought me sustenance and, possibly, even lingered over me while I slept. I smile at the thought before digging into the food like I'm on the attack.

As soon as I'm finished eating, I pack.

It's not like I don't wish all these future heroes well... I do— even Rometra. If it means keeping the mortal population free of the Elders and their evil supervillain plans, I wish this aspiring neo-troop complete world domination, along with a heaping side of moral superiority and kick-ass weaponry.

And, yeah ... I wish I could have a ton more of those kisses that make me feel like I've air-dropped a fifty-foot swell.

But wishing is for people who don't already know what they want. I've known that since waking, long ago, to find that my parents were dead and I was alone.

I want life to be simple and safe.

I want to be free and happy.

I want to spend every day looking out over the ocean ... but even more than that, I want to focus on what's good in life. Not what's evil.

And you can't do that when you're forever looking for shadows.

Tonight, though, I will witness the rise of a new generation of heroes. The claiming ceremony begins at midnight precisely, and since neither mortals nor the conquered can be near the claiming circle at the appointed time, I'll have to watch this particular paranormal party from the safe confines of the comic book shop.

Carl, the other mortal-who-doesn't-belong-but-is-still-here-anyway, will record the proceedings from there. Since they will never be a part of this troop, Thayer, War, and Talus must also watch from afar.

Just after eleven p.m., I ready myself to meet War and Thayer in the grove beneath the cottage. I wear my beach clothes this time, though I shove my mask in my cargoes. Then, I carefully fold the pink bottle Zoe gifted me in the sleeve of my softest t-shirt and bury it back in the backpack. I don't see myself ever opening it, but I don't want to leave it at the cottage, either.

I'm only expecting Thayer and War, so I'm surprised when I drop to the forest floor to discover four initiates waiting in the dark grove. Lanterns have been strung for the occasion, and I stare through the pooling light, unblinking, searing the moment in my mind.

I'll want to remember this later when I'm dozing on some far-off beach, sand in my toes, the knowledge of other worlds playing on my eyelids.

Thayer spots me first.

Smiling, he bounds up to me, so much coiled energy in his step that he threatens to blow. Like mine, his bruises have faded, and if he's upset about his loss, he doesn't show it. He's even refastened the cape that got him destroyed in the arena around his shoulders and shoots me a lopsided grin when he catches my raised eyebrow.

"It's okay. I've hemmed it. See?"

He has chopped it off with what appears to be his teeth. I'm not sure it's an improvement, but who am I to question a future superhero?

"How are you feeling?" I ask instead.

"Same as you, I guess," he says, and only then does a shadow slip across his gaze. He erases it with a shake of his head. "But there will be other troops."

"You okay?" Nia asks me, flanking my other side.

She's dressed for success in a leather skater skirt to go with her button-down, which she's knotted at the waist. She also has a bomber jacket for warmth, with plenty of pockets for her weaponry of choice.

"Wow," I say, looking her up and down. "You look ..."

"Silly?" she worries, tugging at her skirt.

"Hawt?" Thayer responds. His enormous grin earns him an elbow in the gut.

"Like a very lethal fashion influencer," I finally finish.

Frowning, Nia tilts her head to one side. "Thanks?"

"And you..." I say, turning to War, who stiffens when I pause.

She turns the cat-eye slant of her unblinking gaze on me while Beck shoots me a warning look from behind her. He's already told me not to bring up the loss. War is taking it harder than anyone else, and she won't want to get emotional, especially in front of Rometra.

But just because you don't mention something doesn't mean it's gone away. I know that.

"You look even more heroic than the day we met," I finally finish.

Maybe it's just the reflective sparkle of her shirt, but something shines in her eyes. Her shoulders loosen, and a sigh escapes her body.

"My father always told me that there are two kinds of people in the world," she finally says. "Those who see themselves as victims and drown in a river of self-indulgent tears, and those who turn their sadness into wings that will allow them to fly. I will fly."

"I look forward to seeing that in the manuals," I answer truthfully, and she gives me a smile that's still bittersweet—and a bit beaten up—but at least it's hopeful.

I know. I've worn one just like it before.

THE LOS ANGELES INITIATES ARRIVE AFTER THAT, FALLING FROM the cottage chute like acorns from a tree.

They whoop as they hit the ground, obviously excited, and suck in great gulps of the promising night air as if doing so is what will stitch them to their desired fate. Rometra pauses to wait for Beck, but he waves her on, choosing to stay with me instead. Her eyes narrow as she takes in the way his shoulder touches mine, but then she spots the backpack slung over my shoulders, and a smile touches her lips.

"Don't let her get to you," Beck tells me as she stalks away.

"I'm not," I assure him, and it's pretty much true. I no longer care about their shared past because what happened last night between us has already changed that. It's changed him. I sense it in how he watches me and sees it in how he moves. He's like a satellite in orbit, orienting himself in relation to where I stand.

It helps that he and Nia are about to get their own happily-ever-afters. With the stability that a troop provides and the support of strong allies, she'll never again be powerless to help those she loves.

And Beckett? He was simply made for this.

Maybe that's why he tries to convince me once more to stay.

"We'll have so much power after tonight that we can hide you. You'll always be protected. I swear it."

I wait for everyone else to exit the grove, then look up at him and place my hand on his cheek. "There's more to life than hiding."

My time with Zoe taught me that much.

So we emerge from the grove into a swollen night, as if bee-stung by the full moon. It was shining before, but tonight, it seems to take up more of the sky than it has a right to. It's almost like it knows that right now, it's significant in a way the other planets are not. It makes me want to keep my head tipped to the sky as we walk.

Yet my footsteps stutter when we reach the arena. The hermits are there, splayed equidistance around its edges like numbers on a clock face, waiting as instructed. Their backs face the wheat, and their expressions are as impassive as stone.

"Do they look different?" I say aloud before I can stop myself.

"They're humpbacked, drooling, and unable to form a cohesive thought," War deadpans. "Looks normal to me."

Yet something flip-flops inside of me as the nearest hermit flinches at my passing. I want to ask Beck why they're needed at all, but then Rometra rounds on us all. Her mouth curves upward as she makes eye contact with me.

"This is our stop," she says, smirking. "No mortals. No losers."

I roll my eyes. Like I care. Yet I'm the only one who sees how Thayer places his hand at the small of War's back and gives her a reassuring rub.

It's Talus, standing next to Rometra, who protests. "Watch it, Rom."

"Don't like it? Then don't lose." She shoots back, then turns her back on us all. "See you after the Rise, Mother-Lovers."

The four of us are left standing on the perimeter of the cut circle while the twelve chosen initiates take their places on the elevated dais. It has been re-centered atop the shorn wheat and expanded in twelve pie-shaped directions. As the chosen initiates look for their star sign stamped atop the split planks, only Beck glances back at us, his expression unreadable.

It gives me an idea.

"C'mon." For the first time, I'm the one to recover first, and I take the lead through the wheat. "And put on your masks, just in case Carl is already drawing this."

Even Talus shoots me a grateful look. All they have to do now is place one foot in front of the other without worry that anyone else can see their face.

The four of us reach Carl's shop just as the first bolt of lightning cuts across the sky. It makes a dye cutout of the distant mountains, making me want to reach out and pluck them from the air. Instead, I gaze at my diver's watch—it's a quarter to midnight.

Thayer and War greet Carl, who waits on the wooden porch. Talus just deflates atop the steps like his bones have slid from his body. I'd feel sorry for him if he weren't working so hard to ignore the rest of us, so I greet Carl instead.

Except he won't meet my eye.

Instead, he jerks his chin at my backpack and hands me a pair of binoculars. "Going somewhere?"

He knows I am but turns away before I can answer. I busy myself with my binoculars, pretending to bring the now-distant dais into focus while he resettles into the chair near the shop's door. A low rumble of thunder reverberates through the wooden deck as he pulls his drawing pad onto his lap.

"Hey, Ash," Thayer says out of nowhere, binoculars lifted toward the arena. "You're right about the hermits. They look kinda drunk."

"They always look like that," War retorts, arms folded, not lifting her binoculars. Maybe her eyesight's better than ours, and she can see from here. Or maybe she doesn't want to.

I retrain my sights on the arena and use the next bolt of lightning—the closest yet—to search out the hermit facing us. It's a male who's sadly decided tonight's event is clothing-optional. Despite that and the cool mountain air, sweat dots its broad, bulbous brow as it hunches beneath the lowering sky.

Again, baseless worry snakes in my gut.

The hermits are indebted to Beck, and he's ordered them to protect the initiates. If the claiming ceremony works—if it's anything like what *used* to happen when an initiate came into their full-fledged powers—they'll be momentarily helpless.

Yes, being gifted powers by the Universe is transformative, but it also renders you immobile. In short, you really don't want to be ambushed during the transformation.

Meanwhile, ozone thickens in the air, shocking through filling in my teeth that I don't even have. The skies turn muddy above us, cirrus clouds like dough sliding into place overhead. They block out the constellations, pulling shades over the eyes of the sky. Only the moon remains circled directly above as thunder appears from nowhere to slice at the smooth air.

I glance back. Carl's hands move rapidly over the drawing pad on his lap. He has no binoculars, yet each deft stroke brings the scene before us to life. As he draws a bolt of lightning, thunder rumbles in the distance.

The uneasiness I felt earlier now flip-flops hard in my gut, yet I remain silent. Every initiate on that dais has dreamed of nothing but this moment ever since the Zodiac world fell. Who am I to interfere?

"It's time." War murmurs just as the twelve initiates take two forward steps.

They arrange themselves in their positions on the zodiac wheel, Aries to Pisces, and the instant they're all in place, a bolt of lightning rockets from the heavens. It strikes like a cobra, merciless and fast, and sears a hole into the platform's center. The next generation of superheroes, including Beck, turn their faces to the moon and close their eyes.

The storm rises to a torrent around them. Even Talus gets to his feet to watch. Yet the chosen initiates are perfectly still, spotlit beneath the isolated beam of the moon. All is normal.

Right?

"I don't like it," I suddenly say, aloud this time.

Talus huffs and repeats Rometra's earlier reply. "Then you shouldn't have lost."

That's not what I mean, but thunder drowns my response, splitting the sky so that the air around us lifts and swirls in every direction at once.

The hermits all take one giant step inside the perimeter.

"Can they do that?"

No one answers, so I turn to Carl.

Yet he's gazing down at a new, blank page, totally immobile. I lift my binoculars, seeking Beck's reaction, yet every single initiate being claimed still has their head tilted toward the sky.

The hermits have almost reached the elevated dais by now. I search for Bishop, the one I told to jump in the lake, but it's the sweaty one that I again find first. As it takes another step, it shoots the hermit next to it a knowing wink. Then, they disappear beneath the dais.

War finally speaks. "They're too close."

And hermits are territorial. They do not work together. They do not wink.

"Nah," Talus argues. "They're protecting them."

"Then why does it look like they're hemming them in place?" This comes from Carl ... and he isn't even looking up.

You're going to fail. All of you. It's written in the stars, yet none of you know how to look.

"What do you see?" Thayer asks him sharply.

"Trap."

The cracking sky mutes my whisper, but in the flash of light that follows, I finally realize why the hermits look so different. Not one of them carries a talisman. This leaves them free to reach up through the slats of the wooden dais and, in unison, grab onto the ankles of the initiate above them.

Take a hermit's talisman from them and you own them for as long as you possess it.

The wind whips overhead, and I get a face full of rancid decay. Even Carl stands.

Talus covers his mouth and nose. "That smells like—"

"Shadows." Thayer's face drains of color, and lightning cracks open the sky like an egg.

"No." War takes a step forward. "That's the scent of Elders."

And our generation's best and brightest—this world's future heroes—are splayed atop the dais like it's a stage, bound by their ankles in a field of blood wheat.

30

THE SCENT OF SHADOWS.

The initiates on the dais are so married to the idea of what's supposed to happen that they don't begin struggling against the hermits' unyielding knuckles until it's too late. We're watching through binoculars and have a clear view of the entire field—which is suddenly filled with stink and smoke—but even we're caught flat-footed.

None of you know how to look.

"Rometra!" War darts from the porch. She disappears into the field just as icy raindrops begin battering the ground.

"Wait!" Thayer swipes at her but misses.

Like me, he's seen through his binoculars what she can't with her naked eye. The wheat shifting, parting, rushing like a wave barreling down on the shore as dark figures race toward the dais.

Cursing, he bolts after her.

Stunned, I waver in the wake of their flight. Yet Talus has an entirely different reaction. Slowly, he steps down and into the yard. *"Mother?"*

I blink, and suddenly, there's a woman before us, panting hard and holding one of the hermits's scythes. Her white-blonde hair whips around her face in the wind as midnight nears. She must see her son on the porch ... but her gaze lives only for me.

"Hello, spawn of Destruction."

That's a new one.

I swallow hard, backing up until my heel cracks against the step behind me, then freeze. Any move I make now won't be fast enough. If my thumb even twitches in the direction of my urumi, she'll pounce.

"Mother, no—" Talus holds out a hand.

"Cassius told us all how much fun he had murdering your mortal parents." She ignores him to watch her words fall on me, and they do—hard. I flinch with every syllable. "I bet killing you will be triple the pleasure."

She's going for me. I watch her lift the scythe, unable to stop it, and the blade rips through the air to find a home ... deep in Talus's chest.

Of course, I only see this in stop-motion flashes—another impairment of my mortal vision—but the cry that sounds, his and hers combined, is like battling eagles braced with steel throats.

The woman shudders as if possessed. Heat lightning sizzles along her limbs, and sparks of pure energy leap from her mouth as she moans. Her eyelids flip open to reveal corneas glowing like chipped stars, and for a moment, I see Talus spinning in them, like a loosened star spinning in space.

Glowing with all her newly acquired power, Talus's mother again turns my way.

Ignoring the scythe protruding from her son's chest, she steps right over his body. She has taken what she's wanted from Talus and has no more use for him.

I, on the other hand, look like opportunity.

Energy zings along her limbs, raw and snapping ... and then I'm flat on my back.

My head cracks against the wooden deck to reverberate down

my spine. Nose to nose, I can actually hear the woman's hair crackling at its roots. It's as if her deadly thoughts are flames whipping through her mind. Then she pulls back her fist and ...

Is gone.

A tangle of rolling and glowing limbs bursts in and out of view as the sky fires above. In the flash, I sight another scythe poised high and then a wash of fetid decay as thunder breaks overhead. I'm pushing to my feet, readied to run when a muddied figure rises on bowed legs to lift a victorious fist in the air.

"My debt is repaid!" Bishop screams into the angry night. "I am finally absolved of your foul presence and—"

"Shut up." I push Bishop out of my way and reach for Talus.

"Ashlyn!" Carl knows what I'm going to do even before I yank the scythe from the dead boy's chest. I choke back a need to gag, steeling myself against what I've seen ... and what might be coming.

It can all wait until later ... if there is one.

I glance back at Carl. "How long til midnight?"

"You're not fast enough. You're not strong enough. You're just—"

"How long?" I scream.

His face twists and breaks. "Twenty seconds."

It's not long enough for a mere mortal.

But that's not what I am, is it?

"Ashlyn...!"

His cry is already behind me, a terror that mounts and disappears at the same time. I cut a new path directly through the wheat, feet pounding like anvils, crushing stalks as the fetid scent of Elders and ozone burn the lining from my nose.

Ten seconds.

I burst from the wheat into the shorn circle holding the dais and almost crash directly into the first hermit. The moon is bright enough to capture its surprise, pulling its gruesome face wide, but not for long. This is Nia's hermit—the one who killed her entire family—and it might be cross-eyed and drooling, but it's a trained killer.

It releases the ankles of its assigned initiate and lunges for me.

I'm close enough to strike out with my scythe but too close for it to sink deep. The hermit's rough skin acts as a hard shell, and it stutters to a stop before letting out a piercing scream. Then it yanks the blade from its side, tosses it to the ground, and comes at me with its thick, bare hands.

I'm flat on my back, struggling for air, when it suddenly grunts in surprise. Its breath rolls over me in a noxious wave, and I push to my palms, scrambling up as it falls. Behind it stands Nia, eyes blazing.

I want to thank her for saving my life.

She wants to celebrate the death of the hermit who slaughtered her family.

There's time for neither.

Five seconds.

The other eleven hermits eye us with fear, some keening like farm animals, others mewling for mercy, but none can move from their stations beneath the dais. As long as the Elders have their talismans, they must do as ordered and hang tight to the feet of the initiates above.

I'm about to start indiscriminately chopping when Nia points to a hermit on the far side of the dais. "Beckett!"

The smooth arch of Beck's body as he catches waves.

The sweet curve of his mouth as he kisses me until I'm faint.

The resigned sadness on his face when he realizes I've chosen to leave.

I act before any of these memories take hold. Nia does, too. We arrow in on his hermit, who snaps at Nia with its worn teeth.

Meanwhile, I bunch up all of my fear, anger, and *humanity* in my fist and field it like a fast pitch into the hermit's petrified face. Its head rocks back on its thick neck, and its nose blooms red.

Even I'm shocked by the impact as it hits the ground ... until I realize that the sky has shattered like glass.

The entire world is on fire.

Midnight.

White heat lightning cuts the air to ribbons as the Elders seize the initiates, yanking them from their places on the zodiac wheel. Instead of bestowing power, the skies attack those on the raised dais. Right before I have to dodge my own errant bolt, a black-and-white snapshot reveals the Elders using the bodies of the young teens as shields.

It's a snapshot of ruthlessness, and I cower from the image as much as the sky's arrows. Screams begin rising, mingling with the rain.

The cries go on for years. Or seconds. It's all the same when pain rains around you. Yet when my vision finally clears, I am greeted with a dream. Beck, white-faced, wide-eyed, and blood-ied, right in front of me.

He manages only one word. "Run."

A roar sounds above us, right before a furied stomp. Wood splinters, but we have a head start. That, and the path I've already cut leading back to the shop.

The screams behind us alter in tone. The terror is replaced with victorious howls, and from my eye's corner, I spot bright rockets streaming into the sky. I glance back in time to see one Elder pick up a limp body, bend his knees, and thunder up and away. The sound barrier breaks with an ear-popping roar. That Elder is quickly followed by two, then three, more.

"Don't look!" Beck pushes me forward, and I stumble, but fear forces me back to my feet.

We clear the path and then the porch without ever touching the steps. Carl is at the door, screaming and gesturing us inside, and he slams the alarm on just as Beck's heel clears the thresh-old. Beck would protest, but I jerk him around so that he's facing the rest of the room, and he can see that War and Thayer are already there ... and so is Rometra. Nia rushes to hug her friends while Rometra remains huddled by herself, looking dazed.

There's no time to rejoice. Sparks flare at the door, and I cringe against the white sheet of power that shimmers and then dies. A scythe lies in front of the door, thrown and rejected by the shield, but I haven't even sighed my relief before a chuckle breaks through the barrier.

A slow, steady clap takes up the dark beat, and a stewed scent wafts across the threshold in a blend of nightmare and memory.

Then Cassius the Elder steps into view.

31

AND THEN THERE WERE THREE.

Cassius locks his arms on each side of the doorframe as if testing its strength.

Beck moves to intercept so fast that he's faced off against the Elder before the rest of us can even blink. They stand as they did once before, on the beach, toe-to-toe in unblinking opposition. All I could see the first time were their differences—age, clothing, and intent—but Beck now stares at Cassius with such hatred that it sends a shiver down my spine.

Cassius stares back, unmoved. His face blends my nightmares with my memories, all sitting upon a too-smooth mask of skin that I know hides the blackened bone I witnessed underwater.

If he thinks he looks normal, he couldn't be more wrong.

"You don't look surprised to see me," he says to Beck. "Then again, you had to know I'd return. You, of anyone, Mr. Lux, know that I never, ever stop until I get what I want."

He means me.

"And you." Cassius leans to one side to pin Carl with the same look he's granted Beck. "Don't tell me you're playing favorites, record keeper? I thought the shop where the manuals are recorded would be a safe zone for both the Shadow and the Light?"

"Sure." Carl lifts his chin. "Once the Zodiac rises again."

"Which won't be tonight, I'm afraid." Cassius laughs, his breath acidic and pungent as it wafts across the threshold.

Beck shifts, forcing Cassius to look at him again. "You did this? You ordered the Elders to abduct their own children? All of them?"

"You've been gathering your team." Cassius shrugs while jerking his chin at the rest of us. "I've been gathering mine."

"You're going to kill them," Beck says, and it's not a question. "Just so you could regain your place in the Zodiac?"

Cassius leans as close to the shielded doorway as he dares. "I would kill anyone for that."

Beck backs away, dazed, as if he can't even comprehend that kind of evil. Rometra takes up the fight on our behalf. Joining Beck at the threshold, she tilts her head. "Then it's too bad you're stuck on the wrong side of that doorway."

Cassius gives her a small smile. "Isn't it?"

None of you know how to look.

It's like I've been flipped underwater, my reaction slowed by the weight of the ocean, and too late, Bishop's words return to me. All I can do is watch—in seeming slow motion—as Rometra casually reaches over and pushes the button next to the door. My screamed warning is also a sluggish thing ... but everything sure speeds up after that.

Cassius is inside so quickly that he's bulleting my way before I've even blinked.

Beck tries to intercept, but even I can see he'll be too late.

Cassius, at full speed, is unstoppable ... at least until some great blur rockets at him from the side.

Nearer ... "Inside, inside!"

I'm about to shake off the hand until I realize it belongs to Carl. He's shoving me through the threshold to his bedroom, where Cassius can't reach us. Nia is secured in his other hand, and he's reaching back for War when a pained scream slices through the air.

I whirl to find Thayer trapped in the air, in Cassius's grip. My friend is like a cockroach on its back, limbs flailing, his cape wrapped around his head.

Rometra—betrayer, future Shadow—calmly strides forward and punches Thayer soundly in his gut. Cassius drops him to the ground, and he doubles over, his pained grunt exploding in the room. I drop my head and cover my face with my hands.

I can't see this kind of violence. Not again.

"Stop!" It's Beck. He alone is outside the bedroom door now, with Carl straddling the threshold, hand extended in case Beck needs it.

But Cassius is already done. Thayer's cape has shifted, and his head rolls on his shoulders, revealing a bloodied face. Sneering, Cassius tosses Thayer, unconscious, to Rometra. She sidesteps and lets him drop face-first to the floor.

"How could you?" War growls the question but doesn't dare cross the threshold. Cassius has his conduit, that enormous sharpened pick, and he's prowling the room.

"Is 'how' really the question?" Rometra slaps the button next to the door, arming it again.

Awesome. Now we're extra-trapped.

"Why?" War screams.

"Because there are no heroes," Rometra says coolly.

Only survivors.

Those were the words she spoke while looming over me in my bedroom a day ago when she already knew she would betray us. When she was biding her time.

For this.

Meanwhile, Cassius has pulled back the ceiling-to-floor curtain to reveal the hidden room where Carl and I watched movies and pretended to be normal. With a disdainful curl of his lip, Cassius lets the curtain fall and continues to canvass the room, stopping once he reaches Carl's desk.

"Those are not for your eyes," Carl snaps as Cassius scatters the stacked drawings until he finds one that interests him.

"Then you shouldn't have let me in," Cassius replies calmly, studying the drawing. When he finally looks up, it's directly at Beck. "But you did, didn't you? You just told Rometra where your secret hideout was and left the door wide open."

He holds up the drawing. It's a line sketch of the scene in front of us right now ... except for one thing.

Thayer is a lot more broken up than he is now.

I gasp and look at Carl, whose jaw clenches as he swallows hard.

He'd already been drawing this? And he didn't warn us?

The sound War makes in her throat is like a kitten mewling. "Rometra. Please. Stop this."

Cassius tucks the drawing into his back pocket. "What do you think, Rom? Should we stop?"

Rometra, who hasn't seen the drawing, still speaks to its image. "I think we should chop his limbs from his body and then force-feed them to the hermits."

Cassius claps his hands, stake palmed. "Inventive!"

"Enough." Beck straightens to his full height, finally snapping out of his stupor. Growling, he takes a step toward Cassius. "I know what you want."

"And you'll give her to me?" Cassius asks, winking at me. I go lightheaded like all the blood in my body has decided to pool in my feet.

"Not in this lifetime."

"Then say goodbye to your friend until the next lifetime." Cassius waves, and Rometra doesn't even hesitate. She stomps down, caving in Thayer's knees with a brutal double-strike. War isn't the only one to cry out this time.

I get a flashback to the day Thayer and I met, the way he

circled me in pretend flight. I recall how he advised me in the weapons room, shoring me up with coffee and encouragement while he spoke of how hard it was to be neither Light nor Shadow, but gray.

"When I draw you," Carl manages through ragged breath, "I will make sure I pen only your barbaric nature."

"I hope for nothing less," Cassius returns and Rometra laughs. "Yet I am one of the few in this room who hasn't killed anyone tonight. Even the newbie has made her first kill." He turns to me with mock concern. "Tell me, do you feel different, daughter of Chaos? Do you feel super?"

I feel sick.

"Come to me," Cassius commands.

I answer him before my mind can kick in. "Let Thayer go."

Cassius grins. "A trade?"

"NO." Beck growls.

Cassius's entire skull gives a giant pulse, the blackened skull beneath rising to thin out that too-perfect skin. However, he regains his control with a hard swallow and motions to Rometra. I step across the threshold and back into the main room before she can touch Thayer. I'll do anything if it means saving Thayer from the fate depicted on that paper.

Yet Beck steps in front of me.

"No, Ashlyn," he repeats. "He doesn't really want you."

But he does. He wants to kill me. He wants to exact revenge for being tossed into a makeshift black hole when I was twelve. He wants ...

"Promise to let Thayer be?" Beck asks Cassius.

Cassius gives a dismissive shrug. "He is nothing to me."

Inexplicably, Beck turns his back on Cassius. Cassius is behind him before I can blink. Before I gasp. I reach for Beck, but Carl shoves me back into his room, and War yanks me to her side.

"Let go!"

But she won't. She's only thinking of Thayer. Yet I'm thinking of Beck. He must see that! He must, at the very least, sense it.

So why is he standing there, looking more resigned than afraid as his eyes lock on my face? It's like he's waiting for me to understand something I cannot. Then Cassius's hand falls atop his shoulder. Their expressions are identical as they gaze at me.

We both have childhoods that should have been better than they were.

I gasp.

Beck shudders.

Cassius howls with laughter.

The weight of memory—the heritage of stars and centuries— races past me. The repercussion of the Big Bang throbs in my ears. The knowledge of what is real and what is a lie flips, and everything I think I know about what's good and true in the world flips with it.

The villain who murdered my parents is the same one who chased Beck through the forest all those years ago.

The same one who killed his sister, Juno, for failing to claim her birthright.

The same one who began the practice of Shadows killing their offspring.

Cassius the Elder.

Cassius, the Shadow.

Cassius ... Beckett's father.

He doesn't want you, Ashlyn.

My shock infuses the air with a sickly fragrance. I can't smell it, but Nia places a consoling arm around me. War whispers something that buzzes in my ear, and Cassius inhales deeply. The smile that blooms on his face is as close to peace as anything I've ever seen.

Ambling backward, he pulls Beck along by his neck, though his gaze stays fixed on me.

"Leave him," he tells Rometra, who hovers over Thayer. "We've got what we need."

Rometra's lip curls, but she lowers the shield over the door, allowing Cassius and Beck to pass through the unarmed threshold first and then follows. It's only once they're all outside that Cassius finally allows the fragile mask of his human skin to fall. The black skeleton beneath rises to rip through his delicate, paper-thin flesh, and his grin splays wide with decades-old rot.

"And then," he says, jerking his head at us. "There were only three."

And then they are gone.

32

I AM WHAT I AM.

I am no hero.

There is nothing super, powerful, or even remotely awesome about me. I am just a girl who is really good at two things: surfing and hiding.

Wait—I've just discovered something else I'm good at: lying to myself.

"You knew."

My voice sounds the way an ocean cliff-side looks, parched and dry, stroked only by the sun even though the water is only feet away. It's a brittle thing, so maybe that's why Carl doesn't answer at first. Why he doesn't even look up.

Why he just returns to his desk and begins to draw.

"They didn't." He jerks his head at the girls, who are trying to shift Thayer's broken body into a sitting position. The kneecap that Rometra broke will have to be reset, but it will heal. Yet the marks left by Cassius's conduit will likely scar his face forever.

I file the confession away. He knew, and he drew ... but he said nothing to us, his supposed friends, at all.

"You *knew*."

Carl and I alone know and share what it is to be human.

We're the only ones who don't speak of that as a weakness. We spoke of our pasts, and he told me why Cassius hated me so much, and then we watched eighties movies together ... yet he never shared the one thing he knew I'd most want to know.

Beckett's father killed my parents.

"You should have told me."

"Us," War snaps from across the room. I don't look at her. Her voice is already tear-filled.

"I couldn't. It would violate my contract as record keeper."

Because he was only here to record events, not influence them.

I close my eyes and shake my head.

"I'm sorry," he says, and I know he is, but when I don't open my eyes, he adds harshly, "But *he* should have told you."

Beckett.

It explains the tension I often sensed between Beck and Carl, who had to watch Beck watch me at the beach, yet never approach. He knew—as I now did—that Beck was hoping Cassius would change.

If I can throw off my lineage, choose to be good, then others can as well.

I can't think about that right now. If I think about Beck at all, I might just start screaming and never stop.

Carl's drawing again and doesn't bother covering his work when I join him at his desk. Everywhere is slaughter. Blood, not yet dried, sits thickly in my nose, a redolent companion to the carnage he's drawing, one page after page. The one he works on now, pencil flying, shows Rometra meeting with Cassius before the festival, planning her betrayal. Sealing our fates.

"Stop."

Carl doesn't even pause. "I can't."

I yank the pencil from his hand, snap it in half, and throw it across the room. "Stop drawing!"

"I can't stop!" he yells back. Suddenly, he's standing, and we're nose-to-nose, his breath hot in my face. He slams a finger down on the page, smudging Rometra's newly shaded profile. Sadly, it doesn't soften it a bit. "If you want this to change, *you* must do something!"

"What?" I spit back. "Give you something worth drawing?"

"No. Give me something heroic!" His chest is heaving, and his large body is shaking in all that head-to-toe black ...

And he's right.

"We have to get Beckett back."

It's Nia. She standing next to me suddenly, and she's right, too. We have to get them all back.

"They'll wait until another full moon, another of the twelves —the most powerful hour—and use the blood of their children to resuscitate their own power."

Nia says it as we're all thinking it. As Carl begins drawing it. Fate ... pre-ordained.

"It's like placing defibrillators on the heart of the world. They will force the Universe to bring the Zodiac world back to life."

"We don't even know where they've gone," I point out, because it would need to be a place large enough, and private enough, for an enormous zodiac wheel to reflect the heavens.

"Sure we do." War rubs a hand over her face and head. "There's an eager and powerful little audience already waiting for them in West Hollywood."

I shake my head. "No. They wouldn't do that."

The children in the secret playground. And violence ... nobody would do that.

Would they?

My horror is reflected in Nia's voice. "The Universe wouldn't be able to deny them then."

No. Because that horrifying event would forever live in the minds of those children. They'd never be able to escape it. The Elders were planning to fuel their assault on us using the fear and imagination of the most impressionable minds in the world.

They would fire up their lineage by bringing a nightmare to life.

War looks over at me. "So I guess the real question is ... are there really three of us?"

Nia looks up.

Thayer stirs on the floor.

Carl's hand stills on the page.

They smell my fear. My indecision.

"Ash?"

Your failure is fated. It's written in the stars, yet none of you know how to look.

Bishop's prophecy accompanies the thought of Nia, War, and me trying to take on a hoard of deranged hermits and murderous Elders. Not to mention Rometra. Three of us, carrying no real weapons but for the one that I, a half-mortal, can hold.

While protecting the innocence of mortal children.

While saving ten captive initiates.

Doing all of it in the dark ... and in West Hollywood.

It's not a decision. It's a suicide mission.

Closing my eyes, I switch it up a bit and envision a one-way ticket to Kauai instead. It's far away from these bloodied mountains, and LA. And even if the Elders reform the troop system, the island's population is too small to attract any troop. It's the perfect place to disappear back into the life I was supposed to have ... and I could be there by tomorrow.

I'm half-mortal, I remind myself. I'm only meant to be a bridge between the past and the future. My mother broke the Zodiac world, I fix it, and that would be that. That had always been the plan, and everyone here knew it.

I open my eyes to find four pairs of eyes pinned on me. Yes, even Thayer has come around. I don't know how much of the conversation he's heard, but he's shooting me the same questioning look as everyone else.

What will I do?

"Do you know how I started surfing?" I ask, totally randomly. They just stare. "I was having trouble in school. My ... my brain didn't work right, and just being in the water was soothing. But then I caught my first really big wave, and I had a killer three-second ride before being slammed to the ocean floor ... and do you know what I was thinking during all of those three seconds?"

They all look at me. Nia shakes her head.

"*Nada*. Because nothing else existed. There was me, the board, and that wave, and for three seconds, we were one. Outside of three fins and a longboard, nothing separated me from the bottom of the world."

Nia shudders. "That sounds awful."

"It's all I've ever wanted."

Thayer closes his eyes. War's shoulders visibly slump. Nia shakes her head almost imperceptibly, and Carl doesn't move at all. Their disappointment smells like an oil spill in fresh waters.

"But here's the thing about the ocean," I say and watch them all lift their heads. "The water rolls in whether you're ready or not. It doesn't care whether you sink or swim. It keeps coming either way. That's surfing."

"That's life," Nia whispers fiercely, and she would know.

I nod. "The ocean was my home, and I thought it had everything to do with location, but then I met all of you. Initiates in a broken world, not even full-fledged agents, and I thought ... yeah, but what am I?"

"You are someone this world has never seen before." Injury hasn't weakened Thayer's resolve. He shoots me a crooked smile.

"You're the daughter of our world's greatest superhero," War admits.

"You're a first-born female in a matriarchal realm," Nia adds.

"You're mortal," Carl says sharply. He's the only home-grown human here, but for some reason, he looms larger than all of us just now.

"You're a mortal," he repeats, "in a world where even the smallest one is the most powerful thing of all."

I nod. "And no human is put on this earth just to surf through life."

Maybe he feels a story rising, or perhaps he already knows what I will say from his hours of "watching" me as the weirdo, geeky record keeper, but Carl is the first to smile. "So you'll give me something heroic to draw?"

"I'm not sure about heroic."

I shake my head before giving them all a thoughtful frown.

"But how do you guys feel about crazy?"

33

SAY HELLO TO BOB.

Outside, I leap to the field of blood wheat, my footsteps thrumming through the earth like taiko drums. I don't care. I wasn't born to surf through life, and I wasn't placed here to tread softly, either. I was raised by Zoe Archer.

I was reared to leave a mark.

Maybe that's why I don't try for stealth as I crash through the field, red-tipped wheat stalks tangling in my hair and scoring my flesh. No biggie. I'll heal.

Within minutes, I've created a new path just for myself, which War and Nia reluctantly follow back into the clearing.

The sky is still bruised. The ground is still wet and loamy with the scent of the midnight storm. All is silent in the shocked air, and I reach the dais in a world without sound.

It's now three a.m., and the bloodstains across the wooden planks have gone brown. Nia returns to where she stood until I freed her from her hermit and turns her face to the wide, blue sky.

War finds a spot at the dais's edge and sits so her feet dangle. "And what exactly are we doing here?"

I cup my hands around my mouth and show her. "Bishop!"

"What are you doing?" Nia hisses in my direction. War pulls her feet to her chest so they no longer hang over the side. Yet, if anything, the field grows even quieter than before.

I try again. "Bishop, can you come here, please?"

"Who's the bishop?" Nia hisses.

"Bishop is a hermit."

War tilts her head. "Hermits are religious?"

"No, hermits are just … hermits."

Nia rolls her eyes. "Then why did you say please?"

I sense movement behind me and answer loudly enough that anyone near the ring can hear. "Because that's how you address people when you're about to ask them for a favor."

"People?" War leaps to her feet just as the hermit emerges into full view.

His eyes dart, trying to keep each of us in sight, but they're so close to the sides of his head that he keeps having to shift. I don't know if it's clear to Nia or War, but he looks healthier to me. Less stooped. The tilt of his chin is more defiant and squared.

He's even wearing pants.

"Well, well. The prodigal daughter returns," Bishop snarls. "Again."

The new day has done nothing to enhance his disposition. At least he smells a little better. "You don't seem surprised."

"Blood doesn't lie," Bishop spits back.

Grabbing my arm, Nia hisses in my ear. "You can't trust these things, Ashlyn."

"This one is not a thing. He's a person. Aren't you?"

Bishop says nothing.

So I leap from the platform onto the short area of shorn wheat not covered by the dais. Bishop flinches, and both War and Nia cry out, but the hermit keeps his gaze locked on my face and doesn't back up. "You saved me from that, Elder."

"I owed you, and now I don't," Bishop barks. "Now you're free to die whenever you feel like it!"

I nod, pretending to listen. "You could've killed me the night we met in the forest, too, and you didn't."

I've learned a lot since that night, so I'm unsurprised when he doesn't deny it.

"Doesn't make me a good...person," he finally grunts.

I smile. "No."

I glance down, noting that he still carries the talisman that marks him as a law-breaker. I don't know what he did to warrant a lifetime of carrying around a teddy bear, but I do know that if you treat people like the dumbest animals around, they have little reason to act otherwise.

But allow them a little dignity? Allowed that, maybe, despite their past, they could be something more, something better?

Give them a name?

Some of them might even rise to the occasion.

"It doesn't make it a person at all," Nia calls, and Bishop stiffens before me. "It gave up that right when it committed the greatest crime of all."

"Actually," I say before Bishop can snap back. "What makes him a person is free will, which I returned to him when I accidentally gave him a name. Isn't that right?"

War leaps from the dais, and, newfound status or not, Bishop takes a step back. "You gave it a name?"

"Him," I correct, and watch Bishop's shoulders straighten. "And with it came the ability to choose good over evil."

"So?" Bishop spits.

"So now you're going to help us. Duh."

Bishop's gaze is so incredulous that his eyes nearly cross. The look War and Nia exchange is similar. The major difference is that they continue to stand there while Bishop suddenly flings his too-long arms out to the sides, snaps the nearby wheat stalks with scrabbling fingertips, and starts screaming obscenities.

After that, he throws himself onto his back, emitting a breath that makes me wish I'd told him to brush his teeth after jumping in the lake.

Then, after *that*, he rises to his feet and does it all over again.

We wait until he's run out of steam. When he's finally prone and panting on the ground, War shakes her head. "By the stars ... that was pitiful."

"Where are the other hermits?" I ask Bishop.

His head snaps up, and he wipes the spittle from his mouth. "Writhing in their cairns! We prefer to be alone when feeling the agony of shedding innocent blood ... even when it's forced upon us by another party."

Loneliness. Agony. Resentment.

We could use it all.

"Call them."

Bishop stares at me for a moment before his gaze skitters to War. We are both well away from the path that means safety from the other hermits. Then he rises to his feet, glaring at me as he draws a short, blunt knife from his belt.

"Ash," Nia warns, backing away.

But instead of rushing any of us, he begins stabbing the flesh of his stomach repeatedly, making a sound that warbles with each pained beat of his heart.

War glares at me. "Seriously?"

I hold up my palms. "I didn't know he was going to do that."

The tall wheat around us parts. The massive, hulking outlines of half a dozen hermits slither into view, accompanied by the scent of burned compost.

Nia grunts in surprise. I guess she didn't know they could feel sadness.

Wobbling back around to face us, Bishop flips me the middle finger. "All yours."

Most of the hermits are so listless they can barely lift their heads on their thick necks, but they possess their talismans again, and that's enough to keep them aware.

And wary.

"Okay, hermits," I say, hoping I look more confident than I feel. "Here's the deal. We're going after the Elders who stole your talismans, forced you all to attack us, and will soon spill the blood of the captured initiates. Which, by the way, will also stain your souls."

They grumble but don't correct me. More than anyone, a hermit would know that to be true.

"The goal," I continue, "is to get Beckett back—"

"Alive," Nia feels the need to clarify.

"Alive," I agree, "and maybe mete out a little vengeance in the process. So who's in?"

Not even a stalk of grain moves.

"By the stars," War mutters beside me, but I ignore her to turn back to Bishop.

"If any agree," I ask him, "would you be willing to lead them in battle against the Elders' hermits?"

A hiss rises over Bishop's shoulder as one of the larger creatures takes a menacing step forward. Its fingertips are stained with blood, and its face holds newly rent scratches down each cheek. "Why does it get to lead?"

"I am not an it!" Bishop whirls and thumps his chest so that his belly resumes bleeding.

"Idiot," Nia mutters.

"I am once again a person, recognized by the heavens and the stars and the First Mothers by my given name! Just look upon my glorious head—"

"Don't get carried away, dude," I mutter.

"And you'll see it's true!"

The hermits look at him and then look at me. I nod. "I named him yesterday."

The offer sits heavily in the air as the other hermits try to stitch together its implications in their rotted brains.

"I'm willing to name each of you as well—"

"Ash!" Nia hisses it, and I turn to find her eyes burning. War places a hand on her arm, but I don't dare do the same.

"There are only three of us."

And even though she hates all hermits, even though she shakes with the memory of her family dying beneath the fist of the one she killed, after a minute, she swallows hard and nods.

Only then does the giant with the newly scarred face step forward. Its head, shoulders, and arms hang low. Even its knees droop, though its eyes are turned up.

"I used to be a warrior," it grunts, voice heavy with disuse. "It was all I ever wanted. It's what I dream of when I think of escaping this living nightmare."

"No escape," says one hermit, and the others quickly pick up the refrain. It's a dirge. The dark song of their hearts.

"Shut up," I tell their dark, dirging hearts.

The scarred hermit clears its throat. "Yet I could join this army. For the first time, I could fight for what is good. Maybe then I can earn back my blessed nature, one deed at a time."

"Great." I point at him before anyone can stop me. "Then your name is Bob."

War rolls her eyes. "Bob the hermit?"

"What? He looks like a Bob," I say defensively.

"He looks like a fungus," Nia snaps.

Bob doesn't seem to mind, though. He clutches his gnarled hands to his heart, pounding it once before lumbering to Bishop's side. There he straightens, just one vertebra, but a shift shudders through the wheat.

The other hermits gasp and begin jostling each other as they crowd closer.

I turn to Nia and War with a flourish.

"Our army," I say, but only War and I smile as Bishop begins naming his brethren.

"Hold up!" War says suddenly as he's about to name the lone female hermit. I didn't recognize her at first because her bow has gone missing ... along with her ear. War points at her, eyes blazing. "That one's name is Hortense!"

"Dude. That's mean," I say.

War crosses her arms. "She chased me into the wheat last summer and tried to kill me with a sharpened stone."

I point to my left. "Go stand next to Bob, Hortense."

By the time we're done, the night is no longer still. The excitement that seized Bob and caused him to stand taller has washed over the others. The other eleven hermits don't look much saner than before, but that's okay.

Any sane being wouldn't try what we're about to do.

"I do believe," War says, tilting her head, "that we've just created something entirely new."

"What if they turn on us?" Nia has stayed stubbornly silent throughout the whole process.

I turn to her, and this time I do put my hand on her arm. "We just have to trust that they won't."

"Trust hermits?" She still doesn't like it, but just shakes her head as she turns toward the cottage. "That *is* new."

It's better than new, I think, exchanging looks with War as we follow. It's something the Elders will never, ever expect.

34

THE ZODIAC WAY.

I t's dawn by the time we return to the cottage for sleep and supplies. Since we can't be sure the return journey through the wheat is safe, we leave Thayer with Carl, who gives over his bedroom to the cause, just as he gave it to me the day I arrived.

War and Nia fuss over our injured friend, tucking the covers up to his neck and lowering them again. They ask if he's too hot, if he needs water, and if there's anything they can do.

Carl just stands to the side the whole time, frowning at the bandage covering Thayer's forearm. We didn't see it at first, but here Cassius just couldn't resist cutting into his prey with his conduit. It's an etching of his star sign, and since it was done with the magical, sharpened spike, it will scar.

"I'll just get Ash to carve me up with a different conduit and turn it into something else," Thayer says good-naturedly. "Like a butterfly or something."

I nod, even though the last thing I ever want to do is cut into Thayer's flesh.

"Thank the Mothers it wasn't deeper," Nia says, dropping a

quick kiss atop Thayer's forehead, causing a full blush. War hesitates before leaning in to do the same.

Carl finally shakes off whatever deep thoughts or grim drawings are whizzing through his mind and actually grins. "Careful. You'll cause him to pass out again."

This time, it's War who blushes.

Despite our precautions, we encounter nothing but red-tipped wheat and a shock of blue sky spread out before the morning sun. There's not even a lone hermit to funk up the place.

"At least Rometra's not lying in wait," War mutters as we safely reach the grove beneath the cottage. She leaps and is gone before we can reply.

"Nia," I say before she can make her escape, too. "About the hermits—"

She holds up her hands and gives me a tired half-smile. "I know ... and you're right. We need the numbers. But, I swear to the Mothers, if one of them even looks like it will betray us ..."

"I know."

And then she is gone, too.

We're to meet again at six that night. First, we'll eat something bracing and get some sleep. Yet, despite my fatigue, I head to the weapons room instead.

The motion sensor lights up at my arrival, and even though it's silly, I feel like it's been waiting for me. "Hi, honey. I'm home."

The buzzing along my limbs intensifies. It's like being pulled in multiple directions at once. I've been attacked ... and somehow, the weapons in this room know it.

There's an axe that calls to me, its edge dangerously rusted.

There's a whip that reminds me of my urumi, except that it's barbed and longer, and for some reason, it seems familiar.

There's the bazooka Thayer was yanking on the first time I entered the room. The long bayonet is settled next to it like a lost limb.

I wander the room, and this time I let myself feel it all, closing my eyes, flexing my hands, even trailing my fingertips atop each. You'd think this would quell the longing inside of me, but I want to touch everything. I want to run my fingers along the knife blades. I want to slip my palm into the metal gloves and wrap my hands around the pommel of the mace.

I think of Cassius, and I want to wield them all at once.

Yet I'm looking for something specific. I saw it the first time I visited the weapons room and had thought it out of place amidst all the old, rusting, and finished weaponry. Finally, I spot it on the room's far side. A thin metal sheet sits forgotten, half bent against the wall. Stamped cutouts and the mark of steel scissors scar it, but enough remains for my needs.

It gives a bright pulse when my gaze lands on it, like it knows it's been chosen.

But I know it has also chosen me.

"You're beautiful," I say as I lift it in both hands because, in my mind's eye, it already is.

A new weapon for a new generation. A new agent.

Me.

It takes three hours—too long, I know—but I have to proceed slowly—cutting, forging, creating. I need sleep, and fatigue keeps trying to sneak up on me like a seagull spotting a picnic, but my mother's words in my dream keep me going.

It's impossible to mess up when you create from the center of your being.

"Make good use of your worry," I tell myself, speaking aloud to stay awake. "Turn your feelings into something good."

The act of creation is your mind moving through your hands. It's like magic. Or power.

I feel like I've done that when I've finished. I also think what I've created will give me more strength than any power nap I could've taken. It's only as I'm leaving with a new weapon in hand that I realize the insistent buzzing in the room has gone silent. The other weapons no longer pull at me. Instead, they sleep.

This world, I think, is satisfied with my work, and I smile as the light in the room snaps off behind me.

I MEET THE OTHERS BACK AT CARL'S SHOP, AND THIS TIME I'M NOT only carrying my backpack, I'm armed with my urumi and dressed in full battle regalia, playing it safe. Doing it their way.

The Zodiac way.

Carl's jaw drops when I appear at the door, his gaze dropping to take in my leather armor, full black. It almost makes me want to smile. Record keeper or not, I guess he didn't see this coming.

"You look ..."

"Sleep deprived?"

His gaze lands back on my face. "Awesome."

It's something I would say, an acknowledgment of sorts. Maybe that's why I blush.

"Well, don't get used to it," I say, shaking off the awkward moment.

"Why? Because you're not a hero?"

I yank at my pants. "Because I never again want to be on such intimate terms with a large, dead animal."

Yet right now, I need all the protection I can get. That's why I've also donned the new handmade, homemade weapon I fashioned back at the cottage. Thus, Carl's newfound uncertainty around me. Now that he has seen me—really sees me—he knows what I've done and can do. Maybe even how I might use it.

The others don't—not immediately. When we enter the secured bedroom, Nia and War have their backs to the doorway, and it's actually Thayer who sees me first.

He pushes himself up in bed, something the girls have obviously been fighting against. His face has regained color, and his bruises are already gone. Fast healing, yes, but it's more than that.

Even the wounds from Cassius's conduit have stopped bleeding. Thayer's neck is merely scarred with the other man's zodiac symbol.

Like he's been branded, I think, frowning.

Yet when he yells, "No fair!" and points at me from across the room, his voice has regained his former cheer. It helps to scrub his pained cries from my mind, and something unclenches inside me. "None of us get a metal mask!"

Nia gasps as she takes in the armor covering my face. It bends, sloping gently over my upper eyelid and brows so that my eyes are a natural part of the whole, but the softness ends there. My nose bridge is strong, to deflect blows. My vulnerable temples are hidden. And flexible segments flare along my forehead like flames, the sharp, pointed tips a deterrent to grabby hands.

Thayer begins a slow clap. Nia soon joins in, but War gapes. That's how I know Carl is right. I look awesome.

"You look like a daughter of the Zodiac," Nia says, slipping to my side.

"You mean like the daughter of Chaos?" I try to joke, but it doesn't sound funny.

It sounds like a threat.

"Like a proper agent," Thayer clarifies as Nia reaches up to touch my mask. She immediately jerks back as her fingers sizzle at the tips.

"What the--"

Hell.

Thayer tries and jerks away. "I don't--"

Get it.

"By the stars." War breathes, squaring up on me with squinted eyes. She leans close, staring into my eyes. "You made that mask?"

"Only because I didn't have time to make a full suit of armor," I say and shrug. "And after what I saw last night, I figured I could use more protection. Besides, Carl's going to be drawing everything we do."

Back in weirdo mode, he inclines his head in a move that's almost regal. "And you don't want your real identity out there when I do. So you made something no one else could touch."

"That no one can take off," I correct.

I'm tired of people taking things from me.

Thayer practically convulses in bed. "Oh, but I really want to touch it!"

"You realize this is the first new conduit made since the Reordering," Nia says, pushing him back down with one hand.

"What's this?" War points to the mask's center.

Carl leans forward to peer more closely at the carving above the nose plate. "*T T E?*"

They're the letters that showed up in my fever dream after Rometra almost killed me. They waver in my mind like seaweed caught amongst the rocks. They're the secret ones that I think my mother wants me to know somehow, somewhere.

"I'm not sure. But I'm hoping you guys will help me find out."

I reach into my pocket and pull out the pretty little bottle I've tucked there.

"Cassius hates me for whatever I've done to him, but if my gut is right, he fears me too. Given what we're about to do, I think it's time I remembered why."

"What's in it?" War asks, her hand lifting automatically. She hesitates until I nod that it's safe for her to touch.

"My memories."

Her dark fingers immediately tense against the pink bottle, and her eyes flare wide.

"Relax, I trust you."

She freezes, then kinda melts, and I have to smile as I watch a girl named War, my *friend*, go soft.

"It might feel very real," Carl warns, reaching for the bottle. "You'll experience all the emotions you did the first time."

"I know, but it's already a part of my past, and I'm still here."

Still alive. Still standing.

"How bad can it be, right?" Thayer asks and pats one side of his bed, making room for me.

"Maybe not as bad when surrounded by friends," I say and smile as I lay down beside him.

35

GOING BACK.

Here is what happened the day of the Reordering ... the day the Zodiac fell.

Joanna Archer destroyed the evil overlord of Shadows—a being who was supposed to be impossible to kill—and made herself into a legend.

That's why his rudderless minions came after me.

I see it as soon as Nia pipes the oil from the pink bottle into a bowl of purified water.

I feel it as the water warms in the diffuser and the mist of my memories begins to rise.

"Take a deep breath," she says, fanning me so that an oily cloud wafts above my head. My nose itches, nerve endings coming alive beneath the duel scents of peppered rose and something close to lemon cream. My lips tingle as they seek entry there, too. It's a good thing I'm lying next to Thayer because vertigo whips over me, even though I'm lying down.

Nia squeezes my right hand, War my left. I can hear Carl's pencil swish upon his drawing pad.

Thayer whispers, "Get ready to remember how strong you really are."

. . .

I BREATHE IN DEEPLY ... AND HEAR MY MOTHER SCREAM.

"Dennis!"

"Andie!"

I'm back in a steel silo that reeks of Shadows. There's a roiling black hole before me, and Titan the Shadow is across from me, holding out my half-conscious parents to Cassius.

So that he can play.

It is brutal, ruthless, and over fast. Cassius has lifted my father high above his head and heaved him into the black pit while I'm still swaying from his release. The entire room shudders as Dad's body disappears into the thick swamp of darkness, vapor floating from the poisonous pit in tendrils, drifting out.

"No!" I rush after him.

"Now, dear." Titan plucks me from my feet, depositing me just out of reach of the beckoning vapor. "One of the first rules of playing safely in the Zodiac world. Don't stray too close to black holes."

I'm only eleven, almost twelve. I don't know if a black hole can exist inside a steel room or a well. All I know about black holes is that once something's caught inside, it never escapes.

"Nothing!" Cassius bellows suddenly, breaking his own awed silence with a surprised half-laugh. He whirls to Titan, beating his great chest with fists sullied with my father's death. "Nothing happened!"

Everything happened.

Cassius turns on my mother.

"Stop!"

Even I need a moment to figure out where the voice has come from.

My mother doesn't give anyone a chance to recover from their shock. She simply heads my way without looking left or right, spine straight. "I will say goodbye to my daughter first."

The rumble from Cassius's throat sounds like the earth caving in, but it's drowned out by Titan's laughter, which ricochets off the steel walls.

"Let them take their leave, Cassius," he says generously. "It will make for a touching manual."

I'm going to pass out. I'm shaking so hard that the only thing that keeps me from falling to my knees is my mother's warm, familiar arms. Titan steps back, but it doesn't feel like he's giving us space. I think he just wants to see me topple.

"Ashlyn!"

My mother has been repeating my name, and I blink hard, looking for the same fear in her gaze. It's not there.

"I don't understand what's happening."

"Of course you do." She draws back to gaze down at me, even though I don't loosen my grip. "You have your comic books. You have Zoe teaching you about your family history and how to use all of your natural strengths."

"You are my family!" My voice cracks on every syllable.

She smooths my hair from my forehead like she's done a million times. There's fear ... in her shaking hands. "They gave you to us for safekeeping, but now it's time to go back."

"To what?"

"To being an Archer."

"You are my mother!"

I scream it in the past.

I scream it in the present.

I scream it so it'll be recorded for Shadow and Light and mortal, all, to see.

But my mother just leans forward and whispers in my ear. "Remember, *we* are their power."

"That's enough," Titan says harshly behind us.

My mother's eyes dart over my features like minnows, memorizing my face. I start to shake again. "Til the end, Ashlyn Archer. Remember that we loved you til the—"

And there is a blur.

And then she, too, is gone.

Shock waves race over me. My cheeks are still warm from her touch. Yet I'm suddenly alone with steel and stink and Cassius's back flexing hard as his fists brace the floor in front of the pit. He is tracking my mother's trajectory in death.

"Happy now?" Titan asks him.

When Cassius turns, his eyes have turned completely black. Something burns within each iris, a chip of light fracturing that cold, onyx gaze. It sparks something equally cold and sharp inside of me.

I rise to my feet.

Til. The. End.

Titan's gasp causes my hair to billow, and he takes a full step away from me ... from Cassius. Yet blood lust has swept Cassius into his own fantasy world, and he doesn't even sense what Titan and I can already see. Instead, he tilts his head up and roars into the air. "I feel IMMORTAL!"

"You look moronic."

His head whips down, but I don't flinch beneath that newly blackened stare. Half of me wants to pitch myself into the abyss with my parents. The other half wants to take the nascent spark inside of me—the one that matches the chips in his gaze—and light a match.

"Murderer of mortals."

It's the title of a manual. Zoe showed it to me only last week.

"Abomination."

The words are alive in my mouth, bubbling up from the pit of my stomach where I've swallowed down my mother's final vow, my father's death cry, and every epic lesson Zoe Archer has made me memorize over the years.

"Law-breaker."

Fear finally flashes over his face. "Shut up, child!"

I do not shut up. I swat away a beefy black tendril of fog,

causing Cassius and Titan to gasp, and I point directly at his chest. "You've lain hands on an Innocent, and that is the greatest crime in our world!"

It is Law. I know it in my heart ... and Cassius can suddenly feel it.

He opens his mouth to snap at me and opens his palm to slap, but the tiny chips of light flecking his eyes fracture when they land on my mortal face. They are constellations, and they shatter his dark gaze. His cruel smile falls, and his skin keeps falling, melting like wax along furrows I already know will cut down to blackened bone.

I do not turn away, even when he begins clawing at his face. Even when he howls.

Carved in those rivulets is every kindness my parents have ever shown. His brow wrinkles and scars with their love for me— love that he had no right to take. Their goodness wells inside of him, forcing the unnatural light in his charred eyes to spill over his cheeks, creating yet more valleys on the contours of his skin.

Smoke rises from those newly rent rivulets, and Cassius tries to wipe them away, screaming.

"Cursed for eternity," I say, as his hands begin to burn, too. "Cursed til the end."

TTE.

And then I bum-rush him so that he, too, topples over the well's inky side. Tendrils of black mist smother his falling, fading cry. My almost twelve-year-old self thinks he is dead.

My sixteen-year-old mind knows it will be years before he finally claws his way back out.

Yet before either of my minds can wrap around this, a sonic snarl rises behind me.

I turn just as Titan lunges.

36

THE PLAN.

The dam gives way after that.

The memories I've blocked for so long flood my brain so quickly that I feel my eyes bouncing beneath their lids, trying to keep up. The images are terrifying, like when Titan locks me in a glass dome as bait for the other Archer women.

Other memories are fantastic, like when my birth mother finds and rescues me.

And yes, some are even heroic. In some ... I even rescue myself.

I see myself entering my second life cycle, the raw energy forming inside me like a fist. It's the same power I first felt as I watched Cassius fall, and it loops around me in a golden knot of light that links me to every day I've lived since.

This is how my power comes alive inside of me. This is how I reclaim myself.

The days flick by me in blinks. One solid image is all I need, snippets of conversation flowing through me like blood cells, and when I finally reach the present—where I am lying on a bed in a protected room, surrounded by people who are supernatural in nature but with all-too-human hearts—I am a part of that, too.

Nia on one side, War on the other, and me ... all of us part of the generation of superheroes orphaned when my birth mother destroyed the Zodiac world.

I see the whole thing through the eyes of someone who got here, step by step, day by day, good and bad. For the first time since that long ago day when I lost my parents, I look it square in the eye, and I truly see.

I breathe.

I open my eyes.

I remember who I am.

I am finally awake.

"They knew," I say as Nia gently guides me to a sitting position. "They knew what could happen by loving me, and they did it, anyway."

"Of course," she says simply. "That's what parents do."

Yet they'd died because of me, too.

Before this last thought can sour into full bitterness, War is there. She frowns as she looms above me, and I automatically flinch. The characteristic arrogance is there. So is the superiority. Yet her hand on my shoulder is soft.

It's her voice that's unyielding. "Put away your sadness and self-pity, Archer. Not everyone can say that they've known real love."

Til the end.

"I'm not sad," I tell her because what she sees is merely what's on the outside.

On the inside, I am picking up their love for me and placing it on my chest as armor.

"I'm furious."

Smiling, War holds out her hand and pulls me to my feet. Her fingertips don't just rest in mine. No, we grip each other the way people do when they're binding a vow.

"No worries, Archer. Black She-Ra can show you exactly what to do with that."

THE SKYLINE SIZZLES AT THE EDGES, DUSK ALREADY FALLING HARD when we send the hermits forward. They will travel down the mountain under the cover of the trees and underbrush, and from there, they'll be able to reach L.A. under complete darkness, and well before midnight.

Meanwhile, Nia, War, and I will need a much more conventional means of transportation to get to West Hollywood by midnight.

"How did you get this again?" Nia asks Carl when he rolls up in front of the comic book shop in a black SUV with pimped-out stereo and spinning rims.

"It's borrowed."

"With or without permission?" I mutter.

"Does it matter?"

"Not if we hurry." War heads to the driver's seat.

But Carl slams down the lock on the door before she can pull it open. "I'm coming with."

"No." The word's out of my mouth before I can stop it, and all three of them turn my way.

"I'm not going to just sit here, Ashlyn. Not alone." He purses his lips. "Not just ... watching."

Not like last night, he's saying, but I just shake my head and repeat more softly, "No."

Because when I look at Carl, I get a flashback of him drawing everything we've done. His expression had been a blighted landscape of horror. Forget that he's mortal and fragile. I never want to see that look on his face again.

"*You're* mortal," he points out. "And you're going after him."

The last word sours on his tongue.

"I have to."

"Because Beckett saved you?"

"Because it's who I am."

I finally know exactly who I am.

"And I'm the record keeper," he keeps trying. "No one's going to touch the guy in charge of their story."

"He's probably right," War mutters, avoiding my glare. "And we could use the help."

"Especially with Thayer out of action," Nia puts in.

Thayer is staying at the shop where he'll be safe. He's already healing from his wounds, but slower than usual. We can't risk moving him until it's safe.

"Fine." I clamber into the passenger seat next to Carl. "But this is going to be very dangerous. So stay out of the way, mortal spawn."

"You are so power-drunk right now," Carl mutters and shifts the van into drive.

The car falls into an unusually loud silence on the way down the mountain. The air is thick with everything we're not saying, and I alternate between trying to think of something wise or encouraging ... and wondering if crap Los Angeles traffic is one of the last things I'm ever going to see.

Eventually, I let my mind wander to the one subject I haven't dared ponder yet.

Beck.

This guy had been so many things to me—untouchable surfer, heroic savior, leader, friend—yet has he really been any of them at all? His lies stack up like dominoes, all of them predicated on the one that came crashing down last night.

My father was your father's killer.

He should have just said it. Yeah, it would've changed everything between, but at least it would be the truth. Zoe, as crazy as I always thought she was, had at least given me that.

"This is it," War says, too soon, leaning between the seats. The clock on the dashboard reads just after eleven.

"I hope the hermits made it," I say, scanning the darkness for life.

Nia grumbles. "I hope they're as repentant as they claim because otherwise, we're screwed."

All remains quiet as we pull to the side of the sleepy neighborhood and debark. Too quiet. "This doesn't look right."

War's profile hardens. "It doesn't feel right."

"The door's right there," I say, pointing to the handle that peeks beneath the cascading bougainvillea.

"But nothing else is."

She's right. We know we're alone as soon as we enter the private park. No kids are waiting here for a midnight moon.

"I don't understand." Nia checks her watch. "There's not much time."

"Come on." War turns back to the door, the van. "They've taken them somewhere else."

"Wait!" A voice, along with the scent of b.o. and chocolate, rises behind us. "Don't leave me!"

The kid is skinny but running at full speed, and I take a step back to protect myself from his wheedling limbs. Panting, he skids to a stop before us. "Wherever you're going, take me with you."

"No."

"But they left me!" He whines, his prepubescent face squinched up at that injustice. "I was only one minute late, but that's because I had to wait for my mom to get off Pinterest and go to bed!"

"Go home, kid," I say, heart sinking. He doesn't know where they've gone, and we only have a half-hour to figure it out. "We don't know what you're talking about."

"But you guys look just like him."

The kid just blinks when we turn to stare.

"Who?"

"The ugly man. The one that looks like my grandmother."

Nia tilts her head. "Your grandmother's ugly?"

"No, but she's always carrying her knitting needles, too. Like him."

"Like him?" I parrot thinking, *Like my mother did.*

A thought—a crazy one—flashes.

"The only thing is," the kid goes on, oblivious to what he's ignited in me, "this guy never knits. He just whispers terrible things in my ear when I pass too close to the park's edge. But I protect the other kids from him. I tell him to piss off!"

"Good for you, you little runt," War tells him. Nia punches her in the arm.

"So, are you here to say terrible things to me, too?" His voice cracks in the silent night.

"No," Nia tells him. "We're here to kill him."

War punches her back, but the kid lets out a wild whoop and pumps his fist. Then he stops and tilts his head. "So why aren't you at the big house?"

Slowly, Nia and I turn to War.

"Hey, War. That house you grew up in ...?"

I leave the question open.

"You mean where Rometra's been gathering her troop?"

Where she's been plotting to betray them for months.

War gives a brief nod. "Yeah. It's a mansion."

"Please tell me it's close."

WAR'S CHILDHOOD HOME IS NOT ONLY CLOSE, IT'S LARGE ENOUGH to hold an entire army of aspiring Elders, their foul pet hermits, and a bunch of preteens desperate for a peek at the supernatural.

"And I know it like the back of my hand," War says, pointing at a hastily drawn map as Carl speeds for the hills. The mansion that the Elders now occupy is built like a hollowed-out Lego, double-stacked and rectangular, with a center courtyard that is completely cut off from public view.

"Large enough to hold an enormous zodiac wheel to reflect the heavens?" I ask War.

"Totally."

It's also as close as you can get to the Hollywood sign without being in its shadow. Maybe once we pull off this improbable rescue, we'll have time for a selfie.

"Beachwood Canyon is here," War says, drawing a street just above a bluff overlooking a park called Lake Hollywood. "There was a fire in the sixties, and the homes were never rebuilt, though the foundations remained. Our house was built atop one of them, but carved into the hillside in steppes. The basement is on this mountain ridge. It's like the tiers of a wedding cake, all facing the canyon side."

"So nobody knows it's there," Nia comments.

"The coyotes and bobcats do, and maybe the rare off-leash dog... but none of them know it for long." She smiles wryly before going on. "You can only really see the home from the opposing cliff side, where it seems to blend in with the other multi-million dollar properties."

Hidden in plain sight.

Minutes later, War points at a darkened hillside looming above the snaking freeway. We slide to a stop on a gravel lay-by overlooking a grassy field. Above, the vaulting hillside is sepia-still.

Making sure my mask is secured, I hop to the ground with such a resounding clunk that War shoots me a dirty look. Yeah, I'm loud, but that's because I've armed myself with every super-natural weapon I can carry, including the demi-cannonballs.

"You okay?" I hear Nia ask Carl. Sweat dots his brow, and his hands shake as he silences the car.

"I need to draw." He looks nauseous but catches my concerned look and throws some energy into his smile. "Go. And Archer?"

I pause.

Using his one good hand, he taps his thumb beneath his fingers twice, then splays them out, three to the side.

I squint in the dark. "What is that?"

He does it again, saying it this time as his fingers flash. "T. T. E." Then he smiles. "It's how long I'll believe in you."

The back of my eyes sting. Blinking the sensation away, I swallow hard, then nod as I whisper, "It's how long my mother loved me."

"It's how long I'll have your back," Nia pipes up from behind and also taps.

War just nods. "It's how long I'll fight."

"Til the End, then." I tap back before pretending to think. "Hey, War. What was that thing you once told Thayer about having a plan?"

"That everyone's got one." A light turns on in her eyes, and she gives me a slow, snaking grin. "Until you punch them in the mouth."

I mirror her mean smile. "Let's go loosen some teeth."

37

INSERT FART JOKE HERE.

We ascend the Santa Monica mountains near Lake Hollywood Park, using a secret hiking trail cut off from the rest of the valley by the heavy concrete slice of the freeway. We're surrounded by little more than brittle brush and milkweed, and within minutes, the city is well below us, lights like crystals dropped atop grit.

Darkness spreads like a stain, the night so dense with shadows that only the specter of the Hollywood sign looms. It's larger-than-life and ghostly white, the same as the silent movie stars of the past. Then my sharpened eyesight kicks in, and I spot coyotes scrambling between the chaparral, the rabbits they chase cowering beneath ragweed, still as statues.

Hermits are out there, cowering, too. I can smell them.

"How will we tell the difference between our hermits and theirs?" Nia asks as we huddle among flowering gray wands of buckwheat.

"Ours are the pretty ones," War says, scanning the hillside for familiar landmarks.

Nia mutters under her breath. Tonight's partnership with the hermits has done nothing to ease her hatred of them.

"There," War finally says. She points to a rock formation atop a jutting hillock, one that wasn't there before. It's the signal we've been waiting for. The three hermits, stacked atop each other. The world's ugliest statue. War whistles to indicate she's seen them, and the formation tumbles.

"Okay," War blows a hard breath and turns our way. "So we just have to make it that far."

Bishop and company will be set up like links in a chain all the way to the basement entrance. They'll contract around us in a tight ring as we advance and do it before the other hermits scent our presence.

"We won't have long," Nia says, echoing my worries. And the meeting point is farther than it looks. We're just about to reroute to keep our scent downwind when Bishop pops up from behind a bush like a misplaced garden gnome. "Archer. Come."

I don't hesitate. The scent of fermented breath alone—like rotten eggs wrapped in vomit—tells me we're well inside enemy territory. Bishop blows out a deliberate breath to mask any scent that might waft from our bodies. His gaze is stone-hard in the bright moonlight. For the first time in a long while, Bishop has a purpose.

Another of our hermits materializes to flank the rear. I think it's Bob. He also pants heavily into the breeze ... and releases a couple of farts for good measure. I show my gratitude by keeping well ahead of his lopsided gait.

"We marked everything each half mile, beginning as soon as we left the wheat." Bishop's smile looks more like a grimace in the shadowed night.

"Marked?" I whisper to War.

"They peed on everything." She snorts when I draw back.

"We should pee on you, too," Bishop says, catching the look. "You smell too fresh."

I'd stop dead in my tracks, but Bob is still farting behind me.

"Give me death and dismemberment any day," Nia mutters.

Another voice rattles through the night. "Wish granted."

And all hell breaks loose.

AN ENEMY HERMIT LUNGES WITH THE CHARGING FORCE OF A linebacker. Its war cry is a razored screech, dirty claws extended, and eyes burning red in the deep night.

Yet Bishop cries out, too—voice ululating, calling for backup in a way that would make a prepubescent boy proud.

Bob runs interception. The two hermits connect skulls with a resounding crack and immediately turn into a snarling mass of mangled limbs that roll back downhill in the direction we just came.

A half-dozen enemy hermits lope our way in great, lumpy strides. Their throats gurgle in anticipation, and I dig for one of my spheres. Bishop's arm falls over mine. "No! The Elders will hear! And I can't stop them."

No. That's our job.

A descending howl has him pulling away. The enemy hermits are upon us ... but so are those who've fanned out to protect us, and they have *names*.

Maybe it's that. Or maybe it's because Beck has long given them a place to rest and reside in the blood wheat, but compared to the clumsy clockwork motions of the defending guards, our hermits move with almost smooth precision. For every step their opponents take, ours manage two. Every lift of their arm or kick of their bowed, knobby legs puts them farther behind our hermits, who fight with a strength and purpose I didn't even know they had.

War is surprised, too. She watches, wide-eyed, as Bob clamors atop an enemy hermit's back, cringing when he rips out the beast's jugular ... with his teeth. Yet a furied wail rises behind me as the hermit protecting that flank falls under the attack of three enemies.

"There's too many!" Nia panics, caught between warring hermits ... her worst fear.

I don't blame her. The enemy hermits spill toward us as if vomited from the earth. I'd yank out my urumi, but I can't use it with so many allies surrounding me.

"Hold!" Bishop orders his team, and they snap into a tight circle around us. Yet from the corner of my eye, I see one of our smaller hermits stumble, and the shift in formation creates an opening through which I can see the onset of a killing blow. It's aimed right at Nia.

Here's what the readers will say if these events ever end up in a real manual: It was unlucky for Nia that one of those demented hermits had a giant brass candlestick as its talisman.

Shock ratchets through me, blurring my vision as the sound of metal on flesh sickens my stomach. I scream ...right before Nia pulls me away. "Run!"

That's when I catch sight of Bob, bleeding from the skull, the candlestick lodged in his left temple like a new fashion accessory. He turns his head as blood rolls into his eyes. "Run!"

"Shields up!" Bishop screams, running with us, and our own stinky, panting hermits whirl so that their hard-shelled backs and shoulders face their attackers. They grunt and squeal and pant with every blow taken to their thick hides ... but they do not break.

We are fifty yards from the basement door when a bright light suddenly pours out over the earth. The basement door rockets open, a man's silhouette sharp-cut in its center. "What's in the Mother's name is going on out here?"

Our hermits skid on their heels and tighten the circle around us. Nia and War go entirely still, and I forget how to breathe as the Elder leans forward, and sniffs deeply of battle and blood and hermit fart, before keying in on our tightly knotted group. Pointing directly at Bishop, he bellows, "You! Come here!"

For the first time all night, Bishop hesitates. He's kept us safe all this way ... and done it with only one hand. Tucked beneath his left armpit is his beloved, his *essential*, talisman. He can't approach the Elder while holding it. The man will see it, steal it ... and own him.

Careful to stay hidden behind his back, I slip my hand up Bishop's side. He is hot and trembling and sweating, but when he feels my fingertips, he lightens his grip. As I pull the stuffed bear away, a shudder ratchets his body.

"Go," I whisper, bringing the talisman to my chest.

"I said come!" the Elder bellows simultaneously, and Bishop, still trembling, steps forward. The other hermits crowd in tightly before us. Miraculously, or tellingly, the man's appearance in the doorway has caused the enemy hermits to scatter.

Maybe if the Elder bothered to look at Bishop's face, he'd have realized that this hermit is not one of his cowed, raving mad slaves. Maybe all he sees is that Bishop lacks a talisman, and assumes that the hermit no longer belongs to himself. I'll never be sure what the Elder's thinking as he raises his arm to slap Bishop upside the head.

I do know that the last thing he ever sees is the inside of Bishop's mouth, jaw unhinging with a double crack as he leaps at the Elder's face.

Even the hermits surrounding us cringe.

"Mother-Lover," Nia can't help but whisper.

War steadies her with a hand and looks at me. "Let's go."

I let them duck through the threshold first while I pause long enough to hold the stuffed bear out to Bishop. He's no longer shaking, but his back is to me, and when he feels the toy touching his arm, he reaches back with one arm, careful not to look at me.

I enter the basement, vowing never to tease him about his stuffed toy again.

38

INSERT WTF EMOJI HERE.

You know what's spookier than murderous hermits on a darkened hillside? Unfinished basements.

Not even magical ones, but just giant holes in the earth that someone decided to spit a building on top of without finishing it out. This basement differs only in that it's swathed in a cloud of preternatural funk that permeates every surface, even more reason to run the other way.

Instead, War motions us forward.

"I'd rather go back outside and stand in a cloud of hermit farts," I whisper to Nia as War leads us to a half-rotting staircase.

She nods, creeping forward. "We need to be subtle and not just for Beckett's sake. Attacking the Elders in their own home is like entering a beehive. We either walk out with our honey, or we die."

"Comforting," I lie. Because even with our ally hermits, we're outnumbered.

We're all vulnerable to mortal weapons while the Elders are not, and the nine initiates upstairs are likely in no position to help. That means we'll need to ensure the safety of whatever mortal children are here before freeing the initiates, locating Beck, defeating the Elders, and escaping alive.

Basically, if I were texting someone the details of this plan? This is where I'd put the WTF abbreviation and thumbs-down emoji.

Yet our unlikely army shows no sign of turning back, climbing at a steadfast pace that can be considered brave ... or a death march. Maybe it's because what lies behind the hermit and what lies ahead are equally bleak. At least by moving forward, there's hope of salvation.

They surround Nia, War, and me in a noxious shield, with Bishop taking up the rear after locking the basement door. I'm buried in the pack's middle, yet instead of making me feel protected, I feel confined.

The feeling intensifies when we surface from the basement into a slim, well-lit hallway. War's already told us this industrial-chic area hosts bedrooms, yet the doors studding the hallway are all handleless and steel-enforced. I guess that's the only way to feel safe in a house filled with evil, murdering supervillains.

Unless you're us. Then you just feel like a fish in a barrel.

I push forward as fast as I can without stepping on the heels of the hermit in front of me.

War halts us after clearing a bisecting hall just below a steep staircase. This one is paneled in warm wood, which alone tells us we're entering the central part of the house.

"There's a giant courtyard in the home's center. It used to hold our herb and ornamental garden, but there's also a clear view of the stars above, so the ceremony will likely occur there. Cassius will want to see the skies come midnight."

No, I think, remembering how he yelled at the stars from the ocean. He'll want the skies to see *him*.

"But be careful," War continues, "and keep as close to the interior walls as possible. Each of the four sides faces the court-yard, so you'll be visible from every angle."

Thunder rumbles in the distance, punctuating her words. War's gaze touches mine reflexively, probably an accident, and I see right then that she doesn't expect us to succeed. She jerks her head anyway. "Come on."

To our everlasting credit, every one of us does. Yet we don't even make it up the stairs before we spot the first Elder. He's facing the courtyard, surveying the grounds with hands on hips. He's also huge. We all back up.

"Geez," Nia whispers, backing up. "His biceps are wearing biceps."

"It's like a Mack truck mated with a person," I agree.

War checks her watch. "It's eleven-forty."

And Beck is lost somewhere in the reaches of this house with two floors to go.

"Cover me," I say, and I'm climbing before War can swipe at me.

"At least be subtle!" Nia hisses from behind.

I hit the landing and immediately tap the dude's shoulder. It's the size of a skull. "Hey. Old guy."

It takes a while for something other than a blank surprise to register, but eventually, it dawns on me that I'm not supposed to be there.

Before he can lunge, I hold out my unsheathed urumi. "Hold this for me, will ya?"

He smiles like a toddler on Christmas morning and snatches the urumi from my hand. The flexible metal bows as he draws back ... and he immediately impales himself between the tiny outcroppings acting as his shoulder blades. A second later, he drops like a stone.

"Yup." I nod solemnly. "Just as stupid as he looks."

"That was the opposite of subtle." Nia reaches me just as I'm retrieving my conduit.

"But look. I'm the opposite of dead."

I'm wiping the blood on a totally ancient tapestry when a yelp sounds at the end of the corridor. A woman this time. Not as large as the dude, but sinewy and compact as hell. The corner she's standing in looks like the foyer, and she's just come in from outside.

"What the hell are you things doing in here?"

I realized she doesn't yet see us—not past the bulbous backs of the hermits. She also doesn't realize that these are not the same hermits they've captured and enslaved, which is surprising.

Even I can tell the difference between these single-time lawbreakers and the gnarly beasts who've been forced to kill again and again.

"Somebody eat her," War mutters, and three hermits shoot forward.

Elder or not, she's unarmed. One hermit pivots to her back and secures her arms. A second one leaps high, wraps his bowed legs around the Elder's elegant neck, and—clearly a wrestling fan —flips backward. He squeezes his legs together and gives the chick a really mean hug. I turn away before her neck breaks. It doesn't kill her, but she won't get up for a few days.

"Split up." War commands, and three others peel off the other way, including Bob. The enormous brass candlestick is still buried in his skull, giving him a slightly tilted look, but his brain seems to be working. "We'll make our way to the third floor."

Yet Nia steps aside. "I'm with Bob. One of us should cover this floor, and besides ... nobody kills him unless it's me."

The candlestick wobbles at Bob's temple as he swallows hard, but they fan out and are gone within moments.

"Let's go try for a bird's-eye view," War tells me, and we circle up the folded staircase, flanked by the final two hermits.

CHILDREN ARE SUPPOSED TO YELL AND LAUGH AND IMAGINE themselves on epic adventures as they race through a playground, bound through a home, or zigzag through a classroom.

Instead, the twelve the Elders have captured sit stick-straight with their backs pinned to wooden chairs. Of course, they've been secured there with rope. And blindfolded. And, from the tilt of every little head, told to listen carefully for the thunder marking the new world order.

War and I peer at them over the flat ledge of the third floor, which is nothing more than a viewing arcade with arching cathedral windows on all four sides. Each is thrown open to the night. The entire courtyard is visible from here, and the sight makes me swallow hard.

War's right; it's been cleared of foliage, and mortal children and doomed initiates stud the area beneath a sky full of gathering clouds.

Not one Elder is in sight.

In contrast to the children, our ally initiates are not blindfolded, only gagged. They sit cross-legged atop the ground, which has been ripped of fauna and overlaid with concrete. One giant star centers them all, while shimmering lines inlaid with gold extend to the encircling glass walls to create the spokes of the zodiac wheel. Each initiate has been dumped halfway to the bright star in the courtyard's middle, bound and secured atop the appropriate zodiac symbol, stamped into the concrete.

It's all a bit obvious, but then symbolic gestures usually are.

"No Beckett," I say, noting the sole empty spot. From above, it's like a sliver of pie has been sliced from the whole.

"Cassius is keeping him close," War answers. "He won't risk him escaping again."

"So where are they?" And I mean *all* the Elder.

We've done a sweep, and none are on the third floor. Probably because everyone is taking part tonight, not watching. After all, what evil supervillain wouldn't want to participate in the advent of a new world order?

"Probably donning ceremonial robes or some crap like that."

She shakes her head. "Wouldn't want to get blood on your street clothes."

The evilness of what is about to occur suddenly gut-punches me. Lousy timing, I know, but until recently, this kind of brutality hasn't been a part of my everyday life.

"They're going to kill the initiates in front of the children." I say it out loud, just to drive it home. "In cold blood."

"Of course." One of the arching cathedral windows is directly behind War, allowing in a gust of fresh, rain-scented wind. She's framed like a stained-glass silhouette. "That kind of trauma will keep the Elders alive in the nightmares and imagination of those kids forever."

And fear is rocket fuel to the Elders.

War turns to the two hermits who've been waiting for our instruction. "We need to split up, one of us on each side of this balcony. You two take the corners to the south. I'll head north, and Ash will stay here."

"What do we do after that?" asks the ugly one.

Uglier one.

"Wait for the signal, and then jump, of course."

The second hermit scrunches its face. Now it's uglier. "What's the signal?"

"You'll know it when you see it." War turns her attention back to me as they disappear. "You know how Nia told you to be subtle?"

I nod stiffly.

"Screw that."

We high-five, and then she taps her fingers—TTE—before ducking low to slip around the corner, leaving me alone. Counting off the remaining minutes until midnight, I resume my watch over the children and the bound and gagged initiates below.

And I begin devising a plan that will fuel the imagination of those kids in a totally different way.

39

HEROES AND SURVIVORS.

I hear Cassius before I see him.

His voice billows into the open courtyard, causing every muscle in my body to tense. Holding my breath, I peer over the balcony in time to see him striding to the courtyard's center, Beck in tow.

Despair affects people differently. Some bend under its weight, backs bowed like oxen beneath the crossbar of a plow. Others straighten, only an unwilling blink, a forced life-sustaining breath, moving them.

Beckett is this kind, except that his eyelids close over a gaze so dark it's a struggle to remember that they once sparked blue. I don't know what's transpired between him and his father in the hours they've been together, but whatever Cassius has said or done has extinguished anything that once lived inside him. That alone has me forgiving Beck completely.

And I hate Cassius more than ever.

As he dumps Beck atop the Leo star sign, I see that War was right. He and the other Elder have changed into robes. I suppose the first ceremonial killing in five years is cause enough for formality.

They want to be drawn impressively—heroically—if it works.

"Can we take these blinders off yet?" asks a child when one of the other Elders passes close enough that his robe brushes the tiny, bare ankles.

"Soon," comes the growled reply as a bolt of lightning arcs over the sky. It's followed by a far-off rumble that ends closer to the compound than it began. Not long now.

I dip my hand into the pocket of my sturdy cargoes, coming out with three cannonballs.

Looking down on Cassius's vile head, I can't help but imagine his limbs flailing as one of these babies strikes home. More lightning flashes—slivered like the prongs of a fork—turning his profile into a slab of blackened bone. The hair on my body lifts with an electric crackle as thunder claps for attention overhead.

The children are blindfolded, but the gagged initiates sight the impending tempest and begin squirming.

It's too late.

All but three are within arm's reach of an Elder. Two of the missing star signs—the Pisces and the Scorpio star signs—must be the Elders we attacked in the hallway. The others exchange quizzical looks, but it's too close to midnight for them to investigate.

A third Initiate, Emerson, has turned her wild, disbelieving gaze up into Rometra's stony face. My fingers twitch with the need to act.

Above, thunder and lightning align. A single, sizzling spear rockets into the heart of the courtyard. Sure enough, every Elder turns their attention to the bright, burning sky overhead.

Amidst the ensuing sizzle, I hear Rometra ask, "What time is it?"

Her voice, that flat tone, immediately whisks me back to the cottage—the room where she threatened me, the field where she pummeled me. Yeah, Cassius is the murderer of those I most loved, but that was long ago. Rometra's more recent betrayal is about to result in a dozen new deaths.

Except that it's not, I think, and, sparing one last glance at Beck, I stand.

The sky ticks off the final moments in bright rockets of fire ... and I answer Rometra myself. "It's dinnertime, Mother-Lovers."

I throw like a girl.

My matriarchal lineage, along with my heartfelt intention, turns my demi-cannonballs into supernatural fast pitches. Robes go flying as I unload explosive spheres into the courtyard, and you wouldn't believe what some of these guys wear beneath them. Elders begin hitting the ground, and eight ally hermits get to sink their teeth into the first snack of the night.

They don't bother with the entry. They just rush directly through the glass walls to attack. Each hermit scores a solid bite with their brick teeth before the Elders even move.

A movement flickers at eye level, my two hermits poised atop the balcony wall like enormous gargoyles. They wait to see which of the Elders shake free first—in this case, the Libra male and an Aquarius so deformed from all its evil deeds that its sex is unclear —and then they leap from the balcony with roars that are swallowed by cracking thunder.

I save two cannonballs for Cassius alone, and the way his limbs wheedle through the air when I double-tap him is just as rad as I dreamed. His decaying mouth forms a soundless scream while the rapid-fire lightning turns his fall into a stop-motion film.

It's awesome.

It's also a good thing the kids are still blindfolded because between the bones cracking beneath the hermit's teeth, and the raw lightning severing the sky, this battle's getting real. The smoke from the demi-cannonballs rises to obscure my view from above, but I'm a heat-seeking missile.

No escape for you, I think, and blindly tag Cassius again. His fury scars the air in a series of serrated screams.

Meanwhile, Nia is suddenly there with a knife, doing that acrobatic thing she does so well, spinning, ducking, and slicing at ropes, freeing the cringing initiates. Three are free before the Elders regroup.

Suddenly it's a war.

Grinning, I reach for my pocket, face falling when I come up empty. I've run out of cannonballs. I'm reaching for my goodie bag, fingers scrambling for any projectile, when a voice rockets up the stairs behind me.

"To the roof!"

His voice.

I turn in slow motion, instinctively flattening my back against the balcony wall.

Of *course* he's abandoned his allies, I think, just before Cassius heaves himself up the staircase. When has he ever cared about someone other than himself?

Beck is with him, unresisting as he's dragged up toward the watchful sky. He's followed by Rometra and looks resigned, like he just wants it all to be over.

My urumi hisses like a snake as I slide it from its sheath. They all stop cold.

Cassius, so focused on chasing the stars, blinks as if startling awake. He halts in his tracks so that Rometra plows into him from behind. My fist tightens around my urumi, fingers tingling as the flexible blade wakens in my hand. My muscles hum with the need to swing, and I'm just about to whip out a few deadly figure-eights when I see what Rometra carries in her arms.

The girl from the playground. Her name escapes me. Tammy? No, Tavi.

"Ash, get out!" Beck again, still trying to save me, but Cassius silences him with a brutal thwack to the skull. Beck sags, out cold.

I answer him anyway. "No. I'm no longer hiding from anyone."

Including myself.

Cassius's eyes flare, and I think I spot fear glimmering despite the smoke in the air.

"You were right, Cassius Lux," I say his full name for the first time. He can't hide any longer, either. "Titan should have taken care of me five years ago. Guess you'll just have to do it yourself."

He wants to. I see it in the way he instinctively reaches for his conduit at my goading, but a trio of lightning bolts come together at that moment, the electric crack making a hard surface of the sky. Even Beck jolts and rolls his head around at the sound.

One minute until midnight.

"Take care of this," Cassius orders Rometra.

Rometra, who has never seen me work with my urumi, shoves Tavi aside with one arm and takes a giant step forward. "Gladly."

Yet Cassius can't resist one last dig. "Enjoy your final moments, knowing you failed. He will die," he says, jerking his head at his son. "And she will watch."

Tavi yelps as he jerks her to his side, a sound that disappears with her as he flees around the corner.

Faced with Rometra, I'm more distracted than I should be. Yet the muscles in my thighs twitch with the need to chase after Cassius. After the girl. After Beck.

Too bad, I realize, right before Rometra lunges. Because she only has eyes for me.

THE LAST TIME ROMETRA AND I WERE SQUARED UP LIKE THIS, A rope linked us together. I've more freedom to move this time, but she's already closed the distance between us, leaving little room to leverage my weapon. I brace for impact as she plows into me.

Or would have ... if War didn't cold-cock her from the side.

Rometra flies across the room with such force the wall splinters into a crumbling web around her body.

"It's okay, Ash." Gaze fixed on her sister, War cracks her neck. "I've got this."

"You." Rometra wobbles, but finds her feet. "You figured it out."

"That you'd come here?" War says, and her sister nods. "Of course. No one knows you better than I do." War jerks her head over the balcony, where the smoke muffles the screams and cries of pain. "Was that your idea, too?"

"Betraying the others?" Rometra shrugs. "Not initially. I was just tracking a hermit last spring when I came upon the blood wheat. It was so oddly placed that I knew it couldn't be accidental. Sure enough, I spotted the other hermits minutes later, lounging in the field like it was their right. That's when I knew you had to be on the other side. You and the other second-borns. Usurpers." She glances at me. "Freakish spawn."

The barb hits home. It's Cassius's taunts all over again. Yet War intercepts before I can answer.

"Cassius will never be your ally," War tells Rometra. "He used you to get to us, and as soon as he's claimed Beckett's power, he'll kill you, too."

"You're wrong. Cassius sees how powerful I am. He doesn't care if I'm from a different generation. Our twelve agents will form a new sort of troop. An unstoppable one."

"The Universe will never permit it."

"We're not asking permission."

Rometra speeds forward to plant one steel-studded boot like a bomb into War's chest. War's body makes a sound like a balloon being popped, and her head strikes the floor with such force that the reverberations shock up my legs.

Without thinking, I swing out, and the urumi's first bite strikes like a whip. All Rometra can do is hold up an arm in defense, and for a moment, we're bound together like before.

Then her pained cry stains the air. The accompanying stink is like vomit blended with hot tar. I jerk the flexible steel loose, and

Rometra sags against the wall, head down and shoulders heaving with the effort not to collapse.

War, back on her feet by now, moves in front of her. "All I ever wanted to do was love you."

Rometra looks up, pauses, and then begins laughing so hard that blood pours from her wounded arm. "And all I ever wanted to do was hurt you."

Even after Rometra's multiple betrayals, War still wants her to be something she's not. And Rometra knows it. She watches long enough to see the barb strike home.

Then she catapults herself backward and out the open window.

War doesn't hesitate this time, and neither do I. She lunges for the window. I head for the stairs.

Yet not before calling out, "Prove her wrong."

War's reply falls with her as she leaps. "Heroes."

"And survivors," I mutter and race to the rooftop, following my own advice.

Following the scent of Shadows.

40

DAUGHTER OF CHAOS.

Somewhere beyond this last flight of stairs, Beck cries out in the night. Even racing, even with my heightened speed, I know I am too slow, too late. The door leading to the rooftop is cut into the ceiling, locked from above.

Yet the bolt is normal, regular, manmade ... and I am not.

Power fists inside my chest, and I blast it from its hinges in one great shove. It rockets open to clatter against the rooftop, the sound masked by the thunder and lightning still gathering overhead.

The chaos below us is manmade, yet the rooftop is ringed in elemental fury. Clouds swirl, dark bruises crackling with electricity. Thunder rumbles in the giant bellies of those great masses while wind pulls the edges into tattered flags.

It's a magnification of what happened to me on the beach, and exactly what was supposed to happen in the field of blood wheat.

It's what Cassius has been waiting for.

I brace against the turbulence, legs splayed and strong, and shake out my arms like I used to when I surfed, trying to relax. It's difficult amidst the electric charge in the air. Even my hair is stiffening at the root, the very molecules in my body sensing the destruction to come.

I whirl, searching out Cassius and Beck, and spot them right as a gong marks the midnight hour. From this distance, I see—yet can't stop—the upward bend of Cassius's arm. Tavi, holding tight to an air conditioning unit, screams.

I race forward, already too late. "Stop!"

Cassius plunges the enormous stake into Beck's chest. "No."

He does it again. Beck buckles as the stake finds his side, piercing some organ there, but my cry has somehow focused him, and his eyes are on mine. "Ashlyn, no!"

Tavi whirls, eyes gone saucer-wide. "Help him!"

The power of her expectation does something to me. It's like all the energy in the air reroutes to fuel my body and quicken my reactions. Maybe it's just that I want to be a hero for her.

Maybe it's just that I already am.

The sky claps raucously overhead. Lightning sears the air in impossible directions, and though still grounded, I grow weightless in the tempest. I am subject to the elements—that's what makes me human—yet I'm a part of them, too.

For the first time, I actually feel what is super in me meld with what is mortal, like plant and root, one complete whole.

Another flash singes the sky overhead, and I whip my urumi side to side in enormous figure eights. Like a metronome, it picks up pace to keep time with the beat of my strong heart. My circling blade sends rooftop cuttings flying.

Cassius sees, and for a moment, his weapon hand shakes. Then he discards Beck and lunges for the girl. She screams, Beck reaches out, and Cassius's blackened skull pulses in the bright heat. I keep to my slow, metronomic march. Super and mortal. Extraordinary and normal.

Light *and* Shadow.

"Stop! Or I'll kill her."

I'm sure he'd like her to believe that.

I whip my blade faster. Everything falls silent in the relative quiet of the storm's eye. The Universe is watching.

"Now, why would you do that?" I say as storm clouds circle us.

"It's what Shadows do! It's what *I* do!"

No, that's what hermits do ... but I don't say that. Instead, I stop and spread my arms wide. "How about a trade?"

"You'd sacrifice yourself for this mortal child?" His eyes widen in genuine disbelief.

I used to *be* that mortal child.

"That's what heroes do."

"Ash, no!" Beck tries.

Cassius responds by stomping on Beck's head. For a moment, he's out cold.

Good. I don't want him to see what happens next.

"The girl goes free," I tell Cassius, easing forward. My conduit clatters to the roof behind me. "You never see or touch or go near her again."

"Done." Cassius pushes Tavi aside. She stumbles with the force but rights herself quickly. And she watches.

Good.

I remove my mask with one hand so she'll remember my face.

"Watch," I tell her, opening my arm wide, and exposing my chest. "And remember."

Cassius charges, and the stake plunges deep into my chest. My breath both flies from me and escapes from that nifty new hole. Cassius throws me to the ground and pins me beneath one hand and a knee.

I scent the rancid smile stretching over his face.

His laughter is fire on my neck.

He plunges the stake again, and my flesh burns as it tears. The pain flares in an agonizing corona to overtake my entire core.

Mother-Lover, I think, fighting to hold to consciousness. That hurt way more than I thought it would.

. . .

Despite the fiery pain, I hold tight to my mask.

I fix my gaze on it, an assurance that I'm still here. I force feeling into my fingers, and even as I bleed out on the roof—beneath the sky, under a child's horrified gaze—I'm reassured by the weight of the metal mask. Slipping my fingers through the eyeholes, I begin to shake.

"What's so funny?" Cassius asks, because I'm already laughing hard. I can't help it. I'm half-dead, yet the other half is just, like, hanging out.

Marking time.

"Don't you see? You're dying!"

"Oh, dude." I snort, causing air and blood to bubble out of me. That's okay. "This isn't me dying."

This is me killing it.

"You totally forgot ..." I have to spit out blood before finishing my sentence. "Who my mother is."

"I killed her!" Cassius snarls, triumphant. "And your father! I watched as their limbs were torn from their bodies in a black hole of my own creation!"

I know.

"I'm not talking about her."

Cassius freezes.

"Daughter of Chaos, remember?" My turn to snarl. "The woman who was half-Shadow and half-Light. That gives me a direct line all the way back to both of the First Mothers."

"Cool." Tavi's voice has gone breathy. The sky goes silent.

"*Super* cool," I say into the paused hush, "Because that means I can't be killed with a mortal weapon."

"This is a conduit!" Cassius screams, but now his voice has gone reedy and desperate.

"No. This is a conduit."

I whip out at him with the sharp, flaring edges of the mask that I created. A maggot-ridden rot washes over me as even the blackened bone gives way beneath the vicious slash. His pulpy skin pops like overripe fruit, and he lets out a surprised yelp.

Rising, I yank the "stake" from my side, flip it in my hand, and follow Cassius as he retreats. He turns, intending to leap over the rooftop's ledge. I don't think he knows where he'll land on the sloping cliffside. I don't think he cares.

"Sit," I order.

There's a war going on inside Cassius's body. It causes him to waver on his feet before he plops to the ground like a landed trout.

"Ash?" Beck is conscious again, blinking as he tries to take in the changes that've occurred in these last few seconds. The thunder recedes, and the smoke has cleared. Midnight, and the full minute after, retreat in the rearview mirror.

Watching the clearing sky, Cassius slumps.

Tavi, the child whose fear is supposed to fuel a new troop, is unnaturally chill as she eases to my side. "He stinks."

"That's because he's been rotting inside for a long time," I say, tossing my mask onto Cassius's lap. It burns his clothing where it lands and scorches his palms when he pushes it away. Yet when he tries to rise and run again, all I have to do is point. "Stay."

Cassius stays. He looks confused. Beck looks confused.

"Why is he listening to you?" the little girl asks, confused.

But to me, everything makes perfect sense.

"Because of this."

I hold up the stake, causing Cassius to lunge, but I lift it high as I plant a boot back in his chest. I am suddenly way faster than him.

"What is it?" the little girl asks, popping to her toes and craning her neck.

Cassius lunges for her again, and snags one slim, sweet arm. She screams, and Beck pushes to his feet to help, but I just stand there.

"Let her go," I command, and Cassius does. He must.

Knowing it, he gives me the same murderous look he did back in Laguna when he ranted about his lost birthright and held me underwater.

"Can I hold that?" Tavi, reaching for the pick.

I roll my eyes. "No."

Weirdo.

Oblivious to how close she had just come to a totally heinous death, she pushes. "What is it, then? A weapon?"

"It's his talisman."

Despite the wonder in his voice, Beck gets it right.

"That's right." I nod and have to clear the lump that has suddenly risen in my throat. "And it's not really a stake, but something he strengthened and sharpened to hide its true nature. A mere, manmade knitting needle. My mother's."

"So what?" Spittle flies from Cassius's mouth, fury making him rabid. "I'll never pay for what I did to your parents! You saw to that when you shoved me into that black hole after them!"

Beck turns to regard me fully. "How did you know?"

"I remembered."

And memory is power. Memory lets you know what you've already survived.

"But I escaped that black hole as a new man!"

Cassius can't move, but his mind is racing. He's retelling his story like that can make it count.

"I was forged in the black fire of the Universe's loins!"

"Gross." Tavi winces.

I add to his narrative. "But now you've killed another mortal, and for that, you must pay."

Cassius waves dismissively at Tavi. "She's fine!"

"Not her, idiot." I point to my chest. Sure, the wound has healed, but the leftover blood makes my point nicely. "Me."

"You?"

I glance at Beck. "You were out for a couple of minutes."

But Tavi gasps. She knows what's happened, and Cassius

does, too. His hand flutters and falls from his destroyed cheek. His racing mind finally catches up.

"This jerk wad just murdered what was mortal in me," I say, for the record, "but my super side resuscitated me."

And thank the Mothers I was right about *that*.

"But that's beside the point." I turn back to Cassius. "Isn't it, Law-Breaker?"

Cassius's sneer turns rictus. When he finally opens his mouth to answer, his jaw cracks wide and keeps opening. Heaving, he tilts his head to shoot a horrified look at Beck. His neck cracks, then his spine shrinks, vertebrae sloughing off in his body. It fuses together again, and reforms.

This transformation works its way through his entire body in one violent shudder, and a pained howl slices from his shorn throat.

Its throat.

"Nasty," says Tavi.

"Totally."

I wait until the hermit stops thrashing, and then I kneel before it. It's panting, sweaty, and stinkier than ever. "Hey, what's that word for when you're totally destroyed by the very humanity you so revile? Oh, yeah—irony."

It cowers as I straighten and stand. "Don't worry. I'm not going to make a foot servant out of you. Your son can do with you what he sees fit."

I hold my mother's old knitting needle out to Beck. He's still reaching for it when the-thing-formerly-known-as-Cassius shifts. Using every bit of strength left in its gnarled body, it wraps its swollen fingers around my mask, and—fighting off the pain of touching a supernatural weapon—it plunges the high tines of the mask deep into its own heart.

Bile washes over us, and the decay of something long dead follows. The urge to puke rises as something crawls along my skin, venom pressing against my pores.

I'm not alone. We all empty our stomachs over the rooftop's side.

Silence finally falls.

I risk a glance back at the rooftop. Cassius is one big mound of funk and decay.

"You okay?" I ask Beck, next to me.

Brow furrowed, he doesn't look at me. He doesn't look back.

Instead, he shakes his head and stares into the distance, where storm clouds can be seen wheedling away. I put my hand on his shoulder just as I realize Tavi is missing.

Leaving Beck, I find her leaning over Cassius's body for a closer look.

"You're not going to put that thing back on, are you?" she asks, gesturing to the mask.

Huffing, I shake my head, "You really are a weird kid."

41

WE WILL RISE.

It was Cassius's weapon—his fake weapon—that unraveled everything for the Elders. I'd seen it paired up in my mother's hands enough times that nothing Cassius did to make it appear like a conduit could truly disguise it.

The minute I regained my memories, I knew it was his talisman.

"You didn't kill him."

Beck's voice pulls me from my thoughts. It's the first thing he's said to me since we left the rooftop. We're walking Tavi home from the playground, where Carl dropped us all off before rushing off to collect War from downtown LA.

He doesn't have to say Rometra got away. It's there in his bleak expression. Nia offers to drive so that he can draw on the way.

None of us spoke to the failure aloud. It's not just that we couldn't stand the idea of Rometra's escape, it's that we didn't want to say her name in front of Tavi's strong, impressionable young mind.

"That was fun," Tavi says, bouncing on her toes as we stop in front of a dark, Craftsman-style home. Can we get together again soon?"

"No," Beck and I chime as one.

If she's bummed, she doesn't show it. Instead, she claps her hands and twirls. "I can't wait to tell my friends about tonight and the future agents of Light and the Elders with their demented hermit pets. And that you saved me. And that you can touch the conduits. It's all just so exciting! I don't think I'll be able to sleep!"

"Doesn't mean you can't dream." Beck places his palm atop her head until the bouncing subsides. She visibly melts as she gazes at him. I smile, knowing how she feels.

"Goodbye, Beckett Lux and Ashlyn Archer!" She skips up the short steps and into the house. "You are my heroes!"

I sigh when she's gone and turn my head up to the cold sky. It's totally unremarkable in its black velvet coat, a relief after tonight's events, and I can't help but remember what Beck told me the first time we stood beneath this sky together.

The stars shine more brightly because of the darkness, not in spite of it.

Wondering if he still feels the same, I glance over ... to find him tapping on his cell phone. He only smiles when I ask what he's doing, but within minutes, a dude drives up in a Prius. "You guys call a car?"

It's either because it's the middle of the night, or because our driver is obviously training for NASCAR, but we're at the beach within twenty minutes. I shed my black boots while Beck thanks the driver, and the moment the sand touches my toes, I am no longer a child of the Zodiac or the daughter of Chaos.

I am nothing more, and nothing less, than a mere mortal.

Sagging, I stagger to the water's edge and drop down before my beloved waves. I am home.

"You had a chance at revenge tonight," Beck finally says after we've been there awhile. I can feel the heat of his stare on my cheek, but I keep my face turned to the cold Pacific. "Joanna Archer would have done it. Cass—"

He has to clear his throat.

"My father would have. But you didn't."

I breathe deeply of the ocean breeze and simply shake my head.

"Didn't you want to?"

I frown. How to explain that the last thing I want is for Beck to see his father's death every time he looks at me? For one, it's totally not romantic.

It's also not heroic.

"It's enough that I remembered," I reply, pushing my wind-whipped hair from my face.

And it is. By remembering my past, I finally put it to bed. And for the first time in forever, I don't feel like I'm treading water. Instead, I'm moving forward.

But Beck has stopped dead. He drops his head into his hands and rocks a bit in the dark. "I should have told you."

That Cassius was his father. That he's the one who murdered my parents before my eyes.

"Yeah." I put my hand on his back and dig my bare toes deeper into the cold, wet sand. "You should have."

"I was afraid," he lifts his head, the words rolling from his tongue as quickly as the waves before us. "And ashamed and—"

"I'm glad you didn't."

His father's shame isn't his. Beck's a good guy, but he's been hamstrung by his lineage, unable to be an effective leader because of his father. Like me, he needs to find a way to put it behind him.

"Our histories are a part of us," I begin slowly. But that doesn't mean we have to be slaves to them. Besides, it was better that I figured it out on my own."

Opening that bottle was the only way I could've remembered my mother had that needle on her at the moment Cassius tossed her into the black hole. Outside of me, no one else could know that his sharpened stake was really a modified knitting needle. Or a hermit's talisman.

Only I could ever discover that Cassius was just pretending he could touch the magical conduits. That's why I was such a threat.

That, and because I really could.

"So what now, Ashlyn Archer?" Beck gives a deep sigh. He's asked me this once before. On a cliffside. A lifetime ago. "Bora Bora? Phuket? Kauai?"

He's letting me know the choice is mine. With Cassius gone and my memory returned, I'm no longer in the danger that I was ... and I can do it. I can just disappear like Zoe, never to be heard from again.

"What are *you* going to do?" I ask instead of answering. His silhouette is etched against the night, and his breath matches the rhythm of the waves.

"I'm thinking about taking a page from Rometra's playbook."

"Turning on your friends with murderous ambition?"

He manages a half-smile. "Different page."

Moth. Flame, I think to myself.

"I think we should try to rebuild our world with a tribe made entirely of initiates."

And because it doesn't sound entirely crazy, I nod. "A new model for a new generation."

"A whole new world," he whispers.

"Maybe I stick around, then," I say and feel his attention grow still and honed. I meet his steady gaze and shrug. "I mean, I've missed the start of my senior year and need to catch up. No point in messing up now."

"No." The smile blooms in his voice. "No point in that."

"I can always take off for Kauai next year," I say, knowing I probably won't. I mean, dudes, I'm a hero.

And a survivor.

"Yeah, there's always next year," he says, knowing it too.

For now, dawn closes in. It's cold, but all the armored leather helps with that, and although he's tentative at first, Beck finally wraps his arms around me, and we wait for the sun to rise together.

It tries to sneak up on us. Maybe it thinks we're not watching. Or maybe it hears us whispering to each other about our dreams and plans and hopes for the future.

Or maybe it sees the epic kiss that I've been waiting for, the one that has heat blooming over my lips and warming my mouth.

Maybe it also thinks that all of that has made us less watchful, less aware, less tough.

But we are the offspring of the Zodiac. We can feel the light and the darkness rising and falling like waves on the shore. We know the exact moment that day and night evenly split open the sky, and we turn to the horizon together.

We make a promise to that burning skyline.

Our generation *will* see the Zodiac world rise again. We will do our best to protect the human race from the influence of those who would use mortals for their own gain. I'm still not sure what my role is in that, but I do know that for the first time in years, I'm exactly where I'm supposed to be.

"Now that's a sunrise," Beck whispers into my hair.

I watch the sky warm and glow, its light reflected on my face. "Unforgettable."

42

BACK-UP PLANS.

"An everything bagel with cream cheese," I tell the cashier at the village coffee shop. "And black coffee."

Okay, so we're all back in the mountains because we have a few things to figure out.

What to do with the hermits, for one. They're not just our gnarly little pets anymore, and their newfound free will is making for some very interesting conversations about how they should be treated as they work to earn back their humanity.

We're also housing all of the initiates betrayed by Rometra. There's talk of all of us moving to the LA compound since it's located within the thick human populace, but we have to make sure it's fortified against Rometra, who knows its every corner so well. She's still out there, somewhere, living her best worst life.

Therefore, for now, we're hanging out in a mountain village.

"You never did like my tea."

The voice reaches me just as I'm exiting to head back to the comic book shop. I look over to find a woman with nondescript brown hair of indeterminate age staring at me from a corner table. I'm unsurprised to see that her back is to the wall.

It always has been. I know that now.

"You're here," I say dumbly to Zoe, probably because I'm having trouble believing it. I sit down under the pretense of joining her, but in truth, I'm afraid my legs are going to give out. I thought I'd never see her again.

"Carl told me where to find you." If she notes my shaking, she does not comment on it. "He also showed me this."

The drawing is of me being stabbed in the side by a truly foul-looking Cassius.

"So I guess you know everything that happened."

Her expression remains unreadable. She doesn't even blink. "You failed to form a troop. And the Elders drew first blood."

"And I got stabbed a lot in the side," I point out, not unreasonably.

I'm about to add that we saved a bunch of kids and stopped the Elders from Rising, but her I-told-you-so smile stops me cold.

"Don't worry," she says, crossing her arms over a boring gray sweater. "If there's one thing I've learned over the years, it's that one moment in time doesn't forever define you. You can try again."

I give her a suspicious squint. A forgiving Zoe Archer? A reasonable one?

"Who are you," I finally say, "and what have you done with Zoe?"

"I'm still me, maybe just the next version of me. Zoe 2.0." She cocks her head and thinks on that before shrugging. "Or 5.0. I've lost count. Besides, you're different, too."

My knee-jerk reaction is to disagree. To protest out of habit. To claim that I'm the same carefree surfer girl I've always been.

Yet that would mean unknowing my time at the cottage—the black holes, the red-tipped wheat stalks, hermits with unspeakable guilt staining their miserable souls. And I can't do that. Maybe in time, the memories will all fade, but no one's going to take them from me.

I won't let them.

Which means I'll just have to find a way to live with them.

"Will it be hard?" I jerk my chin at her and all her blandness. Gone are the gypsy skirts and clanking jewelry. I get the feeling that this Zoe is still uncertain, still unformed. Not yet what and who she's meant to be next.

"Starting over?" Zoe frowns when I nod, giving it serious thought. "Not really. The hardest thing is trying to be something that you're not."

I think of all the times I've caught her staring off into space, fingers twitching, fists tightening. Maybe the loony grandmother routine wasn't an act. Maybe being blocked from an entire super- natural underworld that she couldn't forget—yet one she'd never be a part of again—*has* made her a bit crazy.

I give her another suspicious eye squint. "You're still acting weird."

"I'm just sitting here."

"Exactly." I frown. "You're, like, chill."

Zoe shrugs, leaning back in her chair. "You know everything you need to know now. You can choose for yourself who you want to be ... or not. That's all I really ever wanted for you."

"You coulda just told me," I mumble.

"Tell a teenage girl who she is?" Zoe laughs loudly enough to have the nearest patron turning our way, but Zoe's no longer an attractive redhead, and he immediately loses interest. "Yeah, that's worked in the history of ... NEVER."

"What if I'm not sure yet?"

I know I still want to surf, I still want to be in charge of my own life. Yet I also feel the as-yet untapped potential in me. It's set to a simmer somewhere deep in my core, but I can tell.

It wants to boil.

"Just put one foot in front of the other. You'll figure it out."

"And if I take a wrong step?"

"Everyone makes mistakes." She pushes the drawing back my

way as proof. "Some of them even become the best part of your story."

"That's how you make a choice?"

Just fumble around and hope for the best?

"No. That's how you make a *life*." Smiling, finally, she stands. "Walk with me?"

We tour the village.

There's a countrified gas station, and a sandwich shop. Clothing boutiques, and a real estate office displaying photos of dream cabins and enormous homes. It's strange to see regular humans doing regular human activities—circling the lot looking for parking spots, sipping lattes on a small patio, getting sandwiches to go. What's it like to be that normal?

I can't remember.

Finally, we come to a car that's two decades out of fashion and so ugly it probably repels the police. Even though I've never seen it before, somehow I know it's Zoe's. Sure enough, she stops, keys jangling as she pulls them from her pockets.

I turn to face her fully. "I won't know you, will I?"

Because I do know Zoe. Now that I've seen her like this, she'll alter her appearance again as soon as she can. She'll take her own advice. She'll keep going.

"Nope." She confirms it with a small smile. "But that doesn't mean I won't be there."

Watching. Waiting. Planning her next move. Backup plans to her backup plans.

She might be mortal, but Zoe Archer still thinks like a superhero.

"Be safe, Ashlyn. And try to remember..."

"Yeah?"

"Some of the people who love you are still very much alive."

It's as if I've been shot in the chest again. It's the closest Zoe's ever come to saying I love you.

Zoe must feel the same because she busies herself with the

rusted driver's side door. I expect her to drive off without looking back, the same as she did in the taco shop, and although I swallow hard, I don't try to stop her.

I just watch ... so that I'll remember.

Yet Zoe pauses with her hand on the open door. Unexpectedly, she turns her back on the whole of the village—the cars and the people and the other beings that may or may not be watching —and she lifts her chin up to mine. Even in the new day's light, unshed tears make bright stars of her eyes.

"I loved being her."

I clear my throat of the tears that spring up. "You mean the eccentric but beautiful boho-chic surf shop owner who crafts poisons on the side?"

I'm trying to give her time to recover, but the joke falls flat. Or maybe, for just one moment, she doesn't care who sees the real Zoe Archer. She just stares at me with an intensity that burns. I don't flinch from the look, and this time?

I don't think she's crazy.

"I mean, I loved being your grandmother. These last five years?" It's her turn to clear her throat. "The best of my life."

And, true to form, Zoe Archer is gone before the first tear falls.

43

IN CONCLUSION, OLD PEOPLE SUCK.

After that, I head back to the comic book shop, studying the drawing Zoe left me with one hand and holding my coffee and bag of bagels in the other.

My flip-flops thwack against the gallery's wooden walkway in a steady, if out-of-place, beat. These are shoes made for summer and a warmer climate, and it's now October in the San Bernardino mountains.

The chill winding its way through my toes is a good reminder that some things change without grand gestures or the big bangs of a demanding Universe.

Sometimes, all it takes is the mere ticking of minutes, one piled atop the last.

These are my thoughts as I reach for the shop's door, and I'm so preoccupied that I don't even notice the person at my side until it's too late. I whirl, then jerk back.

Then I look down.

The kid is a walking sunburn, with chapped lips and skinned knees, and a bowl-cup hairdo that places him around age ten. He points at the shop door. "Is that place open?"

"No," I snap, though I reel back in my snarl. He's just a kid, after all.

"Then why were you going in?" he says, thrusting out his chest, stance going wide.

"I wasn't."

"Yes, you were."

Now I snarl.

"Are you the owner?" he asks, pushing past me to press his grimy fingertips against the window. He shifts, trying to see around a giant cut-out of Spiderman.

"No, dummy. I'm only sixteen."

Almost seventeen.

I start back down the gallery walk. I'll go in the back way. Let the kid fry on the security system if he tries to follow.

"So, are you one of the new agents?"

I stop dead in my tracks. "What did you say?"

He waits until I've turned back around. "You know, one of the kids Rometra plans on smashing like pumpkins."

He demonstrates, stomping his foot onto the wooden porch. I shudder as the reverberations shoot up and into my legs.

"Rometra," says the kid, looking back up into my face, "totally kicks ass."

She does.

"She does not," I say.

"So you do know what I'm talking about!" He rushes me, holding up a sheet of paper that's stained in one spot and ripped at the edges. "Come on, you gotta let me in. Some old guy gave me this last week, and I can't get it out of my head. He said I needed to roommate on it."

"Ruminate," I correct, juggling my coffee.

I hold out my hand for his crumpled sheet. I recognize Carl's work immediately, and, no surprise, the drawing is of Rometra. It's the one Cassius stole the night of the Elders' attack.

Ruminate.

I swallow hard. Forget Shadow and Light ... a child's mind, lit up, is the most powerful thing in the Zodiac world. The whole point of the manuals was to capture the energy of a mortal child's belief. Cassius must have given this to him when he still thought the Zodiac would rise with the Elders.

He's gone now, but Rometra ... she's now receiving all the power of this child's belief.

The kid snatches the drawing back. "I need more! I gotta know what happens next!"

I should've ripped the drawing to pieces when I had the chance. Instead, I say, "Can't. The series is over."

The boy's hopeful expression crumbles. "What?"

"Yeah, the writer died in a car accident that was super-fiery and killed everyone. Plus dismemberment. Lots of blood."

The kid draws back, eyes widening, and I clear my throat.

"Anyway, the shop is closed for a period of mourning."

"How long?"

"A couple of weeks at least," I lie.

The kid's shoulders slump. "I'm going back to LA tonight. I have school."

"Tough luck," I say and watch him turn away, shoulders slumped. "Hey. Wait a minute."

I pull out the drawing Zoe gave me.

"I was going to keep this," I tell the kid, "but you can have it. It's one of the last drawings of an old dude named Cassius."

The boy snatches it from me, the other drawing forgotten. "How old?"

Not the point, I think, but okay. "Like, forty."

His gaze whips back down, drinking in the scene. "Old people suck!"

"Pretty much."

"Why was he hurting this chick?"

I consider lying, but hey. The world's been reordered. A new generation is making up the rules, and that's me.

"Because I kept him from murdering his own son."

The kid's gaze whips up and down, again and again, until finally ... "It is you!"

The breathiness in his voice is a rush of pure, dizzying power. His awe powers through me like a freight train, winding through my body and out my limbs, before circling back again. It's all I can do not to let out a victorious whoop.

"Who *are* you?" the kid says, sending a tingling right up the back of my skull.

Maybe it's because I just saw Zoe, but I recall her words in The Taco Tavern, right before she left me the first time.

This time, though, it makes me smile. *This* time, I give the kid a grin that's too-wide, too-me, and claim those words as my own.

I am Ashlyn Archer, the beloved daughter ... of Chaos.

I am a human, and touching me has consequences.

I am also Light, and I always will be.

Any other stupid questions?

~

AFTERWORD:

Hello, and thank you for reading! If you enjoyed *Zodiac Rising*, please consider leaving me a review at your favorite review site. It helps me a ton and it lets other readers know if this story might ring their bell, too. Thank you!

Meanwhile, I invite you to read the series that started it all, the original—and complete— *Signs of the Zodiac* series.

The battle between Shadow and Light begins with *The Scent of Shadows*.

Joanna Archer's life was forever shattered at sixteen when she was savagely assaulted and left for dead in the unforgiving Nevada desert.

By all accounts, she should be dead.

Now, by day, Joanna masquerades as a photographer in the glittering facade of Las Vegas. But when darkness descends, she prowls a more sinister Sin City, seeing answers ... and revenge.

Yet in a city where the struggle between Light and Shadow remains eternal, Joanna's nightmare is just beginning ... for those in the Shadows have been looking for the girl who got away, and this time they want her for their own ...

Here's a sneak preview ...

Chapter One

He didn't look dangerous, not at first glance. Still, a girl can never be too careful on a blind date, and that's why I'd insisted Mr. Sand meet me in a popular steakhouse nestled in a casino dead center on the Las Vegas Strip. It was, I'd thought, the most public of all public places.

Yet now, watching the way shadows from the muted lighting

sought out the unhealthy hollows beneath his eyes and cheeks, and the way he toyed with his blue cheese and endive appetizer, I decided the most ominous thing about Mr. Sand was a deeply embedded issue with self-control, and the only thing I was in danger of dying from was boredom.

Of course, that was before I really knew him. And before my death the very next day.

At the time I had no way to know of Mr. Sand's true intentions. Not like now. Besides, who knew homicidal maniacs came wrapped in horse-faced packages with little to no fashion sense?

Beyond that, he was so skinny his Adam's apple bobbed like a buoy above the opening of his pressed shirt, while knobby bones protruded at both knuckles and wrists. Ichabod Crane in a poorly fitted suit.

Not exactly intimidating.

Looks aside, the next mark against him was his first name.

"Ajax?" I repeated as our soups arrived, not quite sure I'd heard right. "Like the cleaner?"

His smile was tight. "Like the Greek warrior."

I mean, really.

Cursing my sister for setting me up on yet another blind date —and myself for letting her—I nevertheless planted my feet firmly on the bright side of things. At least *this* one could walk without dragging his knuckles on the ground.

Plus, even if the woman in me had recoiled at first sight, the photographer in me had something to do.

I tried to picture Ajax in a bank, as he'd already mansplained how the world's financial industry would fall flat on its ass without him, but I couldn't quite imagine him languishing behind a desk.

There was too much movement, too much latent energy in those snaking limbs for that. His fingers twined and untwined, bony elbows rose to rest on the table only to drop a second later.

His eyes darted around the dining room, taking in everything but never fully settling.

I'd like to still those relentless limbs with my camera. Take time to study those shifting eyes. See just who Mr. Sand became when seen in two dimensions instead of three.

He looked at me like he knew what I was thinking.

And it was *that* look, those eyes, that sent up the first red flag. I don't mean the color, a blue so light it was near-transparent, but more the way they tried to own me.

I licked my lips, and his eyes dropped to watch my tongue dart out.

I ran a hand through my bobbed hair, and felt him following the movement so that my fingers fisted there.

I exhaled deeply, forcing myself to relax, and for some reason that made him smile.

I was jumpy, I confess, but I recognized that hungry look. I'd seen it once before, long before I'd ever started dating. I'd hoped never to see it again.

"So, what do you do for a living?" Ajax asked, finally breaking the silence. "I mean, you don't just live off Daddy's money, do you?"

He followed this with a shallow "just joking" guffaw, one belied by how carefully he continued to watch me.

I ran my fingers over the stem of my wineglass, wondering just how long it would take Ajax to notice that mine weren't the hands of a debutante, but those of a fighter.

"I take photographs."

"Like weddings or models or something?"

"Like people. Shapes. Shadows. Usually night shots using natural lighting and gritty settings. Reality."

"So..." he said, drawing the word out, "you don't make money at it?"

"Not yet."

He looked at me like I should apologize. Guess he was a fucking banker after all.

"Sounds like a waste of time," he said, then turned away from my stare.

The jab stung more than it should. I don't normally care what people think, but lately looking at the world through a refracted lens--viewing the worth of places and people and objects in terms of light and shadow, black and white--wasn't as satisfying as it used to be.

Restless, I'd recently begun taking more self-portraits than anything else; zeroing in on singular things like my knuckles, constantly red and callused from nylon punching bags, or my eyes—right or left, rarely both—which were tawny and earth-colored during the day, but blackened like a clouded lake in the dark, or when I was extremely angry.

Instead of looking for enemies in the faces of strangers, I'd begun turning the camera on myself ... and I didn't need Freud, or even Dr. Phil, to tell me I was searching for something.

Question was, would I like what I eventually found?

"Banking, on the other hand," I began sweetly, once the server had delivered our entrées, "sounds mesmerizing. Please. Don't skip one fascinating little detail."

Ajax's mouth creased even thinner than his hairline. "Gawd. I should've known by looking that you're nothing like your sister."

I didn't really consider it an insult ... but knew my eyes had gone black as tar. "And how, exactly, do you know what my sister's like?"

"I subscribe to her *Playboy* fan page," he said nastily, and shoved some saffron potatoes into his mouth.

In turn, I settled my own fork on the side of my plate.

So that was it.

I loved my sister, but Olivia and I had taken vastly different approaches to both our sexuality and our general lives. The profile Ajax was referring to had launched three months earlier, and while I didn't approve of Olivia's overt approach to sexuality, I understood the reason behind it.

Ironically enough, it stemmed from the same origin as my own.

Good ol' Ajax here had probably also read the recent article about the Archer family empire in *Fortunes and Fates* magazine:

"Lacking the acute business sense of her gaming magnate father, Xavier, and the brilliant social acumen of her glamorous sister, Olivia... Ms. Joanna Archer seems to have eschewed her public duty as one of the richest heiresses on the planet for a life of frivolity and self-interest."

Self-interest was accurate, but frivolous?

Like writing scathing gossip columns was brain surgery.

So my sister hadn't given Ajax my phone number. Olivia likely didn't know him at all. He'd been counting on someone who looked and acted like a Playmate, and likely hoped my reported self-interest—along with my inheritance—could be funneled his way.

That he'd have a chance with the token black sheep of the Archer dynasty.

Wrong, Ajax, I thought, picking up my wineglass. On all accounts.

"Look," he said, spreading his hands before him as though discussing stock options. "I just came to Vegas for a good time. I thought I'd look you up since we seem to have some of the same interests..."

A.k.a. my money.

"...and see if you wouldn't mind showing me around. That's all. Why can't we just have some fun?"

When I only continued to stare, he dropped his bony elbows on the table with a force that shook the plates.

"Fine. Then you could at least pretend you have a sense of humor."

"But then I'd have been laughing from the moment you showed up."

See? Sense of humor, intact.

"Bitch."

Boring word. Predictable response.

Yet I was surprised my words cut so deep, so quick. Then again, a fuse that short was likely lit long before I came along.

"What's wrong, Ajax? Wait ... lemme guess. You came to Vegas on some sort of pilgrimage, to forget for one weekend exactly how disappointing your life really is, and now mean, spoiled heiress, Joanna Archer, is screwing it all up."

I have this ability—I think of it as a gift, really—to see clean through to people's sore spots. I home in on a bruised psyche and I press.

Not nice, I know, but Olivia had earned the Miss Congeniality title in our family.

Ajax's reptilian features had rearranged themselves as I spoke, and he now looked like a glowering python.

"Thanks for the psychoanalysis, *babe*," he spat, "but all I really wanted from this weekend were a couple of easy lays."

Right, so I *should've* thrown my wine in his face ... but I liked Chateau Le Pin, and took a long, considering sip of the vintage '82 I'd made him buy. Then ...

"And what? Your mother wasn't available?"

Ajax's head jerked, and suddenly a different man sat there. It was the still picture I'd imagined before, a person comfortable in his skin.

A warrior living up to his name.

I surprised myself by blinking first.

"You like to argue," he said, and it wasn't a question. "You like to fight."

I did ... but suddenly I wasn't sure what I was up against.

"Insult my mother again," he said in a ragged whisper, "and you'll get the fight of your life."

And just like that a bolt of lightning speared the gilded room. It arched across the beveled ceiling to snap like fangs between us.

The air became a live wire, crackling so that lights, wall sconces —even the candles—flickered, flinched. An invisible force funneled around us, sucking all the energy in the room toward our table, leaving me breathless.

In the eye of that storm, the flimsy skin layering Ajax's bones melted away.

His face became a slab of bone, teeth, and cavernously slanting eyes.

His smooth skull grinned at me across the table, eyes aflame.

And a banshee's howl sprung from the gaping mouth.

ACKNOWLEDGMENTS

My thanks to Jann MacKenzie, my eternal first reader. Later, Miki Quick, Crystal Parnell, Tiffany Savicki, and Heather Shaw all provided valuable feedback as long-time Zodiac readers, House of Ink members, and fellow writers.

I cherish you all. TTE.

ALSO BY VICKI PETTERSSON

The Signs of the Zodiac Series

The Scent of Shadows

The Taste of Night

The Touch of Twilight

City of Souls

Cheat the Grave

The Neon Graveyard

Also in the Zodiac World

The Reordering - A Signs of the Zodiac Novella

Zodiac Rising - An Ashlyn Archer YA Spinoff Novel

Celestial Blues Trilogy

The Taken

The Lost

The Given

～

Swerve: A Stand-Alone Thriller

ABOUT THE AUTHOR

Vicki Pettersson is a Las Vegas native who always loved to read and write. A post-college stint in PR—along with a handful of Vegas service jobs—quickly revealed that being told what to do was *not* a good fit for Vicki.

So she did what any self-respecting Vegas girl would do: she became a showgirl by night ... and a closet novelist by day.

Fast forward a decade and she also became an instant NYT & USA Today Bestseller with her *Signs of the Zodiac* series. A paranormal-noir trilogy, *Celestial Blues,* quickly followed, and then came SWERVE: a high-octane cat-and-mouse thriller.

After a decade of living part-time in Dallas, Texas, Vicki is back to living—and writing—full-time in her beloved hometown.

PRAISE FOR THE SIGNS OF THE ZODIAC SERIES

"From the one-damn-thing-after-another school of unputdownable books, The Scent of Shadows rockets into the air and explodes like fireworks, with nonstop bursts of action and imagination."
– **Diana Gabaldon**

"The Scent of Shadows came out of nowhere and slapped me silly. Vicki Pettersson is a new voice that needs to be heard."
– **Kim Harrison**

" [A] bullet-train of a book. Read at your own risk—it'll keep you up past your bedtime.
– **Charlaine Harris**

"As original as it is compelling. The action comes fast and furious."
– **Kelley Armstrong**

"Passion and intrigue, heartbreak and victory—nothing is predictable in Pettersson's newest novel."
– **Melissa Marr**

"Moody, fast-paced ... blends fantasy, comic book superheroism and paranormal romance, but holds no promise of a happily-ever-after ... imaginative ... [Readers] will embrace Pettersson's enduring, tough-as-nails heroine and anticipate gleefully the next volume."
– **Publishers Weekly**

Made in the USA
Monee, IL
05 April 2024

56439607R00208